TRICKS OF THE LIGHT

Broom is in her fifties. She is spending Christmas in the Alps, where some years before she had fallen in love with Al, a climber who was subsequently involved in an accident abroad. Lockhart, with whom Broom once had an affair, is returning to the family estate on a remote Scottish island, with painful family news for his autocratic father. As Broom looks back on her life and past lovers, she becomes drawn to Micky Flint, a young executive who is her polar opposite, and an intimacy develops that will wrench Broom out of the past and into her new life.

TRICKS OF THE LIGHT

TRICKS OF THE LIGHT

by

Alison Fell

Magna Large Print Books
Long Preston, North Yorkshire,
BD23 4ND, England.

British Library Cataloguing in Publication Data.

Fell, Alison
    Tricks of the light.

    A catalogue record of this book is
    available from the British Library

    ISBN   0-7505-2074-4

First published in Great Britain in 2003 by Doubleday
a division of Transworld Publishers

Published in Large Print 2003 by arrangement with
Transworld Publishers Ltd.

Magna Large Print is an imprint of Library Magna Books Ltd.

Printed and bound in Great Britain by
T.J. (International) Ltd., Cornwall, PL28 8RW

For Dave and friends

I should like to thank the Royal Literary Fund and the Society of Authors for their financial support during the writing of this novel.

I am indebted to the following people, who generously shared their expertise during the research phase of the book: Sally Musgrove, Les Stern, Louise Ann Wilson, Richard Bridges, Magali Barthélémy, Nigel Fountain, John Hornsby and Pat Devine. Needless to say, any errors the text contains are my own responsibility. Thanks also to Ruthie Petrie and Sarah Westcott, who were, as always, skilled and sensitive editors.

My son Ivan rescued me from two dead computers and coped patiently with my raging phobia. For this I am more than grateful.

The poetry featured on page 43 is by Lennart Sjögren, and can be found in *Five Swedish Poets*, published by the excellent Norvik Press at the University of East Anglia.

On page 307 the text contains a brief passage from Thomas Mann's *Doctor Faustus*, which is intended as a tribute.

That winter, in an apartment that was the smallest of three in an Alpine chalet, on the top floor, under generous eaves, Broom decided that she was born for happiness. The thought was unlikely enough to make her laugh out loud. Fifty years, it had taken her, a mere half-century to reach the conclusion that, in spite of everything that had happened, happiness was intrinsic to her, like flight to a gull or blood-sucking to a tick – her nature, in fact (though not, perhaps, her fate).

Her first bliss had been the radiant blue that struck the ice at one o'clock when the sun, struggling over the summit of the Montjoie, lit the floor of the valley. The snow had come early that year, her landlady, Madame d'Ange, had said, followed by an unbroken deep frost that set the fall solid. Only the Route Nationale, scoured by the ceaseless friction of tyres, cut a wet dark ribbon through the white landscape. In the night the snowy ground gave out its gathered light and shone like noonday under a navy sky – an inversion so magical that she was drawn again and again to the window to stand in darkness with the curtain wound round her, like a monk in a hooded cloak.

It was the light, she supposed, that had done it: light in midwinter, that rare thing. Under such a steep sky even solitariness seemed to sparkle. Unlike sunlight over oceans or forests, the light on the spindle-shaped snow cornice at the summit of the Aiguille du Sud had no softness to it, for what moisture the air contained had turned to frost-crystals that intensified each dazzling ray. Later in the day the warmer tints would come, but right now the sun was no golden orb but a chromatic explosion above the Massif: urgent, immaterial, more event than object. The kind of light that could even redesign a life.

Broom wanted it to last, to be more than a brief winter blessing. If these were her true colours, like charcoal or conté they required a fixative, otherwise they would fade when the light did. Burned by the sun, on her fretted wood balcony, while inside the apartment ancient radiators scorched sooty shadows on the flowered wall-paper, she looked for evidence that might support this sudden shift of frame.

In fact there had been clues. More than once she'd been surprised to find that her friends saw in her some quality of which she'd been unaware. (Something that gleamed out of her, perhaps, like the midnight secrets of the snow.) A quality that was envied, even resented.

Take Veronica, for instance. One day Veronica told Broom she'd dreamt that her flat had been broken into. What hadn't been stolen was completely trashed; in the centre of the living room was a pile of ruins. In the dream Veronica had been devastated – she wept inconsolably, she tore at her hair – but when Broom appeared, she didn't try to help her; instead she fell backwards, laughing, on the rubbish heap that once had been her home. *Careless. Uproarious.* These were the words she'd used. Her tone – sulky – implied that even in dreams Broom was the bad mother who would always fail her.

Lately Broom and her old friend Heather had agreed bitchily and with relief that the trouble with Veronica was that she demanded total allegiance, not only to her precious vulnerability, but to the innumerable defences she constructed to safeguard it. In those days, though, it had never entered Broom's head to challenge Veronica. For years she had pandered to her; to be perfectly honest, she'd fallen over backwards to please her.

The linguistic coincidence stopped Broom short. A reckless stillness emanated from the Massif, not unlike the pause, seemingly infinite, before a theatre erupts into laughter. Maybe that's what the dream had been trying to tell Veronica: that she had a very bad habit of putting everyone in the wrong, that she charged too high a price for intimacy.

At the time she'd felt guilty. Later she was incredulous, no less at being taken to task for her dream activities than at the insouciance Veronica had ascribed to her. In the midst of mourning Al, this version of herself – its crude vitality – had been incongruous enough to shock her. Yet the image with its spice of selfishness stayed with her; the truth was that it made her feel decidedly superior to Veronica. You could tell that the person in the dream was a woman who would always pull through.

Broom sipped her tea, lately made but quickly cooling in the mountain air. Gradually she'd lost patience with Veronica, her allegiance withdrawing itself as her capacity for sympathy dwindled.

But what if the dream had been a kind of prophecy, and she had now become what Veronica, back then, had accused her of being? Useless to deny that in the past five years she had hardened. But what else did people do who'd had the last ounce of stuffing knocked out of them? Perhaps one day she'd end up as a battleaxe, like her redoubtable aunts, those wartime widows who had closed their ears to the disappointed cries of the heart. She understood their brusqueness better now; she understood why they had refused sympathy, and subsequently could not sympathize. She understood something of what had turned them into the women she had known – rigid, opinionated women to whom no young girl would ever have turned for solace.

Squinting in the sunshine, she gazed defiantly up at the Aiguilles. Cold. Remote. Forbidding. The adjectives accused her. Equally, she could refuse to be swayed by them. To her eye the high snow ridges were suavely sculpted, the granite pinnacles more elegant than arrogant. I am what I am, she told herself. After all, who ever said bereavement made you a better person?

Al kept the map in its polythene map-case taped to the handlebars of the bicycle. Folded open, that day, at the eastern armpit of the Mediterranean: Antakya, Adana, Tarsus.

'At last I'm turning my nose west again,' he wrote to Broom, 'and speeding back to you.'

When they dragged him off the road he was almost gone, blood everywhere, his bike a mess of tangled spars and spokes. This she had been told by the

16

Consul, or rather the Honorary Consul, for Monsieur Engin was a local businessman who served Her Majesty only on a part-time basis.

Monsieur Engin did not smoke. He drove a long clean car she remembered as a Mercedes. His pale fingers emphasized with precise, almost pleading gestures not the collision itself but the fortuitousness of the rescue, the probity of the lorry driver who could have fled but chose instead to summon help, the skill and speed of the emergency services.

Broom listened and nodded and could find Al nowhere in this diplomatic narrative.

She saw the police diagrams through an icy fog. Only later, when she held the plastic map-case in her hand, did she feel the impact. A spray of bloodstains, rusty: Al's trace across the dotted borderline of Syria. Then she knew what had happened to him: the eleven o'clock sun on his bare shoulders, the smell of juniper and exhausts, the map riding happily on his handlebars; then and only then did she know what had happened to her.

Broom went back into the kitchen and sat down at the table, which was dressed in a brown oilcloth with a trellis-and-honeysuckle pattern, and spread with an A5 layout pad and the rest of her Faust bits and pieces: the libretto and tapes, her Goethe and Marlowe, and a file of reproductions of the Horned One as portrayed by Dürer and Bosch and Cranach. She had brought the ground plan and elevations of the Opernhaus in Leipzig, which Daniel had faxed through to her, but those were for reference only: the fiddly business of the model box could wait, thank God, until she got back to London. Miniaturization was an unavoidable part of the process but it was one which always unsettled her. She preferred space, a large canvas, five by four minimum. Unlimited pigment. Faced with the frailty of cardboard and balsa wood, she was all thumbs. Even as a girl she'd disliked doll's houses, with their scaled-down settees and teeny cups and saucers. Really she ought to be overjoyed that digital technology was catching up at last and threatening to make the model box obsolete. Already someone at St Martin's was developing the Virtual Stage. Soon you'd be able to put flies, trucks, revolves and so on into a 3D computer model. Add in your scenic elements and you could run a technical rehearsal complete with light and sound cues from a simulated prompt-box.

At half-past one the sun sneaked in through the window and lay across her hands. Her right hand, which held the stick of conté, looked battered and workmanlike; the knuckles were red and rough, the fingernails ragged and seamed with paint residue at the quick. The left hand, by contrast, had the look of a lady of leisure. Its smooth fingers – although not the wedding finger – wore rings; its nails were shapely and patrician, filed to enviable ovals. Schizoid hands, she thought, staring at them. As in the right one doesn't know what the left one's doing.

Her father had had mechanic's hands: square, stubby-fingered, the cracked skin crazed with engine oil. Yet what she remembered was the delicacy of the manoeuvres they performed, the way they bound tiny wisps of feather to the hook

18

for fly-fishing, the adroit surgery they carried out on camshaft or carburettor. He'd known next to nothing about art, but he had steered her towards it all the same, sharing with her his awestruck admiration for the sort of Celtic kitsch you could still see in hotel lounges all over the Highlands. Tea-shoppe realism, all heath and heather and misty crags. They would stand up close and exclaim over the ruts and ridges the palette-knife made in the pigment, while her mother sat tight with her currant scone or port-and-lemon.

For her eleventh birthday he made a palette out of hardboard with a hole for the thumb, and bought her her first tubes of oils. Her daubs delighted him. He mentioned a great painter called Rembrandt and talked with a gleam in his eye about her future. This her mother called 'romancing', her tone implying that it was at the very least a sin against modesty. She could go on to college, he argued, become a commercial artist. Trying, against his nature, to be practical. She imagined greetings cards, prim illustrations of housewives with perms and refrigerators, the furry line drawings of dumb-bells and brassières in the back of the *Daily Herald*. The actual term was 'graphic design', but of course she didn't know that yet, hadn't even set foot in a proper art gallery, for God's sake. Where they lived, roads were scarce and towns were far and there simply weren't such things. Just lochs and hydro-schemes, and the incomparable light and shift and shade of the mountains.

Broom got up and massaged her hand as she

waited for the kettle to boil. The thumb joint was knotty and sore, borderline arthritic. Lately she'd felt that her right hand was resisting her: it did not often seem to want to work. Yet work was what it was all about. Discipline. Praxis. Time and time again you had to remind yourself to get back to first principles, to the pleasure of the stroke, the mark, the colour spreading across the canvas in the same way that the sun spread across the valley and revealed all the brutal and delectable shades of the snow. Work, after all, was the one constant. People might let you down, but work, thank God, was always there. It was also the only way to evade the ever-present critic in the head, which demanded nothing less than total brilliance, immediately and without effort.

She thought of the paintings that languished currently in her Shoreditch studio, their faces turned modestly, girlishly, to the wall, paintings whose only crime was that they didn't glow quite like the luminous versions in her head.

It was impossible, really, to define the kind of light she was after. Except that it was not naturalistic, not an attempt to replicate the single light-source and directional shadows of the earthly beam. A kind of haloed radiance, perhaps, something that lived on the outer edge of the visible range of wavelengths, between infra-red and ultraviolet; an even, kindly light that did away with shame. Something you could sense but not quite see, or at least – for there were times when you simply had to follow your instincts – not yet. It seemed to emanate, if certain conditions were right, either from her or from the mountain she was looking at, or, more probably, from some relationship between the two. More than that she did not know, did not, perhaps, need to know...

All artists, Broom was convinced – all real artists, that is, as opposed to the showmen and the charlatans, the Kleins and Warhols and Picassos – had a template deep inside them, an inkling of some reality so compelling that they'd spend decades trying to salvage it from the shadows. Cézanne had slaved all his life to uncover his own correlative for form in space; Van Gogh had driven himself mad trying to render the agitated energies of nature. Then there was Giacometti, that other great hero, who had seen space pressing in on him like death, like gravity...

She'd tried so many techniques. Mixed powdered glass with her pigment, experimented with gold leaf, mica, anything that might achieve a crystalline surface. She'd studied Russian ikons, Byzantine mosaics, the illuminated scrolls of the early Celtic churches. For a while she took to smashing cheap marcasite jewellery with a hammer and embedding the chips in gesso, but the dazzle that resulted was too lively, too contingent. She played with transparent washes on glass, but drowned in her own reflections.

In her sketchbook was a quote she'd copied from a biography of Giacometti. *The more I work, the more I see things differently; that is, everything grows in grandeur every day, becomes more and more unknown, more and more beautiful.*

Broom supported this credo one hundred per cent. She knew, of course, that you had to be

21

patient. She also knew that it was over five years since she'd had even a small exhibition. Throughout that deathly period Hilda had been a gem. Supportive, forbearing. Far from holding Broom to the letter of her contract – which she was perfectly entitled to do – Hilda had urged her to take her time and stick to her vision. But Hilda had a gallery to run, and these days there was a sigh at the end of her sentences.

Late evening with notes on loneliness: Broom looks out for Venus.

The moon has a cool composure; the clouds fall apart like the last rags of the tide on a black beach of stars.

One day in the third summer after Al's death she became older than Al. Her life going on, his death going on. She who'd always seen him as the older man – no doubt for her own obscure erotic reasons – had reached his age and passed it.

Snow whispers off the trees, like pieces of a past she belongs to.

Standing at the window she remembered the slight sag of the skin over the muscles of his belly, the wrinkled hangdog look about his eyes. Strange now to recall how shocked she'd been, once, by those signs of decrepitude. When later they became so very aphrodisiac.

Always it came back to this, her fingers stretched wide as the claws of a cat, kneading at nothing. The flesh in her mind's eye only. And so this was how it would be. Every year from now on she would get older, and every year from now on the body that once wore the visible marks of her desire would get younger and younger.

He would be away for five months or more, he said, if everything went smoothly. The plan was that he would circumnavigate the Mediterranean, kiss Africa and Asia, complete the littoral and tie the knot. His escape not only from London's grey October but also from her, or so she feared. He'd crossed his heart and sworn that this was his last solo expedition; anywhere else he went in future, she would come too. A short walk in the Hindu Kush, perhaps, or even the Tien Shan. She'd agreed to fly out to Tunis – the mid-point – at Christmas.

Al had an orator's voice; even his whispers carried.

She had taken the dinner plates out to the kitchen, leaving him with Ken McBurney, his old Party comrade: big Brummie Ken, who was to handle his financial affairs for the duration of the trip.

'If I get the chop out there, don't bother bringing the body back. Just have it cremated, right?'

Like most of the climbers Broom knew, Al was aggressively unsentimental about death. The word he used was 'rational'. The implication being that if he didn't give a toss about his last remains, no one else ought to.

She couldn't work out exactly why she was angry. She was not his wife, after all, nor should she wish to be: that much had been made clear to her.

It was their last night. She went back through to the living room and picked up her whisky and continued helping to pack his panniers. If she was allowed so few rights over his life, there was no reason to assume that she would have any at all over his death.

After they made love, however, her mettle returned.

23

'If anything happens to you I'm on the first plane out. Whether you like it or not.' A whisky-promise she'd never expected to keep.

In the morning he brought her tea in bed as usual and set out in a grizzling rain. Knowing that he would look up at the window before he rode off, she threw back the covers and stood behind the curtain. She had let go by then; she'd accepted that he was going, that she couldn't or shouldn't stop him. Down in the street people were putting up umbrellas or getting into cars to go to work. She watched him wheel his bicycle along the garden path. Before he closed the gate he bent to tighten the straps on one of the panniers. When he glanced up at the window she whisked the curtain back and flashed a naked breast. Long after he had gone she could still see his face, wrecked and pale, laughing up at her in the drab London light.

Micky Flint was discriminating about beds. In his Barbican flat he kept a plain pine one from Liberty's, king-size, with very straight flat sheets. His duvet covers and pillowslips were as snowy as his bathrobes, his linen cupboards capacious and concealed. He liked white towels, white walls, women who wore white silk camiknickers.

The french windows of his bedroom opened onto a balcony shaped like the prow of an ark, with a commanding view of St Paul's and the Thames to the south, while to the east rose the graphite glass escarpments of the City.

Lately he'd been toying with the idea of installing a couple of steel struts that could hold a hammock, to emphasize the nautical theme. A hammock would introduce a note of informality, a certain swash of the buckle, as it were. He liked to think that he might doze in the breeze from the balcony and open an eye from time to time to see a bird, a cloud or, best of all, a shipshape passing plane. Open an eye, and snap it shut again like a lizard, or close it as casually as a client in a barber's chair. Supine, trusting. Close shave, nose hairs, trim. You saw them still, these Englishmen – archaic, yet faintly enviable – who left the whole thing routinely to the professionals. One curt glance in the mirror at the end of it, a quick brush-down, and back to business. Later they'd sleep soundly in their marriage beds in Bromley or in Barking, their dreams and limbs entangled with their wives', their souls ajar and unprotected as their open mouths.

Like most insomniacs, Micky was a seasoned scrutineer of sleeping faces. There was something morbid about their quiescence which never failed to summon up in him a small resentful thrill. If he'd attempted to describe the flavour of this voyeurism he'd have had to say it was like discovering that your hotel bedroom affords a perfect view of the worshippers in a parish church, or overlooks a blindless lavatory window. You saw what you should not see; in fact, you were obliged to.

The nights he spent in company were long and problematic. Lovers got agitated so easily. Assuming that the insomniac had something on his mind, they'd enquire earnestly about his troubles. Not only women, who after all were inquisitive by nature, but men too these days, increasingly.

On the whole it was simpler to pretend. For the sake of a quiet life he would lie there with his eyes shut and his brain burning until dawn and his Svensen schedule gave him an excuse to slip away. Did you sleep well? his bedmates would ask tenderly as he emerged from the spanking shower, and he'd nod back, rosy and relieved.

Of course you couldn't entirely escape the little intimacies. Nice dreams? he'd enquire, and listen sagely while they unburdened themselves. Micky was a good listener. Listening, like kindness, cost nothing. Often he found that he was genuinely interested. Looking at it cynically, you could even argue that there was a professional pay-off. Market research, if you like. Keeping a finger on the deeper pulses, tracking the parameter of changing needs. He'd often thought he ought to toss it around with Damien: dream as desire in its formative stages, dream as an index of global consumer tensions to come. 'Let nothing in heaven or earth be strange to you,' as Damien would say, 'with the sole exception of boredom.' Damien liked his creatives to be zany. The weirder and wackier the idea, the more it tickled his fancy. Damien was that rare breed of CEO who knew that the only way to inspire a team was to give them a free rein and demand that they always, *always* excite you.

Sometimes Micky's lovers asked about his own dreams, but fortunately these could always be invented. He'd discovered that even the most sussed among them could be fobbed off with the most appalling schlock, so hungry were they for intimacy. 'I dreamt I was a lightning bolt,' he'd say. 'I dreamt I was an angel.' 'I dreamt my laptop had an ass's head and eagle's wings.' In the white bedroom he'd fold his hands and suffer a gaze of such sincere concern that he was within an inch of being worried about himself.

The interpretations that followed – ingenious, scholastic, or inept – had one common denominator, or so it had begun to seem. All of them were tainted by the same blatant self-interest. How solemnly his lovers strained to know, and to know more, to be close, and even closer; how avid their inspection of his can of worms. 'You've got my number there,' he'd lie and laugh, feeling that he'd been quite right not to trust them. The fact that they had opened the wrong can quite contentedly seemed to prove that they deserved no better than a counterfeit.

And there, thought Micky, was the downside. Once you convinced yourself you were surrounded by idiots and incompetents, you cut yourself on the twin blades of triumph and despair. Sometimes he even felt it would be preferable to be found out, to be pinned like a rabbit in a single beam of predatory light. The confessional bit. Forgive me, Father, for I have sinned. Then again, forget it. Even if people pretended to believe you they'd only make a fool of you behind your back. In London's fair city it didn't pay to be a bleeding heart; in Momo's and in Mosimann's you could expect no quarter. No way, thought Micky. If you were going to be laughed at, it was far better to be laughed at for your fictions than your facts.

In the Hôtel des Aiguilles the bed was high and wide, the brass bedstead gleaming and ornate. The reading lamps that flanked it had been lit for him, the sheet turned down in readiness. Gold-wrapped bittermints lay beside the Room Service menu on the tasselled day-bolster.

The Aiguilles wasn't exactly what Micky would have called his dream hotel. The cuisine didn't approach Four Seasons standard, nor did the ambience compare with the Chêvre d'Or above Cap Ferrat, where every year, at the end of the International Adfest, he and a few other discerning suits caucused for R & R – although that, of course, would be asking for the moon. On Micky's personal scale of one to ten, the International Group came in around fifth. Their hotels were, on the whole, well managed. They aimed for, and generally achieved, a tolerable marriage of retro luxury and high-tech efficiency. And, at the very least, they were reliable. When the Room Service trolley appeared it would bear a tablecloth of white damask and a single rose in a crystal vase; the cutlery and coffeepots would be uniformly silver. In the marble *salle de bains* he'd find cute little jars of gels and essences, and thick white bathrobes sweetly warmed and aired.

The room was soundless and smelled faintly of freesias. Beyond the closed curtains there was a balcony; in the morning the Montjoie view he'd specified would no doubt be superb. Not that he had any compelling interest in the mountains themselves – on the whole the High Alps were too bright and dizzied him – but he did like to know he had them at his disposal.

He surveyed the handsome walnut desk. His leather driving gloves, pulled off with pleasure, lay on either side of the blotter. Standing over the telephone, he stabbed the buttons at random. Laundry. Ski hire. Valet parking. In each case the response was immediate.

'*Bonjour, Monsieur Flint.* How can I help you?' Neither his name nor his room number was requested.

Warmth spread through Micky's body. He felt safe, he felt welcomed, he felt winning. As he had anticipated, the hotel had passed his test – a childish indulgence, for sure, but one that never failed to tickle him.

'*Je m'excuse,*' he said to each obliging voice. 'Must've keyed the wrong button.' His face smiled back at him from the Second Empire mirror. He wiggled his toes in his Bass Weejuns, whistling a bit. Odd, isn't it, how the little triumphs are so important?

Micky set his Zero Halliburton on the desk and keyed the combination. It had crossed his mind that he shouldn't be using digits from his birth date, not when any young Turk with half an ounce of brain could suss his secret at a glance. To the self-styled *Wunderkinder* of Svensen Grabinger, anyone over thirty-five was a sad old git – which presumably, as of this year, also included Damien. It was perverse of him, he knew, not to have changed the numbers. Almost as if he actively wanted someone to decode them. Maybe what worked for him was the small but tangible risk run daily and wilfully, the personal 'fuck you' that kept the juices flowing...

He retrieved the bumf Estelle had faxed through from Paris and leafed through it. According to the hotel brochure the Hôtel des Aiguilles retained the original balconies and balustrades of its predecessor, the noble old Windsor, haunt of Victorian alpinists like Alfred Mummery and Edward Whymper. Given his assignment, the pedigree was pleasing. An engraving on the flyleaf showed three gents in felt hats and knickerbockers negotiating a crevasse by means of a grotty old stepladder.

One of a brand-new breed of daring free-climbers, Sophie Sauvage is at the cutting edge of her sport.

No ladders or alpenstocks for Sophie, then, and no ropes either, according to the résumé. He noted that she'd already had a couple of sponsorship deals: Cassin, Le Grimpeur – print media mostly. But she wasn't with one of the fat-cat agencies, which was definitely fiscally advantageous. There was a half-hour documentary, which Estelle was bringing down tomorrow, but all in all Sophie was hardly what you'd call overexposed – another plus, in view of the tarnished credibility of the big star megadeal approach. Anyone could see that if Nike and Adidas weren't hurting now they soon would be – even without the media-friendly antics of the fluffy hordes, who thought they could strangle global capitalism with a few Victorian sampler slogans and a couple of strands of tinsel! Bless, thought Micky.

Trampa was an upstart in the Sports and Leisurewear field, which suited him just fine. Micky liked working with the underdog, because you got the opportunity to stir things up a bit, disrupt the market. These days positioning was all, and if you wanted brand integrity you had to dig deep, ruthlessly define your strategy. The line Svensen was taking – which Micky happened to believe was correct – was that if Trampa didn't go all out for the passion brand they were dead in the water. And Trampa liked it. They liked it a lot. So much, in fact, that after the initial chemistry meeting Toby Rhodes had practically begged Damien to pitch for the account.

Micky's highlighter pen flew across the page, emboldening quotable quotes. Of course at this stage he was only scouting but already he could feel the concept firming up. High risk. The Zen extremities of experience.

An adventure is a baring of your soul, not your wallet. Nice one, thought Micky. *Millionaires in zircon-coated balloons aren't adventurers.*

Since the assignment meant being out of town for Christmas, others would have hesitated, but not Micky. Damien knew his team, and he knew what counted: experience, good instincts, and the sort of people skills that quite frankly were in short supply these days. Damien took the view that the real creative stuff lay in the engagement with the individual, and in the hands-on department, well, Micky was his man. For the moment to the average punter Sophie Sauvage was little more than what'shername, that girl who swings off precipices by a finger. But Micky's was the yea or the nay, and if it was yea he had *carte blanche* to take her to the limit. An enviable position, whichever way you looked at it. He decided that he was really looking forward to meeting Sophie.

Over and above the Trampa campaign there was a gratifying sense that it was within his power to stamp her on the consciousness of the TV-viewing multitudes, to launch her into the thin bright air of celebrity. For you could certainly see it that way; it wasn't simply a daydream. First the money would trickle, then it would flow like rivers of milk. All the mega-companies falling over themselves to lay votive offerings at the feet of the newly minted ikon.

Always presuming that Svensen got the account, of course. Which we will, Micky assured himself, as he nibbled the corner off a bittermint. Clients didn't want you just to do the job, they wanted you to exceed their expectations, which was exactly what he intended to do. As always Damien was hoping for a pitch-winning campaign, but this time Micky would go further: he'd give him an award-grabber. It so happened that he had a very good feeling about that; in fact, right now he'd literally lay a bet on it.

When they sunbathed, not quite reading, on the flat-shouldered rock on the horn of land that is the Cap Afrique, they looked north, like the Arab boys who yearned for all the gleaming goods of Europe. Except that she and Al stared more or less vacantly at the sea, demanding at that moment neither to cross it, nor that it provide them with anything more than an everyday pleasure, like a yawn or a stretch or a glass of greeny wine. While a few feet below them, in the shallow glassy waters of the cove, men to whom they were invisible hoisted their robes and squatted to relieve themselves.

In the Hôtel Panoramique they dubbed the cleaner Queen Dido, for her spear-straight back and her astonishing Punic profile. Dido was, perhaps, in her mid-twenties. They marvelled at the aristocratic grace of her gestures, at her precise and gliding steps. Dido lived with her mother in a whitewashed cube on the flat roof of the hotel. Every morning they watched admiringly as she hosed down the marble tiles of the patio outside the room where the guests took breakfast, her small feet clad in high-heeled rubber galoshes.

Tourists go to Tunisia believing they can escape the winter darkness. Like Broom, they peek at the strip of skin beneath their watchstraps to see the way it bleaches, the way the freckles mass on its edges, dark and eager as flies. Particularly in the south, in the furnace glow of the desert. Automatic narcissism. As if they were souls foreign to themselves, or about to be.

Broom looked critically at her Faust roughs. She'd drawn the cantilevered glass towers of a financial district, which could have been in London, but equally in Hong Kong, Frankfurt or New York. For Faust's study – in this case, his executive suite – she'd decided to go for a bank of computer consoles, blazoning their numerals:

33

stocks and bonds, the ups and downs of the Futures market, the Nasdaq, etc., etc.

She found herself wishing that she could pick up the phone and have a word with Lockhart. Broom didn't know her FTSE from her elbow but Lockhart certainly did. Lockhart the investment banker, with whom, sadly but, she supposed, inevitably, she'd lost touch. Everyone narrowed as they got older, she reflected, went their separate ways. Pushing their lifestyles ahead of them like desert beetles rolling balls of camel dung along the dunes towards their separate nests. She remembered with a pang that even in the short time they were together Lockhart had had a peculiar flair for never being around when she needed him.

Broom drew a kind of plinth, and on it a skinny statue in a stretched tube of a dress: a boy-girl with a concave chest and breasts not big enough to furnish the scooped neckline with a cleavage. Her nipples and hip-bones poked at the material like tent poles at canvas. She stood knock-kneed, her toes turned awkwardly but fashionably inwards, her shin-bones sharp as rulers. Broom imagined the statue standing downstage, revolving constantly on the fragile stilts of her heels.

She lit a cigarette and surveyed the storyboards through narrowed eyes. The signifiers of wealth were too brash, somehow, to be convincing. Marguerite, being poor as well as pious, was easier to visualize. She drew a dark Punic profile: Dido in a wraparound overall with straps that crossed between the shoulderblades and looped around to fasten dowdily at the front. She added

34

a cramped roof terrace with a threadbare sunflower in a pot, although in fact she had no memory of flowers up there in Dido's garden on the roof of the hotel: just a few dry window-boxes, and in one of them a child's plastic windmill spinning on a stick.

The tape-recorder was an aged beast whose sole virtue was that it was small enough to be transportable. In the upper registers the loud-speaker gave out a strained vibrato; the mezzo could have been gargling in an aeroplane toilet.

Combien il est triste, de vieillir seul, en égoïste, sang Marthe to Mephistopheles, flirtatious and pathetic, a middle-aged woman making a fool of herself. *Prenez mon bras un moment.*

Anticipating Mephistopheles' crushing response, Broom felt sorry for Marthe. She slipped a straw table mat under the tape machine before his infernal bass could shimmy it sideways, like a glass on a Ouija board.

Fuck me, the old bag's so desperate she'd marry the devil himself. Or words to that effect.

Broom felt suddenly sad and wintry. Prejudice lay upon her like a pall. '*Et maintenant, vous êtes célibataire?*' her landlady had asked the night before. She was sipping *le vrai* Scotch Broom had bought in Duty Free, recalling her first stay in the chalet, years ago, with Lockhart.

Broom hadn't known how to reply. She was all too aware that Madame d'Ange had three daughters, a husband and, to cap it all, a *beau-fils* who was *un véritable guide de montagne.* She wanted to say the word 'widow'; she wanted to claim that status. Struggling for a subtlety her

35

French fell short of, she hung above the chasm between then and now. So many things had happened in the interim, and most of them were incommunicable: relationships with men she could barely remember, and then the one with Al, which she couldn't forget. In the end, defeated, she shrugged. *'Oui. En ce moment.'*

Madame d'Ange smiled politely, her pale grey eyes alight with curiosity. *'Mais comme ça vous êtes tranquille, n'est-ce pas?'* Her plump hands described a space indefinite and calm, free of the constraints of partnerhood and parenthood. Such solitude, they implied, was enviable.

Touched by her tact, Broom smiled wryly and said, yes, *oui*, well, *quelquefois*.

There had been other questions, other pleasantries. *'Et votre fils, il a quel âge maintenant? Trente ans? Non! Vraiment? Mais, madame ... vous êtes si jeune, la belle ligne,'* and so on, and all very flattering too, but none of it altered the fact that it was *triste*, bloody *triste*, in Broom's opinion, to grow old alone, *en égoïste*.

She saw that she had been doodling. From the end of her pencil a memory had flowed, the kind of thing she used to scribble mindlessly in school exercise books. Back then it was the era of Monroe and her voluptuous predecessors – Hayworth, Bergman, Ava Gardner. Dresses clung seductively to every curve; necklines plunged, deep and precipitous, like crevasses. She'd practised the curved V between the breasts over and over until her execution was fluent. Finally she left out the dress and filled her margins with the sign alone, her own obsessive hieroglyph. My very first artworks, she thought. V for vanity. V for voluptuousness.

At that age she'd been too young to wear such frocks, and in any case she had no breasts to show. The irony being that now, when she did, she was supposed to shroud every inch of her that was no longer taut and perfect. It was as if there was some unholy contract women signed which placed their beauty always out of reach, always in the past or in the future, a hope or else a haunting, never to be savoured in the fulsome present tense.

One more thing our mothers didn't prepare us for, she thought, lapsing into an ingrained habit of resentment. One more turn of the screw. For she could see clearly now that she'd been lovely, in her late teens, twenties, even into her forties, and it was galling to realize that she hadn't seen it then.

A dull explosion echoed high up in the Massif. Another crump followed within seconds. They must be dynamiting to clear the avalanche slopes before the skiers arrived *en masse* and took to the pistes. She put down her pencil and went to investigate. Now that the snow had stopped falling the wind had an easterly edge to it; the Christmas bandeau had blown down from the neighbours' porch and frisked about in the kitchen garden. From the balcony below came the laughter and foot-scufflings of Madame d'Ange's grandchildren. Her lips were dry. The sunlight peppered her eyes with black spots. Under the snow cornices of the Massif the blue gashes of bergschrunds were a measure of the day's brightness.

Her father had called her Con more often than he had called her Connie. She'd pretended that it was short for Connor, a boy's name. Connor rhymed with honour. Connor was the wild one, the tearaway her father really wanted. Connor had a gun belt, holstered, with white-and-silver sixguns, and a knife he threw often and accurately at fence posts and garden gates. Connor went poaching with his father and fishing up the loch; his face and hers twinned in the mirroring water, before the twilight rise of the fish; he leaning out from the alder-shaded bank, his rod angled and nodding, the firs on the far side of the loch long horizontal cliffs of light.

One day – soon, perhaps – she'd have to give up on love and settle for being needed, as women did. Zipping her fleece up to her chin, she sighted along the arthritic knuckle of her thumb at the red satin bandeau. She imagined the recoil of the gun against her shoulder, the flat crack of the report, like the sound of planks being dropped on concrete.

Inside the apartment the duet became quartet, as Marthe and Mephistopheles were joined by the star-crossed lovers.

Mon coeur parle, écoute! sang Marguerite the innocent, sublimely offering her heart to Faust. Even on the decrepit machine the notes were pure and piercing. Broom felt tears sting at her eyes. As a counterpoint to the profane, the middle-aged, it was cruel and brilliant. Gounod and his librettists had done a terrific job. They had made art, and they had made an utter fool of

38

Marthe. Poor old Marthe, she thought bitterly. Mutton dressed up as lamb, and all that. Break the bloody contract and the devil has the last laugh after all.

In the flat bottom of the night Lockhart goes walking. Under the bare trees the shadows of sycamore leaves imprinted on the pavement are a last residue of autumn. On his left loom empty factory buildings where things were made, once; on his right there's a council block, a tower, with Christmas trees high up and dainty. All the shouts flung from the day's windows silent now.

Gusts of wind chill the orange-lit street corners and ruffle the waters of the canal. Back at the house Agneta is sleeping, exhausted by the last day of the school term, but happy, or so he hopes. Earlier he watched her opening the presents from her class – scented candles, initialled hankies from Woolworths, After Eights she doesn't eat. There was a sheaf of home-made cards, each one laden with love and pasted glitter. She'd tossed her head, chortling at the messages. *Oh that Mahmoud, what a little rogue!* The memory of this sustains him.

Lately he's been noticing that men mourn in a different way from women. Their posture doesn't give away their shame like women's does. A white unhappiness around the eyes, a lack of conviction in their handclasp: these are the sole symptoms he's discovered in himself and others like him who belong to the one secret society nobody wants to join.

He remembers that in the consulting room he let out a hooing sound, like a broken-hearted owl.

I'm sorry, the consultant said, *I'm really very sorry*, his head and shoulders silhouetted against the window, his face in shadow, so that you couldn't see the expression in his eyes. They weren't to think it was anyone's fault, he told them; it was damned hard luck, that was all. Behind him the slim arm of a crane swung through a shallow arc, like a windscreen wiper. The past wiped clean. In his mind's eye Lockhart saw an egg in a glass Petri dish, smaller than a full stop. *Punkt*, in German. A transparent smear of sperm. He thought of the abortion Agneta had had when they were first married. What a busy, busy couple they had been since then, always procrastinating, living on easy assumptions. Their bodies uncreasable, they'd imagined, by gravity or time.

Afterwards, cycling to Finsbury, he looked up and saw the truant swallows leaving. It could have been the last day of summer. Across the blue gymnasium of the sky little clouds marched like children to their first assembly. Soon the grey lessons would begin. Behind closed doors rulers would rap out their rude reminders. Soon the weather itself would smell old: damp and musty, like a chewed pencil.

That afternoon he'd noticed a new arrival in the gym; a boy, or baby dyke, he wasn't sure which. The blond hair was strictly shaved but for a Tintin quiff upstanding at the front. He counted six earrings, a nose stud, ten aluminium finger rings, chunky as knuckledusters. The press-ups were perfect. Thirty; thirty-five; forty. The small strong body pumped relentlessly; it was labouring now, but clearly determined not to stop. If there had once been breasts they had been exercised away, but it was, he decided, definitely a her.

He felt angry then, and caught himself thinking that the imitators always took the thing too literally. Transsexuals who wore twinsets and carried dour brown handbags like the Queen's, dykes with shaven heads and body-builders' pecs. There was something desperate about their constant petitioning of the inner man, the inner woman. Not very pc of him but there you bloody are. Consciously he held that gender was contingent, no longer a fixed category, and so on, but all he wanted at that point was to yell, 'For Christ's sake, why don't you just *stop trying?*'

A door in his chest swung open, funnel for a sudden wind. For a moment he couldn't feel the moulded seat beneath his bum or see the digits on the read-out panel. Weightless with rage, he floated an inch above the rower. Somewhere nearby an unseen church clock chimed brightly, and love rocked him on the heights like an eagle. Loath to forsake the horizontal, he clung on grimly to the handles, while outside the window the morning bent before him. He saw his business suits float up like angels in the wardrobe, each empty sleeve a benediction. Knowing beyond a shadow of a doubt that whatever anguish he was suffering, Agneta bore a hundredfold, spoke it in the night, perhaps, to her heedless pillow, but never, ever, shared her grief with him. Her breath so sick and heavy with it that he dared not speak his own.

So what did it matter if he was angry, if he felt cheated of something he'd always assumed to be his birthright? Compared with Agneta's pain, whose gravity was so great that nothing, not even light, could escape from it? So what if he cried frozen tears behind the lavatory door, his thighs spreadeagled on the closed lid of the pan, his penis soft and trivial?

It was ironic, he thought, that of the two of them he with his easy easy life had always been the weeping one.

Turning into New North Road, he felt the first blown needles of sleet. There was a trickle of traffic: taxis, night lorries heading for Dover, their high glass cabins strung about with fairy lights, like Christmas cribs. Tomorrow when Agneta woke she would go into overdrive on her gift lists – exactly what to buy for sister Claudia and brother Max, the spouses, her nieces and nephews. Manny and Elsa, Fuzz, Ramona, and the twins. Then she'd embark on a two-day raid on Hamley's and Selfridges and High Street Ken, so enlivened by the logistical challenge that Lockhart needed to do no more than trot along behind. It was a role he'd come to relish – the pack-horse, the bumbling husband. Begging her advice on what to get for Fraser, and his father.

On Thursday she'd drive the parcels down to her brother's in Brighton, where Claudia and

Manny, having flown over from Hamburg with their brood, would already be ensconced. A gathering of clans he'd miss, unfortunately, having agreed that he was going home to Callasay.

Last week a card had arrived, the sort that comes in cheap packs of twenty-five or fifty: a snowy village with a Star of Bethlehem improbably enormous in a pitch-black sky, and, inside, a poem called 'Light', which was, he supposed, Fraser's idea of a Christmas greeting.

Birds wounded by shot
are more often to be seen
on our coasts
along with the more strong-winged.
Sometimes the rainbow spreads out its light
behind them

He'd stared at the words for a long time. Then he picked up the phone and called Callasay. There was some kind of fault on the line. While he waited for the operator to make the connection his ear explored an airy world of whistlings and winds. He heard the wings of the signal flap across the peat and schist of the mainland and the great grey acres of the tide, and when at last his father answered, his voice, by contrast, sounded wooden and oppressed. He said that Fraser had at first seemed better. But he really would prefer not to discuss family matters on the telephone. He said, *I think it would be best if you came home for the holiday.*

Whenever he thought of the island the same

image swam back to him: a summer evening, a summer field, the buttercups still bright beyond the great spreading shadow of the house. His mother's skirts fell in stripy op-art folds across her knees; the high-heeled sandals she'd kicked off lay empty on the tartan rug beside her. And in her lap little blond Fraser held up his posy of buttercups and peered at the yellow shrine beneath her chin, shrieking triumphantly, *You like butter! You like butter!* This he set against the other, more perturbing memories: the mouse-light of winter afternoons, his father, black-suited at the Sunday dinner table. The clipped silences between the purposeful chime of his words.

Unlike his brother, Lockhart reasoned that his father didn't ask much of him. Which was perhaps why, unlike Fraser, he generally managed to do what was expected of him. Fraser who knew the boundaries of propriety by now, but still seemed compelled to cross them; his eyes at thirty-something still importunate, still saying, 'Look, Daddy, see what I can do.' Fraser who had been painter, poet, wine-importer... Fraser upon whose essential brilliance Lockhart still stubbornly insisted, snapping at anyone who dared to demur, as if the sheer fervour of his love could force Fraser to forgive him for being the firstborn. The son and heir. Lockhart did not want to think of this, but there it was. The unalterable factor.

Broom was one of the few people who'd shared his view of Fraser. 'Talented?' she'd said. 'He's a star! Although whether he'll do anything with it remains to be seen...' It was Lockhart who had steered Fraser towards her class at St Martin's. He had done so not only for his brother's benefit but also for his own; it was the closest he could come, he supposed, to taking her home to meet the family.

Of course he had not told Fraser what was going on between them – he had presented Broom, vaguely, but not entirely dishonestly, as someone he'd met through the Fell and Rock Club – but Fraser had guessed anyway. He was, as Broom observed, frighteningly perceptive. She admitted that she was drawn to him; there was, she felt, a definite bond. She also worried about him. 'The more I praise his work,' she said, 'the more he seems to punish himself.' He'd begun to turn up hours late and jaunty with a can of Export in each pocket of his donkey jacket; on piss-wet days he'd arrive in bare feet and ragged espadrilles, looking ill and medieval, like his paintings.

To Lockhart Broom's concern seemed more than professional. Listening to her, he suffered unreasonable pangs of jealousy. Fraser had become her protégé, her lovely problem. 'He might not paint like Francis Bacon yet, but he's certainly trying to drink like him.' She thought Fraser needed help. Finally she told him straight out that he could continue with the course only on condition that he saw the college counsellor.

It was hard to believe, now, that he and Broom had been so blind. It was not alcohol that was the problem. Fraser had already found his vocation, and its name was heroin. He was on the threshold, in fact, of a brilliant career in drugs.

45

Lockhart plodded south heavily and without intent, while the wind brought gritty tears to his eyes, and Fraser moved ahead of him like a bright insubstantial angel.

Was it July when he'd last seen him? Certainly it was in the hot hub of the summer, during what he now conceived of as 'the time before'. Fraser had arrived one day on the doorstep, accepted Agneta's offer of dinner, and announced that he had discharged himself, finally, from the clinic. He'd had it up to here with London, he insisted. London was toxic, London was full of shit. This time he was going home for good. He ate a grapefruit, segment by segment, without flinching. Then he looked defiantly at Lockhart.

'So what d'you think, Lucky? I don't see why I shouldn't learn to manage the estate, do you? Even if I didn't exactly get the grounding you did.'

Lockhart did not look at Agneta. He knew exactly what she thought of Fraser's hare-brained schemes. 'If that's what you really want, man, then go for it,' he mumbled, hoping against hope, fearing in his heart that it was a disastrous idea.

For a while he'd heard nothing. Then there was a terse letter from his father. *Since this is the first time your brother has expressed an interest, I do not feel I should discourage him. We shall just have to see whether or not he makes a go of it...*

As the weeks went by and autumn shivered into winter, he'd told himself that no news was good news. This, of course, was wishful thinking. Although it would be fair to say that he had problems of his own at the time. Not to put too

46

fine a point on it, he was gutted. His days were dull and tremulous and clumsy; he woke wretched in the morning and lay down wretched at night. At the moment, however, reminding himself of this didn't help. It simply didn't seem to amount to a good enough excuse.

Above Canary Wharf tower the sky was unstable: great bales of cloud closing and clearing to show a skinny peeping moon. On windscreens and the plateglass of bus stops there was a fret of rain. Lockhart stepped into the gutter to avoid a splash of newish vomit, and at the last minute saw the car swerve, the horn-blare plucking at his nerves. He caught a glimpse of the driver, still chattering into his mobile. Lockhart skipped onto the pavement – not as smartly as he would have done a year ago – feeling his bulk surround him like an outline of the future: his father's build, strong and square and heavy as a headstone. It was Fraser who'd always been the slender one, narrow of shoulder and fair of face, like his mother. As for his own shoulders, Lockhart could hardly blame those who saw them as a solid shelf to set their burdens on. Not that he had any particular objection to being dependable. The way he tried to look at it was that giving what's asked of you was a kind of privilege, and although nothing in his life would ever be quite right again – or perhaps *because* it would not – it might also become, one day, a kind of pleasure.

Near Old Street roundabout he spotted an illuminated sign down a narrow side street. CAFÉ OPEN. Lockhart was tired. His feet were wet. No part of him was shining. Already he sensed the onset of pre-emptive nostalgia, the thought of Callasay filling him with a need to cling to the city, to dive his nose into some shabby aproned essence. Picturing the rain driving horizontally across the moor, he turned into the alleyway and let his feet take him towards the comforts of gingham curtains and greyish coffee.

When he opened the door the sprung bell tinkled a welcome. No one in particular looked up when he entered, or at least no one looked him in the eye. Boundaries were observed more carefully at this time of night; so far from the zone of the day, nobody liked to be caught out or startled. The waitress gave him a valiant lipsticked smile. Her ice-cream-coloured hair was whipped steeply up on top of her head, where it curled out in overhangs, like the snow cornice on the summit of the Aiguille du Sud.

On the counter was a cardboard collecting box with a snapshot glued to the side: a young boy, bald-headed, on a beach that looked like Clacton. A polaroid of someone's son and heir, grinning in red waterwings. The legend was hand-printed in felt-tip pen; Gavin's illness was one of the few words that wasn't misspelled.

There was no *cappuccino*. Lockhart ordered a Nescafé, reflecting on the ordinary goodness there was in people, when you got right down to basics. He dropped some coins into the box and trained his will on Gavin. Gavin would run along the beach again, his hair would grow thick, his heart would beat as powerfully as Lockhart's own. Only a fear of being conspicuous stopped him adding a ten-pound note from his wallet.

A blue haze of bacon smoke hung above the kitchen door. He heard the rattle of an iron frying pan against a stove. When his coffee materialized he carried it to a corner table and sat snuggling his hands around the mug to warm them. Just then the door swung open to admit a tall and sloping youth, and Lockhart felt the heaviness of preoccupation leave him in a rush, mysteriously, as if sucked out by the circulation of fresh and frosty air. Bewildered, he stared at the guy, wondering what was familiar about the buck teeth, the pale-lashed eyes, the fashionable straggle of the forelock. Was he an actor, perhaps? Some kind of media celebrity? None of the other customers had done more than glance at him, but Lockhart was convinced that a coherent – if for the moment indecipherable – connection existed between himself and the newcomer, who ordered a Full English and sat down with the late edition of the *Standard* and minded his own business.

A warm wool smell rose from Lockhart's wet donkey jacket. He felt a smile of puzzlement shaping the corners of his mouth. Foolishness aside, sometimes the feeling of the arrival of angels was very strong. Not that he would ever think of mentioning it to anyone – not even, as it happened, to Agneta. Agneta had no patience with wishful thinking. It would not have been easy to convince her that a good and meet destiny hovered somewhere nearby, refining itself, preparing for a surprise entrance.

49

He sipped his coffee, covertly observing the youth, indulging the pleasant flowering of his fantasies. For wasn't this exactly how they would come – unheralded, unremarked, in a mildewed tracksuit and a pair of Nike trainers? He imagined you might recognize them by a blue glaze round their bodies, perhaps, in certain lights, or by a kind of laugh they'd leave inside you as they turned away. And maybe after they'd gone you'd see some sign or other: for instance, when you looked at the sugar bowl it might be changed, and changed utterly. You'd glance down idly and the joke would blind you. In place of the tea-tarnished contents you'd see a white mound, cold and pure and glittering, the sugar crystals transformed into snow.

If you were to have asked Broom what, at this point in her life, she most wished for, very likely she would have replied that, at her age, she was learning to expect less of the future, that she had become, by force of circumstance, a creature committed to the past.

Micky, on the other hand, had a little motto he was fond of. Whenever he was asked what his field was, his line of work, *'Qu'est-ce que vous faîtes comme travail?'* etc., he'd come out with it. Profession: Futurist. Hedging his bets with a laugh and a shrug, although in actual fact he saw no good reason why the term shouldn't pass into common parlance. Futurist. It was a word with wings, which evoked like no other the air and space of the new communications industries. A word, moreover, that promised a synthesis of advertising, marketing and PR – those quarrelsome siblings which in his honest opinion were far too concerned to fence off their territories and define their identities as separate. Futurist. As an umbrella term, it had dash and attitude and lifestyle connotations. It lit up a better world to come and plunged the nostalgic non-subscriber into twenty centuries of darkness.

At about 2 a.m. Micky wheeled his supper trolley out into the corridor and hung his breakfast order on the doorknob. He watched Satellite for a while, then he sat down at his laptop with a litre of Badoit and logged on. First he checked his email: a few bits and bobs from Alice in the office; nothing crucial. Some spam that had slipped through – 'Say yes to Jesus', free loans, the usual. There was a message from Iceboy, which reminded him that he hadn't replied to the last one yet, but nothing, disappointingly, from Damien.

He emptied the rubbish into the cosmic garbage can, ran his hands through his hair and prepared to enter a zone between worlds. The night stretched ahead, exciting as an empty motorway. On the net the flesh was made word and words had free assembly. They flew far off and settled like black birds on a white ground, assembling a personality upon the screen.

Invent a history and you invent a person, as Martinson had written, or was it Berghof? You

51

could be who you wanted to be; you could be the devil himself if it pleased you.

It was like the time as a boy when he'd discovered the terrible gullibility of his mother. On the TV screen he had seen sky-divers for the first time, and his chest had tightened with excited recognition. They dropped out of the deafening deep blue of extreme altitude, and as the silence echoed in his ears he was aware, suddenly, that this was a pond in which he, too, had swum once. As they fell, he fell with them, until the bright wings of the air fluttered and faded and finally burned out.

By that time he had already seen the apartment blocks of Ras Hamra collapse under the shelling; he'd seen their inhabitants plunge from the shattered storeys in a blizzard of pillow feathers. He'd seen many things falling: inventories of things, an alphabet of items drifting down onto the streets of the city. Mnemonics, *aides-mémoire*. He had seen adzes fall, and Bibles, clocks, colanders, shoe-trees, sewing machines. He'd seen people fall, burning, the flames blown straight up like skirts by the draught of the drop. Civilians for the most part – slaughtered lambs, mute with surprise. But he had never really been able to identify with them. Like any Beiruti boy of that era, he'd preferred to think of himself as a lion.

One day he told his mother that he remembered falling, that he remembered being thrown. He must have been nine or ten at the time, old enough to know that remarks like these were guaranteed to have an impact. Latifa was a

Druze, and so ingrained is the Druze belief in the transmigration of souls that no child of theirs was ever slapped down for telling fairy tales. In the foothills and fastnesses of the Chouf, you could disown your parents with impunity. Even nowadays you could still find youths who conducted themselves with the dignity they thought appropriate for the reincarnation of such-and-such a fighter struck down – at the time of their own birth, naturally – by a Phalangist bullet, or pulverized by an Israeli mortar shell. These ghost boys didn't play noisy games or rough-house with their peers. They smiled seldom and warily. With patient good humour they submitted to lengthy interrogation sessions, knowing, no doubt, that the longings of the bereaved were enough to ensure that they would pass the test and be welcomed eventually into the bosom of their chosen 'family'. They seemed to know, mysteriously, in which drawer 'Mother' kept her gold and turquoise jewellery, and under which floorboard 'Grandfather' had hidden the deeds to the house and orange grove in Palestine. Young though they were, the old folks deferred to them and sought their advice on important family matters. Gifts were showered on them. They became celebrities overnight, inflated with the honour of fallen heroes.

Micky had watched their antics with interest, but although he remained convinced that he had somehow tumbled into his life – so convinced that he could still feel the delicious downrush of the fall – he stopped just short of claiming that he was one of them.

Needless to say, he'd mentioned none of this to his father. If Latifa was content to live in a world of half-hints and possibilities, Jerome was a Catholic with a capital C, and his tolerance of his heathen in-laws did not extend to blasphemy. Only with Latifa could Micky share his secrets, which made her sad but seemed also to make her proud. Perhaps she had taken them as proof that Arab blood flowed more strongly in his veins than European. Otherwise why would she have let his fantasies take such a hold? He had seen it happen before, the way mothers in their maternal passion could tailor their tenderest memories to fit, even persuade themselves that the phenomenon had started with the first baby breath, that when the midwife laid the infant in her arms his eyes had focused on a point beyond her, as if searching for the other one, the mother who had gone before.

When he first realized how thoroughly he had duped her, he was horrified. It was the one and only time he'd come close to hating her, because he had been forced to ask himself how she could renounce him so stupidly and so sweetly. She had shown no backbone, mounted no solid opposition. Instead, she had conjured up a changeling and placed it in his baby cot.

On the net, however – and this was the beauty of it – everyone could choose to be a changeling, no questions asked. There were those who saw it as the last bastion of liberty–equality–democracy, and perhaps they weren't so far off the mark. Perverts and poets and A1 plonkers, all were cyber-pilgrims in the blackness of blue. Some wore masks, while others, like Iceboy, simply poured out their complicated souls; all were searching, as far as Micky could see, for something like permission. Permission to love, permission to hate. He had stopped being astonished by the trust that tumbled towards him through the hush of space. The trust of strangers. There was something about him, apparently, that inspired confidence. It was as if the beam of his heart spread out to encompass a larger kindred who could be warmed by it, their agitations soothed, and if he found this more touching than troubling, no doubt it was because distance, in this case, was the saving grace.

Scorn I can work with, said Mephistopheles cheerfully in the middle of the long night.

Broom clutched at darkness and found the switch of the standard lamp that stood behind the bed. At first, glancing round the room, she recognized nothing. She had the sensation that some part of her had not quite returned from a long way off. Her body felt bedevilled and blubbery, as if it had wakened in some hostile element. Her mind was a chair-lift that kept passing and repassing the same pylons; again and again it chuntered up to the summit but couldn't get off.

She saw the familiar pelt of the nylon rug in the middle of the floor, the leatherette sofa, brown and plump and ugly as ever. The cuckoo clock on the wall kept up its arthritic tick.

She closed her eyes and tried to trick herself

into believing that Al was there, surrounding her. So big and hot, like a polar bear.

Al had never felt the cold. In winter he'd walk naked out of the tent to piss in the snow: Wales, the Cairngorms, it made no difference to him. Dank, slimy quarry-faces were, perversely, his particular delight, and the particular despair of his climbing partners.

But of course above all else he loved the sun. The sun on the open road. If he'd written from the Alhambra of the way the Moors worshipped water and the enclosed space of courtyards, he himself was pure European and, like all those from northern countries, his soul turned for nourishment to fire, to the sun burning in the sky. There was nothing he relished more than to follow it as it mounted to the top of the highest mountain and plunged into the sea at dusk. The sun on hot rock, on sheer cliff crags, on shingle sloping to the tide.

Broom really couldn't bear to think of this, of his freedom, his feet burning on the pedals, the dust thrown up behind his wheels. All the ways he had of not belonging to her.

She tried to think of something that would make her brain a better place to be. Her body, for instance, which knew the wind's knock against its shape, the pleasure of soft hair blown across the face. Her body, which she still intermittently loved, was wise; it seemed to know a lot. What it didn't know, however, was how to be fifty and some kind of widow. Or else it did, and tried to tell her, but she couldn't or wouldn't listen. Perhaps it didn't know – any more than her infant self did – how to speak its hunger in a forbidding adult ear...

She jumped up, pulled on her fleece, put the kettle on and waited. The one yellow eye of the street lamp glimmered on the cypress tree outside the kitchen window. The snow, constant and crystalline, reminded her of some airy fracture of her self, how it tried to assemble itself around the sullen music of her mother's voice. Become a little china cup on a tiny perfect shelf: the lightest entry, small and slight and irreproachable as snowfall.

She remembered a concentration of effort, a holding action. It was rather like trying to keep a plane in the air. Breathe out for a second and you can be sure the ailerons or struts or whatever will snap and the whole shebang will hit the deck. The feeling had lasted until her father came home from work at night and hugged her closely in his brawny arms. Diesel and grease and engine oil. The smell of the Swarfega he used to scrub the dirt of the day from his hands. His face was big and convex like a hub-cap when it came close and gleamed at her. He'd hitch her onto his knee and give her a beardie with his spiky stubble, until she squirmed and squealed with joy, and then what a laugh would rumble up from his insides. Her father was a flier. He had flown over a place called Germany but when she tried it from the bed-end he told her that people could not fly, only birds and angels could. He was the one who'd cried at her wedding, not her mother. Standing on the steps after the reception to see them off. 'My wee girl, so young, I just canny credit it.' *A man who will be missed*, the minister had said at his funeral, although since her father had never had any time for Bible-thumpers she didn't know why her mother felt she had the right to have him there.

To be without. To be in need of. To lack. So what's new, thought Broom. Whenever she tried to work out what was happening to her the same numbing vertigo seized her. She didn't exactly feel, nor did she not feel; rather, she fell prey to nameless inner events that for all she knew might even have been violent. There was a kind of undifferentiated pain, but there was no meaning. She could put nothing in its proper place.

Behind her the big fridge shook itself like a wet dog and clicked off. She caught a glimpse of her reflection in the window glass: fleeced, hooded, her hands circling her cup. Her body was hunched and mistrustful, anticipating the alarms of each and every hour to come before the dawn. Her watch said 1.30.

The duty-free whisky, bought for emergencies, stood, stoical, on the kitchen dresser.

It could have been worse, she told herself. I could have turned to drink: the slippery slope. It wouldn't have been surprising.

It was a hot night and a wet one when she first set eyes on Al. Thunderclouds hammerheading up over the city, rain battering periodically at the petunias in Roz's window-boxes. Since the flat was barely big enough for Roz and Simon, not to mention their paintings, the doors were wedged open to let the guests spill out onto the landing. The windows were open too, admitting mosquitoes.

She stood in the crush with a glass in her hand and a sweat slick spreading down her spine. The art critic who reviewed in the Sundays, and should have known by now that she disliked him, was bellowing in her ear. Roz had told her that she should network more, and it was certainly true that the critic had clout and could be useful to her, if she played her cards right. But Broom went to parties to see friends, to drink and dance and let off steam; she didn't go to play her cards right, nor to cosy up to hollow men whose waspishness was avid for accomplices, and the thought that she was required to – worse, might even be tempted to – filled her with the darkest kind of claustrophobia. She had tried for Roz's sake to be polite, but by this stage the critic had her backed up against the drinks table and she was losing patience. Before she could stop herself she snapped at him and wheeled away, and made an enemy.

The man she did want to talk to had a tall weather-beaten face and a greying quiff that was pure Jerry Lee Lewis. He was sitting on the floor between the window and a stack of canvases. His back was wedged against the wall and his knees were jammed against his chest but he looked impressively relaxed. Earlier he had seemed to be with a woman friend of Roz's, a journalist Broom knew slightly; she had overheard him saying something about mountains. She struggled through the crowd towards him.

'Did I hear you say you were a climber?' She realized that he was alone. When he stood up he

59

loomed above her, craggy and huge, like a cliff face.

'It's possible.' She saw bright speckled brown eyes, a solid jaw, chapped lips spreading slowly into a questioning smile. 'Alan Hargreave.' He held out his hand. 'And you are?'

'Fed up talking to dickheads, actually,' she said, returning the handshake. 'Sorry. I didn't mean you. I'm an old friend of Roz's. We were at college together.'

'Another painter, then?'

'Yes. Mostly.' She was aware of being given a rather thorough physical. Here was a man who looked, and didn't care to hide it.

'Of repute?' His tone was teasing.

'Well, I don't know about that...'

'Don't believe a word of it, Al!' cried Roz, shimmying by with a bottle of Cava and squeezing her in passing. 'She's pathologically modest.'

Broom laughed gratefully. 'I've got a lot to be modest about.'

Apart from the comely glow of the outdoors, what struck her most about him was his voice: rusty, sonorous, deep as a tanker's hull. A voice, she thought, that was made as much for reassuring as for laying down the law. She learned that he used to be a history teacher, but was presently in charge of a referral unit for disruptive pupils. A sin bin, in other words. He assured her that he liked the work, and she believed him. She pictured disturbed and disturbing youths coming at him with their whirlwind needs and purposeless rebellions, the wedge of his chest stopping them in their tracks, his sizeable arms pinning them into a bear-hug.

Around midnight she collared Roz in the kitchen and pursued her researches. Roz was dragging baking

60

trays out of the oven, her round face slithery with sweat. He used to be on the Executive of the Communist Party, she said: when there was such a thing. As Youth Organizer, she thought, or perhaps it was National Organizer. He and the journalist were no longer an item; as far as she knew, the affair had foundered because Al refused on principle to be monogamous.

'So technically he's a free agent?'

Roz took a palette knife and began to prise off a batch of burned puff pastries. She looked at Broom doubtfully. 'Listen, my angel. Al's an old mate and I love him dearly, but between you and me he's a bit of a handful.'

Later, piecing together the early stages of the encounter, she remembered how he had hitched up the belt of his trousers – gleefully, purposefully, like a man getting down to business. At the time, though, she was conscious mainly of the smile that had somehow got inside her stomach and was spreading upwards. As if her system had o/d'd on junk food and was thankful to be faced with something wholesome.

High up in the eaves pigeons plumped out their chests and strutted along the gutters. It was May, the mating month: she knew something was due to happen.

If, like the ancient Greeks, you'd tied strips of red wool to each part that Al had wounded or broken in his search for adventure, he would have been a flaring field, a scarlet tatter. Both ankles, left knee, wrists, left eye, thumb: she never could keep track of the inventory.

When he arrived at her door she noticed the limp

61

immediately. He hauled up his trouser leg to show off a vivid V-shaped scar above the knee. A block the size of a chest of drawers had come off the buttress above him – a glancing blow, he told her. Luckily. Otherwise he could have lost the bloody leg.

Broom was irritated. Did he really think he could impress her with boyish bravado? Lockhart was a climber too, but his reserve had always been exemplary. If he had narrow escapes he kept them strictly to himself.

In the pub Al fired his questions gruffly, as if expecting her to account for herself. Had she ever been married? Children? Had she ever joined a party? What did she think of Green politics? (Yes. Yes. No. Maybe.) Less of a date, she decided, than an interview. Evidently passing the physical hadn't been enough. It was on the tip of her tongue to ask him if she'd got the job. She'd assumed the preliminaries had already been dealt with; instead, here she was, dutifully comparing notes – demos they'd both been on, picket-lines: Vietnam, Grunwicks, Wapping, the Miners. It was the sort of conversation that could easily go on all night: at their age, after all, they had a lot of ground to cover.

Once again it was a hot evening, too hot and languorous for ideologies. Her eyes drifted. She nodded and smiled with restraint. Couldn't he tell that he was boring her? After a while she leaned her chin on her fist and said truthfully that if she was the sort who joined parties, she would have joined the CP, but she'd always been more of a libertarian, herself. Libertarian, she thought. Such a slippery word. On the right it meant rampant free-marketeering; on the left it smacked of anarchism. She felt like telling him

62

she'd had socialism with her mother's milk. Well, OK, her father's. Not that he'd ever been in the party as such, but contempt for the landlords and bosses of the world had landed him in hot water often enough. On Sundays, to rile her mother and her grandmother, he'd insist that Jesus Christ was the first Communist. 'Easier for an elephant to pass through the eye of a needle than for a rich man to enter the kingdom of heaven,' *he'd intone with a triumphant grin, the declared atheist who wasn't above misquoting the Bible when it suited him.*

'Nice pub,' said Al, glancing around restlessly.

Broom began to wonder if he was as nervous as she was. 'For London,' she agreed, 'it's civilized.' A poster on the bar threatened Quiz Night, but there was no jukebox or Sky TV to up the volume. Two white-haired Jamaicans were playing chess. A Labrador lay hopefully before the empty fireplace. Through a broad bay window the Domesday church was visible, nestling in its leafy graveyard. 'People actually come here to talk.'

She found herself relating an incident that had happened during the construction of the Hydro dam. A Polish labourer had lost his legs while clearing a defective chute on the crusher. Her father knew that the construction company would try to wriggle out, and offered to testify in court on his behalf. Thanks to his evidence the company were found liable and forced to pay compensation. There had been other witnesses to the accident, but her father was the only one willing to risk his job for a principle.

Al nodded judiciously. 'And he lost it?'

'Oh yes.' She could see that she'd impressed him, and for a moment she felt obscurely resentful, as if he'd

somehow manipulated her into trotting out her working-class credentials.

'...So when he runs along the traffic jam looking for a phone to call the emergency services he sees this woman in her car, talking on her mobile.'

At the next table the owner of the Labrador, a young man with blond dreadlocks, was telling an apocryphal tale. There were two girls with him, in halter-necks and frayed shorts. They had their elbows on the table and they were drinking pints. From the fireplace the Labrador watched fixedly.

'He raps on the window and asks, you know, if he can use it. But she shakes her head. So of course he insists. I mean, the guy's frantic. In the end she winds down her window sort of shamefaced and tells him that it doesn't actually work!'

The dark girl stopped rolling her cigarette. 'But she was talking on it.'

'Yeah, but she was faking.'

'Like, for security?'

'More like for show.' The blond guy shrugged. 'It happens.'

They began to argue about fashion statements and the situation of women and the pressures of both. Their cheeks were dewy, their gestures young and loose and eager.

Broom felt Al's eyes on her, and heat rose to her face.

'So what about feminism?' he said abruptly. 'I hope you're not another backslider, like all these trendy ex-feminists who just want to dash off and get married!'

She laughed, assuming, naturally enough, that he was joking. 'You make it sound like a major conspiracy!' Then it registered that he was knitting his

64

brows at her. He really is knitting his brows, she thought wonderingly.

'Feminists used to have principles, for God's sake. Anti-monogamy was the central tenet of the movement.'

His voice was hectoring. She laughed again, uneasily. Oh, here we go, she thought. A complete throwback, an absolute dinosaur. She waited for a twitch of the lip or a comic inclination of the eyebrow, some little hint that he knew how truly idiotic he sounded. 'I think you mean the Sexual Revolution. Wrong movement, right?' Her tone was scathing but he'd put her on the defensive. Skeletons she'd almost managed to forget were stirring in her cupboards. She felt faintly fraudulent, and did not like it.

She studied him critically. He was no longer a young man. Already his eyelids had a definite droop. She decided that his reputation for womanizing bothered her a good deal less than the quiff, that antique badge of vanity. If he had any sense at all he'd be as embarrassed as she was by the excesses of the past, the old rigorous utopias. 'Typical of a man,' she said sweetly, 'to focus on the one thing that suits him.'

Al swilled down the last of his beer, glaring at her over the rim of the glass: a man in middle age, she thought, with froth on his lip and a bee in his bonnet. But one who occupied space well, she had to admit – if not his shirt, which seemed to be a size too small for him. The sleeves, rolled up, cut into solid muscle. There was a tanned V at the open neck which made her glad.

She pointed to his empty glass. 'Foster's, is it?' He placed his hands flat on the table and levered himself

65

up. 'Sit,' she commanded, whisking away the empty glass.

Leaning on the bar, she was conscious of her bare brown shoulders. Fallen May blossoms, stirred by the draught of passing traffic, whirled in through the open door. A wilful energy surged in her. She felt feisty and combative, and just drunk enough to enjoy showing a guy like Al that he had met his match. It was a long time since she'd had a decent fight with a man, since she'd felt like a contender.

She went back to the table and placed the pint within the compass of his arms. 'So...' she said, sitting down with her Chardonnay and squaring up to him. Al nodded and sipped. A bullish energy bristled back at her.

She began to chuckle. It wasn't so much that she couldn't take him seriously; rather, that some enthusiasm inside her was determined to come out. Perhaps her genes had forgotten that she was nearing the end of her child-bearing years, for they seemed to be decreeing that he was the right stock, the right stuff, the perfect combination of warrior and peasant. Or perhaps some brand-new bio-system had kicked in, some radar peculiar to mid-life which told her that with this man she would never ever have to worry about her wrinkles.

Later she would have given anything to see him guzzle down a pint, the big leonine head tilted back, one eye on the clock for last orders. Not drinking his beer so much as inhaling it straight into his bloodstream, into his thirsty soul.

Impossible to forget his appetite for pleasure, the way he sighed and sucked it into him. His love of women, their curved shadows and their smells. His love and his suspicion of their power, or at least that part of it which threatened to ensnare him.

Broom told herself that anyone could change. In the interim she flew to Munich to attend the opening of Daniel's Don Giovanni. *Then she went down to Brixton for dinner.*

On the way to the tube station the bus was almost empty and the black conductor was playing the fool. He reeled a strip of ticket-tape from his machine, coiled it into a crown and then perched it on the blond curls of a little girl.

'Now you're a princess,' he said, beaming. 'Lady Di.'

The girl and her mother got the giggles, and Broom, who was never happier than when filled with unrealistic expectations, laughed with them.

The rush-hour Northern Line was an abomination. There had been signal failures, a breakdown. She squeezed into an overloaded carriage and tucked her head in like a tortoise, but the doors refused to close.

'Move along, please,' begged the intercom. 'Get closer.' A sardonic chuckle crackled over the loudspeaker. 'Snuggle up. Make new friends.'

Broom laughed. London, she thought. City of dirt and closet anarchists.

When Al set a whole salmon ceremoniously on the table, Liam and Robbo smirked at the sight of it.

'Old Greavesy's really making an effort.'

The fish steamed in its foil, princely on a bed of fennel. Liam and Robbo were fifteen or twenty years younger than Al. They were climbers too, Lost Boys

67

who kept their sleeping bags and stereos in rough-and-ready rooms at the top of the house, and did casual work on building sites to support their habit. They greeted her with nods and monosyllables, 'Hi' and 'Cheers'. They had a flushed shiftiness that made her feel self-conscious. Lost Boys implied the presence of a Peter Pan, and she had never really seen herself as a Wendy.

The phone hadn't stopped ringing since she arrived. Liam and Robbo, who were squatting on the floor sharing a pre-pub joint, took turns to shout messages through the kitchen hatch to Al.

'Ken McBurney can't make the Democratic Left meeting.'

'Kevin from the Climbers Club says do you want a fast lift to Pembroke this weekend?'

'Ercan's coming down for the Campaign Against Racist Laws. Can he doss?'

Some calls, it seemed, were more personal, and required Al to be fetched from the kitchen. She declined the joint and stood, awkward, by the fireplace, trying to hide the fact that she was listening. Al's telephone manner was uniformly brusque and breezy. There was no way of telling whether the calls were from lovers.

On the mantelpiece was a framed photograph of two infants: a boy with blue eyes just a fraction too large, too luminous – 'There's a wean that'll be spoilt,' her mother would have said – and a little girl with an extraordinary head of ruby-auburn hair.

'Al's grandchildren,' Robbo supplied obligingly.

Liam grinned. 'Oh yeah. Greavesy's the proudest grandaddy in the whole of London town!'

She was relieved when Al turned landlordly and

68

shooed the lodgers out.

'So how was the opera?' he asked as they sat down at the table. Then the phone rang again and he swivelled his seat sideways to answer it. He scribbled rapidly in his diary, grandfatherly in half-glasses.

The fennel was underdone, and no wonder. She poked at her fish, thinking of Don Giovanni's little catalogue of conquests. On his fingers Leporello ticked them off wickedly. 'Ma in Spagna, mille e tre.'

'Is it always like this?' she asked when he put down the phone.

Al shrugged. 'On and off.' But he fussed with the plates and looked pleased. In his warm brown eyes a sweetness she suddenly wanted to get close to.

After dinner he sat her down on the sofa and organized the music. 'What would you like?' He had everything, he assured her proudly, that the connoisseur could possibly require: jazz, country, rockabilly, TexMex, bluegrass.

'You choose,' she said, smiling blankly at row upon row of records. The hi-fi was the only modern item in the room; otherwise it was a strictly no-frills establishment, with shelves of climbing guidebooks, coiled ropes in a tea-chest in the corner, and furniture that was a few years short of the V&A – a utility dining-suite, two bucket-shaped armchairs in dark red leatherette, and a veneer radiogram from the Thirties, presumably defunct. Above the bay window hung a desolate strip of cretonne which didn't match the curtains.

'It's a pelmet,' Al explained with a grin. 'It makes the place respectable.' He had fetched a tray on which stood a blue coffee jug and a bottle of Jameson's. With loving deference he slid an LP from its cover.

69

Broom had the feeling that she would soon relax: it was high time, after all, that she was courted. She sipped her whisky, anticipating intimate exchanges, anecdotes of childhood. Surely whatever odylic forces had brought her this far must soon reveal their hidden form. Patterns would emerge, coincidences, elements that at first looked random but turned out not to be.

She smoked a cigarette while Al stacked and cleared the plates. Even without the limp his walk was stiff and lurching, like a cowboy who'd ridden clean across Wyoming. The message – sent not only by the music – was rugged and retro, dustbowls and distance and Texas yearning. His meat and drink were sex and action; Hank Williams's slide guitar supplied the syrup on the side. She thought she could detect something dry and friable in him, a place that had never been watered with milk or tears.

When he sat down opposite her she felt her stomach tense. He had big square feet, big hands planted on wide-splayed knees. On the wall above the fireplace hung a black and white print that showed the confluence of two high glaciers. She gazed at it silently, while her mind filled with divergences – musical, doctrinal, maybe even moral. She confessed that Hank Williams made her cringe.

'You're joking!' Al exclaimed. 'The Master?'

She made a rueful face. 'The Velvet Underground's more my kind of thing.'

Al's eyebrows scaled the heights. 'That's not music, it's decadence!' He flapped his hand derisively, his fingers flicking at her, as if sprinkling her with holy water. His grin broadened. 'Take the shame!'

'At least you could play me some blues. Something with a bit less of the buckskin and fringes.' Something,

70

she thought, that wouldn't make me feel so old.

'Try this,' said Al, as a saxophone trailed a long note across the silence. 'Albert Ayler.'

'Ah yes,' said Broom, who hadn't heard of him. She felt suddenly melancholy, disappointed in Al and in herself. Or perhaps it was the shabbiness of the room, seeping muddily into her. She hedged her breasts in with her arms and heard herself complaining that she wasn't as fit as she used to be, that she'd found it heavy going last summer on the Haute Route in the Pyrenees.

Al sat down again, formal and upright in the ruined armchair. His eyes swept her appraisingly. 'Judging by the bits I can see, you look in pretty good nick to me.' Once again his grin swept wide: white and gold-capped and truculent. 'So how about it?'

Broom gaped at him for a second, wondering whether she should or shouldn't feel insulted. She blushed and looked away. A curt laugh came out of her. 'Don't you think, with relationships, it's better to get to know people a little bit?'

'Who said anything about a relationship?' he barked back. 'I was only talking about a fuck.'

A shocked resonance from the past said that she had provoked the attack; almost simultaneously another voice leapt to the defence, protesting that she'd done nothing to deserve it.

Al tossed back his whisky, eyeing her. His chin jutted. Everything about him now looked brutal. 'Well, if you want sex, why beat about the bush, that's how I see it. And don't tell me women aren't as antsy as men. Even your married feminists aren't averse to a bit of rough, take it from me!'

His smile harangued her, brazen, ridiculous. A bit of

71

rough indeed, she thought. 'Excuse me. I thought I heard you say you went to Cambridge!' It struck her that her instinct, which was to like him enormously, had been crudely and wilfully obstructed. He would not do, could not be made to do. Of course Roz had warned her, but like a fool she hadn't wanted to listen. Marooned in the evening she had so looked forward to, she could have wept hot tears.

Al put down his whisky and leaned forward, shrugging defiantly. 'Look. You can always say no. I'm used to taking it on the chin. But if you're asking me to be a hypocrite...'

Something inside her had locked tight. She stared at the glacier print. It looked like the Noir and the Blanc on the Ecrins but it was now too late to ask. With an acute pang of sorrow she realized that she should go now, exit, slam the door in his face. There was a vibration in the superstructure of her shoulders, like the shudder of a decelerating plane.

She stood up abruptly, throwing her cigarettes into her handbag. The edge of her sandal caught the whisky glass and spun it across the carpet. Al reached under his chair and retrieved it. Then he rose heavily, cupping the empty glass in his hand. 'You're not going?' There was a glaze of shock on his face but strangely no surprise. It occurred to her suddenly that he had expected this, that in some weird way he'd been setting himself up to be rejected.

'What do you think?'

'No, listen... You're right. I was out of order there. I'm really sorry.' He took her hand and coaxed her towards the sofa. When he had sat her down he patted her shoulder swiftly once and retreated to the far end, leaving a notable gap between them. 'We'll do it your

72

way, OK?' She watched his hands fly up, palms flattened and neutral, like a footballer swearing that he hasn't fouled the ball. 'I mean it. Scout's honour.' His grin flickered, droll and sheepish. 'I know a terrific climbing hut in the Peak District: we could have a walking weekend. Just, well, get to know each other...' His torso inclined towards her but he dragged it ironically back. 'Just friends,' he promised.

Broom eyed him. Any idiot could see it was a tactical retreat. He wasn't even going to pretend that he was pleading. 'So you'll fix it all up, will you?'

Her sarcasm went unnoticed. Al let out a kind of war-whoop. 'Will I!'

For a clever man, she decided, he was extraordinarily naïve. He really expected everyone to behave like good boy scouts. 'OK,' she said, 'fine,' knowing already that she was lying, and that she was going to let him down. While he played straight and made honesty his policy, she would wait and play dirty. Let him make all the phone calls, clean out the old Fiesta, bundle his walking gear into the boot: she would give him just long enough to taste his pleasure. And then she would teach him that she wasn't anything like his other women, who swallowed his notions of the level playing field and were no doubt oh so rational, reliable and comradely.

Welcome to the sex war, she thought. Nothing like hurting a man to make him start to pay attention.

By now it was well past midnight; the tube stations were closed and twenty-five pounds was the cheapest quote Al could get on a taxi. He offered his spare room, which she accepted warily. Once she'd made her choice, however, he was punctilious about respecting it. Upstairs he showed her the bathroom and gave her

73

a towel and a brand-new toothbrush. When he handed her the smaller of two matching bathrobes that hung behind his bedroom door she took it without a word. Girl-size, she thought. For the girlfriends.

The spare room was a cubby-hole off the kitchen with a chill linoleum floor. When she switched on the light she saw that a bare bulb swung above her. In one corner there was a heap of toys, board games, and a large red plastic pedal-car. On the wall hung a blown-up photo of a teenage Al in corduroy climbing breeches, poised on the vertical edge of some murderous mist-shrouded buttress.

She lay in the narrow boy's bed and raged. She punched at the lumpy pillow, thinking of Al's large grey sleeping head and the heat that came off him.

Earlier she'd caught a glimpse of his bedroom. It had a deep pile carpet, soft-shaded lamps, a blue duvet cover patterned with lotus flowers: luxury that was markedly absent from the rest of the house. When she ran upstairs to use the toilet the self-satisfied sound of male snoring issued out from under every door.

In the claustrophobic room her anger ricocheted like a bird in a box. Her mind traversed the evening, revisiting again and again every wound that had been inflicted, every broken wing. A cold sweat filmed her neck and throat. She wrapped the thin coverlet around her and tossed, groaning, in the strange house, wishing she could throttle him or shout.

At around five in the morning the anger began to transmute into something else, something humiliating that was in her. When the first flight out of Heathrow trundled overhead like a shadow of her childhood she saw her father's plane cut the light into colours, make red nights melt over Dresden: his plane, fit only for

74

heroes, which had held her in its high arms on sufferance.

She thought of Al's grey hair, and the younger men she'd been involved with, and what she might have been avoiding. Her body thirty years beyond boyishness, and all this time she had been kidding herself.

What she couldn't do was go up and get into that bed with him, any more than she could have crept in needfully between her parents, and every thought that entered her brain was both a grave and obvious mistake and a current she was powerless to prevent. Which was, she thought, exactly why he had to start to suffer.

It was getting light. Bird sounds seeped from the bushes in the back garden. Her feet itched to be on the move. If she got the first tube she could avoid the unbearable embarrassment of breakfast, and seeing him.

She leapt up and dressed and tiptoed down the hall. Then she saw that the front door had a Chubb lock on it. With tears of frustration in her eyes she searched the kitchen for a key, opening and closing drawers, rummaging in the living room like a burglar.

When Robbo got up at six he found her drinking Nescafé and eyeing the front door accusingly. He gazed at her, barefoot and bleary and curious. Then he padded down the hall and swung the door open. 'It's never locked.'

'Oh, right,' she said, mortified. She let out a silly tinkling laugh. 'Thanks a lot.'

'Cheers,' said Robbo. 'No problem.'

Later she heard how Robbo had split his sides over the whole misadventure – the spare room, the salmon,

75

and the one-night stand that got away. The joke was on Al but by then he could tell it against himself spinning it out and chortling when he got to Robbo's punchline.

'Well, Greavesy, you certainly blew it this time!'

Acc: nighthawk@freeserve.co.uk
Re: guilt

Your encouragement will not fall on deaf ears. It is manna in the desert of this devotee, who asks you one more question only. Why do the stars look younger every year from here, where the sun's angle is so low and no rock is fixed and the flattened glaciated ranges seem to boil and billow?

For now it's a long night in which our part of earth turns dimly. A few hours only of daylight or so. I'm not bored however but resolved to bite the apple again and again thanks to your words, for I'm no longer so churlish as to refuse all teachings, merely preachings. There was a beloved teacher once who urged me to follow my star, and to serve Art – but with discipline. This is the price she wanted to exact, and when I could not compromise she took the path of convention and washed her hands of me, although I could not see then, and cannot now, how exactly one's supposed to grasp one's demon *with discipline...*

In the meantime my telescope is trained on the

heavens and tonight – on the horizon – a new
star. So young it hurt my heart. Its advent was
prefigured by a bombardment of sunstorms. Of
course we're so near the Arctic Circle here that
plasma clouds penetrate the atmosphere with
ease and buffet us like giant boxing gloves. The
intensity of greenness in the north aurora gives
the measure of the state of excitement of the
oxygen particles. It's predicted that some damage
will occur due to the electricity generated by the
magnetic fluctuations. Usually the satellites bear
the brunt of the electrostatic charge, but we on
earth are far from immune, particularly in areas
like this where granite predominates. And so I'll
be quick, since am wary of power surges.

Nighthawk, this star is tender
as a boy-child whose skin glows
a pearly pinkish-gold

He comes surely
from those coronal mass-ejections
potent enough to escape
the sun's gravity

These are the sunstorms
I spoke of

I tell you he is born
of sun, is spawn
and atom of him
Pure fire and not quite formed,
yet more perfect thus

Sunlight so red
through his transparency,
like through a fragile ear

I am sad for him and proud,
to be thrown out so,
to be ejected like all of us

Bright ear of the heavens
I call him Puer in dedication
and tribute

Grace approaches!

Iceboy

Micky's head felt cool as coins and spacious. His
face was lit bluish and alert. At times like this he
felt rather like the driver of a night train, who has
a sworn responsibility to keep his vigil at the
wheel. The whisper of the heating vents lulled
him. He heard the easy rustle of his fingers across
the keyboard.

Acc: iceboy@demon.co.uk
Re: happiness

Who created the reprobate but God?
And why, but because it pleased him?
O man, who art thou that disputest with God?

There's Augustine for you, Iceboy – God's wasp
busy in his pear. God hoards his light jealously,
he grudges us a larger portion.

Just consider this paradox. Ever wondered why people at a high point of happiness break down in tears? Parents with a newborn, lovers reunited, champions clutching their medals on the Olympic podium? One minute they're smiling; the next, you see their faces crumple up and tears pour down their cheeks. Since it seems to me that a kid of five or six will weep, but you never see him weeping for joy, the inescapable question is, surely, where does this shadow come from, this envy, this spoiler out to make us wear a crown of thorns?

In response to your previous question, my advice to you as per usual is to be true to your desires, and be strong in the fight against self-censorship. I'm sure you're aware how many people allow their creativity to be stifled or even crushed altogether by the triumvirate of family–school–religion. In your case your father is the suppressive factor. There are so many forces out to prevent us experiencing *that genuine inspiration, immediate, absolute, unquestioned, ravishing, where there is no choice, no tinkering, no possible improvement; where all is as a sacred mandate, a visitation received by the possessed one with faltering and stumbling step, with shudders of awe from head to foot, and tears of joy* (sorry, there it is again) *blinding his eyes.*

Maybe your sunstorms are in fact a good sign. Maybe they're trying to remind you of your own untapped powers and energies. Maybe they're also trying to indicate that there are forces abroad that could eventually sweep away the whole patriarchal problematic...

79

Many thanx for the poem, which is much appreciated. Of course I'm not the poet you are but will try to return the compliment as soon as pressure of work permits.

Nighthawk

Micky pressed Send and sat back pensively. Sometimes he thought he could grow genuinely fond of Iceboy; certainly he did not like to see him so unhappy. The possibility filled him with a kind of serene anguish.

When he thought of Iceboy he imagined a slight, fair figure, numbed by the north, adrift in the abysses of the night. It felt like a natural instinct to surround him with the warm breath of his confidence, but was there also a wish to recast him, rescue him, even to adopt him? On the whole he thought not. Once or twice he'd almost suggested they meet IRL but so far he'd managed to check the impulse. He knew Iceboy's suffering, his universe, his inspiration; what, then, was to be gained by getting acquainted with his age, his toothpaste brand, his shoe size?

No, for the present he had no desire to get closer in. He drank a glass of water and decided to pay a nerdy visit to the Colditz site, do some virtual escaping. He would launch a blue gingham glider from the battlements, let the thermals drift him east across the Czechoslovak border. Experience had taught him that even nerds had their moments of eloquence but when the word became flesh you could be drastically disappointed.

When the great white bird of the north touched down at Stornoway, Lockhart stepped out onto the soil of another country. It was the sky that held dominion there, keeping the foreheads of the buildings pressed to the ground, like serfs abasing themselves: oceans of sky, striped with high horizontal ice-cloud, sky that stretched his lids until his eyes watered and told him that it had been the worst of all ideas to go to Miles's Christmas party.

Lockhart zipped up his Goretex against the uncompromising wind; he had the queasy feeling that his soul stood waiting here, forsaken and reproachful on the tarmac, even if his heart was still in London, drinking black coffee with Agneta, eating bananas under protest, blinking out at the drizzling Hackney dawn. *Get them down you. Tryptophan metabolizes into serotonin. You don't want to turn up there with a hangover.*

On the Callasay ferry he found a seat in the downstairs buffet and ate two floury rolls filled with bacon. The Minch swelled darkly under the boat's keel; the bow rose and fell. Through the salt-speckled glass he watched the island begin in the distance, a snail-grey smudge that the porthole scooped up and set down again. Closer in, he saw the low glinting dome of bald rock with its fringe of gingery-green turf, and the silver sandy stretches of the shore.

As the boat approached the southern tip of the

island he went out on deck. Rubha na Starragan, the Headland of the Crows. Sometimes you could see seals here, in the rich feeding grounds where the currents clashed. This was the point in the journey home for vac when he and Fraser would lean over the rail and shout to each other over the wind. *Starragan* meant hoodies, Fraser insisted; *feannagan* was the proper word for crows. Fraser had always been inordinately proud of his Gaelic. At six he'd been considered too delicate to board, and was sent instead to the village school to be a day-boy with his satchel and his sandwiches. Finally, having sailed through his eleven-plus, he was allowed to join Lockhart at Fettes.

Lockhart bandaged his Polartec scarf up around his ears. On the plane he had dozed, entering a warm and welcome blankness that protected him from morbid thoughts. Bad news – for however often he reran the conversation with his father he could draw no optimistic inference – would come soon enough, but for as long as he could he would stave it off, keep a door in his mind shut against the incalculable. The midwinter sun was low: even at noon the darkness bled its inky blue onto the outer edges of the day. He squinted across the water and counted four dark heads bobbing among the waves, four doglike inquisitive snouts. Under the surface their coats would be slick and black as bin-bags.

The boat rounded the promontory and entered the relative shelter of the bay, at the western end of which lay the town of Morrisdale. Lockhart made out the creosoted wooden piles of the old jetty and the concrete slipway of the new, and, at the seaward limit of the car park, the forlorn cheese-yellow outpost of the public lavvies. At the town end stood the war memorial, and beside it the Christmas tree the Lockhart family in the person of his father donated every year from the small plantation on the estate, for Callasay was a place not of forests but rather of scrub and heather, and brief hawthorn bushes welded to the steep diagonal of the wind.

Lockhart collected his bag and waited for the ferry to dock. Under the hull the waters ground and grumbled as the boat toiled round on its axis and began to back in. A few cars queued at the top of the slipway, and at the last minute the red mail van drove on to the quay and parked at a casual angle, but he could see no sign of Fraser.

He joined the other foot passengers in the narrow stairwell that led down to the car deck. In the bowels below, engines were already revving, the stink of their exhausts becoming more overpowering with every step he descended. It was a place you simply had to suffer, breathing through your scarf or your handkerchief, trapped there in the nauseous dark until the winch began to squeal and the first fresh air rushed in through the opening jaws of the exit.

Lockhart was halfway down the ramp when his mobile rang. Under his soles the ridged metal was steep and slippery. Above his head seagulls scissored and screamed. He balanced his holdall on the railing and fumbled in his pocket.

'Come in, Lucky. Over.'

A Spar truck thundered past a foot from Lockhart's ear. He shouted into the receiver. 'I'm here, all right, so where are you?'

'Running a bit late. Sorry and so on. Be right with you. Over and out.' There was a peal of caustic laughter.

Into Lockhart's mind came the image of two tin cans joined by a taut length of string. He could not recall whether the experiment had worked but he was fairly sure that Fraser would. Fraser remembered most things, at least in the long term. Fraser was the keeper of their boyhood, the repository of what had gone before; when his brother was in this role Lockhart could only defer to him, listening bemused or amazed to tales of exploits that had the vague ring of truth but whose details he had long since obliterated.

He put his feet on the island and the island shimmied sideways, refused to stand its ground. Light-headed, with the cold striking at him, he took himself to the bench by the war memorial and sat down to wait. He himself was incapable of being late. Always at the airport or the theatre with a good hour to spare, seated at the restaurant table before the other guests had commandeered their taxis. Agneta found this quirk of his more irritating than amusing, and it seemed that she was not alone in this. The punctuality Lockhart had regarded for most of his life as a mark of politeness or respect – ergo, a good thing – was dismissed by most of his friends as obsessive-compulsive. He'd seriously begun to think they might be right. It wasn't as if he actually enjoyed the amount of waiting he did.

To be honest, it made him almost as anxious as the thought of being late. He was unable to wait in good heart and with confidence, and this, he could see, was a fatal flaw. Lockhart the automaton, old Lucky Lockhart, programmed for punctuality. He glanced wistfully at the portico of the Town Hall, almost hoping that the iron hands of the clock would prove that it was he and the ferry that had arrived too early, and were at fault. He didn't think that Fraser really *meant* to let people down; he simply had a more relaxed approach to time-keeping.

The tide was high. Foam-mottled waves rolled in across the shallows and crested on the blackish boulders on the small Town beach. Behind Lockhart the lights of the Christmas tree clinked against one another in the wind. According to Fraser the tree had been their mother's idea, not their father's. Since Fraser was the one who had been there, Lockhart had to believe him.

What she'd really wanted, Fraser said, was to get the Hogmanay dances going again, as they had in Uncle Boz McFadzean's heyday, with everyone mixing and mingling regardless of rank or station, the fatted calf, the piper at midnight: the whole feudal business. But their father wouldn't entertain the idea, his line being that, unlike the McFadzeans, he had no desire to patronize the local folk, and that any responsibility he felt on their account began and ended with providing employment and treating them with ordinary decency.

Uncle Boz McFadzean had died in the Fifties, 'a bachelor without issue', in the euphemistic

85

phrasing of the times. With Boz gone it had fallen to the son of his sister Nessa to take over the estate. Thus John Lockhart, called back from Hong Kong, had brought his young wife Frances – a girl born and very gently bred on the suaver seaboards of the Far East – to share the draughts and debts of Gillinish.

Since Frances's death, in the spring of 1989, Lockhart and Fraser had coincided rarely at Gillinish. He had an image of Fraser on the *chaise-longue* in Uncle Boz's room. The *chaise-longue* was upholstered in black velvet appliquéd extravagantly with moons and stars and, like most of Boz's relics, had been left to moulder under dust-sheets. On the wall above his head hung a portrait of Boz in a tartan deerstalker with a cocked gun and, at his side, a sleek Red Setter. *Sir Brian McFadzean with Nineveh.*

Lockhart couldn't recall what year it had been but he could see Fraser clearly. He was finishing off the Jameson's Lockhart had brought him for Christmas, tilting the bottle to his mouth, sucking on it like a thirsty calf. "Well, at least give them a Christmas tree," Mother said, but of course His Nibs wouldn't entertain the idea. God, she was mad at him. So in the morning she runs down to the wood and says to Donald, "Cut me a tree, a good big one." The poor guy must've been shitting himself, but you know what she was like, wouldn't take no for an answer. So somehow they get the tree on the tractor and the upshot is she drives it right across the terrace and past the library window, so that when Father looks up he sees this bloody great fir tree sailing across the lawn like a cruise missile...'

In the firelight Fraser's face – the Viking cheekbones, the nose narrow as a hacksaw blade – was fluctuating and feverish. 'That's why Morrisdale gets its fucking tree every year. Guilt. Because if he'd let her win more often when she was alive he might not have lost her, right?' He looked pugnaciously at Lockhart. 'He never even let her have her own chequebook, did you know that? Like he wanted her to have to ask for every fucking penny.'

Lockhart hadn't known, and he was shocked. He had an impulse to defend his father, but his tongue stuck stubbornly to the inside of his mouth. He felt drunk and alone and suddenly purposeless. The business of the tree had happened long ago but this at least his mother might have told him.

The silence between them had grown glutinous. Fraser's chin rested pensively on the neck of the empty bottle; his face, drained of anger, wore an intimate, tremulous smile. 'Can't you just see her on the tractor, though?' he whispered, and for a moment, with an effort, Lockhart had been able to. Mother with her pearls, who painted a bit, and would have loved nothing better than to dance the eightsome reel at Gillinish, Mother who had acquainted her younger son, but not her elder, with her star maps and her secrets.

The old green and cream Land Rover nosed out of Bank Street, accelerated along the Front and, after turning a showy circle in the deserted car park, slammed to a halt beside him. Fraser leapt

87

out. 'Hey, Lucky! Happy Christmas, man. Welcome to Robben Island.'

Lockhart hugged him briefly and clapped him on the back. 'All right?'

Fraser smelled of sheep. He wore a flat tweed cap that must have hung in the lobby of Gillinish for thirty years. His weather-beaten wrists protruded from the too-short sleeves of an Aran sweater whose cuffs were as frayed and frilled as coral. Fraser had always been the leather-jacket-and-Levis type, maybe the odd linen suit in summer.

Lockhart grinned apprehensively. 'Well, you certainly look the part.' The trouble was that Fraser looked the part exactly; he looked the part as it would be played on a West End stage. Wyndham's rather than the Royal Court. The casually decaying gentry.

Fraser shot him a wry and glinting glance. 'You know me, always the local yokel at heart.'

Lockhart flushed. 'What I meant was you look really well. Bloody cheerful, actually.'

Fraser chortled. 'Great to see you too, Lucky!' He gave the bonnet of the Land Rover a proprietorial slap. 'Better make tracks. Retta's got lunch waiting – if you're still up for mince and tatties.'

No one had thought to shield Gillinish from the westerlies. It was as if the McFadzeans – who had built it at a time when sheep were the new cash crop of the emptied Highlands – had exhausted their pragmatism in the making of profit, and proceeded to turn into the kind of dreamers whose main aim was to assure themselves of a clear view across the Sound to the sunset. The house stood on a rise and faced onto lawns which, protected only by a sparse hawthorn hedge and a handful of rhododendron bushes, sloped starkly down to the shore. Although built of granite, the house was styled for the softer Portland stone of the south, with a pedimented portico supported by fluted pillars. The reception rooms, which included a ballroom, now disused, and a drawing room with gracious french windows giving onto a paved terrace, faced southwest, into the teeth of the weather. On the terrace stood a sundial and several wrought-iron benches on which summer guests – in the days when the Lockharts still invited them – would sit and shiver with their sherries.

Fraser parked in the gravelled yard at the back of the house. The yard was flanked by two single-storey extensions, which accommodated the pantry, cold store and laundry on one side and, on the other side, the boiler room, woodshed and gun room. When he tooted the horn Retta emerged from the pantry and stood on the doorstep, drying her hands on her apron. Lockhart plonked a kiss on her powdery cheek and gave her a squeeze, which made her giggle. She had aged considerably since Lockhart had last seen her; there were age spots on her face and neck, and her reddish-grey hair, now thinning, was permed to the brittleness of lichen.

She pushed him away, the better to examine him. 'Here you are, then! Aye, and looking grand, I must say.'

Retta was of the Old Caledonian school of aesthetics: either you were sonsy, or you were a skinned rabbit. There had never been any doubt which category Lockhart belonged to.

'Your bed's all made up. Your father said to put you in the Blue Room, next to Fraser,' she said, bustling him inside. She would even have taken his bag from him if Fraser hadn't intervened.

'Archie's a big boy now,' he scolded, as she biffed him playfully. 'I'll take him up.'

The Blue Room was a recent family euphemism. Before Frances Lockhart's death it had been known as Mother's Den. Here she had kept her easel and paints, and her astronomy charts, and the brass telescope that had once belonged to Uncle Boz. It was the only place, she said pointedly to all and sundry, where she felt free to be herself, to think her private thoughts, explore her creativity. In that crazy Montjoie summer, the summer before she died, he'd spilled it all out to Broom: his mother's thwarted energy, her constant search for satisfaction. He'd watched Broom try to stretch her feminism to include the spoilt wives of the landed gentry; slate-faced, shrugging. She too had grown up on a Highland estate, but she was quick to point out that she'd seen things from the underside, the serf's perspective. 'So many women,' she said, 'settle for being potterers.'

Fraser had installed himself in the nursery next door – an east-facing room that caught the morning sun and enjoyed some shelter from the night-whinings of the wind. A bathroom connected it with the Blue Room.

Lockhart showered quickly, decided against a tie, and knocked on the adjoining door.

'Yup,' said Fraser.

The blinds in the nursery were drawn halfway down. There were modern divans in place of the iron-frame beds he remembered, but otherwise little had altered. The big mirrored wardrobe was still there, and the old mahogany commode with the lid that lifted to reveal the chamber-pot inside. On the wall was a poster of Yuri Gagarin, yellowing to parchment. Above the boarded-up fireplace hung two framed photos of Fettes' First Eleven. Fraser was sitting at a spanking-new workstation by the window. The iMac was turquoise blue and semi-transparent; all its hi-tech innards were just visible enough to be provocative. 'Business investment.' Fraser swivelled his chair round, grinning. 'Look.' His fingers floated over the keyboard. 'www.gill-fish.com. *Voilà le* website!'

'Hey, impressive,' Lockhart said dutifully. Unlike Agneta, who was a card-carrying technophobe, Lockhart had no quarrel with the digital age, but secretly he found it boring. Agneta said people talked about their gizmos in place of themselves: their peaks and troughs, their moods and quirks and viruses and superhuman powers. 'If you pulled the plug on their PCs, what would be left of them? It's as if they think, where there's all this communication, there can be no emptiness.' She could get quite het up about it, her English – perfectly colloquial as a rule – an inadequate conduit for what he could only codify as a lofty German pessimism.

91

'It makes sense,' he agreed. His eye fell on a stack of computer games. He recognized Tomb Raider and Final Fantasy. There was something called Neutrinos for Windows.

'Well, nowadays.'

'Yeah, right.'

Fraser stood up and, pushing his chair back, bent tenderly over the machine to key the shutdown. 'We should go down.'

A modest fire had been lit in the dining room. John Lockhart was down on one knee at the hearth, fussing at the coals with a poker, when they came in. 'Well, Archie,' he said warmly, 'flight all right? Ferry?'

'Fine, sir. Good to see you.'

His father heaved himself up with an effort. Lockhart shook a slightly sooty hand. His first impression was that his father hadn't drawn himself up to his full height; then he remembered that for some years now he had been the taller. 'Agneta's really sorry she couldn't come up,' he lied.

'Och, not at all. She's her own family to think of.'

John Lockhart's white hair crested strongly on the crown. His cheeks were red and coarse-grained, his upper body still broad, even bulky. His whole appearance suggested *bonhomie* and brandies and good living, but Lockhart knew that this was deceptive, for the fact was that a small cool wind accompanied him everywhere, and those who made the mistake of being too familiar quickly felt the chill of it. Years ago Agneta had

92

commented that he was the sort of man women couldn't help finding attractive. 'I bet he had plenty of offers even before Frances died,' she said. According to her it was exactly his severity that would be the challenge: any woman worth her salt would want to dismantle the invisible rules that placed a brake on his desires. Lockhart had never been able to envisage his father flirting, let alone being unfaithful. When he was with Broom he'd tried to imagine his father in the same state – guilty, aberrant, in sexual thrall – and he had failed miserably. John Lockhart wasn't the sort who would ever understand or condone adultery; to John Lockhart, lies and deceit had always been, and would remain, anathema.

'Still keeping on with the teaching, is she?'

'Loves it,' said Lockhart emphatically, as the tension settled into place between his shoulder-blades. The words carried an implicit criticism. In a moment his father would trot out his *Daily Telegraph* spiel on the horrors (undeniable) of inner-city comprehensives, and once again Lockhart would feel obliged to point out that Agneta taught Infants and Juniors, which was another ball game altogether.

His father glanced at the door and coughed drily. 'Aye, well...' A momentary blankness crossed his face. His smile came almost on cue, from a quota that was not inexhaustible. 'Must be a vocation, eh? Isn't that what they call it?'

Lockhart had been poised, as usual, to defend a whole generation of working women, but when the attack did not come his thoughts foundered. *When you have children you'll see things*

93

differently. London's no place to bring up weans. This was the real issue, and Lockhart knew it. His father still clung to the belief that in the fullness of time his elder son would come back to Callasay and take over the reins of Gillinish. In his eyes his daughter-in-law was simply part of the package.

In the grate the fire struggled fitfully for life. Above the mantelpiece hung an engraving of a Jardine's ship in some turn-of-the-century harbour, Cochin or Shanghai or Singapore. His father slid his hands into his trouser pockets and rocked on the balls of his feet. What his father didn't know, and would not understand, Lockhart was sure, even if confronted with it, was that Agneta was one townie who entirely lacked the gene for rural fantasy. The idea of her playing lady of the manor was enough to make a cat laugh, although right now Lockhart didn't feel at all like laughing.

Three places had been laid at the bay-window end of the long oak dining table. There was a vase of tight red tulips, a jug of water, and another of orange squash. John Lockhart disapproved of the excessive use of alcohol. In the alcove by the chimney-breast the grandfather clock loomed like a sentry-box. Seconds fell from it with the sound of sandbags dropped from a height. The room seemed bleak and bare: not a carpet or a cushion to absorb the echoes. Presumably Retta had saved the Christmas decorations for the sitting room.

Fraser hovered, smiling perilously. Fraser was always on edge around his father. He would be looking to Lockhart to pass the ball; then and only then would he run with it.

At last Retta appeared with the tray. 'Thank you, Retta,' his father said, as they drew up chairs which squeaked in unison. 'Retta has a new grandson, Archie, did she tell you?'

'Oh, really?' said Lockhart, as the word 'grandson' hung in the air between them.

Retta dimpled proudly. 'Callum, they've called him. Only six months and he's blethering away already!' She set before them plates of mince and mash, already served out, like school dinners.

'Aye. Bright wee chap,' said his father.

'Sounds like it!'

The door closed behind Retta and for a moment there was a weight of expectancy Lockhart couldn't bear. Obscurely he felt that it would be up to him, now, to save the day from its encroaching darkness, to be the eggnog and the fairy lights and the Christmas cracker. He heard his voice boom out, like a man bellowing across a golf club bar, 'So how's the fish farm going, sir?'

'Oh, not so bad, considering... They've had a terrible time with the salmon anaemia on the mainland, but out on the islands we've been clear so far, touch wood... But no, we're not short of orders. Smoked salmon mainly, and now the oysters...' He glanced warily at Fraser, who was pushing carrots round his plate. Fraser hadn't changed for lunch but the lapse had been passed over without comment. Silence furled round him like a flag. He had hardly eaten anything. '...Aye, we've enough to be going on with.'

With his mouth full of mince, Lockhart nodded frantically. Outside the window the sun had vanished behind cloud. Through the angled pane of the bay he could just see the stone bird-table on the terrace; there were seeds on it, but no birds.

'According to your brother, there's a new eatery opening every day down south. Times change, eh? In my day we'd a day off University to go back to the Highlands and fetch the barrel of oatmeal and the herring!'

Lockhart had a sudden vision of Agneta at the other end of the country, drinking *sekt* and talking fast and laughing in German. 'It certainly seems to be the big growth sector.'

Abruptly Fraser returned from his stony dreamtime. He leaned across the table, his face all animation. 'Sky's the limit down there, isn't it, Archie!'

'You'll have heard how Fraser's hell-bent on dragging us out of the Dark Ages?'

'I knew I'd cracked it when Father found out even the Church of Scotland had gone on line. Till then he thought everybody still did their business by snail mail!' He grinned at Lockhart. 'No, really. I mean, *what?*'

John Lockhart wiped his mouth with a napkin and replaced it in his lap. His lips were trying to involve themselves in a smile, but he looked tense and aggrieved.

Fraser, who'd always had the capacity to flash in seconds from despair to unreasoning joy, was already revving. He leaned back in his chair; his foot tapped jauntily. 'It isn't just the UK supermarket outlets, it's the European market. In fact there's no reason why Gillfish couldn't eventually break into the East Coast US markets if we played our cards right.' When Retta brought in dessert – tinned fruit salad topped with maraschino cherries – he slid the jug of evaporated milk towards Lockhart. 'Cream, Archie?' he said sarcastically. 'I mean, look what our competitors are up to. Down in Loch Fyne they're growing scallops in lantern nets and mussels on ropes; they're branching out into langoustines and squat lobsters. OK, so we're undercapitalized, we've got a lot of catching up to do, but you have to agree the possibilities are endless...'

'Today Glasgow, tomorrow the world, eh?' Lockhart laughed uneasily. The prospect of Fraser going global was faintly ludicrous. He resisted an urge to tell him to stick to his art and leave the capitalism to his big brother.

'Well, exactly!' Fraser fixed him with a brilliant questing gaze. 'Maybe you could rustle us up a few investors, Lucky.'

Lockhart laughed sharply. 'Oh, sure. Rivestre would really go a bundle on that!'

'Yeah, yeah. What I'm saying is, you must have some mates with a bit of liquid, the odd grand or two...'

Lockhart felt trapped. Was Fraser serious? He reached for the jug and filled his glass with orange squash. The nursery drink was sweet and cloying on his tongue. 'I might.' As soon as he had said it he regretted it, for with the best will in the world his brother could hardly be seen as a safe investment, and the thought that he might be required to present him as such filled him with an embarrassment that bordered on dread. Avoiding his father's eye, he said sternly, 'Of course, you'd need to have a serious business plan.'

'Of course,' said Fraser. 'But, come on, think about it. Gourmet fish meals with all the fresh ingredients in the pack – your tarragon and your hazelnut butter and your capers or whatever. Recipes, menu suggestions. I don't see how it could fail, do you?'

John Lockhart went on scooping sliced peaches into his mouth; although he believed in plain food, he did like puddings. It was Frances who'd been the gourmet. Given half a chance she'd spend an entire day preparing a meal, the kitchen counters groaning under a battery of ingredients. Bowls of minced pork and king prawns and sliced beef fillet, dried mushrooms soaking in rice wine, grated horseradish, diced ginger, bamboo shoots. One weekend after his A levels, she'd come down to Edinburgh to take Lockhart out to lunch. The restaurant had been reviewed in *Tatler* and she had high hopes of it. He remembered the precise pincering grasp of her fingers on the chopsticks, her magenta fingernails, the way she'd called the waiter across in her peremptory colonial voice. Every head in the restaurant turned to watch – in these days food wasn't the sort of thing Scots thought you should make a fuss about – while she criticized each dish in fluent Cantonese, and Lockhart sat sweating in his Fettes blazer, scourged by shame and foreignness.

His father's silence pressed on him. Lockhart felt a surge of irritation. Fraser's delivery might be manic, but that was par for the course these days, and, to be fair, Gillfish was as feasible a project as many he had fielded for Rivestre. It didn't deserve to be strangled at birth, which, he suspected, was what he'd been brought in to do. In any case it was fairly safe to assume that like most of Fraser's enterprises it would wither away by itself, as the State was supposed to do after Communism.

He folded up his napkin, nodding his professional nod. 'With all the refrigeration, you realize you'd be looking at huge transport costs?'

'I'm computing those at the moment,' said Fraser, in the patient tone of a person of consequence. 'It's early days yet, Archie.'

'Good, uh huh, great. Well, we'll see, then.' Lockhart tried to expunge the doubt from his voice.

'What I was saying to Fraser is that luxury goods are all very well but you don't want to rely on them. You only have to look at what the salmon anaemia did to the industry...' John Lockhart's voice was heavy with the plodding rhythms of the dogmatist; it brooked no argument. Fraser raised his eyes and communed silently with the ceiling rose. 'In the meantime we've the farm to keep going. That's the major consideration.' He stood up and began to clear the dirty crockery onto the tray. 'I've asked Retta to serve coffee in the library, Archie,' he said, as Lockhart held the door open. On the threshold he turned and looked wearily at Fraser. 'I expect you've some jobs, have you?'

Fraser's lips parted in reproach. He flashed Lockhart a glare of outraged appeal. 'Oh, right,' he said and, driving his hands into the pockets of his body-warmer, barged brusquely past, leaving Lockhart stranded and smarting in the doorway.

The library had been his father's office for as long as Lockhart could remember, although he'd never seen him open any of the volumes on the shelves that lined the walls – the complete Shakespeare and Sir Walter Scott, the Waugh and the Wodehouse, the biographies of Churchill and Mountbatten. On the desk was an old Adler typewriter, a blotter, and two wire trays labelled IN and OUT. There was also a framed photograph of his parents' engagement party in Hong Kong; John Lockhart in white dinner jacket and carnation, Frances blonde and winsome in a strapless satin cocktail dress.

Through the window he saw Fraser striding purposefully across the lawn, a shotgun crooked over his arm. There was a red-headed boy with him.

'They're after the hoodies. We lost a fair few lambs last spring. You remember Davie Donaldson? That's his boy Ronnie.'

Lockhart watched them go through the beach gate and head east along the path that hugged the shore. The sea was dark and roughening. He turned from the window. 'I saw Hydro Seafoods had to pay off a hundred workers last month,' he said, as if talk of a far-off disaster might somehow stave off one that was closer.

'Aye. If you've one fish infected you've to destroy the lot, and you can kiss goodbye to your compensation! There's talk of a nine-million-pound fund as long as the industry matches it, but we're small players, well spread out. It's a nonsense.' John Lockhart paused to pour the coffee that had slopped into the saucer back into the cup. He handed it to Lockhart. 'But that's not why I asked you to come, Archie.'

Lockhart sat down on the leather pouffe, balancing the cup and saucer on his knee.

'There's a cigar if you'd like.' His father pushed a black-lacquered box towards him.

'Thanks, sir, I'm fine.'

'You see, he's up till all hours on that machine. Surfing, isn't that what they call it? I'll come straight to the point, Archie. Something's not right. I didn't want to raise it with the bank until I was sure – even with the telephone banking, you know what Morrisdale's like.'

The oily dark leaves of the rhododendron chafed against the window; the few remaining flowers were pale purple coronets, wind-torn, anaemic. Lockhart waited numbly; he might have been back at Fettes, queuing in the vestibule to read the exam results.

'The trouble is I'm not up on this high-tech stuff, as you know. It just doesn't appeal to me, but that's by the by.' John Lockhart raised the small cup to his lips and, frowning, drank decorously. 'It would be a weight off my mind, Archie, if you'd check over Fraser's accounts.'

The baldness of it shocked Lockhart. 'Do you really think that's necessary?'

'As a matter of fact, I do!' There was a dark flush beginning on his father's neck. 'I want to give him the benefit of the doubt, you understand, but if it's the drug business again I swear it's the finish!'

The room was lit suddenly by a maverick shaft of sun; simultaneously a barrage of bright hail slammed against the window.

'Have you asked him straight out?'

'You know what Fraser's like.'

There was a harsh note of disdain in his father's voice. Lockhart got up and went to stand at the window. He felt his heart pounding. He thought of the tin can, its reverberation, the string between him and his brother tautening. The hail was slanting diagonally across the lawn. He stared at the cypress tree that stood at the edge of the terrace, remembering its great inner blackness. From the outside it looked solid, like a fat green cigar, but inside it was hollow, a cavern of dry and broken twigs. The sky was ochre-yellow, the colour of a toad's back. Beyond the lawn the sea was invisible. 'We're in for a storm,' he said mechanically.

'Looks like it.'

'But if it means going behind Fraser's back...' He turned and saw the dead weariness on his father's face. He was rotating his cup in his hands, staring into it, as if the contents might reveal his future. He looked drained, beaten; he looked as Lockhart had never seen him look, not even at his mother's funeral. He looked as he would look, Lockhart realized with desperate remorse, on the day he learned that his elder son would never be laird and master of Gillinish.

Lockhart felt the void nudging at a spot between his shoulderblades. When he shrugged his elbows lifted and flapped, like truncated wings. 'OK, sir. I'll do my best. Take a look. See what I can find out.'

His father nodded tightly, but did not thank him. The message being that Lockhart should know how much it had cost him to ask. With sudden vigour he rose from his chair and went to the trolley on which he kept a decanter of whisky for his clients. 'You'll take a dram?' He was already pouring one for himself.

Lockhart was conscious of a sudden feeling of relief, if not of a particular desire to celebrate. 'I think I will, actually.' He took the glass and sipped. Tears came up from the depths and stung his eyes. 'Strong stuff,' he muttered.

'Aye. It's an island malt.' His father held his glass up to the light, turning it this way and that. 'Smoke and peat.' Narrowing his eyes, he considered the colour gravely. 'Of course I don't need to tell you, Archie, that all of this is in the strictest confidence?'

That night, pole-axed on the narrow bed, he dreamt that oysters had taken over the world. In their black and grey rubble they bristled on every shoreline, like colonies of clerics. Their tight old lips were clamped into rigid frills that sipped parsimoniously at the salty influx of the tide. The communions they held were wordless. They had passed an edict that prohibited speech. They had sworn the world to silence.

Broom sat with her back against the elephantine radiator and a glass of rouge on the rug beside her. Wearing a pair of cheap chemists' glasses in the too-dim light, she read:

Hell also hath a place within it called Chasma, out of which issueth all manner of thunders, lightnings, with such horrible shriekings and wailings that oft times the very Devils themselves stand in fear thereof. For one while it sendeth forth winds with exceeding snow, hail and rain congealing the water into ice, with which the damned are frozen, gnash their teeth, howl and cry, yet cannot die. We have also with us in hell a ladder reaching of an exceeding height, as though it would touch the heavens, on which the damned ascend to seek the blessings of God, but through their infidelity, when they are at the very highest degree, they fall down again into their former miseries. Yea sweet Faustus, so must thou understand of hell, the while thou art desirous to know the secrets of our kingdom.

The telephone, modified to accept only incoming calls, let out an old-fashioned trill. She had been expecting the call, and jumped up eagerly.

'*Also, liebste*,' boomed Daniel. A scramble of German followed.

'Talk English,' she scolded. Over the years it had become a joke between them. *You've been away so long you don't know what language is coming out of your mouth.*

In the days when art took to the streets and people did things for love not money, she and Daniel had been involved in agit-prop theatre. Daniel had moved to Germany in the late Seventies to live with his girlfriend. Quite quickly he'd scored a surprise hit with a play co-written and performed by Turkish immigrant workers, and within a few years had built a reputation not only in avant-garde theatre, but also in the opera mainstream. Meanwhile, back in London, Broom picked up what work she could, and when she couldn't, she painted. She supported herself and Sean, but only just. From time to time she designed sets for embattled fringe productions; occasionally she obtained a residency in what was still quaintly called 'the Community'; once she had even been placed in a cathedral.

Since her accommodations with the market were made so rarely, and only by necessity, she watched Daniel's trajectory with censorious surprise. Daniel became defensive. He told her scathingly that she was an anachronism. The Seventies had turned into the Eighties and it was no time to be starving in a garret. She could see now how naïve she'd been, how slow to grasp the scope of his ambitions.

Recently she'd found a snapshot in her desk drawer: the two of them in a London squat, under a poster of Rosa Luxemburg, long-haired, leather-jacketed, and in deadly earnest. In the photo they looked gaunt and glamorous; they looked, in fact, terribly modern. Skimpy ribbed

105

sweaters and flares. In the meantime fashion had come full circle and at a glance it seemed that nothing had changed, when the truth was that everything had. Like so many of their generation, they'd been socialists, activists. Unlike some of her erstwhile comrades, Broom saw no reason not to be proud of this. *Committed.* For so long the word had had an archaic ring, like a Latin prayer-chant. Luckily she had Sean to argue her out of old-fogeyish thoughts, to point out that things were stirring again, the younger generation mounting its inchoate challenge to corporatism. And none too soon, she thought privately but usually managed not to say. 'Save the Trees', 'Reclaim the Streets', 'Stop the City'. There were Met. officers who, when they saw Sean lugging his camera bag down Piccadilly or Park Lane, would get on their radios. 'Sean-boy's on the move. Must be something cooking.'

Daniel was ranting. '*Ach ja, Herr Intendant Maier*, popular appeal, *Herr Intendant Maier*, marketability, *Herr Intendant Maier*. A youth Faust? Well, why not indeed, *Herr Intendant Maier*. I see needles, nose studs, a smackhead selling his soul to sustain his habit ... or why not a transsexual one, if it'd pull in the punters? Faust wants to *be* Helen of Troy, not fuck her. Mephistopheles to the rescue. *Oopla!* No operation, no problem.'

Broom laughed. Daniel's grumbles were never less than operatic. He himself would have been the first to admit that his attitude to his adopted country was ambivalent; but there he was, stranded in Lower Swabia, and since he was

106

married now, with two small boys, there, presumably, he would stay.

For an East End Jew it was a bizarre choice, to say the least. Whenever Passover came round he would scrape together a handful of New Yorkers from the Musiktheater and drive over to the Seder at the US Army base. She'd gone with him once, out of solidarity. During the Rabbi's address – he was an ex-boxer from the Bronx, just back from Operation Desert Storm – she didn't dare look Daniel in the eye. She ate the spiced apple and the horseradish and drank the too-sweet wine, but couldn't bring herself to say the responses. Afterwards Daniel had been crestfallen and aghast. 'To the right of fucking Genghis Khan,' he muttered, gunning the big Merc back to Aryan Stuttgart.

On the other end of the line she heard the roar of a football match. In all his years of exile Daniel's loyalty to Spurs had never wavered. '...*Arschlocher*, the lot of them,' Daniel said viciously. 'I tell you, my darling, this is the very last time I sell my soul to the subsidized theatre... By the way, did you remember the slides of your paintings for Maier? It would be a whole lot easier, you know, if you had email!'

'I had copies made. Email might take longer. Say, another fifty years.'

'But anyway, tell me, how *are* you? How *is* it there?'

'Oh, you know – minus ten, sun, snow. Bliss, in other words. So when do you think you'll make it down?'

'I'd thought Tuesday, but it turns out I have to

shoot over to Munich on Wednesday to check out the state of play on the *Shrew*... Before I forget, the good news is that Maier's managed to sign Zeinab Guterson, so you could say we'll have our *Gastarbeiter* Marguerite after all...'

'That's great,' said Broom. 'That's terrific.' The chill she felt was small but irreducible. Outside in the lane a car door slammed: Madame d'Ange's neighbours, back from picking up the last batch of fresh bread from the *boulangerie*. It was a gloomy early-evening sound, which spoke of shop lights going out one by one, the town settling in for another long December night.

'Let's see... Friday's Christmas, so if I left Saturday early, I could make it down in two, three hours... Think you can amuse yourself till then?'

'What, me?' she said quickly. 'In the mountains?'

Daniel let out a bracing laugh. 'That's what I figured.'

The force of her disappointment shocked her. Obviously he wouldn't leave the kids at Christmas, but she hadn't realized how much she had been counting on his company earlier in the week. 'In any case, I'm supposed to be working. I'm still thinking along the lines of Broadgate Circus, basically – did you know they've built an ice rink in the middle of it, among all the merchant banks and see-through skyscrapers?'

Daniel snorted. 'Faust on ice, *ja?*'

'I thought of an anorexic statue for the piazza: Eternity as seen by Calvin Klein, that sort of thing.' In her voice there was a peevish tremolo that made her try even harder. She started to tell

108

him about her idea for Marguerite's room – no casement window here, but instead a glass hutch full of mops and brooms high up among the ventilation shafts; a cramped place fit only for minions. But Daniel was already fading, eyes and ears on the TV screen.

'*Ja*, good, good. We'll talk, though. *Ja, ja, natürlich*. Friday, hopefully.' In the background a child's voice rose fretfully, pleading in German. 'OK, darling, *bis Freitag, ciao, ciao*.'

'*Wiedersehen*,' Broom muttered, to the dead receiver.

Broom stared across a gulf of pigment-scarred floor at the unfinished painting.

The six sacred mountains of the Navajo had marked the limits of their tribal homeland. Dook'o'oostüd, the mountain of abalone; Sis Naajini, the mountain adorned with white shell; Tsoodzt, the mountain of blue-green turquoise.

She bridged her hands across her forehead and squinted. Lead-white and cadmium yellow for the central sun-eye. A sepia glaze could work, but the rock-flakes should be darker in tone, a blue-black fringe, like lashes. From the beginning she'd had the title in her head: The Mountain Looks Back at You. Which was exactly, glassily, what it was doing. Like Al, it was giving nothing away.

She'd kept him dangling for weeks. On his fiftieth birthday he had walked Bleaklow bracingly in wind and rain. She, on the other hand, had spent the holiday heaving Veronica's suitcase around the Dodecanese, and she was full to the brim with sun. On one of the smaller islands there was a ship in the harbour she kept smiling at: a rusty blue dredger that made her think of him. She spent two days under a tamarisk tree, painting it, thinking of framing it when she got back, thinking of calling him immediately.

August Bank Holiday. Calm weather, hot as the breath of hell. It was their first weekend, although it would hardly be accurate to say that they'd spent it together. Not only were Liam and Robbo in attendance; the entire British climbing fraternity, it seemed, was clanking along the cliffs of Pembroke, and Al was on first-name terms with each and every one of them.

On Monday they'd headed back to London, a sunburned, wise-cracking crew, packed into Kevin's Audi. The M4 was chock-a-block, nose-to-tail at ninety. In the wing mirror the sky behind them was western and on fire. She'd felt charged and changed, bewildered by the terrible importance of sex. In the back seat Al kept glancing at her oddly, as if everything depended on making a correct appraisal of her.

Camping was like playing house. In the small makeshift homestead of the tent Al was housewifely: rucksacks stowed away at the foot, sleeping bags lined up, basic foodstuffs stacked neatly in an orange-box under the flap. He'd even brought pillows, for her benefit.

When she thought of the umber light inside she felt the sea-change working in her stomach. A certain kind of sex, a certain kind of mirth. 'An old man like me,' he'd yelped, collapsing from his knees into a kind

110

of salaam. 'One more scintillating fuck and it could be curtains!' A certain way of sitting – sated and rooted – on the puritanical wooden benches of the climbers' pub, knowing that she didn't have to please or put on a performance, because she had pleased, did please, was pleased. The homing heat of Al's hand was still an imprint on her shoulder: the bare arm that lay along the back of the bench staked a public if ironic claim.

She'd watched his charm at work on others. The way men turned to him expectantly, their eyes lit up with excitement. The boy racers who chuckled into their pints as they listened to his sportsplan – no unethical imports from the Continent, where impassable routes were simply bolted into submission, just fun, good style, British adventure-climbing at its purist best – but who deferred to him all the same, won over, evidently, by his barnstorming good humour. Al might be the old bull, but it was clear that his was the team everybody wanted to be on. Herself included, to be perfectly honest. Because, despite all his blokeish bluffness and his flirty tricks, she couldn't help finding something foursquare and fine in the big face that shone at her like a dog-daisy from a cornfield.

Outside, the light was already fading: half an hour's work left in the day, if she was lucky. Any longer and she'd be tinkering, gnawing at a dry bone. You could be too eager to predict the outcome, too greedy to get the painting right. The emptier you felt, the stronger the temptation to turn the damn thing into a totem. Most misjudgements happened in late afternoon or evening, when your energy was flagging but you couldn't admit that it was time to give up, go home in good faith, try again tomorrow.

111

What was hardest to grasp was the way the city had come between them, full of noise and distances. A landscape marked out in diary days, businesslike. People meeting and parting. He'd pencilled her in for the weekend but pencil, as everyone knew, wasn't indelible, and the phone was a barrier she couldn't seem to cross.

She carried a stool to the centre of the studio and sat down with her mug of milkless coffee. Did men miss differently? Or did they suffer the same loss of significance that women did? She didn't have a clue what Al would be doing in the interim, but he had mentioned summit talks with Miranda, his journalist ex., on Friday night. Perhaps a compromise was being hatched, a return to an entente cordiale. *The idea repelled her. No wonder her mind was in a state of limbo, a kind of dismay-in-waiting.*

The coffee tasted of turps. She got up and threw it down the sink. There were tea-stained mugs on the draining-board; on the window-sill stood a jar of Nescafé and a sugar-encrusted spoon. She scraped the paint off her palette and sluiced it with white spirit. She would end it, of course, if they did start up again. Withdraw – gracefully, if possible. No point in entering a contest you couldn't hope to win.

The dabs of pigment swam muddily together: primaries, secondaries, tertiaries. She tore a length of kitchen paper from the roll and scrubbed at the autumnal sludge. When she'd first learned that light split into the spectrum of colours she'd been childishly delighted. It was a pity, she thought, that the miracle couldn't be managed in reverse.

Al rang on Saturday, just as she was about to ring

112

him. 'I'll be late,' he said gruffly, 'owing to several major developments in my life.'

The committee-speak was hardly reassuring. 'Oh yes?'

'One of which is that I have to finish an article Keith and I are doing for the Statesman.'

She waited to hear what the others might be but he didn't enlarge. Perhaps they weren't telephone material. Or perhaps that's what he wanted her to wonder.

He arrived at nine, filling the doorway, apologizing. He had a briefcase and a bottle of wine in a bag. When he bent to put down the briefcase she glimpsed the bright grey hairs on the sunburned nape of his neck. He caught her up in his arms, then held her away, to appreciate her. His smile was roguish but strained.

I should come right out with it, she thought, get in there first. Disengaging herself, she said coolly, 'I made an onion tart. It's probably turned to caramel.'

She lit the candle on the table and served the pissaladière and drank a lot while he ate it. The two feet of table-top between them had turned him into an actor. His compliments were effusive, theatrical. OK, she thought, I get the picture. He's minding his manners, trying to sweeten me up. She remembered Pembroke, and exactly how his arm had lain across her shoulders but not what it had meant – not reliably, that is, in that she didn't know what it had meant to him. Or what any of it had meant, for that matter. Or whether he was going to work his way politely through his dinner and afterwards, as politely, let her down. He was explaining that the Statesman article analysed the splits that had led to the demise of

113

the CPGB – the Euro-Communists versus the Stalinist brigade – and seemed utterly unaware of her edginess.

'The Tankies,' she said, leaning back in her chair and slotting her hands between her knees. Every remark she could now think of had a certain sneer to it.

'The Tankies,' Al agreed primly. 'We were trying to sum up the prospects for the Democratic Left – which I joined, I have to say, but out of principle, not conviction.'

'And Keith?'

'Didn't. Also on principle.'

At any other time she might have asked him to elaborate, but the longer he talked the longer she would have to contemplate the frightening fact that he now seemed to bear the responsibility for her happiness. He plucked a bunch of watercress out of the salad bowl and munched on it. His composure intimidated her. Her breathing was shallow, her chest and shoulders rigid with impatience. She managed to light a cigarette with a fairly steady hand.

'So how did it go with Miranda?'

There was a brief, incalculable silence. His shoulders jerked up into a shrug. 'Well, the upshot is...' A look of bewilderment crossed his face. 'She says I make her feel utterly impotent.' He blew out a yard-long sigh. 'I can't actually think of a worse indictment.'

She tried to discipline her voice. 'So you didn't sleep with her?'

Al looked at her. He didn't seem surprised that she had asked. 'No.' He shook his head slowly. 'We didn't.'

Broom's ears drummed with relief. She poked a spent match into the candle flame and watched it

114

catch fire, nodding mutely, able now to remember the dead skin of the week and let it fall from her. The starkly single nights, the productive days punctuated by small but strenuous attempts to treat herself. In the space of a moment the future had changed its shape. She wouldn't now have to steel herself to go back to how things were before. She could put it all behind her. She said impulsively, 'You know I was going to break it off, if you had?'

Al's shoulders were wary and hunched. His mouth pulled down into a frown. After a moment he said, 'But I did sleep with Alex.'

'Who?' There was a sensation of annulment, and then a sharp and puncturing grief. He was eyeing her anxiously. 'You mean, she's a lover?'

'Yes. Well, we … see each other sometimes.'

Mutiny froze her; she could not even shake her head. It was, she knew, beyond her: to want someone and be with that person and then proceed to wanting someone else. To reach some cusp of betrayal and, with no fuss or bother, simply step across.

Al's scowl was a millimetre short of sheer exasperation. 'Look, I did say I'd cancelled sex to take you to Pembroke!'

He had, of course. She remembered now. But she'd been so determined to go that she'd hardly heard his objections. Lust had blocked her ears and turned her into a creature of instinct, so that gaily, confidently, she had brushed his protests aside.

She shoved her chair back and grabbed the wine bottle and carried it through to the living room. She could see through the net curtains that the neighbours across the back courtyard had guests. She started to pull down the blinds. It was Saturday night, they

115

would be partying. She heard herself shout, 'I mean, how much bloody sex do you need!'

Al came after her. 'Well, I wasn't going to lie to you!'

She turned on him, astonished, the bottle hanging from her hand. 'Don't you understand, I want to marry you!' The words were supercharged; a stupid heartfelt roar. She knew instantly that they were true.

Outside, an ambulance blared past, hee-hawing towards Hackney.

'Marry me?' Al grabbed the back of his neck and stared at her in comic disbelief. 'Marry me?' He let out a squealing laugh. 'Give me a fucking break!'

For a second she stared back in bafflement, some childish part of her still convinced that the sheer truth and force of her feeling could and should sweep everything before it. She watched him step away and flap his arms and turn a pirouette and shake his head at her.

'You've got to be kidding!' There was a look of sprightly outrage on his face, as if she'd insulted his intelligence. His frown deepened, accusing her. 'You're asking me to throw all my principles down the pan, just like that?'

'Principles?' She flushed in angry shame. 'I don't give a toss for your so-called principles! You prove to me they aren't just a cover for Don Juanism and maybe then I'll take them seriously!'

The heresy had hit home, and she was glad of it. Al stood stock-still, his body angled, like a man leaning into a gale. His face looked buffeted, the features flattened and spread. 'If that's the line you're taking, then there's nothing to discuss, is there?'

'So go, then!'

She watched him pull on his jacket. It was the old

116

green fleece he'd worn in Pembroke. His shoulders were bunched and rigid. He was no longer looking at her. She shrugged furiously, thinking of his callous honesty, how it had shocked the declaration out of her. His fault, not hers. It serves him right, she thought. There were exultant words on the tip of her tongue, words that could prove to him that he wasn't only cruel, but stupid. 'Equality!' she jeered. 'You know fuck all about equality. No wonder Miranda feels impotent!'

He zipped up his fleece with a decisive snap and stared distractedly around for his briefcase. He bent heavily and picked it up. The light had gone from his face, which she knew now was both dear to her and hateful. No way, she thought, am I going to stop him.

Taking a couple of steps towards the door, he turned, with the briefcase clasped to his chest. 'Well, there's absolutely no point hanging around, is there?'

But hang around he did, and the wrangling had gone on, bitter and euphoric, past the point where either of them could walk away – although both threatened to more than once – past the point when all the wine in the house had been drunk, past the point when the Rastas in the next-door flat turned off their Rap tapes and retired, so that they had to tone down the shouting: a torrent of scorn that abated only when Al lurched across the floor and went down on his knees before the sofa and, hearing the click of his joints, she took his head in her hands and said they were getting a bit too old for this.

Then they went soberly to bed and made starved love, and at some point in the broody dawn she leaned over and punched him once, massively, because the

117

choice was crystal clear and the hurt was still in her, and it was either land him one or leave him.

After a drink or two she'd tried to sum it up for Heather. 'It's the new love-promise. I won't marry you, I won't be faithful, I won't promise to be around a whole lot, and I won't be yours for ever. But if you're patient enough I might open up a bit and reveal a few emotional needs... Talk about pricing yourself out of the market!'

Heather grinned back delightedly. She waited until Broom had stopped laughing to give her professional opinion. 'Give it time, though. No, seriously. It's early days yet. Don't let the bad things wipe out all the good ones.'

Stranded in London, she went to the park and drew skies and animals. A white goat with a crescent for a beard. The straight-eared deer. A tree split by summer lightning.

Al had gone to Scotland with Keith for two weeks – a regular commitment – in expectation of clement autumn weather. A postcard had arrived, of Buachaille Etive Mor. Glencoe was awash. It had been raining for days, he said, and he was missing her in the damp. 'The rivers are in magnificent spate,' he wrote. 'PS I am dining out on my black eye!'

Geese flew in a wide circle overhead, crying their raucous goodbyes. Sun sheeted coolly across the wet grass. The rowanberries glistened and encouraged her.

The blinds of the business suite had been pulled down. Estelle sat by the contained spot of the anglepoise, pad and Powerbook at the ready.

The footage from the North Face of the Faille had not impressed Micky. For a start, the density of the cloud obscured the drop, so you couldn't see how far a climber could fall. Padded, balaclava'd and mist-shrouded, Sophie Sauvage could have been anyone or anything; she could have been a yeti or a bloody yak.

He watched Sophie swing herself up out of the overhang and flop onto the snow of the summit. Below the glacier goggles her nose was purplish, the skin on the bridge peeling off in shreds. He glimpsed the unshaven profile of a guy with a ponytail. A sunburned hand came into shot, offering an aluminium flask. Sophie drank thirstily, water dribbling down her chin; then she fell back in the sunlit snow and unfastened her hood and screamed something, and Micky saw the famous auburn hair at last, and also that she was crying.

He leaned forward and peered intently at the screen. This was where expertise came into its own. You had to be a good judge of character; you had to see what others missed. You had to look straight through the skin and spot the flaws and foibles that made someone a bad risk. Above all, you had to trust your instincts and listen to what they were telling you. If Mauritz Stiller hadn't trusted his instincts, Greta Gustafsson would have lived out her days as a Stockholm shopgirl. Without von Steinberg's perspicacity, Dietrich would never have existed. He pointed with his pencil. 'The guy. Is he a boyfriend, or what?'

'A friend only, I believe.' Estelle made a note on her pad. 'I shall find out.' Her smile was glassy and eager. From her pearlized stockings to her asymmetrical oyster-coloured bob, Estelle reflected light. Despite a dawn flight from Paris and a testing drive up into the mountains, she was bright and shiny as a new ten-franc piece. Shadows, it was clear, simply would not stick to her. She was dressed expensively in fine pale wool and underneath he could imagine the secret scented folds of silk. He let his gaze rest on her legs for just long enough to be appreciative.

'To be perfectly honest, the winter stuff doesn't grab me like the Mali footage. I can't pretend that shorts and a sports bra aren't more scenic than layers of duvet. I mean, if you've got it, flaunt it, I always say.' He waited to see if Estelle would rise to the bait. You could tell a lot about a woman by the way she reacted to sexism.

Estelle inclined her head a neutral inch. Her smile sat tight. *'Bien sûr,'* she allowed, in a voice straight from the boardroom.

Point taken, thought Micky. OK, she was a career girl. So now let her see how the real professionals got down to business.

The film had cut to an interior shot. Sophie sat cross-legged on a divan that was covered by a shabby Mexican blanket. She wore no make-up;

120

her hair hung loose in a foxy frizz.

Slipping his shoes off, Micky slotted his knuckles together and free-associated. 'That frown. It's like a red rag to a bull. With a jaw like hers it gives the wrong signals. Also – there, she did it again. She has a habit of sniffing. Did she have a cold? My impression is that it's a nervous tic. And when she's listening to the interviewer she looks depressed. No control over her expressions at all. Sometimes she even looks hostile, as if she resents the camera. Does she? Because I've got to know whether it's worth going ahead with this. Otherwise I'm wasting her time as well as Svensen's. I've got to be sure she'll make the commitment.'

Estelle regarded him gravely through gold-rimmed glasses. 'Sophie is a shy girl, but very motivated, I can assure you. Very serious about her career.'

Micky gave her a sidelong smile. 'Like all your generation, huh?'

Estelle's mouth briefly formed that maddeningly attractive thing the French call a *moue*. Her shrug was self-deprecating but she didn't challenge his emphasis in quite the way he'd have liked. Either she hadn't yet learned the art of flattery or else she sincerely saw no need for it. Micky decided to give himself the benefit of the doubt. All the same, he felt a little piqued by the exclusion.

'Oh, don't get me wrong. It's admirable. You're realists. You outline your goals and you go for them. I can relate to that.'

The crazy thing was that he meant it. What age

was she? he wondered. Twenty-six? Twenty-eight? He reflected morosely that there might come a time, after all, when he no longer identified with youth. When he would think of himself as the older man. Sophistication, then, would be his new season. He'd grow a grey stubble and step imperceptibly into subtler shoes. No doubt age had its own peculiar compensations, although he couldn't at this moment imagine what they might be. When he tried to envisage a future subject to the ravages of time the idea was insubstantial as mountain mist and every bit as chilly.

Estelle was looking at him uncertainly. 'She has a great neck, no? I have suggested she should have a crop – more *clavicule*, you understand?' She tilted her head back and outlined her own collarbone with a copper-polished fingernail. Her straight hair ran along her jawbone like mercury.

'Oh no, I'm sorry, Estelle,' Micky said quickly. 'Perhaps I didn't make it clear. We're looking for glamour, not gloss!' She looked so crestfallen that he decided to be gracious. 'I take your point, though, about the Afro. Just a touch too much of the Woodstock, you think?' Draping his legs over the chair arm so that his stockinged feet swung fancy-free, he smiled at her comfortably, from the other side of a great divide. It would be too galling if she seriously thought he was flirting with her.

'*Pardon?*'

'I'm talking Sixties,' said Micky, all geniality. 'No reason for you to remember.'

In the luxurious gloom they stared in silence at the screen, on which Sophie was describing a solo ascent of something called the Mitchell Spur on a mountain called the Juron.

'So where did she learn her English?' he asked.

'Sussex University, I understand. She speaks like a native, don't you think?'

Micky pounced. 'And that's exactly my problem. I'm hearing Home Counties, I'm hearing Radio 4, I'm hearing Sue Lawley on *Desert Island Discs*. What I'm saying is, our clients will be looking for an accent. It appeals to them, you see, that *je ne sais quoi* you French have.'

Estelle regarded him with a puzzled frown. 'You are suggesting she makes ... an exaggeration?'

'Well, I'm not saying she should do an Inspector Clouseau,' Micky replied equably, before lapsing into a judicious silence.

On the screen Sophie took out tobacco and papers and began to roll a cigarette in her lap. When she held the paper to her lips to lick it, Micky saw with a thrill of dismay that her left forefinger had been amputated at the first joint. Nailless, it stuck out obscenely. It looked blind and wormlike, resembling a small boy's penis. 'Uh-oh,' said Micky. 'We'll have to keep the finger out of shot.' He thought squeamishly of scalpels and stitches. He could not take his eyes off it.

'Frostbite,' said Estelle, glancing at him significantly. 'Sophie suffered badly last year in Norway. She had two toes amputated also.'

Understanding that he was supposed to be impressed by Sophie's battle scars, Micky felt exasperated. He opened his mouth to object, then thought better of it. Because in fact she had a point. Cringe factor aside, you could see the finger in another way. The finger as signifier of the martyred body, as sacrifice to passion. As a badge of identity, he had to admit, it was rougher and tougher than body-piercing: unarguable, unfakeable...

Sophie was telling the interviewer that she suffered from clinical boredom. She was saying that everyone had a rat in their belly which needed to be fed and that hers required regular doses of excitement. 'A rat with a habit,' she said, on the crest of a wild guffaw.

'And between expeditions? Do you train a lot?'

Sophie stared the camera in the eye. 'Oh, no,' she said emphatically. 'I laze around, I eat chocolate. I don't see people. Just get fat, you know, get depressed.'

'Oh, please! Spare us the true confessions, ducky!' Micky turned irritably to Estelle. 'Does she *want* everyone to know she's a slob?'

Estelle's face contracted. As the footage faded the screen filled up with electronic snow. They stared at it in silence for a few seconds before Estelle hit the rewind button. She studied her nails; her sleek hair swung down to shield her face. Her shrug would have been helpless, Micky thought, if helplessness had been in her nature. There were wounded hollows under her cheek-bones but he looked in vain for the sheen of tears.

At last she got up and smoothed her skirt and went to raise the window blinds. 'You must remember that Sophie is an individualist, like all great climbers,' she said defensively.

An Alpine sun surged into the room. Estelle stood with her back to it, her stark silhouette so narrowed by the glare that she seemed almost transparent.

'OK, OK.' Micky sighed. He had made his point, secured his position; he could afford, perhaps, to ease up a little. Through the window he saw a cable-car cabin slither towards the summit of the Aiguille du Sud. It was nearly lunchtime, and perfect skiing weather. 'Just as long as she's prepared to meet us halfway...' Palming the arms of his chair, he swung lightly to his feet. 'Look, love, let's call it a day, shall we?'

Estelle nodded crisply, snapping her Powerbook shut. When he helped her on with her jacket she looked at him with a prim uncertain mouth.

'You do see, don't you, that we can't afford to give our clients the wrong impression? But let's talk again after I've met her, OK?' He rested his hand on Estelle's shoulder for a moment and allowed himself a rueful grin. 'Well, we've got our work cut out for us, is all I can say!'

Every morning Broom worked at the kitchen table until the sun was high and handsome over the Montjoie; then she put on her boots and went walking.

Broom loved to walk. She relied upon it, not to make her feel blithe and gay, necessarily, but rather to release her from the responsibility of feeling anything in particular. Things in the landscape merely lived; they neither resented the fact nor treasured it; in fact they took no position on it at all. Surrounded by this pervasive neutral intelligence, you escaped all obligation to dwell on what you lacked or envied or what was lost to you. Nothing more was required than to breathe and plant your feet sensibly and swing one leg past the other. It was enough simply to allow your limbs to move you along. The rest, she supposed, was chemistry.

She had been reading too much about the Reformation; her brain was begging for mercy. Marlowe and the new sense of the isolation of the human soul; Marlowe and the weight of individual responsibility; *Dr Faustus* as embodying the Renaissance spirit of enquiry, but also the Calvinist sins of presumption and pride. Yards of turgid commentary. Not that any amount of exegesis could tame the text itself. Marlowe's daemons were alive and well and sizzled from the page five centuries later. Goethe's *Faust*, on which the Gounod had been based, was undoubtedly a masterpiece, but it was the Marlowe that reminded her she was still a superstitious Scot, and simply scared the pants off her.

Muffled up, she took the back lane which led from Madame d'Ange's chalet up the valley towards the hamlet of Les Cristaux. After a kilometre or so she turned under the railway bridge and followed a level track through fir trees to the boulder-strewn banks of the river, from whose waters icy gusts of air rushed up at her. On the west side of the valley the Couronnes range rose graciously enough, flanked by the Casse-Noix and its consort La Charrue, but her eyes were drawn, as always, to the higher Montjoie *massif* on the eastern side, with its beetling pinnacles and ridges. She ticked off the names of the Aiguilles, from south to north, as Lockhart, years ago, had taught her. The Sud, the Juron, the Blatte, the Jongleur. She had brought her map to check but found she didn't need it. Then came the Aiguille du Diable with its attendant *gendarme*, the Sans Pitié, and, facing them across the great cleft of the Cristaux glacier, the graceful pyramid of the Faille. To the northeast, just visible behind the Faille, the peak of the Paradis marked the highest point on the barrier ridge of Les Grisailles, where Switzerland and clouds began.

On the opposite bank two Sécurité Civile helicopters stood idle on the tarmac of the heliport. It was lunchtime. The windows of the wooden mess-hut were too steamed up for her to see the crews but she thought she could hear their laughter.

The Rochers des Cristaux loomed up on her right; above the tumbled moraine-boulders she could see the ragged green ice-fringe of the Cristaux glacier. Meltwater from the glacier snout eked down the slope to form a tributary that joined the river further up the valley. The junction of the two streams was spanned by a wooden bridge, split-level, to take account of springtime floods. Under the bridge lay a deep pool where plates of ice which had calved from the frozen plates at the river's edge circled on the current, their contours smooth and rounded as waterlily pads.

When she stepped onto the bridge her boots

127

made a hollow squeaking sound on the snow-laden planks. Above her the Diable and the Sans Pitié rose like sentinels, but on the other side of the glacier the Faille was stark, aflame. She had come at exactly the right time of day, when the sun, emphatic on the triangle of the great west face, warmed the rose and ochre heart of the granite and honed the Arête des Cristaux to the sharpest possible serration.

La faille (geology): a fault or fault-line. No blame attached. As opposed to *le défaut*: an imperfection or failing.

She lit a cigarette and leaned and wondered. If you truly lacked desire, if you had no ambition to conquer a mountain, did it reveal itself differently? If you were a climber – which she was not – the Faille would present itself as a sporting challenge, a worthy adversary. But she had done just enough climbing, with Lockhart and with others, to recognize her limitations. She was older now, if not wiser. She'd learned to accept that it was art, for better or for worse, which was her big adventure. When she stood before the Faille what she saw was a peaceful pyramid. Safe. Solid. Patriarchal, somehow, in its strength...

The equation – borne out by little in her experience – was wistful enough to irritate her. You could idealize to your heart's content but in reality mountains were fickle and changeable, prone to rock-slide, avalanche and treacherous weathers. It wasn't as if she'd ever been the religious type – monotheism, certainly, repelled her – but she could understand the impulse to put a name to the mystery – the sense that love's fluency moved in you, passing easily between the poles of masculine and feminine, the presence of a harmony, wounds healed, and so on – to dress it in canonicals and package it in creeds. People needed comfort, and she was no exception. Even sceptics, after all, had their sacraments. Each to his own path was her position, and let them follow Allah or Jehovah if it pleased them, as long as they left her free to find her own.

Smoke rose perpendicularly from her cigarette. The trees on the steep slope below the Rochers were motionless, misted by light; not a breath of wind. In the pool under the bridge the ice-flowers circled endlessly.

She buried her cigarette butt under a stone and headed for the path that traversed the wooded slope below the glacier. After her amble along the valley floor some serious exercise was called for. As she struck uphill, lactic acid snarled in her calf muscles. Her breath came short; her head was mired in half-remembered dreams.

The old mule-path she was following led up to the disused forest station of Les Gorets. From there it was possible to descend to the town via the rack-and-pinion railway line that served the Cristaux glacier. She spurred herself on through the thinning trees. Birch. Rowan. Grey cut stumps of dead firs marking the outer edges of the path. On a bald black branch, red clumps of rowanberries wore startling caps of snow.

She was high now, high as the Charrue ski-station on the other side of the valley; soon the path would level out and start to descend. But not too soon. She had no desire to return to the chalet as long as there was light in the day.

Generally she came down from the hills with a sinking heart, as if her dreams were doomed to die a death on the doorstep; some child-part of her still refusing to forget, perhaps, how houses had hemmed her in, their shadows full of a melancholy that seemed to emanate from her mother. Roz had once pointed out that her London flat was a place which ached towards the great outdoors: the interior doors were wedged open, the curtains drawn back to the maximum, allowing the light to ricochet from room to room. It was Roz who'd drawn up her astrology chart in the days when such things were still taken semi-seriously. 'Sun–Venus conjunct Uranus at the mid-heaven. Sweet Jesus Mary, no wonder you're such a claustrophobic.'

In a fire-break in the forest, the new saplings bore a two-inch wedge of frost rime on their skinny branches. The slight draught of her passing was enough to disturb a shower of motes, which flashed and died before they reached the ground. A cascade of light-atoms, gone in a millisecond. For a moment she was filled with a calm so remarkable that she didn't trust it, and it struck her then – out of the blue it came to her – that grief had a half-life, like spent fuel. You mourned still, but you began to be able to imagine a time when you might not...

At the end of every term her evening-class students had to fill in self-evaluation sheets. Please tick the column that best describes the progress you have made. *I can do this/I am working towards this/I have decided not to work*

130

towards this. Mourning, stage one, she thought: complete beginners. But if she were honest, wouldn't she have to admit that she no longer found it impossible to believe that five years had passed since the accident? Already there were times when she didn't actively resent being alive ... which suggested, didn't it, that something had shifted; implied, even, that one day she might be able to think of Al, not without sadness, of course, but without the kind of pain that compressed memory to something dense and crystalline, like a mineral deposit?

She stopped on a level section, open-mouthed. The sound that slipped out of her small and nasal, like the whine of a whipped dog. Her boots had broken through the frozen crust of the snow to the insubstantial powder beneath. She stared at her sinking feet, rebellious, her eyes steamed up with tears.

It wasn't as if he didn't know the score. It wasn't as if I could have stopped him.

For the hundredth or thousandth time she told herself that she had no reason to feel guilty. A mountain of a man, he'd convinced himself – as he'd almost convinced her – that he was super-human. Despite his injuries, even the consultants seemed certain that he would recover. 'Heart like a twenty-year-old footballer,' they marvelled; 'you'd never guess the fellow's fifty.'

The image of him as he rode: great bullish shoulders in a torn green vest. And when he stopped he talked to everyone. To Syrian poets and Greek sailors on shore leave in Alexandria and Palestinians in the Friday frenzy of the barber's shop; to Moroccan roadsweepers and Berbers tending their herds and Bulgarian cleaning women on the tourist boat to Haifa. Each day he set himself to learn twenty new words in the tongue of the host country. No one could deny that Al was a man of the people. Sometimes she felt that he could talk to the whole wide world in all its languages but not to her.

Every week, along with his letters, came the journal instalments, which were to form the basis of his book. Always there was a seizure of envy when she read them, because, unlike the letters, they were addressed not to her alone but to the public at large, but also because of what they conjured up. Sights, sounds. Scents she couldn't smell, flavours she couldn't taste, no matter how conscientiously he tried to convey them. A meal of *chai* and dates with the Jordanian Army on the King's Highway. Damascus dumbstruck under snowdrifts, the fronds of the palm trees loaded and sagging, icicles on the statues of President Assad. The long freewheel down from the plateau with the Lebanon to the south and the Crac des Chevaliers tempting him from the hills, and in the distance, drawing him on, the shimmering line of the sea.

A goat bell tinkled faintly on the slope below. She sensed a subtle withdrawal in the landscape: the sun's face hardening, the branches whispering to themselves but not to her. She stared at the path ahead, suddenly panicky, convinced that she had lost her bearings. Her breath made loose white clouds before her on the empty air. Could she have passed Les Gorets already? She didn't

132

remember seeing the chalet with its tarpaulin-covered log stacks, or the bend the railway track made before it vanished into the tunnel.

Look right, look left, look right again, and still the shock of the lorry slamming into him. Her *faille*, her fault-line, her fallibility. Scar tissue might thicken over time but beneath the skin the wound lived on, dark, delinquent, exclusive; lipped with shame, like solitary sex.

If it was intolerable to rage at the dead, it was even more intolerable to desire them.

She sidestepped urgently, needing to touch something, a stone or a larch cone, or a stick with which to pattern the blank white page of the snow. All around her the white, white mountains and the gross estrangement of the sky. There were fragments of glassy sound: tiny things echoing and falling. She snatched an icicle from a bush and sucked on it, her tongue feeling the sharp point, the slipperiness: sensations that had the effect of holding her in. From a cool distance her mind observed that it wasn't very clever of her to come to France alone. Veronica, being a woman in full command of her weaknesses, would have been quick to point this out to her.

Six thousand feet up an Alp, she thought, with no one but your own worst enemy to rely on. Predictably the cheap jibe braced her. Now was neither the time nor the place for a *crise de nerfs*. Safer not to think at all, in the circumstances; safer just to keep moving, like a prayer-wheel, hiding your madness behind sunglasses.

The path sloped down, gently at first, and then acutely, to a bare rocky bluff that looked across the valley to the Charrue station. Broom edged down sideways and stood on the rim. The bluff overhung a gulley fifty metres below, where shattered trees indicated an avalanche slide-path. The thought of jumping was no more than a reflex, a familiar signal from the sympathetic nervous system. Give it a good belt round the ear, said Al, who'd never had much patience with her brainstorms.

She stepped back and saw through the trees a smudge of smoke rising from the squat chimney of Les Gorets. There was a wind-iced dog-leg she took cautiously, and then, directly below, the toothed rail of the narrow-gauge snaking up out of the forest.

Two pairs of new skis leaned, incongruous, against the decrepit lathe-and-plaster porch of the chalet, their orange laminate emblazoned with silver and black. On the doorstep sprawled a pair of child-size wellingtons. The sight of the settlement steadied her. As she passed she smelled hay, woodsmoke, the red onions that hung in a net bag under the roof of the porch.

Just then a goat stepped, tinkling, out of the forest and stopped on the path ahead. She saw that it wasn't young. Its hair was long and matted. Brief icicles dangled from its ginger beard. Its yellow eyes regarded her disinterestedly, the black apertures of their pupils narrowed against the sudden sun.

Broom did not always talk to animals. Often, though, she found herself listening hopefully to them, as if expecting them to provide a fresh perspective on her ills. She liked the beasts of the field. She liked the way they shat and pissed where they stood. She liked the different set of words they spoke inside her head: not trickster words, not words that refused to name the things you needed most to know. She thought they should get more credit for the comfort that was squeezed from them. She thought they carried a loving animus to a world which sorely needed it and didn't even know.

She stood quite still, paying attention to the animal, whose interrogative eyes were trained on her.

Loneliness is no disgrace, she heard it say.

Loneliness, she thought. Now there's a good plain name, like Mary or Margaret. Surely I can manage with that.

The goat stood motionless; she saw the pulse that beat at the base of its throat. Its beard steamed gently in the sunny clearing. It was telling her that it was hot-blooded, like she was. It was telling her that everything wanted to connect with something warm and alive. It was telling her, also, that she thought too much and knew too little.

When she blew her nose the goat sped away, leaving her with the regret that she'd had nothing to offer it, not a square of chocolate or a single hank of hay. She sent a kind of thanks into the empty space where it had been, marvelling at the fact that it took a goat to let the tears fall down, a goat to tell her to forgive herself.

Consciousness is a kind of curse, she thought – they hear the call, these animals, and then they come.

After lunch – tiger prawns in aubergine batter, taken with a glass of Chablis in the panoramic restaurant on the top floor of the hotel – Micky zipped himself into his Moe one-piece, collected his skis from the lobby and strode out into the jarring sunshine.

The mountains, radiant, bore down on him. In the Place du Sud a minibus had just finished disgorging a group of Italian tourists, who stood stock-still and silenced, their little moley snouts pointed skywards. Light flashed on the mirrored lenses of their sunglasses; their lips were stretched into dazed transcendent smiles.

Micky traversed the square without looking up. All through lunch his mind had refused to relinquish the theme of slash, bite, severance. From the restaurant windows the summit dome of the Montjoie looked like a blank white breast without a nipple. The stubby *séracs* of the glacier below it were amputated torsoes; the Aiguilles might have been sharpened by a god the size of a *Hauptbahnhof*, with a mossy beard and arms like massive carving-knives.

He crossed the bridge and paused outside the windows of the *confiserie* to examine a pyramid of fruits made from *pâte d'amandes*: peaches, bananas, little blushing pears, slices of passion-fruit complete with purple seeds. He propped his skis outside the door and went in whistling the 'Marseillaise'. He'd had a successful morning, after all; he was entitled to his just desserts.

With the triumphant precision of a surgeon removing a gall bladder, the shop assistant plucked the kiwi fruit he'd asked for out of the display. Her smile was intimate and Christmassy. 'You wish that I make a ... *presentation?*' she enquired, holding the sweet between her silver tongs.

Micky was abashed. *'S'il vous plaît,'* he muttered. Clearly the girl assumed that the thing was for a child, a *petit cadeau* to hide in the toe of a stocking or hang among the baubles on the tree. In this context a solo sweet seemed mean. Too late, he considered buying four or even six. Already the girl had eased the sweet into a narrow cellophane bag embossed with a grinning Santa Claus. She folded the top over several times, stapled it carefully and fiddled with a spool of scarlet ribbon.

Micky glanced through the glass door to check on his skis. Out in the square two post-office clerks had leaned a ladder against the front of the *bureau de poste* and were tying fir branches and gold lamé bows to the portico. Despite the chill in the wind, the man on the ladder was in shirtsleeves and the girl shouting instructions from the ground wore only a thin blue suit. On the bridge beside the *poste* the flags of all nations fluttered in the rushing draught from the river; only the red cross of Switzerland was motionless, weighed down by a yard-long beard of icicles.

An elderly couple – Germans, Micky assumed, from their green loden coats and their vaguely apologetic air – came into the shop, but the assistant wouldn't be hurried. She had wrapped the cellophane packet in an outer casing of gold paper; now, reeling ribbon off her spool, she began to construct an elaborate rosette. With two swift strokes of her scissor blades she curled the loose ends of the ribbon into spirals that sprang up pertly, like childish ringlets. With a flourish, she set the article on the counter. *'Voilà, monsieur!'*

The Germans stared admiringly at the parcel.

'Ravissante!' cried Micky, who was genuinely impressed by the scissor trick. He bore the *petit cadeau* off in a routine festival of *mercis* and *bonne journées*, and remembered only after the door had shut behind him that he hadn't actually paid for it. Briefly he considered going back in, to see her face light up like a Christmas tree, to wear his Christmas halo: at ten francs, a cheap enough salvation. On the other hand, the girl had discomfited him, or as near as dammit, and on that score alone he owed her nothing and didn't care to keep her in his mind a second longer than he had to.

As he shouldered his skis he risked a sidelong glance at the window and saw that she was fully engaged with the Germans. Her smile looked eager and forgetful. Blithely donning his sun-glasses, he slipped round the corner and hurried along the Avenue de la Gare, where, without slackening his pace, he stripped the ribbons and wrappings from the sweet with impatient fingers and let them fall on the cobbled street behind him.

Ralentissez, skieurs! screamed a red notice. *Piste débutants.*

A few hundred metres beyond Les Gorets a cutting in the forest marked the top of the nursery slope, which led down to the outskirts of the town. There the *télésiège* began, and the orange netting of the perimeter fence, and every few metres the snow cannons, silent, iced.

When Broom came out of the trees the great mass of the light filled her, and she stopped on the brow of the slope, shielding her eyes with her hand. Overhead the yellow seats of the *télésiège* cranked along between the pylons. Here and there disembodied legs dangled, wearing the scissor-blades of skis. She marched on down the slope, keeping to the outer edge, in the lee of the fence. Too late, she saw the compacted gleam of ice under the snow cannon, and her boot skidded away sideways, and she tumbled forward onto the piste.

For a moment the cry behind her enveloped everything. Then a decelerating shadow showered her with hot frost. A ski-boot thumped into the small of her back, in the region of her kidneys. When the solid body fell across her she was already sliding, her chin ploughing into the crusted surface of the snow. Half of her mind told her this wasn't what should have happened, but the other half said she'd invited it, if only by relaxing her vigilance.

139

Broom's habit had always been to anticipate situations, as if their potential for harm could thus be neutralized in advance. One result of this was that reality, when it arrived, was so wildly different from her imaginings that it disturbed her far more than if she'd simply taken things as they came. Her mother used to say, obscurely, 'You're frightened of the day you'll never see.' The words had borne out her worst apprehensions, denoting as they did a day on which the sun would fail to rise, a day which there was every reason to fear, precisely *because* you wouldn't see it. Her mother made a conscientious effort to explain. She only meant, she said, a day that would never arrive. Broom's child-mind had been swayed, if not entirely comforted, but not for long. Quickly forgetting the gloss, she'd revert to her old habits and in no time would be scaring herself just as badly as before.

Now, taken by surprise, she whizzed down the slope, face first and too fast for fright, her body locked into a kind of cruciform arrangement with the unknown other, her mind as free as can be of constructs.

When at last they came to a halt she saw one ski escape and surf off down the slope, silent and singular and stately. She was winded, and seemed to have lost her sunglasses, but she did not feel exactly injured.

The man in the silver ski-suit rolled over her and struggled to release his ski-binding. His face was tanned and goggled; he wore a stripe of white zinc on his nose like a badger, which struck her as both absurd and magical. Adrenalin-boosted, she started to laugh, for no damage seemed to have been done and a close shave is such a clean thing compared with self-inflicted torments.

'Fuckssake!' the man spluttered. 'I hope you're insured for this!'

Broom was glad that he could see the funny side. She gasped her apologies, exuberant, wiping the snow from her mouth. Then she saw that he was clutching his ankle, his lips twisted into a grimace of pain. Now it sank in that he might be serious.

She peered helplessly at the ankle – invisible inside a vast immaculate ski-boot – and then at the person she had wounded. The mirrored lenses of his goggles reflected two pursed, remorseful versions of her face.

'Oh God, is it broken?' Shock made her voice flat and formal. She didn't stop to ask herself what kind of man was this who in his first breath threatened litigation, or at least not yet; for the moment his anger was unbridled and crushing. Generally speaking, Broom didn't regard herself as someone who was easily crushed. Then again there was her age, which made it all too easy to assume that he regarded her as a poor investment, not worth wasting good manners on. She accepted, of course, that he was in pain. But had she suddenly become so very old?

The man eased up and tested his weight on the ankle. His sigh was explosive. 'No, I don't think so. Sprained, more likely. Give me a hand, will you?'

When she scrambled to her feet to help him up, thick wedges of snow fell from the creases of her

141

jeans. Under the open parka her sweater was crusted and sodden. A few metres away she spotted her sunglasses perched on a nubble of snow, staring inscrutably down at the *terrasse* of the *relais du ski*. She gathered up his ski-poles, wondering if she ought also to offer to carry the ski, whose runaway partner had now come to rest against the orange mesh fence at the bottom of the piste.

Invited to lean on her, badger man leaned heavily, grunting and cursing as they hobbled down the slope. She was aware, suddenly, that her chin was raw and stinging. When she saw the blood on her glove her mind cleared and it dawned on her that according to the code of the slopes, the skier above is responsible for the safety of those below, who – obviously – can't see him coming. The bugger wasn't in control, she thought: he wasn't skiing within his limits.

'There's a first-aid post,' she said coldly, 'at the back of the *relais.*' Listening to his groans, she decided that a bit of stiff upper lip wouldn't come amiss. He might sound English, but he certainly didn't act it.

They negotiated the *terrasse* with difficulty, overturning several plastic chairs, clanging the ski-poles against the metal hoarding that advertised *Glaces.* The *coupe de banane* was daubed with nail-varnish pink, to represent the Melba sauce; the *Mont Blanc* was a glum chestnut-coloured turd with a tampon of cream on the top.

In the *bureau du ski* the goggles came off, and Broom took a covert look at the casualty. He was neither tall nor short, young nor old, and if she

142

formed any opinion of him it was that he had the sort of Mediterranean good looks she'd never managed to find attractive. His face was tanned; his hair was vehemently black, as if it had been dyed. His one identifiable flaw was that his eyes were red-rimmed and inflamed – a touch of conjunctivitis, perhaps, from the snow-glare. Undoubtedly he was expensive; just looking at him was enough to remind her that she lived in a rented flat, smoked her cigarettes too close to the butt. She couldn't help noticing that every item on his body (no doubt his underwear as well) boasted its designer's marque.

Providing free advertising for the mega-companies came high on Broom's list of inexplicable behaviours, on a par with stealing supermarket trolleys or watching TV pro-grammes about hedging-plants. As far as she was concerned, it was yet another symptom of the prevailing epidemic of money worship. These days people tended their money with a craven passion, exalting it, fearing for it as once upon a time they might have feared for their immortal souls. Like her father – that happy-go-lucky man (her mother would have said feckless) who throughout his short life had owned no more than a fishing rod – she'd never been able to understand why something so utterly trivial should be taken so very seriously.

All surplus value was created at some point by the labour of an exploited majority, or so thought Broom, who'd read her Marx and still believed it. Odd how in the nineteenth century this had been clear to everyone: then, the rich had responsibilities; nowadays, on the other hand, only the poor had. No soul-searching in the boardrooms of today, she thought, eyeing Micky – who was being prodded, and wincing awfully – without sympathy. No earnest philanthropists there. Those who prospered were, by definition, productive; by implication, morally superior. Those who didn't were weak, antisocial, even vicious. That a man might work hard all his life and die in poverty was no longer acknowledged.

It was true, of course, that she hadn't exactly been sensible. Every year she told herself, OK, I'll just scrape through this summer and when it's over I'll really sort my finances out. Sometimes, looking to the future, she panicked. Hang on to your hat, she'd tell herself, facing, in not so many years, a penurious old age. And then – thinking of Al, thinking of her father – well, I should be so lucky, to live that long. Sometimes she considered the lilies of the field, *for Solomon in all his glory was not arrayed like one of these*; sometimes she simply felt she was a failure, and at fault. The important thing, however, was to keep your integrity. Let them write that on her tombstone if they wanted.

'Micky, is it? Well, Mick, no clubbing for you for a coupla days, right?'

The paramedic was that admirable sort of Australian who, when the plane falls five thousand feet over the Pacific, will be ready with the repartee. 'Jeez, mate, not more bread rolls.' The sort of man who is good for morale. To Broom's relief he didn't seem particularly impressed by the injury, although he listened

144

patiently enough to Micky's worries. Holding to her chin a wad of gauze soaked in disinfectant, she watched him ease a tubigrip bandage over the swollen ankle.

'Sure, you can get an X-ray at the Polyclinique – it's up to you. But frankly I wouldn't bother.'

She couldn't help noticing that Micky was putty in the paramedic's hands. He fussed a stray hank of hair back behind his ear while his eyes appealed for reassurance. His badger nose wrinkled into a bashful smile. Outside, in the Gare de Montagne, the narrow-gauge cranked up in preparation for its last trip up to the glacier. A smell of burning diesel wafted through the open door of the office. This rich man, she thought, this Micky – he's gay, of course.

'You recommend I rest it, then?' said Micky, pulling on a long fleecy sock with a design of little red skiers.

'Two, three days should do it. If not, you might need physio.'

Between them Broom and the Australian helped Micky to his feet.

'How's that feel?'

Micky limped experimentally across the room. 'Better.' Nodding. 'Yeah. Not bad at all.'

The paramedic waved away his offer of payment. 'No worries. Buy me a beer sometime.'

Micky shot him a bright and wistful glance. You're barking up the wrong tree there, thought Broom with pleasurable spite. She thought she ought at least to offer a taxi, but Micky wouldn't hear of it. His shoulders were jaunty; his dark face sparkled with a light she suspected would last no further than the door. His hotel, he insisted, was just a stone's throw away, a few hundred metres at most, it really wasn't a problem. Suddenly devil-may-care, he announced that she looked as if she needed a drink and he could certainly fucking do with one. He held out a feeble arm to her and said self-mockingly, 'Shall we?'

Outside, the mountain train had gone, taking with it the tourists and their cameras. Since there was no longer any sun on the terrace of the *relais* they made their way inside, where the banquette seats were of shabby plush and the petunias in their wrought-iron pot-stands unapologetically plastic. As she settled the invalid into an alcove seat a muffled electronic rendering of 'The Ride of the Valkyries' issued from his jacket. He fished a red cellphone out of a zipped inner pocket, punched a button and barked, 'Flint.'

Broom went over to the bar, where the waitresses looked quickly at her chin and then away, and ordered coffee and a *pression*. When she returned to the table Micky was talking about a guaranteed audience of five hundred million viewers across a hundred and ninety-five countries. He nodded his thanks for the beer. There was a silence in which he totted up a column of figures on a beer mat. 'I don't know what advice you've had,' he went on smoothly, 'but there's still a lot you can do that doesn't infringe FIFA's copyright.' His eyes swept the café, flickering blankly over the locals. They were men, mostly: railway workers and a couple of middle-aged *gendarmes*.

Broom took out her pocket mirror and checked

her chin. It looked bad. It looked as if it had been grated.

'Take Nike back in 'ninety-six, before the Brazil deal. They bought so much poster space around the stadia that most people assumed they *were* an official sponsor... Yeah, ambush marketing. Where there's a will there's a way, Miles.'

She swatted at her cigarette smoke, which was heading, predictably, for the one man in the room whose pearly teeth proclaimed that he'd never been a smoker. Micky's voice was annoyingly loud. She was aware that people were staring. She shifted the salt and pepper pots around, lined them up with the toothpicks and vinaigrette bottles, building a mini-barricade that marked her off from him. He was listening hard, his pen poised and erect, like a little soldier at attention. He said carefully, 'I really don't think we should go down that particular road, Miles.' By now the beer mat bristled with black question marks. *Chris Hymns*, he wrote, frowning. She watched him crown the name with thorns. 'Svensen pitched in good faith for that account! We thought it was a free and equal tender.'

Outside, the Aiguille du Sud gathered the dusk in around its lower slopes. The summit spire glowed its splendiferous sunset pink, but Broom found that she had lost the taste for it. It looked puffed-up and vulgar, like an outsize strawberry ice-cream cone. Micky's voice had become impatient. 'Well, *of course* Damien's pissed at Chris. How do you expect him to feel? Nobody likes being dicked around by a client, specially when said client rips off your pitch ideas and foists them on the agency that does get the account!'

Broom's embarrassment was giving way to a feeling of unreality. She began to feel like someone who, in her own home town, has managed to take a wrong turning.

On the periphery of her mind a thought lay in waiting. Perhaps at the heart of every accident lies an invisible fork where fate pauses to deliberate between two paths. An instant in which the mishap – still ludic and absurd – might or might not turn out to be deadly.

Al was a slow climber, painstaking. In Pembroke he deliberated so long at the crux of a route that Broom, who was staked out on the beach below with her sunscreen and watercolours, had plenty of time to paint him. On the midway ledge Liam and Robbo sunbathed and creased themselves. Still life with cliff face. It was a great opportunity for a wind-up.

In the second summer he'd begun to make mistakes. At Land's End she'd seen him snatch his body sideways when a block he'd dislodged slid past on a runnel of stones and shattered on the rock platform forty feet below. In September, a month before he set off on his trip, there was another incident.

He'd spent a fine Saturday bouldering on the sandstone crags at Eridge; nothing more testing than Hard VS, he'd assured her on the Friday night: in other words, a breeze.

When she arrived at the door on Saturday evening Robbo was buzzing with excitement. 'Would you believe, the stupid git forgot to tie on properly! He's thirty or forty feet up and we spot the rope-end dangling…'

148

'*Fucking Alzheimer's,*' Liam agreed. *He was laughing, but he looked shaken.*

Al shrugged at her, shamefaced. Clearly she was expected to play the outraged girlfriend, to read the riot act. 'First time in my life, cross my heart and hope to die. Can't think what came over me.'

Al spent the rest of the evening buttering her up. He was still trying to mollify her when they climbed the stairs to bed. On the landing he stopped and put his hand on his heart and gazed at her. 'VSL,' he said, with a tortured grin.

'What?' she said crossly. He was laughing, waiting for her to get the joke.

'Very Severe Love...'

It was Liam, as it turned out, who'd saved him. He'd been climbing in parallel, and had launched himself across the rock. In her mind's eye she could still see him, small and nimble as a monkey, swinging towards Al on a crazy pendulum of rope.

The fall, relived, was a kind of freedom. A long sashay down the snow slope with the sky blue and circling overhead. Maybe that's what Al had felt, just for a second. Like a player in an unknown game.

When a wave of excitement hit her she began to shake. She felt nauseous. The gold rim of the coffee cup rattled against her teeth.

'Look, I'm out of London right now, so why don't you call Alice Marks at the office; she'll fit you in. Yeah. No sweat. *Ciao*, Miles.'

Broom shut her eyes and breathed strongly through her nose. When she opened them again Micky was tucking away his mobile.

'Sorry about that.' He stared at her with concern, his smile fading. 'Hey, are you OK?'

'No, honestly, I'm fine.' She put her hands up to her cheeks. 'Just reaction, I guess.'

'You look pretty peaky, I have to say. Gave me quite a scare for a minute there. Sure you don't need a cognac or something?'

'No, really. I'll be OK.'

Micky cocked his head on one side and said, with a mimicry so suave and flagrant that she was caught off guard, and laughed abruptly, 'No clubbing for *you* tonight, mate!'

It was dusk when she turned into the lanes. She saw Madame d'Ange's youngest grandchild trundling towards her on his tricycle; his father, Guy the mountain guide, was several yards behind. Guy called out something cautionary, which made him pedal faster. Just then the front wheel hit a rut and the bike bucked sideways, tipping him off. There was a second's silence and then a wail from the infant, who lay face down on the ice and didn't move until his father picked him up and set him on his feet. Giving the trike a glance of purest hatred, he grabbed his father's legs and buried his head in the trousered nook between his knees. Guy stood immobile, his hand on the child's shoulder, his face patient and rueful.

Broom made sympathetic noises as she passed. When she looked out of the window five minutes later Guy hadn't moved an inch. The boy had stopped wailing, but he was still clinging to his father, still blotting out the hard and hurtful world.

150

Once and only once, after much prompting and with relentless cheerfulness, Al had talked to her about his childhood. His father had been a civil engineer, based at that time in the Gulf. At seven Al had been sent off to a Jesuit school in Beirut – his mother believed that boys should be given the best education available – while his younger brother and sister remained with their parents.

Maybe if he had been seventeen ... but he was not. He described the taxi journey across the desert and, at the border, tanks, roadblocks. Listening, Broom was appalled. It was 1948, when Syria and Jordan were at war with Israel. Half a million refugees were on the move through Galilee. His mother had given him a kiss, put his brand-new passport into his hand, and sent him, wittingly or unwittingly, into danger.

'For God's sake,' she said, 'weren't you terrified?' Al said that he couldn't remember. He had a feeling that it might have been exciting; had even, possibly, given him a taste for adventure. 'Maybe it made a man of me,' he added, trying, as usual, to provoke her. He couldn't recall much about the school, he said, except that he'd had to learn French; nor did he remember missing his family, although at that age, OK, he'd concede the point, presumably he must have done.

151

Acc: nighthawk@freeserve.co.uk
Re: fraternal love

A new trope. My brother the watchdog has descended. 'Overpaid, overweight and over here' is the phrase that comes to mind. His barriers have grown more solid (literally) over the years, so that he now seems positively burgher-ish (or do I mean burger-ish?), and tho I don't believe he has ever actively intended to be cruel to me – which is more than I can say for His Lairdship my father – communication is, as it always has been, a mega-problem. In my father's eyes oor Archie can do nae wrong, whereas when he (they) look at me I feel the word 'reprobate' branded on my forehead.

Nevertheless, I am trying to keep faith with my 'untapped powers and energies', as you suggest, and include for your amusement a brief (true) fairy tale I've been meaning to send you, on the theme of happiness.

Stopping off at the café-cum-winebar down by the harbour one Sunday after church, I saw a young lad waiting in the queue with a woman I assumed to be his older sister. The boy was sixteen or so, dark-haired, with soft fresh skin. His face was heart-shaped and elfish, his eyes deep-set, blue and sparkling. Clearly he had 'Learning Difficulties'. What we used to call ESN. His sister was shorter than he, frumpy, with

152

a bitter put-upon look, and in the fifteen minutes or so they were queueing at the counter – the café was very busy, because of the filthy weather – she didn't say a word to him.

The rain was firing off the sea that day like a weapon. Down by the ferry our huge local gulls fought to keep their balance on the roofs of little foreign cars, while inside bored Italian tourists opened the windows an inch or two and offered up their inedible Scottish sandwiches.

I could see that he was finding it seriously difficult to wait, yet he did so with good grace – in fact, with a great deal of it: raising his arms, at first, as if conducting an orchestra, then swaying into a kind of ballet, his feet in the position called *demi-pointe*. Every so often he gave a deep bow, flashing his jacket open to reveal its brilliant scarlet lining to everyone who cared to look. Once or twice he bent to peer into the eyes of those of us who were seated at tables near the counter. His face was full of light. He had an air of the purest, most delicate enquiry. His smile radiated such a generalized delight that people smiled back, for once more touched, I believe, than embarrassed.

Here was grace and here was sweetness. I could hardly bear to watch him wait a second longer. If it had been up to me he would never have waited for anything, in this life or the hereafter.

When the woman finally reached the cash desk, she didn't say, 'Here we are!' or 'What are you having?' She said nothing at all. In fact she appeared not to care one way or the other. It was almost as if she wanted to disown him. Without a

153

glance at him she turned away and headed for the door. She may have been carrying a packet of crisps. She may even have been eating them.

The boy stood at the counter for a moment, utterly nonplussed. Then he turned, empty-handed, and shambled gracelessly after her. I couldn't bear to see the transformation her cruelty had brought about – for it did seem to me a deliberate act of cruelty. It seemed so wrong that that chalice he held inside could be so easily broken. I wanted to believe that it was the one gift he'd been granted in perpetuity, by way of compensation for what had been denied him in terms of rational consciousness. I wanted to believe that whatever else he lacked, he had at least been granted a perfectly unbreakable happiness.

Watching through the window, I saw him catch up with the woman in the car park, although once again her response was to ignore him. A little later I glimpsed them on the upper deck of the ferry, standing side by side, silently, at the rail.

I have honestly tried to find my place here, but His Lairdship my father has no kindness in him. I go to church only because he asks it of me. What is it, Nighthawk, when a man won't even raise a glass with his own son?

Iceboy

There was no immediate urgency, the Foreign Office had assured her. According to their Ankara bureau Mr Hargreave's injuries were not life-threatening, although he was, yes, unconscious. They would not therefore advise her to fly out at this juncture. The implication being that she was over-reacting.

After the shock of the call came mistrust. Broom sat on the floor at the end of her bed while the telephone trembled in her lap. She rang Keith and Barbara's house in Manchester, and couldn't understand why Ercan answered the phone. When she tried to tell him what had happened her voice was not at home, its signals faint shots that exploded elsewhere.

Ercan was distraught. His brother-in-law was a neurosurgeon in Izmir, he said; he'd ring him immediately. More than likely, he'd have colleagues at the Adana hospital.

'Cerebral oedema,' she said. 'Ask him how bad it is.' She waited, motionless. There was a flaw in the glass of her bedroom window, a kind of thread-line, which snagged the clouds and slid them north, like washing on a pulley. A few minutes later Ercan rang back with names, contacts in the area. The roughness in his voice told her that the Foreign Office was wrong and she was right. There was no time to waste. She should get the first flight out.

On the BA flight to Istanbul miniatures arrived, unasked for, one after the other. She could tell by the way the cabin crew peeked at her from the galley that

155

her story had spread.

The cabin was almost empty. She'd never flown First Class before and wasn't sure whose credit card had paid for it.

At Heathrow Ken McBurney had given her such a gruff send-off that she'd seen herself suddenly not as Al's lover but as a delegate who represented the hopes of many. Friends, family, comrades. When they parted at Passport Control he called her 'mate' and hugged her in his hard builder's arms and gave her to understand that they were all depending on her. In a strange way the responsibility had been a blessing: it was as if duty took over and dried the tears in her.

There had been an hour's delay in take-off and after they got clearance and were airborne a stewardess called Pamela knelt down beside her seat and asked her if she was afraid of flying. Normally this would have been all too true, but for once the thought hadn't entered her head and it was impossible to convey the irony.

Pamela was extremely blond. She was as blue-eyed and flaxen-haired as the Angles pictured in Our Island Story. *For some reason Broom had always remembered the illustration: Julius Caesar or some other Roman general, encountering British slaves for the very first time, on a sandy beach reminiscent of Bournemouth with a bright green grassy sward behind. She thought there had even been a coracle.* Non Angli, sed Angeli. *They are not Angles, but Angels.*

The great engines drummed in her ears. She heard herself say the word 'oedema'. She heard herself tell Pamela that if she missed her connecting flight Al might be dead when she got there. With a bleak surprise she

156

realized that Pamela was holding her hand.

Blankets arrived and armrests were raised and Broom stretched out across the seats, looking down sometimes at mountains. They flew through cloud and above it and when it cleared the Transylvanian Alps were blue and white all the way to the brilliant shores of the Black Sea.

After some time Pamela came back and bent over her, filling the air with minty breath. A small gold St Christopher dangled from a chain round her neck. The captain had radioed ahead, she said: BA would have someone standing by to rush her through Immigration and get her to the domestic flight. 'We can always give you a whiff of oxygen,' she whispered. 'Sometimes it really helps to calm you down.'

Broom was far from sure that she deserved such tender care. She refused the oxygen and drank more whisky, to make herself deserving. She felt safe and stranded, up there in First Class with all her British Angels. Their angel-dust rubbed off on her; she was charged with light and didn't recognize herself.

The plane banked sharply and showed her the Bosphorus. To the south a haze hung over the city, bluey-white, like wood ash. The sun's searchlight swept the cabin as they circled, levelled out, started, oh so gently, to descend. There were gold-bellied clouds in the far west and it struck her low down and darkly that she really had no right to be so swaddled and so spread. She could see now that she'd been lulled into a false security, and had forgotten that the sympathy she'd received from the crew invited the one and only extremity that could justify it. The thought of this act of betrayal – soft, savage, slipped into – sucked the breath out of her. She shrank herself back into her

157

single seat and buckled her seat-belt. Far rather live on fright, she thought. Eat it and drink it and wake in its clammy arms each day, rather than forget that nothing in the world was safe if Al was not.

Broom stared straight down on St Sofia's dome and bargained sickly with a Reformation God. Far rather be a hysteric, who'd had all that First Class fuss and bother under false pretences. This is what she wanted and would settle for: to feel like a fraud, to have spent someone's money stupidly and be scolded for it. To see Al frowning at her from his hospital bed, Al the big bear with the sore head, Al the ageing, heavy-handed flirt with all the pretty nurses.

On the plane from Istanbul her request for a whisky was summarily refused. The Turkish stewardess had eyed her with dislike. It was, of course, a Muslim country: she should have realized that the domestic airline would be dry.

It was dusk when they touched down at Adana. Broom came through Arrivals with no idea what she was to do next. She'd printed the name of the hospital on a piece of paper. BALCALI HASTANESI. The best teaching hospital in Asia Minor, the Foreign Office had assured her.

Outside the plate-glass windows of the terminal a small excitable crowd was being held at bay by two military policemen. An old Kurdish man pushed past her with a crate of hens. Then she saw, jammed up against the glass, a roughly printed oblong of cardboard. MR ALAN HARGREAVE. Below the letters she made out her own name, in smaller print.

When she reached the door the wind of winter hit her, smelling of eucalyptus and exhausts, blowing her

158

long tweed coat hard against her legs. The man who held the sign was shorter than she was, bald as an egg, with startled black eyes.

'Where is the hospital?' she said clearly.

The man pointed to the rank of taxis on the other side of the road. 'Monsieur Engin,' he muttered.

She dropped her bag at her feet and took out her sign and showed him. 'Balcali Hastanesi.' He looked at her as if offended. 'Do you speak English?'

He shrugged and bent to take her bag, which she had no intention of surrendering. She grabbed one of the handles and held on. One of the military policemen eyed the tug-of-war from the exit, fingering the trigger of his gun. 'Balcali Hastanesi,' she repeated.

By now the driver looked thoroughly alarmed. 'Monsieur Engin,' he said desperately, waving an arm with frantic grandeur towards the faint orange lights of the city, as if to say he served a lord at least, and must obey his orders.

Broom gave in; she let him have the bag and trotted after him. He bundled it into the front seat of a low-slung taxi, indicating that she should sit in the back.

She lit a cigarette and peered out into the characterless dark. They drove along a flat, unlit stretch of road bordered by heath. There was nothing to indicate which way was south, or where the sea was, although she'd glimpsed it from the plane as they circled before landing. The same sea that had glittered off the Cap Afrique, dotted with lazy garish caiques. The same salt lips of the Mediterranean, licking its littoral.

In the suburbs grey apartment blocks loomed above houses whose flat roofs bristled with metal reinforcing rods, as if waiting for extra storeys to be added. Their sad scarecrow look reminded her of Tunisia. It was a

159

scam, Al had said: *they weren't waiting for anything. Houses that weren't finished were exempt from land taxes.*

It seemed important, suddenly, to lay her eyes on some ancient fragment of the beautiful, a minaret or cupola, a single glimpse of something that would steady her.

A frosty fog hung over the town, through which sparse street lights shone like sulphurous little moons. The taxi swerved into the inside lane and stopped abruptly before a tall modern building faced in black marble. In an illuminated display case set into the wall were tinted photographs of a mirror-lined ballroom and a casino where women with beehive hairdos played roulette. A commissionaire in red livery hurried to the kerb.

She leaned forward and stabbed the driver's shoulder with her finger. 'Balcali Hastanesi!' *she protested. He darted out of his seat and thrust her holdall at the doorman.*

The failure of communication was breathtaking. She was blonde, she was Western, ergo *she was rich. For a moment she felt the kind of frustration a pilgrim might feel who, on fire for Mecca, finds himself delivered to the door of a McDonald's. Yet there was no way of telling him that luxury was the last thing on her mind. It struck her then that she hadn't thought about where she would stay, and frankly didn't care. She would sleep in a police cell or bed down in a ditch: it was all the same to her...*

The passenger door swung open. The doorman smiled fixedly and tipped his hat. She threw her cigarette into the gutter and followed the two men into the lobby.

Inside, some kind of reception was in progress – a wedding or a funeral, she couldn't tell which. Guests were arriving, the men in dark suits and cashmere coats, the women in floor-length furs. Bouquets on beribboned poles were propped against the walls of the lobby, but the demeanour of the guests seemed more grave than gay.

'A room has been reserved for you, Mrs Broom.' The receptionist took a key from a hook and passed it across the desk. He was young, crop-haired, with a six-o'clock shadow and soft brown eyes. His smile was competent but troubled. He leaned towards her and spoke in a low voice, as if to protect her privacy. 'The Consul regrets that he is called to a business meeting this evening. He will come next morning at nine thirty prompt to drive you to the hospital.'

'You don't understand,' she said. 'I have to go immediately.'

The girl pointed to a name badge on the lapel of her white coat. Underneath she wore an Oasis T-shirt. 'Narmin,' she said. There were butterfly slides in her short dark hair. She looked far too young to be a doctor. A nurse, perhaps, or a medical student.

Broom's brain said that Al was alive. Only the extraordinary good fortune of this allowed her to take in the head, huge and shocking in a turban of bandages, the swollen and featureless face. She saw then that he was naked, his body shifting restlessly beneath a single tangled sheet. The sheet was stained with spots of bloody mucus from a plastic catheter that snaked from his penis. Somehow this was only slightly less bearable than the way his long and lovely legs were exposed to all and sundry, as if they really

161

didn't matter.

'Mr Al-an ... husband?'

Broom gripped the metal frame at the end of the bed. 'Yes,' she lied. 'Husband.' Her heart sickened with jealousy. The blood was rushing in her ears.

The young nurse touched her arm gently. 'Is ... what years? Forty?'

She felt a fierce surge of pride. 'Fifty.' She printed the numerals 50 on the air.

Narmin's eyes widened. 'He is strong man.'

'Very strong!' Broom nodded vivaciously. 'Cyclist.' She bent over an imaginary racing bike and pedalled as if her life depended on it. She thought of all the smudged and sleepless nights she'd spent keeping this particular bike on the road.

'Cy-clist,' Narmin echoed, on a note of wonder. They stood at the end of the bed, marvelling. As a man he was, undoubtedly, marvellous. Hard tears pricked Broom's eyes at the thought of him. He had put himself in harm's way – her too, if it came to that – but the fact was that he absolutely had not died.

'May I?' she asked, shuffling closer. On her feet were two elasticated blue bags, like shower-caps. Narmin drew up a chair for her.

Broom pulled the immodest sheet up to his waist. His left shoulder was black with bruises, the left arm plastered across his chest. She took his right hand fearfully. It felt warm and lively, a familiar outdoor animal. She stared down at it. The skin was tanned, leathery. You could always tell a rock climber by the backs of the hands, the white blotches where repeated scarring had destroyed the pigmentation. 'Darling,' she whispered, 'you've really been in the wars.'

Al's mouth flickered. A dry heat came off him.

She turned to Narmin in triumph. 'He can hear me!'

Narmin smiled steadily. 'May-be.'

Something in her eyes embarrassed Broom, as if she were glass the girl might see straight through and break.

A low moan came from Al's grossly swollen lips. His left eye seemed to be straining to open. The white was bloodshot, leaking a yellowish fluid. She could see a tiny sliver of iris, but the pupil was hidden. Pity filled her. He'd hate it so much, lying there trussed and pierced and helpless. Drips flowing into him, urine trickling visibly out.

All across the surface of his skin there was a delicate fluttering. She watched his mouth intently, willing it to speak.

Only two nights ago they'd talked on the telephone, the echo of his words tangling with hers in the long-distance delay. He'd been jubilant, stuttering with excitement. Her letters to Damascus and Amman had gone astray – lost or stolen or censored – but in Adana he'd found two fat envelopes in the poste restante, and now the rush of actually talking to her. Silences thicker than blood, and then the little yelps of lust and frustration as the final pips went down. 'I love you,' he said. 'I want it to work. Just because I'm a Communist doesn't mean I have to go on being a blockhead!'

There hadn't been time to tell him about the documentary. In Shanghai, a city just opening up to all the blandishments of capitalism, everyone was listening to a new phone-in programme that was famous for its unusually frank treatment of personal issues. One caller confessed that friends had been

163

teasing him about the length of his penis. 'I measured it,' he said glumly. 'Erect, it is two inches. I'd really like to read up on it, but the thing is, well, you see, I'm a Party member.'

An infant wailed violently from a barred cot in a corner. Broom looked for Narmin, but she had vanished into a curtained alcove on the far side of the ward and didn't reappear. She saw with horror that one of the child's arms had been amputated above the elbow.

When the wailing subsided her eyes filled suddenly with tears. Al had been badly mothered, therefore he was suspicious of tenderness. QED. But at least she was here, whether he liked it or not! She stared at the clear, unwounded slope of his forehead, wondering if it would be invasive to kiss him, just to sneak one in.

A few feet from the bed a window had been wedged open, admitting a freezing draught. She pulled the sheet up further, to cover his chest. For a moment his legs thrashed convulsively, as if to fend it off; after they stilled, his left foot went on twitching, regularly, like a signal. She realized that she had no idea how nurses knew when comatose patients were in pain, or why, for that matter, she assumed they even cared, since everywhere she looked people moaned and shifted in their cots, and were left unattended. She'd seen a notice on the door that strictly forbade visitors at any time, but with the arrogance of a colonial she'd simply barged past it. Now it occurred to her that the patients were being left to sink or swim – or maybe even to find their own exit, peacefully or not – without the comforting presence of their loved ones. No wonder there was hostility in the eyes of those who were awake enough to watch her.

She swivelled her chair to block their collective view of Al, made a karmic shield of her shoulders, for it wasn't her fault that she'd had to flout the rules; nor was it any fault of Al's, who suffered as they did and was just as deserving of pity.

Through the window came a smell of asphalt and the sound of televised gunfire. The channel changed to the gargle of a Turkish soap opera. Al stirred. His lips – so parched – formed a little pout, opened a millimetre. She tried to assimilate the meaning of this. Somewhere outside the window a moon shone ignored on the country where he'd lost his bearings; meanwhile, down in the abyss he swam darkly and was all at sea.

The thought of this dream-state made her panicky. What if he was experiencing himself as a series of discrete agonies, random and without reason? In his ears only the incomprehensible ebb and flow of Turkish. If she could at least explain his injuries in plain English, re-member him to himself. That much she could do for him. Put all the parts back together: the two dramatic black eyes, the semicircular stitched cut above his ear, the left shoulder dislocated or broken, the legs, torso, arse and penis all perfectly intact.

She bent over him and spoke clearly into his ear. For the sake of his vanity she didn't mention the size of his head, that terrible livid football. Under the bandages his scalp had been shaved. His quiff was gone, his foppish sideburns. He'll be seriously pissed off at that, she thought. She felt cheered and useful, chattering to him.

It seemed OK, suddenly, to be angry. 'You stupid bastard,' she hissed. 'You knew what Turkish roads

165

were like. So you couldn't just get yourself on the train?' He'd always prided himself on taking it on the chin. He'd expect abuse, he'd expect no less of her, and she didn't want to scare him with too much sympathy.

In her purse, folded like a banknote, was the phone number Ercan had given her. She released his hand and settled it on his chest.

Behind the curtain Narmin sat at a chipped Formica table with two male orderlies, one of whom was smoking. She brought out her Silk Cut with relief. 'You would like one?'

The younger of the two lit up immediately. He was twenty, perhaps, plump-cheeked, with a narrow moustache. He examined the cigarette from all angles, then puffed on it with respect. 'English,' said Broom, with a deprecating smile. 'Not strong.' A glass of tea was poured for her, greenish-black and flecked with mint.

On the wall was a telephone, black and archaic, with letters on the dial. There was a way of translating them into numbers but she'd forgotten what it was. She looked at Narmin and, pointing to the telephone, made dialling movements in the air. 'You will help me?'

Narmin raised her eyebrows when she saw the professor's name. When she'd dialled she thrust the receiver at Broom, as though afraid that it might sting her. Broom heard a woman's voice, fretful, French-accented. 'The professor is at his meal. It is his wife speaking.' In other circumstances she would have apologized. There was a discouraging pause.

'Please wait.'

When the professor answered she sensed that he'd already taken offence.

166

'Yes, of course I am familiar with the case. The oedema is the result of the injury to the brain caused by the impact. One must simply wait for the swelling to subside.' His voice had a right and a duty to his supper; every word squeezed out of him a concession to the importunate foreigner.

She heard her own voice grow feeble. His silences made her stunned and forgetful. Realizing that she had no clear idea what questions she should be asking, she became querulous. 'I need to know, you understand, how soon he will be well enough to travel.'

The professor's reply was guarded. It was impossible to say. It depended upon... There were factors that... She listened, rigid, fingers winding in the telephone cord. Certainly not sooner than two weeks, three.

She turned from the phone. Narmin and Co. were watching with interest, as if waiting to see what she would do next. The weight of their expectations pressed on her. In thrall to action, she smiled severely and asked to use the lavatory.

The sink was stained and scaly. When she looked at herself in the mirror she saw the strange pinpoints of her eyes. Her earrings dangled, incongruous: plain silver dolphins, each with a single turquoise stud. Her mouth, which tasted of mint and tannin, already belonged to another country. Her own bed, her own bad dreams, were so far away that she no longer felt entitled to them. Her mind flickered with images of exile. The young Arab on the Tunis plane who, sighting the lights of the coast, leapt to his feet and danced madly in the aisle; his companion clapping to keep time, singing out: 'Tunisia, O my mother.'

When she emerged from the cubicle the younger orderly stood up to offer her his seat. He had picked up

167

her Zippo lighter and was fingering it admiringly. 'I go ... London. Two years before.' He held up two fingers. Just then a cockroach appeared from under the table, brushed past Broom's sterile footgear, and advanced unhurriedly across the linoleum floor. She looked away quickly. Perhaps the others hadn't seen it. Or perhaps they had, and were pretending not to. 'Carnabee Street,' said the orderly. 'Bucking-ham Palace.' Broom smoked and nodded, trying to understand the Mall and Piccadilly and what tourists saw in her city, did in it. Their aimlessness on winter days, their little day-sacks, their maps consulted anxiously on gusty street corners, their outsize umbrellas bearing the logos of hotels.

The cockroach arrived unmolested at the lavatory door, where it passed out of sight. Narmin mimed a pillow with her hands and laid her head on it. 'You sleep?'

'Yes,' said Broom, realizing that she had forgotten the name of the hotel. 'You will take good care of Mr Alan?'

'Oh, yes,' said Narmin. Her smile was young and dazzling. Broom smiled back to seal the bargain. She shook hands all round, forcefully. 'I come again. In the morning.'

Down on the deserted boulevard a damp curling breath of rain hung over the street lamps. The heating in the room was punitive, the carpeting an unfriendly synthetic that clung to the soles of her shoes. There was a desk with a telephone, a coffee table in the same light veneer, and two voluminous chairs in mock leather. A huge faux-goatskin rug lay across the double bed.

168

The note pad beside the telephone showed cartoon characters enjoying the various facilities in the hotel. A couple with shovel-shaped smiles clinked champagne glasses over a pock-marked chicken; a man reclined in a barber's chair, the buttress of his nose protruding from a snowdrift of shaving-foam. At the top of the page a finger pointed straight at the reader. SIZI NEREVE BULABLIRIZ? (Where are you?) Below, a list of convenient boxes waited to be ticked.

I am at:

Lobi ☐
Night-clup ☐
Swim-pool ☐
Berber ☐
Casino ☐
Outside ☐

I will come back at: ...... hours

She called Al's mother, whose voice betrayed nothing. She had met Jennifer only once, at a weekend gathering at his sister's house in Dorset, and remembered a small combative woman with bright black optimistic eyes. Al's father was tall and mild with a depressive's wistful smile. He spoke seldom and haltingly; it was easy enough to see which one of them ruled the roost. Jennifer, clearly, had the social savvy; she also had a portfolio of fairly ball-breaking opinions. Broom had the impression that she saw emotions as suspect things, best kept out of the picture, for which, at this exact moment, she was grateful.

Jennifer's voice was cool and respectful. She asked few questions. 'I see,' she said, 'I see.' Just before she rang off Broom thought she heard her say, 'We don't know how to thank you,' or, more probably, 'We don't know how to think of you.'

She stared at the notepad, fascinated by the sheer silliness of the faces. Automatically she noted the repertoire of marks: the crude cross-hatching of the shadow between the croupier's breasts, the stippling that signified the tweed of a man's jacket, the swift wiry curlicues to represent a woman's hair.

She checked for a minibar and, finding none, put a call through to Ken McBurney. His voice was slurred with drink and what she sensed was shame. 'Now, you're sure you're all right, honey?' he kept saying. 'You're sure you don't need me to come out?' He had booked Sam, Al's eldest, onto the morning plane. 'I'm putting the bugger on it myself,' he blustered, 'or else he'll never make it!'

She gave him the telephone number of the hotel and waited. Within half an hour the calls began to come in. The switchboard operator announced each one by city. London, Manchester, Birmingham. 'You have a call from...' 'I am putting you through to...' There was a clarity to the sequence that promised to keep her intact. She told a dozen people what had happened, repeating the bare facts again and again in a voice that denied their right to sympathize. She was glad that they did not ask for more. In the lull between each call her words floated above her head, capricious in their cartoon bubbles.

When Heather rang, Broom could hear her listening hard, like a professional. 'But are you remembering to look after yourself?' she asked at last. Broom was irritated. The question seemed quite cosmically irrelevant; she resented, too, the implication that she

170

was turning herself into a martyr. When it comes to a real catastrophe, she thought, trust a therapist to get the wrong end of the stick.

'Take care,' said Heather, 'and remember, call me any time.'

Afterwards Broom took off her shoes and stared at the small hole in the toe of her sock, knowing that she should breathe, drink something, go to the window to check on the moon. She lay down on the opulent goatskin and saw herself on the plane back from Majorca, her head buried in Al's lap after a terrifying take-off into crosswinds. Above her head he went on reading the Guardian, *half-glasses perched on his nose, his hand flat and quiet on the triangular section of back between her shoulderblades. It had been their first proper holiday, a winter climbing trip with Keith and Barbara. The image that now detached itself – Al goosepimpled on Christmas morning, in leopard-print Y-fronts, poised in mid-air above the glacial water of the villa swimming-pool – was so vivid that she turned towards him in her mind, as if he were on the bed right next to her, as if to say, 'Do you remember these terrible underpants?'*

Footsteps passed in the corridor outside, rattling the door in its frame. A woman laughed shrilly. Broom imagined the puffed-up height of her hairdo, the brush of her fur coat against the walls. A man's voice said, in heavily accented English, 'No, tell him. Tell him where I made love to you last time.'

She got up and went to the bathroom and flicked the switch. The light that flooded out jarred her fingers and flickered up her arm. Her eyes absorbed the grainy gleam of marble: black tiles on the floor, greyish-green on the wall above the bathtub. She leapt back, afraid of the message her mind was sending.

The force of her anger propelled her to the telephone. 'The switches in Room 511 are live. They have given me an electric shock. Please send someone immediately.'

The electrician wore a maroon boiler suit that matched the receptionist's jacket. It was the same receptionist she had met earlier, the soft-eyed one who had been kind to her. She noticed that he had shaved. The two men stood awkwardly in the doorway. She stood aside to let them in.

'It gives a shock.' She reached out as if to touch the light switch and at the last moment leapt back, grimacing.

The electrician tapped the switch with a small screwdriver. She folded her arms and waited. Shrugging, he tested the switch with his finger, and spoke over his shoulder to the receptionist.

'He says there is nothing.'

'There is a fault,' she insisted.

The electrician gave her a look which implied that the only loose wires were in her head; if there was a fault it was not his, but hers. He switched the light on and off and indicated that she should do the same. She shut her eyes and stabbed at the switch, although it was going to take more than that to convince her. The two men were watching her expectantly.

'Nothing,' she conceded. They seemed to be waiting for something else – a tip, perhaps, or an apology. She looked at the floor and saw, through the hole in her sock, the intimate red peep of her toenail. By her reckoning she hadn't slept for forty-eight hours and there was no way she was going to say she was sorry.

When they'd gone she double-locked the door and went to stand by the window. The mist had cleared a

172

little and the moon was out. By crushing her right cheek against the glass and peering sideways she could see, framed in a rectangular gap between the office buildings at the end of the boulevard, a rim of distant mountains. A major range, ten thousand feet or more, by the look of them. She wondered what they could be. The Atlas? No, of course not. The Atlas were in Morocco. They had to be the Taurus.

A caged headache throbbed behind her eyes. Her watch said 3.30. The glass was cold and foreign against her skin. She remembered that Atlas was the Titan who'd defied Zeus; he'd been condemned to hold up the sky for all eternity.

She stood before the breakfast buffet, irresolutely studying cereals. She had slept for four hours and in her dream Al had woken up. He was completely conscious, coherent, cracking jokes with the nurses. Broom, however, he treated with indifference: his eyes passed over her and his big grin flashed for absolutely anyone else. When she demanded his attention he became sulky and withdrawn; when she tried to entice him with sex he pulled the covers over his head and said, 'I'm thinking of convalescing in East Bengal.'

Convinced that the dream was a sign, she rushed down to Reception and asked the young desk clerk to telephone the hospital. She saw her smile flare in the mirrored wall behind him, her eyes terrible and brilliant, like a drunkard's.

When the clerk put down the receiver he laid his fingertips lightly on the polished surface of the desk, like a pianist preparing to play. His thumbs flickered apologetically up and out. 'Stable, but no, not yet conscious.'

173

She chose sweet buns from the buffet, ham, a cold hard-boiled egg, and, having settled herself at a table by the window, ate conscientiously, as if in rebuttal of Heather. The point being that the stodgy food would make her strong.

The breakfast room was full of businessmen; she counted three married couples, no other women on their own. Agitation rose in her. At least half of the dream had made her feel a failure, and now she felt like a spare part, spare as the time she couldn't spend with Al, every moment of which ought surely to be working for its living. The red-haired waiter who had refilled her coffee cup was watching her inquisitively. She called him over. 'Excuse me, will you tell me the Turkish for...'

Koça, çoçyk, hanim. *Husband, son, wife.* She opened her notebook and spread the pages flat. It was a Muslim country. Al would just have to forgive her for lying.

The receptionist, who told her that his name was Akil, seemed to be surprised that she had asked. 'Monsieur Engin is waiting,' he announced, emerging from behind the desk and leading her importantly across the foyer.

The Honorary Consul rose from the folds of a deep sofa, his right hand outstretched, a fawn raincoat draped neatly over his left arm. A gold pen glinted in the breast pocket of his navy-blue blazer.

'I am sorry about last evening – a business matter, I'm afraid. My driver was satisfactory? And the hotel? Shall we take coffee?' Monsieur Engin snapped his fingers and a waiter flew across the room towards them. Once the order was given, Broom had the

174

impression that the waiter was literally backing away, as if after an audience with royalty. The Consul, it was clear, was a man who took his station seriously.

When she sat down the Consul followed suit, with a gesture she hadn't seen in twenty years: the swift and delicate pinch that lifts the knees of the trousers to preserve the crease. 'I have arranged that we will go to the hospital at ten fifteen.'

'Thank you,' she said. 'I have gone there last night already.' The perfect tense rang quaintly in her ears. 'Went' seemed too crude, somehow, too colloquial; 'have gone' promised to reposition her in the neutral space of diplomacy, where the word 'accident' might yield more easily to 'incident'.

A faint frown hovered on the Consul's face. 'You were permitted to see Mr Hargreave?'

'I have seen him, yes.' She remembered the forbidding sign on the ward door. Surely he wasn't going to make an issue of it? Her mind filled with all the practicalities such a paragon could solve for her. She brought out her list. The hotel was too expensive; she would appreciate it if he could help her to find a cheaper one. There was the question of banks, and foreign money-orders, and Sam, who would arrive, God willing, in the afternoon... She seemed to be talking and talking. Monsieur Engin nodded forbearingly, making notes. She said finally, 'You see, I have no idea how long Mr Hargreave will be here.'

'Ah yes. That we will ask the doctors this morning.' He replaced his cup in its saucer and set it on the table. 'I am afraid there are also some formalities. I have been yesterday to the Military Police at Tarsus, where the accident happened – about twenty kilometres from here, a terrible road, terrible...' Tutting

175

energetically, he reached into his briefcase and produced a passport and a wallet of traveller's cheques.

The cover of the passport was dark Euro red, the same shade as the bellboy's pillbox hat and the satin stripe down the outside of his trousers. She was struck by the improbability of the colours that had been brought together by the situation: the acidulous blue of the American Express wallet, the sienna-yellow coat of the stray dog which limped briefly in through the revolving door, its claws clacking as they skidded on the marble floor, the particular depth of violet in the shadows under the hotel portico. She took the passport and held it between the tips of her fingers. Monsieur Engin hadn't realized that she wasn't Al's legal representative. She'd have to hand it over to Sam.

'The contents of the bicycle panniers will be released by the police when they have completed their investigation. The driver is still being questioned. There is, however, no doubt that he is entirely to blame.' *The Consul paused to clear his throat. His eyes, sorrowful, appealed to her.* 'The bicycle, I fear, is not salvageable...'

Broom stared at him in alarm. 'No, no, throw it away, by all means.'

'If I may ask ... did Mr Hargreave have insurance?'

There was a drizzle of ash on her black trousers. She brushed it off impatiently. 'Yes, of course.'

'I have searched, but have found no such document in his effects.'

It struck her that she didn't know for sure. 'Well, he would have had, wouldn't he, for such a long trip'

The trouble was that the elements simply didn't add

up. The businessman-diplomat with his bureaucratic details, the militant with shaved-off sideburns, comatose in his hospital bed. The 'wife' dressed too casually, jeaned and booted, her hair unstyled to the point of impertinence. She should have taken more care; in a foreign country you had to observe the proprieties, pay attention to detail. Your behaviour had to be above criticism. For a moment she was convinced that this was what the whole outcome depended upon. She said reluctantly, 'I will ring his colleague in London. There must be a copy of the policy.'

The passport and traveller's cheques lay on the coffee table, waiting to be claimed; she had only to reach out her hand to take formal possession. Outside the window, above the roof of the apartment block on the other side of the road, was a wedge of cold blue sky. On the street, traffic jousted at the intersection. A boy with a box of tomatoes on his handlebars wove in and out of the trucks, his torso angled back in the saddle, arms swinging loose, knees pumping. Look, Mummy, no hands. Traffic lights turned orange and red and were ignored by all and sundry. Pedestrians were hurling themselves into the road with what appeared to be a total disregard for life and limb. She scowled at their stupidity, a dull rage rising inside her. Perhaps they were offering up their trusting souls to Allah. 'Your traffic's certainly anarchic!' she said accusingly. It was as close to an insult as she could come.

'This is very true!' All at once Monsieur Engin became animated. His eyes sparked with anger. 'Let me tell you, last weekend our Minister of Transport opened a new stretch of motorway near Ankara, and

177

yesterday he was killed on this very same road!' With a wave of his white hand he dismissed his errant countrymen. 'It is madness, of course,' he said fastidiously, 'utter madness. But now, if you are ready, I will drive you to the hospital.'

Al lay quite still in the meagre dry-dock of the bed. Broom wondered what she'd expected – that the sleep would slip from his head like water and he'd emerge like a cheerful buffalo, spouting and snorting? The bruises round his eyes seemed fainter. There was a growth of salt-and-pepper stubble on his chin. When she bent over to kiss his cheek his lips parted; she heard the tiny geriatric click of tongue on teeth. His breath smelled vinegary, of stale vomit; only his skin retained the gladdening smell of health.

She caught a whiff of carbolic which reminded her of his ablutions. The vehement all-over lathering, the punitive scrub with the nail-brush that turned his skin bright scarlet – such a ferocious, gratuitous expenditure of energy. Shaving, too – that was another performance. After he'd finished he'd refill the basin with cold water, cup his hands together and hurl the water at his face. Invariably he managed to flood the bathroom floor. One day she'd sketched him in action – the bunched-up biceps, the eyes squeezed shut, the lips pursed up against a fusillade of droplets. For his Christmas present she'd had the drawing blown up and printed on a T-shirt, under the logo 'Macho Face-washing'. She wondered if the police had discovered it in the bicycle panniers, and at this very moment were holding it up, dwarfed by the big baggy garment, frowning, failing to get the joke.

Nurse Narmin came to join her at the bed.

178

'How is Mr Alan today?' Broom tried to keep the urgency from her voice.

Narmin's smile was dazzling and doll-like. 'Oh ... OK!' Broom smiled back doubtfully. She was pleased that Narmin was so happy for him. 'He is very ... quiet?'

Behind her the Consul cleared his throat. 'Mrs Broom.' He ignored the little nurse, who hung her head and slipped away.

Broom turned and met the incurious eyes of the doctor. She had expected to see the professor, but this man was thirtyish, with long layered hair that slithered over his collar, and he spoke no English. Taking her cue from the Consul, she shook hands with frigid politeness. She looked at Monsieur Engin. 'Please ask, when does he expect Mr Hargreave to regain consciousness, and how soon will he be fit to travel.'

The Consul rendered this in a respectful whisper. In the time lapse between utterance and response Broom stared at her silly shrouded feet. The correct placement of things seemed so important. She had a vision of Prince Philip with his hands clasped awkwardly behind his back, the Queen with her handbag arm riveted across her chest. She wondered why no one had asked the Consul to wear the shower-caps on his shoes.

'He says perhaps the day after tomorrow, perhaps the weekend. It is difficult to predict. But he would not wish Mr Hargreave to travel before ... one week or ten days at the earliest.'

Broom nodded. The day dragged at her eyelids, full of the potential for awful surprises. The doctor watched her, volunteering nothing. She fixed her eyes *on the chart that hung at the end of the bed. 'Please ask, what treatment Mr Hargreave is receiving for the head injury.'*

The doctor unhooked the chart and tapped it with his pencil.

'Two types of drugs to disperse the oedema,' the Consul translated. 'Antibiotics – five types – to fight infection.'

A blankness settled on her brain. The three of them stood silently, surveying the figure on the bed. For a moment she saw it dispassionately: the foreshortening of the sheet-shrouded feet, and beyond that the tapering vista of the chest, and beyond that the head, bandaged and immobile, heroic as a study by Ingres.

Monsieur Engin, whose manner throughout had implied that the doctor was a busy man who should not be importuned, now transferred his raincoat from his right arm to his left, ready to shake the doctor's hand, usher her punctiliously out. For a moment the thought of his protection filled her with such lassitude that she was sure he knew exactly what it cost her every time she had to leave the bed.

'One minute.' She smiled at them and dodged away and kissed Al's forehead, avoiding tubes. 'I'm going, darling,' she said, her voice pitched on a register the whole world could hear if it wanted, 'but I'll be back later, when I've picked Sam up from the airport.'

Broom settled back into the accommodating leather seat of the Mercedes; she had stopped trying to read the road signs, to chart her progress. For a mile or two the highway was smooth and blue. Dry earth banks rose up on either side; here and there she saw plantations of tamarisk saplings, whitened by a limey

180

dust. A great white bolster of mountains lay along the north horizon.

'The mountains are so near!' she exclaimed. 'There is skiing?'

The Consul nodded. 'Some, yes. Mainly local as yet, but, with investment, who knows?'

Sun struck the windscreen as they turned south. Monsieur Engin adjusted the air-conditioning. 'I have thought that you may wish to see ... the location,' he said delicately.

She was surprised that he would think of this. He didn't seem the sort of man who'd willingly take the risk of appearing tactless. 'As a matter of fact, I would.'

'When Mr Hargreave's son arrives, perhaps you will permit me to drive you? The coast at Mersin is most attractive. You are an artist, I believe? There are some very fine examples of ancient Anatolian ceramic work in the museum.'

'Thank you. I would like that very much.' His calm seeped into her. Subtly he was suggesting that the situation was not, after all, so very grave, even that her own reactions had been, perhaps, excessive. It was soothing to see him as the arbiter of normality, and to imagine that once the initial shock had worn off she might be able to look at things a little differently, might even consider taking a day or two to be a tourist. 'Mr Hargreave was on his way to visit the high-school teacher there,' she volunteered.

'Ah yes?' said the Consul.

It occurred to her that she didn't have the teacher's address. It was on the tip of her tongue to ask Monsieur Engin for help. Then she remembered that the man was a Party member, and that the Turkish

181

Communist Party was illegal.

They passed a cement works. The car moved suavely on oiled wheels, placing itself at her disposal, just like the Consul, who hoped hospitably that she would not leave his country without first sampling at least a few of its many pleasures.

It was day now, and although the city was still ugly it was stroked by feathers of light. There were lemon groves, rows of pruned vines. The sight of a donkey tethered to an orange tree filled her with a wild gratitude. 'The motorist who stopped to help,' she said: 'can he be contacted? I'd really like to thank him personally.'

At Reception there was a message asking her to call Al's brother. It was an Oxford number; Philip's research project was based at the Radcliffe.

'You're doing a first-class job,' he said. 'We're all behind you one hundred per cent.' The unaccustomed emotion made his voice husky. For a moment she couldn't speak. Her mind swooned off wanting to pour out everything, to swear that she would stay in Turkey for as long as it took, that the people were so kind and the mountains were so beautiful and the Consul was, well, an absolute godsend.

She opened her notebook and read off the names of the drugs.

'Fairly standard,' said Philip. 'What about oxygen? Is he on a ventilator at all?'

'Oh no,' she said enthusiastically. 'He's breathing really well on his own.'

'Listen. Have you got a pen? There are some things we need to know. First, has he had a CAT scan? Yes, C–A–T. Second, has he ever, at any point, been on a ventilator?'

182

His curtness startled her, the expertise buffeting her like a reproof She crossed out the cheery face beside the 'Night-club' box. With one continuous line of her pen she drew a cat, curled up, comforting. She wrote CAT, VENTILATOR. 'I can ask this evening,' she said.

'Also, do you have any idea what insurance he had? It could make all the difference.'

'We can't find the policy. At least we haven't, yet.' She had an idea that the Consul had said the police wouldn't release the panniers until the investigation was complete, but her mind refused to focus on the whys and wherefores. She said unwillingly, 'I've asked Ken McBurney to check his files. I can't believe Al didn't leave a copy.'

Two sleepless nights had furred her brain. Whenever she closed her eyes she saw illuminated digits: alarm clocks, flight numbers, last calls for boarding. With each question her confidence sank lower. Philip was probing her about standards of nursing care: did she think they were adequate?

'It's not the NHS, of course,' she conceded. She thought of little Narmin and her kindly smile. Only when she put the phone down did it occur to her that she'd forgotten to mention the cockroach.

A new stretch of motorway, built for speeding. She imagined the asphalt, the unmade verge. Location Tarsus. The name resonated. She went to the window and knelt by the low sill, a light and bounding excitement starting up her spine. Somewhere out there a perfect stranger had dragged Al bodily into his car and driven him to Casualty. For a moment she was transfigured, aglow, the winter sun piercing her. The

183

coincidence was simply too bizarre. It was on the road to Tarsus, surely, that the Good Samaritan had stopped, and hadn't passed by on the other side...

When she reached up to open the window the metal lock kicked her back. Her fingers came away trembling. She stared at them stupidly, hearing the electric click of her bones. Too much static. The room redefined itself as an adversary, its metal fitments gleaming at her, like a mouthful of fillings. She shouted at it, fucked and blinded, but it wouldn't take the blame.

The smell of frying bacon stalked the corridors of the ground floor, mounted the stairs of the east wing, and stole under the door of the Blue Room. Lockhart rolled onto his back and opened his eyes on darkness. Evidently it was morning, although nothing in his body concurred with this hypothesis. His head was thick and indignant, his flesh slow and substantial as the winter night.

In summer, night here was more of an idea than a fact, a two-hour parenthesis in the elongated days. Around midnight the sun slid reluctantly below the horizon and lolled in the shallows of the southern sky until, at 2 a.m., it sprang up again, glowing lugubriously, so that sleep was restless, and dreams scarce and slippery. In winter, however, the sun at its midday height hardly cleared the tops of the hawthorn bushes, and shortly after lunchtime dusk closed in and lights came on in all the houses. Daylight

184

saving, in fact, was a complete misnomer, because nothing at all was gained. Dusk at three or dawn at ten, that was the choice. The dark was like bookends at either side of the day and all you could do was shift them.

Lockhart thrust himself out of bed and, yawning, drew back the heavy blue velvet curtains. Outside, the eastern sky was softening to an opaque pigeon grey. It was 9 a.m. His father would have been up since five for the milking, unless Fraser had turned over a new leaf and was knuckling down to his responsibilities. Lockhart's City friends lamented their City hours, but let them try mixing cattle-cake at dawn, mucking out and re-strawing the byre, rolling freezing churns across the yard to the dairy. In school holidays he and his father had taken turns. It had been a point of pride to Lockhart that no matter what kind of night he'd had – pubbing illicitly in Morrisdale or snogging some local girl in the old boatshed by the bay – he wouldn't miss his date with dawn. Unlike Fraser – who could be bribed, in hungover extremities, to take his place – he'd put up no resistance to the strict regime of farming; nor had his mother showed any inclination to protect him from it. Unlike Fraser he was not considered delicate, and therefore meant for higher things...

In any case, the truth was that bringing the cows in was one chore he'd always liked. Stumbling out with an old coat pulled over his pyjamas and his bare feet thrust into wellingtons, to meet the queue of beasts – who told the time less by the rising or setting of the sun than by the

185

imperative of their straining udders – already forming at the field gate. Their dark eyes fixed on him with such gratitude that sometimes he wondered if some sensor deep in their brains associated his appearance with the promise of a calf to suckle and ease them, when in fact all that was on offer was a cold byre-stall and a rank of stainless-steel milking machines. The cruelty of this was something he considered only insofar as it imposed an even greater duty of care, which went, he supposed, by the name of husbandry. He thought of their patient eagerness, the warm barrels of their bellies suspended from the ridgepole of backbone and the cross-trees of shoulderblades, the feel of the coarse hair of their hides under his hand as he moved them along. Not that they needed herding as such. Once through the gate they took themselves along the track in single file, and always in the same order, like well-drilled schoolchildren.

Lockhart sat on the edge of the bed, feeling guilty and becalmed. The word 'holiday' was on his mind and he knew that nothing would be asked of him but as always he would offer. Nothing, that is, except the hardest thing. When he thought of what he'd agreed to do he felt like a complete pillock, the sneakiest of prep-school sneaks.

Last night Fraser had asked him to come to the pub, but he'd excused himself on the basis of tiredness, the journey, etc. Instead he'd fallen asleep in front of the nine-o'clock news and wakened at eleven before a dead fire and a Gaelic quiz show, feeling sullen and lonely and compromised. He hadn't heard Fraser come back, but he'd been conscious at various points of a background busyness: a chink of light under the bathroom door, the global beep of computer traffic.

A haze of frying-fat hung in the few sunrays that had cleared the low ridge of the gun-house roof and penetrated the kitchen window. John Lockhart looked up from his *Telegraph*. 'Aye, Archie. Slept well? Your breakfast's here.' He pushed back his chair and stretched an arm towards. the range.

'No, no. I'll get it.' The plate was covered by an aluminium lid. Underneath Lockhart found bacon, egg, sausages, potato scone, black pudding, sweetbreads, and tomatoes. He set the plate down on the oilcloth and looked at it with a mixture of nostalgia and regret.

His father quirked an eyebrow. 'Quite a plateful. Not on a diet, I hope? You know Retta.'

'Maybe I should tell her I've got an ulcer.'

'Have you?' His father's voice was sharp.

'No, no,' Lockhart said hastily. 'A bit of heartburn now and again, that's all.'

'Well, then. When you get to my age you'll have time to worry.' His father's eyes returned to the newspaper. He frowned at an item but did not comment on it. His spoon clanked against his bowl: he still took his porridge, Lockhart noted, with a tablespoon of Golden Syrup.

In the silence, Lockhart ate. Silences like this were what had driven him away from Callasay in the first place, to the city's constant background noise, to the talk and the trains and the television, and the mobile phones that never seemed to stop. It wasn't even a question of judging the moment when the silence stopped being companionable, for he couldn't remember a time when it had been. The truth was that his father wasn't a companionable man. He tried to imagine Fraser sitting down to dinner every night with him, washed and changed and trying to adhere to the conversational codes of the dining room. The kitchen, being a staging post on the journey from one job of work to another, had no such codes. Without Retta – who had presumably gone to the shops – an anarchy of silence reigned. He glanced at the old servant-bells which still hung on their wooden board above the cellar door, each one numbered according to a system no one could remember. As boys, he and Fraser had tried the bell-pulls in all the rooms, but most of the mechanisms were rusted. With the exception of the one in the dining room, they had never managed to make them tally.

On the shelves of the kitchen cabinet, glass jars which had once contained Shitake mushrooms, ginger-root, and the bitter twiggy Oolong tea his mother swore by, now held white flour and sugar and pale grey wrinkled peas – foodstuffs so basic that for a moment Frances Lockhart stepped out of the silence of the past and stood with her hands on her hips and her pencilled eyebrows arched in condemnation.

Under the sink stood a cat's dish, licked clean. In the gap between the sink and the cabinet Lockhart spotted an old-fashioned steel-sprung mousetrap, which appeared to be baited.

He had started on the sweetbreads when Fraser came in from the scullery, rolling down his sleeves. Automatically Lockhart's eyes were drawn to the unfreckled inner arms, the paleness in the crook of the elbows. There were no track marks. The boy was clean as a whistle.

'Hey, if it isn't the Sleeping Beauty!' Fraser's smile flared at him. His teeth were white and very narrow, like the petals of a daisy. He spooned Nescafé into a mug and flicked the switch on the kettle. 'If you fancy a look at the new icehouse, I'm just off down the plant.'

Lockhart glanced at his father, who hadn't yet acknowledged Fraser's presence. Nothing seemed more desirable at that moment than to be out under the wide sky with its small mutualities of wind and gull, to race boyishly along the shore and frisk with his brother in the bracing air. 'Love to,' he said. 'Maybe later, OK? It's just that Dad's asked me to do a bit of an audit.'

Fraser shrugged. 'Sure.' He shoved his hands into his pockets and leaned against the counter. There was a pause in which coins clinked in the depths of his pockets. Behind him the kettle noise surged and stopped. 'No problem.'

John Lockhart folded his paper and slapped it down on the oilcloth. 'No good having an expert up, eh, if you don't get the exploiting of him!' His voice was jovial, but the manner of his frown had changed, as if he was beginning to measure its effect.

'No, indeed,' said Fraser, with instant heavy sarcasm.

'If you're saying we couldn't do with your

189

brother's help...' There was no sagging of the shoulders now, no escaping the vigour of the threat.

Lockhart got up hastily and tipped his leavings into the swing-bin. He could gauge his tension by the sour hole the grease had begun to burn in his stomach. Instinctively he stood beside his brother, who had rolled up a slice of pan bread and, without buttering it, was shoving it into his mouth. 'It's all right, Father, he didn't mean anything.'

Exhaling audibly, John Lockhart stood up to put his porridge plate in the sink. 'All right, is it?' he said as he pushed past. 'Would that it were, Archie.'

Lockhart took the full chill of his stare, which contained not only a reminder of their conspiracy but also a flash of fear, which shocked him. Fear of what, though? Of alliances that might be forged against him?

His father shrugged on his body-warmer and took a heavy step towards the door. Then he turned back. With his face suddenly ablaze, he grabbed the marmalade jar from the table and smacked it down in front of Fraser. 'For God's sake, man, act your age!' With that he was gone, slamming the scullery door behind him.

They stood for a moment in silence, listening to the crunch of his feet across the gravel yard. Fraser looked as shocked as Lockhart felt. 'Go on. Ask me. Is it always like this.'

Lockhart shook his head. 'Shit, Fraser.'

'I'm telling you, he's really losing it.'

'You wind him up,' Lockhart said flatly.

190

'You try living with him, Lucky.'

Lockhart hesitated, wanting to come clean, wondering also what on earth had persuaded Fraser that he could ever make a go of it at Gillinish.

Fraser was studying him, amusement twitching at the corners of his mouth. 'By the way,' he whispered, 'why are we whispering?'

Back in London, Lockhart would have seen the funny side, but London was a million light-years away and no wish on earth would bring it closer. 'Don't fucking ask me!'

Fraser rested his coffee cup on the crown of his head and narrowed his eyes, like someone who stands back from his painting to get a better look. Lockhart saw them suddenly, Broom and Fraser, across the strip-lit space of the college studio. He'd arranged to meet them for a drink but had arrived, as usual, too early. He'd paced, fretting, in the corridor outside, until the model emerged, wrapping his Chinese dressing-gown around him, followed shortly afterwards by the students. He'd peeked through the panes of the door and glimpsed them, standing close together in the empty room, staring intently at an easel whose back was turned to him. The intimacy hit him like a blow. Broom's hands were in the pockets of her jeans, her shoulders slumped. He had always envied her capacity to submerge herself completely in the matter at hand, but now, seeing Fraser beside her, seeing the still seriousness of him, the self-forgetfulness of his pose, he felt an ulcerous jealousy, his mind colliding with the knowledge that before too long he was going to

191

have to make a choice, and that Fraser, being well aware of this – sensing, probably, that when the chips were down he would choose Agneta – was moving into position, getting ready to stake his claim.

Fraser glanced at him, his cheeks ballooned out in a mammoth sigh. 'Aye, we're all fallen creatures, are we not?' he said inscrutably. He balled his fist and landed a featherweight biff on Lockhart's arm. 'See you down the shore, then, eh?'

'Right you are,' said Lockhart.

Outside Arrivals, Broom lost her temper with the guard. 'Çoçyk!' she yelled. 'If you do not let me through he will not see me!'

The guard spat out his cigarette and cleared the pavement in reprisal.

She stood on tiptoe in the road, craning for a glimpse of Sam's blond ponytail. When the hall had almost emptied she saw him, his head towering over the Customs man, his kitbag unzipped and held wide open for inspection. And Dexter, suddenly, was behind him, even taller than his older brother, his handsome face set in the coldly mocking expression young men use to conceal their hurt. It was Dexter who saw her first and signalled her presence to Sam.

'Dex came too!' Sam boomed, shouldering through the crowd towards her. His breath went ahead of him, fierce with alcohol. 'We missed the connection. What a fucking fiasco!'

She kissed him quickly, rallying a smile. Sam, who was naturally demonstrative, managed to hug her back. She looked uncertainly at Dexter.

'How's Dad? Is he still unconscious?' His voice was muted, almost an undertone.

Around them the night air was full of shouts and laughter. A football team had returned garlanded and triumphant; children who'd been kept up too late were hoisted onto their fathers' shoulders, their faces full of bewildered expectancy.

'The doctor says it could be a few more days.'

Sam's features drooped with tiredness. She hoped he wouldn't cry, or at least not here. Dexter produced cigarettes, which he and Sam lit simultaneously, with separate lighters. She spotted a taxi with its door open, and shepherded them towards it. 'Look, he's fairly banged up, so don't be too freaked out. I mean, he's not a very pretty sight...'

As she detailed Al's injuries the smoke of their cigarettes filled the car. Sam was listening with frantic attention, his body swivelled round in the passenger seat. Beside her in the back Dexter stared out of the window, his arm elaborately casual on the ledge, his whole body exuding refusal. She fought an urge to tell him that it was not her fault. There was no way, she realized, that she could possibly prepare them.

When they entered the hotel lobby, Dexter stopped dead and dropped his holdall on the marble floor. 'We can't fucking afford this!'

Broom felt like saying that she hadn't exactly had a choice. 'Philip's wiring a thousand,' she retorted. 'If you just stash your bags we can get straight off to the hospital.'

'Sons?' Akil asked pleasantly, sliding registration

193

forms across the desk.

Broom nodded. 'Çoçyk.' Not mine, she thought grimly. Sam had his passport clamped between his teeth. Dexter scribbled his details at top speed, slammed the form on the desk and stared around with studied indifference. For a moment she saw them through Akil's eyes: Sam shambling, disreputable, in layered sweatshirts and fleeces, Dexter sleek and debonair and furious. Chalk and cheese. No one would ever have suspected that they were brothers. Dexter had been brought up by his mother after she and Al had split, while Sam and his sister Didi had lived mainly with their father. Didi was big-boned and gap-toothed like Sam, but her hair was Irish-dark and her skin had a pearly sheen.

Last spring she and Al had gone to dinner at Didi's council flat in Feltham. It was an awkward first encounter. Evidently Dexter had let slip that Al had loaned Sam money for a van; Didi, therefore, demanded a washing machine. 'You owe me, Dad,' Didi said menacingly.

In the summer she'd met the whole clan at Al's sister's house in Dorset: his parents, Vicky and her husband, Philip and his wife Cressida, who was a child psychologist, their assorted teenage children. Four generations of Hargreaves. She and Al had driven down in the old Fiesta with Didi's daughter Nina, and Louie, Sam's son, who had been staying with him while their parents took a break.

For a week Al had had his hands full, and although he hadn't asked for help he didn't refuse when she offered.

Nina and Louie adored their grandad. They squirmed against his legs and stared up at him with

194

shining eyes. Broom cooked scrambled egg on toast and watched from the kitchen window while they played ball in Al's cramped back garden.

Al was trying to teach Nina to throw.

'Come on, darling, show that old Louie what you can do!' Louie, a stocky, competent boy, scowled from the shadow of the hydrangea bushes. He had no patience with the idea of taking turns. Nina flapped her arm and ducked away. The ball sighed up above her head, faded, and plopped between her feet. Al picked it up and knelt on the grass beside her. Taking her hands, he brought her wrists together and cupped her fingers.

Ignored, Louie clouted the ground with his cricket bat. 'To me, Grandad! Throw to me!' Nina's eyes were on her cousin. Her face was crimped and white. Watching, Broom remembered the moment when her father's hand no longer held the bicycle saddle and she was singular in flight and shrieking, for there was nothing to separate her father's triumph from her own. The ball, floated from three feet away, slithered through Nina's fingers. Al's smile grew fixed. 'Just keep your eye on it, darling,' he urged. Broom watched her fail three times, four, before she knocked on the window and called them in for tea.

'You only value the things she fails at,' she said, when the stories were read and the children slept neat and sweet as hazelnuts on their mattress beside Al's bed. 'You ignore what she succeeds at. To her the choice is clear. Either she throws a ball straight, or she keeps her relationship with Louie.'

'You're kidding,' Al said.

She shook her head. 'Think about it. She loves her cousin. You saw the fuss he kicked up when she had

195

the ball. Give the girl credit for some intelligence.'

Al looked at her respectfully. Clear reason, she knew, could always stop him in his tracks. She could almost hear his brain ticking as it tested the new concept for truth. He sat on the edge of the bed with his trainers in his hand. His smile was shy. 'It suits you, you know. The Grandma bit. I'm surprised.'

Broom was delighted. 'Grandma by proxy,' she said, laughing. She felt like a potentate propped up on the pillows, bare-breasted, influential. 'To be honest, so am I!'

As soon as they arrived at Vicky's, Sam and Didi announced that Nina and Louie were to go on sleeping with their grandad. 'A week free of childcare,' said Didi: 'that's what we negotiated, right? Well, the week's not over till Sunday.'

'Fair enough,' said Al, with a sheepish glance at Broom. Stealthy sex had a certain retro charm, but it wasn't exactly their favourite.

Sam grinned at his father. 'We learned our bargaining skills in a hard academy. You didn't really think we'd let you off the hook?'

After dinner, when everyone else had gone to bed, Broom sat on in the dining room with Al and the three siblings. It was the first time she'd seen them in action. All three were twenty-somethings, but in their father's presence they behaved like piglets jostling at the teat. They competed shamelessly, outdoing one another in a recitation of ancient deprivations. On some issues, however, they formed tactical alliances. There were grievances that had to be redressed, things they insisted that climbing and the Party had stolen from them: ordinary things, like holidays abroad and family Christmases. Things that should have been, *still ought to be, their right...*

Broom was embarrassed. Listening, she thanked her lucky stars for Sean. He was of an age with them and his life hadn't exactly been a bed of roses either, but in terms of maturity there was no comparison. Then again, Sean was an only child; unlike them, he'd never really had to compete... She watched the shift of feelings across their faces: hot colours, cool. From time to time she made an intervention which was disregarded.

Al sat there stolidly, taking it on the chin. She thought of the statues of Lenin with his wedge of iron beard, lassoed, succumbing to the block and tackle. The table was awash with nutshells. All the wine they'd drunk was furring up her brain. She felt Al's pain and wanted to reach out and erase it with one stroke of her hand.

She tried to make allowances. It was possible, after all, that Sam and Didi and Dexter didn't actively resent her presence, rather that in their game of Trash the Patriarch she was simply irrelevant. It's because of Al's trip, she thought: we all want our pound of flesh. They were resentful, but perhaps they were entitled to be. By middle-class standards – which they both did and didn't subscribe to – they hadn't done particularly well for themselves. Sam did some labouring for Ken McBurney, Dexter worked for a hardware firm, in sales, Didi the single mother was on Benefit. As the night wore on she began to feel sorry for them, for their hurt and aimlessness and lost Utopias. They were hungry, they were angry, and under their father's jovial bullying lay a seam of guilt they were determined to exploit.

Later that night Didi had had the grace to

197

apologize. 'Don't let it get to you,' she said with a laugh. 'I'll tell you this: if I ever make it to college – some hope, eh? – I'm doing my dissertation on "The Dysfunctional Family"!'

They'd gone out into the garden to smoke a cigarette. Didi's lighter flared and then her lipstick was black in the moonlight. 'Oh, you'll make it, Didi,' Broom said gratefully. 'I'm sure of that.'

Sam and Dexter followed her across the lobby, waif-like, trailing luggage. She wondered if any of the girlfriends had ever tried to mother them. As the lift doors slid across to seal them in she decided that it was unlikely. They'd have their own place in the sun to consider, she thought, with a stab of bitterness which unnerved her. They were too bloody busy competing for his attention.

Broom jerked the sheet up to Al's chest but she knew that they'd seen the urine catheter, the vulnerable penis. There was no escaping the look on their faces, an expression midway between outrage and disgust. Sam's eyes filled up with tears. Dexter sucked in his breath and held it. The swollen head, the livid bruises, were unanswerable. They were staring not only at the absence of the father they knew – someone who towered over their lives, maddening and indelible, who named them for his jazz greats, who undoubtedly diminished them – but also at the interloper who had supplanted him, a changeling with a crumpled, gnomish face, who had betrayed them. They didn't deserve this, she thought. None of us deserved this.

The heat of the ward pressed against her neck. She bent over the bed and whispered. 'Darling, the boys *are here.'*

She watched the small dark O that had formed, oracular, between Al's lips, willed it to speak. Her hand moved slowly on his good shoulder, deliberately, like a masseur's. 'It's OK.You can talk to him.'

'Will he hear us?' Sam's voice was muted with shock.

'Just talk anyway. I'm sure he knows you're here.'

Dexter stared at her for a long unforgiving moment. An indistinct sound escaped from him. He walked to the far end of the ward and stood, dreadfully, with his forehead pressed against the wall. His hands were in his pockets, his shoulders absolutely rigid.

Broom looked helplessly at Sam. She motioned him to come round to Al's good side, the side that wasn't wounded. He drew the chair up close and leaned his elbows on the bed. For a moment he sat silently, palpating his father's hand. 'Hi, Dad,' he said in a high, rattling voice. 'It's me, Sam... Louie says when's his grandad coming home, he sends you a big kiss, and Nina does too, OK?'

Al's lids flickered. The ghost of a groan came out of him. Sam's eyes widened.

Broom nodded. 'You see?'

Sam rested his head in his hands for a moment, the big balls of his thumbs pressed against his eye sockets. Then he sat up straight and shook his head. 'Thank Christ Didi didn't come!' His voice was deep, invigorated. Some of the colour had returned to his cheeks. It was the thought of Didi's vulnerability, she realized, that had done the trick.

Here and there in the narrow beds, eyes observed the melodrama happening by the far wall. Dexter's dark head was bowed, his arms were stiff and straight as

199

oars. His hands, balled into fists, strained at his pockets. She thought she should go to him. On the other hand, just looking at him made the courage drain from her. Sam, as the elder son, would do his level best, but it would be a mistake to expect any help from Dexter.

In the taxi he exploded. 'The place is filthy! It's a bloody tip!'

Broom put an appeasing hand on his arm. 'You have to remember we're not in England. We just have to get him out as soon as we possibly can.'

'Oh yeah? So when?' He shrugged away from her and lit a cigarette, his dark envious eyes saying that he hadn't asked for comfort and would take none.

The taxi sped on along the avenue of fledgling tamarisks. At last Sam turned from the passenger seat and said in a teasing bark, 'Typical, eh, Dex? First time in our lives we get to go abroad and look what it's fucking for!'

'Right!' Dexter snorted. But his face, momentarily, had lightened.

It would take time, of course. She would have to be patient. It was ridiculous to expect them to step blithely off the plane and take the catastrophe in their stride. That might be their father's style, but it certainly wasn't theirs.

When she got to her room she wore her leather gloves to turn on the lights. In the next suite a shower was running. Her skin felt scratchy and bereft, her hair stuck to the back of her neck. What she needed was an open fire, something to lie grimly down by. Not this neutral foreign room, heartless and heartless. The

200

lampshades were shell-shaped and clung to the walls like barnacles to rock; their opaque glass dispersed the light equally around the room, in the way that mist at altitude diffuses the rays of the sun. There was no focal point, no chiaroscuro. Vermeer, she thought, would have hated it. It wasn't sympathetic; it certainly wasn't humanistic. Perhaps it was the light of the future – corporate, rather than corporeal. Like the polynuclear glow of ceiling lights in Bond Street galleries, which showed the artworks off to good effect but not the guests. Impossible not to notice how it was only the youngest and loveliest faces that escaped unscathed.

She checked the voice-mail but there was nothing. Then she realized that she'd forgotten about the time difference. The calls, presumably, would come later.

The hotel notepad pointed its finger at her. *SIZI NEREVE BULABIRIZ?* At first glance she misread the question. *WHO ARE YOU?*

She stretched out on the goatskin rug and the answer came to her. The long nylon hairs shivered towards her, rippling like seaweed on the invisible currents of her body. When she lifted her arm from the bed the fibres relinquished the wool of her sweater with a sound like a sigh of regret.

She could convince herself, perhaps, that she was calm, but she couldn't convince the room, whose stringent stillness pointed unerringly to her own private vortex.

She remembered the length of him, their nimbleness, how lust or love invariably made them fit. In the hotel in Tunisia they'd made love on frayed sheets. Trains rumbled down below on the *Rue de Grèce*. Through the window she could see white doves icing the dome

201

of the Catholic church and, high on the roof of the Miramar el Hana, the winking blue neon palm trees of the Bar Jamaica.

After three months of travelling, his hair, cropped short by a Moroccan barber, was noticeably greyer. 'Bravo, le vieux!' the young sports-cyclists had yelled in Algeria, tossing oranges to him as they passed him on the road. When the sun went down a chill descended on the room and he loomed behind her in the wardrobe mirror, noble, tall as a camel. He dragged a sweater on over his money-belt and pulled in his stomach, patting the bulge. 'Folks will be asking, what's this dishy woman doing with that paunchy old git!' He grinned, rueful, his gold caps gleaming at her. 'Little do they know what a vital beast lurks beneath the clobber.'

There was a knock at the door. Broom got up and put her gloves back on to answer it. Sam stood there frowning, holding a duty-free carrier bag. His face was pink and washed. He had combed his hair back and tightly secured the ponytail. She saw a rash of acne on his forehead, just below the hairline. He looked enquiringly at the gloves.

'Static,' she said, with gallows gaiety.

'Oh yeah? That's the trouble with composition soles. Try taking your shoes off.' From the carrier bag he produced a bottle of Bell's and, unaccountably, six packets of shortbread. 'Ken got it at Heathrow. He swore blind that's what you really, really wanted.'

She stared at the little tartan packages. Scottish she might be, but had she ever, at any time, expressed a craving for shortbread? She went to the desk drawer and took out Al's passport. 'You should have this. As next of kin.'

Sam took the passport, cupping it in his hand so that the pages fell open. He flattened them to examine a visa made out ornately in Arabic. Something funereal in the droop of his mouth oppressed her. His sigh was long drawn out, exaggerated. She looked at him severely. It was neither the time nor the place for dramatics but that was Sam all over. Feelings couldn't simply be felt, they had to wave placards, make sure that they elicited the sympathy they deserved. She handed him the traveller's cheques. Count yourself lucky, she thought. Count yourself lucky he's still living and breathing!

There was another knock, and Dexter stood in the doorway, damp-haired, in pressed jeans and a loose cotton shirt whose whiteness startled her. When she stepped aside to let him in he skirted her awkwardly, avoiding her eyes.

'Well, we can't just live on shortbread!' she said, in a voice she hoped would inspire confidence. 'I'll ring Room Service. You'll need a sandwich or something.' She took off her shoes as she rang the order through. She padded round the room, fetching toothmugs for the Bell's, laying the shortbread packets out on the coffee table, her movements crisp and bossy, like those of a relief worker in an emergency zone. As if to impose order, or quell potential mutiny.

Sam and Dexter took over the grey globular armchairs, collapsing into them and spreading themselves in a leggy male way. The leather cushions huffed and puffed under their weight.

'OK, Dex?' Sam poured whisky, clanking the neck of the bottle against the glasses.

They drank silently, staring at their feet.

Their listlessness alarmed her. It seemed suddenly

203

like an infection she could catch. She looked at their hot, wary faces. Perhaps they resented her, for getting here first, for stepping into the breach. Or perhaps they simply wanted to be alone, to give vent to their complicated grief.

She lit a cigarette and sat down reluctantly, facing a half-tumbler of whisky. Like it or not, they were in this together. 'So, I guess we should make a sports plan, as your Dad would say.'

Sam's shrug blanked her. 'Bugger all we can do, is there, till the insurance turns up!' He ran both hands over his forehead and dragged the skin ghoulishly downward, revealing the livid inside of his eyelids.

When the coffee came she poured, kneeling down before the table, smelling the sharpness of her sweat. She watched them eat soft rolls filled with haloumi. Dexter shunted the garnish disdainfully to the outer extremities of his plate. Black olives, a radish, pickled green chillies. The Englishman abroad, she thought. At any other time she'd have pulled his leg about it.

'The Consul's coming first thing. Nine thirty prompt. He means it. He's a very busy fellow.' As she handed two paper sachets of sugar to Sam she heard the click. The current jangled up her arm.

Sam dropped the sachets and wiggled his fingers in the air. 'Shit! You really weren't kidding!'

Broom laughed despairingly. 'It's not funny!' Stockinged feet or no, she was still lethal. She thought of the morning and panicked. Monsieur Engin's manners. He was so punctilious on meeting and parting that it would be impossible to avoid shaking hands. Sam and Dexter were watching her.

Dexter greeted the information with a xenophobic shrug; she might have been talking about Mithraic

204

sun-symbolism, or court protocol in the reign of Suleiman the Magnificent. Sam's face broke into a grin, all the untidy features wrinkling up with glee.

'What?' said Dexter suspiciously.

'The Electric Consul...'

This took a second to sink in. Then the penny dropped and Dexter let out a kind of bray.

'Oh don't,' Broom begged.

'Nice one!' cried Dexter, tipping his chin back to give full vent to his laughter.

Broom saw immediately that things had changed. At every door the Consul was the picture of courtesy, holding the wings of his coat aside to let her pass. Otherwise he strode ahead with the boys. It was Sam he now addressed on all official matters, Sam who sat in the front seat of the Mercedes as they drove back from the hospital, Sam who was told sotto voce that the bicycle panniers were ready for release, if he would go to the police station to collect them.

'Mrs Broom?' There was a wariness in Akil's eyes as he handed her the key. 'There is a person wishing to speak to you.'

She turned and saw a middle-aged man waiting at a little distance from the desk. He wore a cheap acrylic sweater patterned with lozenges under a worn tweed jacket. His nose was bulbous and open-pored, his cheeks seamed by weather. Beside him stood the doorman, red-uniformed and ramrod-stiff like the Guard at Buckingham Palace. She expected Akil to give a name but he did not.

'It is the brother-in-law of the driver.'

She heard the word 'driver' and thought immediately

205

of the Samaritan. When she realized, there was a queasy rage that vanished as quickly as it had come. She looked accusingly at Akil. The man took a step towards her and let out a salvo of Turkish.

'He comes to say on behalf of his brother that his family deeply regrets for the accident to your husband. They beg your forgiveness.' Akil gazed at her with sorrowful concern. 'You wish to speak to him?'

The doorman had laid a forbidding hand on the man's arm; she was struck by his expression, that fixed No Hawkers glare. Sam and Dexter had gone ahead of her and waited, smoking, by the lift.

Cornered, she felt something akin to vertigo: a thrill of morbidity that started in the toes, an answering quake in the pit of the chest. It was as if she were standing too close to the parapet of the World Trade Center, or the viewing gallery in St Paul's. She looked at the brother-in-law. He was shabby and on sufferance and his eyes, shockingly, were full of tears. She said, 'I will speak to him.'

Akil translated. He nodded curtly at the man, who darted forward and grasped her hand. His fingers were brown and hard as horn. He spoke ardently, his eyes fixed on her.

'He begs that the Court may take into consideration his brother's sincere efforts to aid your husband.'

She understood then that she was powerful. A word in the right ear, a reminder of the mitigating factors. His brother-in-law was in jail and this is what he wanted of her. He was standing so close to her that she could not focus on his face. In the side pocket of his jacket was a rolled-up newspaper, the black and white squares of the crossword section just visible. The concept of a Turkish crossword puzzle struck her as

206

bizarre. It had been completed in red ink. She wondered just how long he had been waiting.

'His brother is a poor man with a family to support.' Akil recited the words in an embarrassed monotone. 'He is praying in prison each day for your husband's recovery.' His gaze slid towards the door. A low battered car was parked at the kerb, its wing- and door-panels streaked with agricultural mud. Inside, Broom glimpsed two women in headscarves, and several children.

Her face felt stiff and stony. The man had clasped his hands together and was watching her beseechingly. She forced herself to look him in the eye. 'Please tell him I will speak to the Consul.'

Akil had begun to translate. She didn't wait for the handshake or the thanks, but turned away brusquely and marched towards the lift.

Dexter was lounging in the doorway with his finger on the control button. Sam looked at her enquiringly. 'What the fuck was that about?'

When she came to the word 'mercy' her hand went up to her mouth. Then the lift rose and her knees dropped away from her. She fell against Sam, the gasps rising from their hiding place in her chest. The wool of his sweater was hot and rough against her cheek.

Sam thrust his arm out to support her but he didn't hold her to him. He was silent, breathing fast. With a pang of surprise she realized that he was warding her off, willing her to right herself.

Dexter leaned his head back against the wall and closed his eyes. 'Fuckssake!'

She flattened her palms against the wall and eased herself up. 'I'm all right,' she announced, although no one had asked. She understood that they were angry, that she wouldn't be allowed to lean or cling or weep. What she didn't understand was why they couldn't see the principle of the thing. The driver was going to jail in any case. It was simply a question of how many years.

Sam's jaw was set, his face flushed. 'How did the fucker get in here?'

'Well, what do you think?' Dexter rubbed his thumb and forefinger together, streetwise and scornful. 'Palms oiled, old son.'

The ugliness of this disturbed her. If she hadn't consulted them it was because she didn't think she needed to. She shrugged helplessly. 'He's a working-class guy, for Christ's sake! You know what Al's like. You don't seriously think he'd want his pound of flesh!'

Philip's voice erred on the cautious side of triumph. 'I have some good news. The policy turned up. In Al's desk, no less. I just spoke to Europ Assistance and they're getting straight on to the hospital. When the scans are faxed through they'll establish whether he's fit enough to fly.'

'Thank God for that,' said Broom.

Philip hesitated. 'How does he seem to you at the moment?'

'About the same. Stable. That's what they keep saying, anyway. No sign of a ventilator, though.' The silence made her feel defensive. 'Lost in translation, I expect.' If no ventilator had appeared it hadn't been for want of trying. How sick and tired she was of blaming herself for asking the wrong questions, when clearly it was the answers that were at fault. Suave, *evasive, slippery. Sick and tired, too, of shaking hands with strangers and peering at name badges that meant nothing to her. She could hardly tell a consultant from an orderly, for God's sake; no wonder the little racist worms were stirring in the compost heap that once had been her mind.*

The cement mixer on the roof across the road had started up again. Day and night, the construction went on, the demolition. Hotels going up, apartment blocks coming down. Always the sounds and smells of progress.

'And the boys?'

'Well, you know ... coping. They've gone out to do the sights. Check out the bars. Or something.'

For several days the three of them had kicked their heels. The trip to Mersin hadn't transpired, since the Consul had gone away on business. The shortbread was gone, as was the whisky. The hospital had become almost routine: the shower-caps pulled over the shoes, the figure on the bed they addressed in whispers, taking turns.

She no longer believed it mattered particularly what was said, but thought of it rather as a kind of singing. Sam related nursery-school news, messages from Louie and Nina; he told laddish tales of nights on the town, peppered with terms like 'rip-off', 'rat-arsed' and 'pathetic', from which she gathered Adana didn't have a lot to offer. She recited daily lists of those who'd sent their love, the tips of her fingers testing Al's skin tone, feeling the changes. His chest was taut and smooth, apart from a sparse outcrop of hairs high up on the breastbone, some jet black, and others wiry white.

When Dexter's turn came he would hunch over the

209

bed, his palm flattened along the back of Al's hand, as if enacting some arcane ritual of measurement. Occasionally he murmured a word or two. Mostly he just stared, in rigid concentration.

It was easier, perhaps, for Sam. People who had children were used to repeating the same things day after day, hoping that some of them would stick. You didn't expect reciprocity, simply that the one-way traffic wouldn't last for ever, because one day they'd grow up and answer back and be the world to you.

Sometimes Al made a little mouth-sound which led the three of them to stop dead and look at one another, convinced that he was about to wake and hold a conversation. Sometimes he farted silently and the intimate smell drifted across the bed like a reproach. She wondered how Philip would cope with the truth of their vigil – the boredom, the spasmodic hopes, the sheer daily volume of bewilderment.

'So how long is all this going to take?' she demanded.

'They'll get him out as soon as is humanly possible, but judging by what their doctor said I'm afraid we can expect a bit of push-and-pull with the hospital.'

'Well, fuck that!' she said furiously. She didn't care if she was testing his patience. The initial impression she'd had at the family gathering was that here was a man trying very hard to make allowances. The contrast between the two camps was glaring: Al's brood hectic and hard-drinking, Philip's teenagers clever and kind and praiseworthy, like their parents, and ever so slightly disapproving.

Philip coughed lightly. 'Hang in there,' he said, with bracing emphasis.

He should steer clear of the casual-speak, she

thought: it really doesn't suit him. 'Oh, I am doing, believe me.' Her laugh sounded spinsterly and sour. It bore a grudge across Europe and deposited it, unreasonably, at Philip's door. Reality kept sliding away from her to make way for a brimming anger that couldn't tell an ally from an enemy. Philip wasn't to blame, any more than she was. So why was it that everywhere she looked she saw her own disgrace?

Up they go, Micky and the two pretty women, the angle of their ascent increasing to forty degrees, and when they enter the tunnel of Les Gorets the lights in the carriage come on, until they emerge high above the valley and Micky has never seen such snow. Not a blizzard exactly, for the word 'blizzard' implied the presence of a wind, but a soft vertical opacity, a curtainfall that absorbed the frequencies which even through sunglasses could make his eyes itch and stream, that blotted the sun out first and then the light and then the landscape.

The only other occupants of the carriage were an off-duty railwayman and his elderly mother. Evidently it was her birthday, and he was taking her up to the Cristaux restaurant for lunch. After a polite nod of greeting, the old lady had eyes only for her son. She sat in her thick coat and best earrings with her handbag on her lap and a shy, satisfied expression on her face. Every so often she touched him lightly but possessively on the wrist, under the guise of drawing his attention to the steady vanishment of the landscape.

Micky envied the stolid-looking railwayman and felt quite affronted by the paucity of his response. In his place Micky would have held her hand and packed her day with little luxuries. Orchids for her lapel, a sable hat (bugger the animal brigade), shower upon shower of compliments. He would have linked his arm through hers and whispered tales to bring a laugh to her lips and girlish blushes to her cheeks. Unlike the dour railwayman, he would never make the mistake of taking her for granted. The guy didn't know how lucky he was, to be sitting pretty, basking in the single-minded adoration of a mother.

'*Quels flocons merveilleux*,' Estelle murmured, gazing out at flakes as big as fifty-pence pieces.

Flocons, thought Micky. A flock. A floss of sheep's wool spun in the highest regions of the air. A kiss on the tongue, a million kisses on the pine branches, a smother of kisses on the featureless mounds of furze and heather as the small red train crept above the tree line. The sound of its engine was sealed in, like the shadows; all sensations were muffled by this soft agreeable fog, this snow that cosseted his softened heart.

'But we'll see nothing!' Sophie Sauvage protested. 'Not the Faille, not even the glacier!'

Up close, her skin was fresh and freckled, her eyes clear pewter grey. Damp curls shambled over the collar of her blue fleece jacket. He'd decided that if it weren't for the unyielding chin she'd be a dead ringer for Sylvia Kristel in the old *Emmanuelle* movies. Her looks had that particularly

212

contradictory quality which poses a sexual challenge – wholesome as the driven snow, but with a dash of voluptuous curiosity. Undoubtedly she was better in the flesh than on the screen, which could just be a problem. In terms of Trampa appeal, however, he was home and dry, since he knew for a fact that Toby Rhodes had always had a retro thing for Sylvia. Micky smiled patiently. 'In that case we'll have to settle for a damn good lunch. Unless you have some objection to serious food, that is?'

Sophie's frown was perplexed. 'Sure, the food is OK, for a tourist place...' This earned a reproachful glance from Estelle, who sat, sleek and alert, on the slatted wooden seat beside her. If Sophie had no idea how business relationships must be fostered, Estelle most certainly did. Estelle, Micky reflected, was no fool. She was like a pale vole, with those sharp eyes of hers. Not to mention those long, sharp, shiny claws. On balance Sophie's gaffes and gaucheries held more appeal, although it was hard to imagine getting used to the frostbite. Women were too watchful these days, in his considered opinion. Or perhaps they always had been, and the only difference was that nowadays they took less care to conceal it. Liberated they might be, but happy they were not. They swore too much, they were wary and aggressive, like animals who've lost their protective cover. His mother, who'd had some of their aspirations but none of their advantages, would have felt sorry for them.

He rotated his damaged ankle with a stoic's sigh. 'So tell me, Sophie, you're from...'

'Lille,' said Sophie.

'Ah,' said Micky, who could think of absolutely zilch to say about the city. He imagined it to be an unpromising place, rather like Belgium, where people worked in coal or chemicals and ate greasily and enormously. On the other hand, Sylvia K. had come, he thought, from Brussels.

'Sure, I know, what could be more boring?' said Sophie, shrugging dismissively in the direction of the invisible glacier.

The train rounded the shoulder of the Massif, passed through an avalanche shelter and came in sight of the station, which was minute, built of grey granite, and seriously snowbound. When they stepped out onto the platform their boots made no sound. Enveloped in undifferentiated white, the pillars of the Diable and the Sans Pitié towered unseen above them. As Sophie had predicted, there was absolutely no sign of the Faille.

They followed the railwayman and his mother round the corner of the building to a concrete terrace from which the snow had been partly cleared. A coin-operated telescope on the parapet spied out across a gulf of pearly fog. At one end of the terrace a billboard painted with purple prisms advertised the Galerie des Cristaux. A workman with a vacuum machine was clearing the snow-drifted steps that led down to it. He smiled at the sight of Micky, limping along between the two women.

Inside the café-bar there was nothing to indicate that they were perched on the edge of a precipice at an altitude of two thousand metres.

The central heating beamed its warmth at them. The tables were precisely set, the aperitif bottles twinkled from the shelves behind the bar. In one corner stood a Christmas tree festooned with starry lights. They could only be in France: a civilized country. If you couldn't tell by the food you could tell by the engineering.

Apart from the railwayman and his mother, Micky and his party were the only diners. The room was bright and welcoming. The slow movement of Beethoven's Pastorale trickled from unseen speakers. Eloquent odours promised that somewhere in the nether regions clever mountain chefs were grating celeriac, truffling ducks, slicing *saucisson d'Arles* for the *salade composée*; they were folding cream into the *mousseline du jambon*, studding the *gigot* with rosemary and garlic.

Sophie rolled a cigarette and asked for a beer. Micky held a brief conference with the miniskirted waitress, sizing up the merits of the *gigot* as opposed to the *sanglier*. Estelle had agreed to share a half-bottle of 1985 Beychevelle.

The waitress studied him with a cool curiosity. 'But you, *monsieur*, you're not English?'

'I'm Lebanese, as it happens,' said Micky, sipping the wine and signalling his approval.

It was a statement that, in his experience, never failed to have an effect. People thought immediately of car bombs and Kalashnikovs; they thought of Amal and Hezbollah, of the faces of fanatics broadcast by the Western media, the posthumous messages recorded on videotape. Bilal Fihas, *arrous al jnoub*: the bridegroom of the south. Sana Mheidi in her combat jacket and red

215

beret, lipsticked and lovely and smiling radiantly. *We are the soldiers of God and we are fond of death.*

'Ah, *Beyrouth*,' Sophie said lackadaisically, squinting at the Christmas tree. 'But it's not so dangerous now, I think?'

Micky was nettled. 'Now that the "theatre", as they call it, has shifted further south?' Inwardly he accused her of a lack of imagination. Here you had it: the old-colonial arrogance of the French. 'You can change the players, of course, but the game itself doesn't go away.' He decided to tell her a Beirut joke. 'Question: How do you avoid being abducted? Answer: Point a gun at a friend's head as he drives you across town. No one kidnaps the kidnapper. Alternatively, wear a black hood in the back of the car. No one kidnaps the kidnapped.'

Sophie choked on her beer. '*Merde!* That is not so very funny!' Estelle's lips produced a disapproving bleat.

'*Je m'excuse.*' Micky knew that he had gone too far. He made a show of remorse. He pretended to be stricken. He shook his head morosely and stared out at the whiteness beyond the window, seeing, with a dreamy sense of inconsequence, the luminous blue washes of the sea off Raouche, the Corniche fringed by feather-palms, water-skiers zipping through the natural arch of the Pigeon Rocks. He pictured himself falling through the darkening air, Israeli Skyhawks shelling the apartments of Ain Mreissé, the streets of Hamra canyons of ruins. He sees, yes, he even sees the tiny fists his mother once pressed passionately to her mouth. He is bruised, he is shattered; when he turns back to look at Sophie his eyes are full of wounds. 'You forget what it does to you. You get hard. They say if you live in Beirut for long enough your tears freeze.'

Sophie was a climber; she risked death daily. There was a rat in her stomach that fed on danger. She had pushed one hand up under the sleeve of her sweater and was pensively kneading the muscles of her upper arm. Her eyes drifted. Her roll-up died in the ashtray. He waited in vain for the shadowed stare of fellowship.

When the *salade composée* arrived she smiled a welcome to it in that French way and fell to like a lumberjack, her knife and fork agile, trimming and lopping and bundling. Her plate was a plan, a set of priorities. Beirut was already forgotten. The *saucisse* must go with the melon cubes, the radishes with the butter; the matchsticks of beet-root were stacked more neatly than all the wood-piles of Montjoie. She and Estelle pronounced it *une très bonne salade*, with such emphasis that across the room the railway worker rolled his eyes in agreement and raised his glass to them.

Micky was disappointed in Sophie. He watched her plough through the *mousseline*, the *sanglier aux pruneaux*. She was behaving like a little *bourgeoise*, when, fool that he was, he'd expected better.

He addressed himself to his lamb, but without enthusiasm. It was, he decided, overdone, and the chef had been a damn sight too lavish with the rosemary.

He found himself thinking of the woman who'd knocked him down, the one who called herself

217

Broom. When he'd asked if it was her Christian name she said, no, her name was Constance, but since she was neither constant nor a Christian she'd given up on it long ago. Sharp, my dear; so sharp she might cut herself. Her self-presentation was that of a woman with a past, but he discerned about her a timid willingness to be entranced. Looking at the tired skin of her hands it had been impossible not to feel, on the surface of himself, a gleam like polished brass.

Lining up his knife and fork, Micky paid laughing tribute to Sophie's youthful appetite. 'So what say you we segue into a spot of dessert?' he said spitefully.

'*Mais non!*' Estelle looked girlish and guilt-stricken, as if he'd invited her to a full-scale orgy. 'For me, no. But Sophie, perhaps? She is so lucky, she does not have to worry about her figure...'

Well, give it a year or two, thought Micky: a few more beers, a few more bars of chocolate. He spread his hands and pantomimed the essential Gallic shrug. 'Without dessert, how can we talk business?'

Sophie patted her stomach and groaned. 'Oh well...' She reached for her tobacco. 'Only if they have profiteroles...'

The dessert arrived promptly, steaming in its velvet sauce.

Outside, the ice. A thousand feet below, the glacier mooched along invisibly, keeping its secrets. The weather was, perhaps, lifting a little.

Micky looked at Sophie appraisingly. Like Michelangelo facing a formless block of marble,

218

it was the anticipation of the end product that always kept him going. The thought of what your average human being could look like when the cellulite had been pummelled away to reveal the clean lines of muscle, and the teeth had been whitened and capped, and the gentle arts of *maquillage* had emphasized the planes of the face, so that studio lights fell in love with the modulations of forehead and cheekbone, and struck sparks from the eyes, and proclaimed the lips a masterpiece. It moved him, to be honest. In most people the transformation was amazing. It was as if you'd fought a war on their behalf, had turned them into winners.

Estelle stopped torturing her sorbet and laid down her spoon.

'Shall we?' said Micky.

It was time to talk business, explain the schedule. Six weeks to Words and Pictures was the norm, but in the meantime he wanted to make sure that Toby Rhodes was well and truly tempted. For that he would need shit-hot sample footage, and soon, which meant that Sophie must be persuaded to do it on spec. She didn't look to him like the trusting type, but she'd just have to accept that for the moment there simply were no guarantees.

'Of course, eventually we'd shoot the pilot in London, although we could probably get a crew over to Geneva if you'd prefer. The mountain stuff, of course, we'll do here. Then there's make-up, hairdressing, that sort of thing. We've a man in Milan who works miracles. Luca Tiziano. All the top tennis players swear by him...' He grinned easily at Sophie. 'Nothing to be afraid of. They're a terrific bunch – very *simpatico*. Luca particularly.'

'You want to cut my hair?' Sophie looked at Estelle and snorted. 'Sure. I don't care so much.' Grabbing a fistful of ringlets, she stretched them to their full length and sawed at the hair with the stem of her spoon.

'Not at all, not at all!' Micky gazed earnestly at Sophie. 'We absolutely want to preserve your individual style. Trust me on this. Your hair is your trademark.'

Sophie eyed him with a steely humour. 'I'm not a tradesman, Monsieur Flint. I don't have a trademark.'

'But you do have a public, Sophie,' Estelle reminded her, in the apologetic tone of a teacher forced to reprimand a brilliant, wayward pupil.

'Depends how small she wants to keep it,' Micky murmured.

'Monsieur Flint only wants to maximize your potential,' Estelle chided.

'So I have to be some Ginola-poodle appearing at hairdressers' balls, or what?'

There were chocolate smears at the corners of Sophie's mouth. Micky controlled his temper with an effort. 'Sophie, you don't have to do anything you don't feel comfortable with.' The rough with the smooth, he told himself. He focused on his nostrils and counted down from ten, feeling the breath wash lightly in and out of him. 'You have Estelle to vet any contract you eventually sign with Trampa. Frankly, my advice to you would be to look on this as your launching pad. After that, it's really up to you. If this works out I'd say you should be able to pick and choose. The sky's the limit, really.'

Sophie glanced at Estelle. *'Vraiment?'*

'I absolutely wouldn't bullshit you.'

'So I'd be able to climb full-time?'

'That's the whole idea,' Micky said magnanimously. 'No more waitressing or – what was it? – PE teaching.'

'Fucking hell,' breathed Sophie. A smile of incredulity passed across her face. She plucked a wet strand of tobacco from the tip of her tongue.

'Oh, I wouldn't say it was as bad as that.' Micky grinned, stretching out his hands and limbering up his fingers. They looked slim and tanned and intact. In and out clicked the double joints of his thumbs. 'So what about a cognac,' he suggested, 'to celebrate. Or maybe one of these local liqueurs – *mireilles*, or whatever?'

The little glasses of liqueur arrived and were duly clinked. Estelle was wreathed in smiles. Even Sophie looked relieved. *'Bonne fête,* madame!' cried Micky, toasting the railwayman's mother, who blushed and fingered the burnished brooch on the lapel of her cardigan.

Sophie was bundling up her wiry hair. She screwed it into a rough rope, knotted it on top of her head, and lanced the knot with two toothpicks. She turned her head from side to side, grinning skittishly at Estelle. *'Chic,* huh?'

Micky smiled, avuncular, at her play-acting. 'Perfect!' he cried, but he knew that she was not. What ought to have been a moment of triumph was tinged with a nagging sense of *petite mort.*

221

The initial contract would be signed, the pitch, no doubt, would win, the money would be made, but history wouldn't. For Sophie Sauvage was hungry, but she was not hungry enough. Under that *louche* exterior he suspected something shrewd and stubborn. Since it was not in her nature to be dazzled, she would not truly dazzle. Light would be in league with her – for she was sure as fuck a pretty girl – but it would not wholly love her, for there was no camera on earth which could convey an excitement that was wilfully withheld. Whatever Sophie's agenda was, she would stick to it; what's more, she would keep it to herself. The rat that lived in her belly would be petted selfishly in private.

Outside, the snow was still falling, but there were breaks or at least transparencies in the cloud. With a jolting recognition of the scale, Micky glimpsed the glacier below: the deep smudge-marks of crevasses, the grey ice-boulders riding on the hump of its back.

They put on their coats and went out. Even the modest brightening in the sky was enough to start up the itch in Micky's eyes. When he retreated behind his ski-goggles the landscape took on a sulphurous tinge. The shifting mists became a desert sandstorm, the crevasses were the cinnamon-coloured canyons of a *wadi*. He made a weird piss-yellow snowball and weighed it in his hand.

Sophie was leaning over the parapet, pointing out an invisible feature on the face of the Faille. The nape of her neck was bare and vulnerable under the upswept hair. He heard her telling

Estelle how she'd been forced to bivouac on a ledge, in a thunderstorm, for eight hours, unbelievable, the way the crashes echoed, the flash of the lightning bolts. She drew Estelle closer and made her sight along the line of her forearm and the peremptory stub of her finger. The pair of them looked happy and excited, their booted feet scuffing up the snowbanks at the edge of the terrace.

For a moment Micky was tempted to bowl the snowball at their unsuspecting backs. Instead he hurled it out into the ochre abyss, where it spanked against a larch tree, spilling a cascade of snow from the upper branches. The result was so disproportionate to the effort that he felt childishly gratified. It was a long way down to the glacier. He watched the snow fall, in gobbets, in slithers, in runnels. Suave and silent, it disappeared into the depths. Micky wiped the slushy residue from his gloves, remembering an open-air café on the Corniche where a stick hurled by an Arab boy missed the pigeon it was meant for and hit a rose-bush instead, scattering scent and petals. The roses had been so blush-pink and perfect, yet in the space of a second the bush stood bare and blackish, like a blighted city...

The image filled him with an energetic melancholy. He felt light-headed; the altitude was charging him up, threatening to make him do something rash and reckless and playful. Creeping up behind Sophie, he barked, 'So what d'you reckon to being disgustingly rich?'

Sophie gasped and spun round. When she

lowered her hand from her heart her eyes were narrowed against Micky or the light. 'You know, Monsieur Flint, you really shouldn't miss the Gallery of Crystals. They have rock-amethysts there as big as refrigerators!'

The wake-up call of the muezzin floated in from the half-darkness. Then the telephone rang and someone in Croydon informed her that the Europ Assistance team would arrive at the airport at 1300 hours local time.

Broom lay on the bed, waiting for the fog to lift, trying to calibrate the time zones. Her battery alarm clock turned out to have a tick, a faint thunk, toneless. A dull sound, like the keys of a toy piano.

She turned on her side and drew her knees up to her chest, storing up the minutes before she would have to move. If the plane had taken off an hour ago, it would be over the Alps. In four or five hours it would float down and scoop Al out of Asia Minor. After that, the sequence of events was so overlaid by previous plans that it was almost too confusing to contemplate. Al had scheduled his return to coincide with spring, but in the meantime winter was hardly weakening. He had promised her an Easter trip to Cornwall: no camping or climbing, no Lost Boys tagging along, just the two of them on the coastal path, mild winds, the flowering gorse a golden rival to the sun. Touching base, he'd called it. Quality time on the stony seashore with their bare feet out to air like buds. They'd eat cream teas and fuck in beds with frilly valances and

224

drink warm white wine in Cornish euro-restaurants.

She shut her eyes and tried to tease out the under-
lying logic. Ever since Christmas she'd been living in
the future tense, egging the calendar on. She'd set her
body clock for April, but now Al had managed to pre-
empt her, as if there was something in him that simply
couldn't wait, some ardent homesick essence that
made sure he would touch base six weeks early.

At Tunis airport she'd cried so uncontrollably that
her nose had bled. She leaned her head back and held
tissues to her nose, but still the flow wouldn't stop. Al
had almost caved in. At the Libyan Embassy they'd
refused him a visa. With the coast route to Egypt
barred, what he'd conceived of as a clean circuit was
beginning to look like a jigsaw puzzle. So why get on
a ferry to Sicily and skid around the Med. like
Sinbad when he could bale out with a clear conscience
and fly back with her to London? Dismay made him
think aloud, but still she didn't press him. Perhaps she
should have done. Another woman would have said it
loud and clear, gone down on her knees and begged
him to come back with her.

Messages from the body. Those racking public sobs.
Were there other premonitions she'd shouted down?
OK, she hadn't asked him to abort the trip but she'd
longed for the phone call or the letter that would say
he was coming home. Perhaps too much longing could
lasso and be lethal. It could slow the reactions, drag a
person down. Perhaps she'd wished so hard to have
him back that even though he stopped his ears with
wax he was unable to block out her siren call...

In a moment she'd get up and let the day drive out
the demons. Stop torturing herself with might-have-
beens, or seeing herself as some kind of Cassandra,

225

harbouring the sickly power of prophecy. The trouble with magic thinking was that it promised to explain the inexplicable, but at a cost – its brilliant spirals usually spun you downwards. Far better, surely, to be a rationalist like Al, and treat such regions with a healthy disrespect. The real world had its own implacable laws, to which both of them were subject. Cause and effect, good luck and bad. A driver passing on a blind bend, a moment's crucial inattention. Looked at that way, it was totally ridiculous to blame herself.

In the lobby the light dazzled her, sun striking bright as a bell on the marble tiles and glass-topped tables. She held up her hand to shield her eyes and stepped gingerly towards the fray. At least half of the floor area was occupied by the sort of aluminium crates used to transport film equipment, around which guests on their way to lunch detoured respectfully. At first glance someone might have been setting up for a location shoot.

A man she assumed to be the team doctor was supervising the stacking; with him was a nurse in a navy uniform with a company scarf pinned neatly at the neck. The doctor was rugby-pitch beefy, with the kind of Cadet Corps voice that expects to be obeyed. Not the type she imagined would apologize for the disruption.

She went over and stood beside them. 'What should I do?'

The doctor was straddling a metal case; when he crouched down to swivel it into position the hem of his duffel-coat flooded out across the floor. 'Hi,' he said curtly, peering up at her. She hadn't said who she was and he didn't ask. A galvanizing energy came off him.

The nurse said in a quiet Yorkshire voice that she thought they could do with a hand outside. She had strictly plucked eyebrows in a small pale face, and an expression of fixed neutrality, as if she'd spent long years learning forbearance.

Through the window Broom caught a glimpse of an airport transit van with the back doors open, from which two men in flight uniforms were manhandling equipment onto the pavement. Sam staggered through the revolving door with a console clasped to his chest, his wild hair haloed by sun, his trainers fashionably but perilously unlaced. Dexter followed with what appeared to be a collapsible stretcher. His step was light and brisk; in his eyes there was a feverish focus.

In the part of her mind where decisions floated, trying to shape themselves, she felt the lightness of relief. For a Monty Python moment she wanted to burst out laughing. 'Well, I never expected the Fifth Cavalry...'

Al knelt on the floor beside the bath, grabbing a last kiss from her before he hurried off to work. She heard his feet galumph down several flights of stairs. She lay listening to the morning sounds of neighbours: babies, Hoovers. After a few moments there was a commotion in the flat below, which belonged to Kieron the caretaker. Presently Al reappeared. He stood in the doorway, gasping with laughter. He had nipped back up, intending to surprise her, but he'd mistaken the third floor for the fourth. He'd burst in shouting, 'Well, you never expected the Spanish Inquisition,' at a big hairy Irishman, who lay naked in the bath, his beard full of soapsuds, gawking up at him.

The transit van was blocking the inside lane. Cars swerved, hooting; exhaust fumes pumped out in leaded blue clouds. One of the pilots was handing gear out of the van while the other piled it on the pavement. They looked rakish and retro in their uniforms. Dirk Bogarde and Donald Sinden, but without the Brylcreem. Very Battle of Britain. She fixed a frown on her face and tried to look as if she was concentrating, now that she no longer needed to.

The pilot on the pavement handed her a bundle of chrome tubing bound with masking tape. She took it fearfully, expecting to get a shock. He had crinkly red hair that wound into tight little curlicues behind his ears. He told her that his name was Greg. 'Sorry, but we had to bring the kitchen sink. Security at the airport's beyond a joke.' His smile was civil but encouraging. From the open window of a huge metal-toothed lorry a man with tattoos stared out at her. He hawked up a gob of spit, leaned out, and spat accurately into the gutter.

In the lobby she presented her bundle to the nurse, who was organizing a stack of equipment to take to the hospital. The doctor introduced himself as Glen. He didn't actually order them to gather round but it was clear that he preferred to address them as a single entity.

He looked at Broom, his eyes bright and snapping in a strangely boneless face. 'So who's next of kin?' She pointed to Sam.

Sam straightened up. There was an unlit cigarette in his mouth, which he removed. 'I am,' he said.

'So he comes to the hospital with us. Right, Sam? We

228

need you to co-sign the release papers. Do you have your father's passport?'

'Yep.'

'Good man.'

'Take yours too, Sam,' Broom interjected.

The doctor nodded brusquely. 'Do that.'

His terseness was infectious. It whittled her down, imposed a military rhythm on her thoughts. Indisputably, she felt safer. Dr Glen was Al's kind of guy. His mandate was action, time measured in monosyllables, rather than squandered on emotions. In her mind she was already surrendering Al to him, or at least the listless wounded version in the cot, signing it over to his expert care.

Dexter frowned down at the unscuffed toes of his DMs. She saw the dark shaven bristle under the surface of his skin, the delicate curve of his lip. Once again he was making himself into a stranger, spreading round him a silence that went beyond rudeness, a silence, she thought, like a tree's. He raised his head and licked his lips, deliberating. 'So you're flying Dad out tonight.' It sounded less like a question than a non-negotiable demand.

'A.s.a.p., really. Of course we have to examine him first. No sense hanging around when there's an IC bed waiting at St Thomas's.' Dr Glen thrust his hands into the deep pockets of his duffel-coat and jerked his head towards the pilots, who were standing to one side, gulping the coffee that Akil had sent over. 'These guys can take off at a half-hour's notice, and that's just the way we like it, isn't it, Delia?'

The nurse smiled tightly and nodded with professional emphasis. Greg raised his coffee cup and toasted them, on his face a daredevil smile.

Dr Glen shouldered an oxygen cylinder. 'OK, let's get organized.' He glanced at Broom and Dexter. 'Better get packed. We'll let you know what the score is.'

'Phone Didi, Dex.' Sam laid his hand briefly on Dexter's shoulder. Delia and the doctor were already heading for the door. He swung away and followed them.

Broom emerged from the lift with her luggage and scanned the lobby. She could see no sign of Dexter. Akil beckoned her from the desk. With him was a man in a camel-hair coat, who appraised her blatantly for a second before disappearing into the office. She went over anxiously. 'There is a message from the hospital?'

Akil shook his head. 'No message, I am sorry.' He plucked at his lapels to settle his jacket on his shoulders. A smooth white inch of cuff showed at the wrists. She saw silver cufflinks in the shape of anchors. 'And so, today you are leaving us?'

'I think so. I hope we are. We have to be ready, you see, just in case.' She realized that she had no idea when to check out, or how to say goodbye, or whether a tip would be demeaning. The clock on the wall said 4.30. There was a stack of crates behind the desk. Elsewhere in the hotel the pilots were showering and resting expensively, in preparation for the long flight back to Gatwick.

Akil's eyes did not leave her face. His smile was glassy. 'Excuse me.' He brought the back of his hand to his mouth and coughed infinitesimally. 'You have found the staff ... helpful?'

She said sincerely, 'Absolutely. Yes. Very helpful!'

'The manager has asked a favour...' Akil's voice

was an intimate whisper. There was a pause. 'He asks if you may perhaps write some words to say this...'

'Yes, of course.' She waited, expecting Akil to produce the visitors' book.

'This is very kind.' Akil almost bowed. 'Such a letter is very useful, you understand, for the hotel?'

A bleariness descended on her brain. She looked at Akil's tidy hands, and then at her own, frowning at the reddish shabby knuckles, the absence of important rings. She imagined her own bad handwriting, framed like a painting and hung up proudly, for promotion's sake. 'I understand. You mean some kind of testimonial.'

Akil almost bowed.

Outside, a metallic dusk was falling; at the kerb a string of taxis waited, purring out exhausts. She carried her bag to a window seat and sat down to wait for Dexter.

Two cigarettes later, Akil called her to the phone. It was Dexter, ringing from his room. 'It's no go,' he said. 'They're refusing to reopen the airport.' His voice was breathy with contempt.

'The airport's closed?'

'At five it is. Because it's fucking Saturday, Sam says. So we're stuck in this shithole for another night!'

None of this made any sense to her. 'But how can they do that? Don't they know it's a mercy flight?'

'Mercy, my arse. Sure they know. The bastards.'

'Par for the course, eh, Greg?' said the dark-haired pilot, whose name was Declan. Greg smiled sympathetically at Broom; he had insisted on paying for her drinks. He and Greg were lounging against the bar counter, as if to maintain a certain independence

231

from the others, who occupied two tables in the cramped seating area. The small room was circular, like a drum, the walls lagged with a suave blue pile that deadened sound.

When she set the pint glass down in front of Dexter he lowered his face over the lager, as if he was trying to see his reflection in it. He pursed out his lips and extended them, proboscis-like, into the froth. The downward movement seemed to go on for ever. She wondered how far he was going to take it: all the way, perhaps, so that when he raised his head his face – nose, chin, eyebrows – would wear a clown's mask of froth. She wondered if anyone had ever been seriously worried about Dexter.

A sluggish orchestral version of Presley's 'Wooden Heart' issued from the speakers above the bar. Sam and Dexter were both smoking furiously. The smoke rose up and orbited the ceiling, as if searching for a way out. She swallowed her wine in two gulps and immediately wanted more.

The atmosphere was too subdued. An adrenalin low. She wondered how much alcohol it would take to banish the collective lassitude. Sam flipped a beer mat back and forth between his knuckles, and did not look at her. She sensed that he and the doctor wanted to resume a tête-à-tête that had been interrupted. Their lowered eyelids were careful and suspenseful.

Nurse Delia sipped quietly at her shandy. Even the doctor looked exhausted. Broom found herself wishing that Al would stride in and liven things up, Al the invisible axis around which they'd revolved, an hour or so ago, when they'd been a team. Now that they no longer were, the disconnection opened up a deep moral strangeness, as if each one of them was a separate *planet, circling in a sunless universe.*

When Delia announced that she was going to bed Broom got up and said that she would go too. In the cramped silence of the lift Delia smiled at her. 'You look all in. Get all the sleep you can. It's going to be an early start.'

At 8 a.m. she was to check out and take a taxi to the hospital, where Delia and Glen would have been since dawn, getting Al ready for the journey. There was one free seat in the air ambulance, which Sam had agreed – reluctantly, although he and Dexter had return tickets – that she should take.

In Room 511 she went straight to the desk and sat down. Pulling a sheet of hotel notepaper from the drawer, she tried to be businesslike, for Akil's sake.

I have been staying at your hotel ... on family business? For family reasons?

I have enjoyed... Its considerate staff? Its excellent facilities?

Night-clup. Swim-pool.

It was no good, her pen refused point blank; there was not a shred of gratitude in her.

Static shock, *she thought, crushing the letter into a ball and dropping it into the wastepaper basket. If enough of a charge built up, maybe she would just ignite, become a bolt of lightning.*

The envelopes Sam laid on the bed were held together by an elastic band. She recognized the scrawl of her own handwriting.

'We had to chuck his clothes. The panniers were just...' *He stopped calamitously, as if unable to own*

233

the image. He handed Al's rock boots to her by the laces, without looking at them. 'We thought you'd want those for company.' His voice broke on the word 'company'.

Broom felt a quick rush of fear, remembering how he and the doctor had sat so quietly, like lovers trying hard to be polite, but wishing everyone would vanish. 'Did they say something when you were at the hospital?' Her voice was faint and rasped in her throat.

'They didn't have to, did they? I'm not a fucking idiot.' Sam shook his head, some vast pessimism weighing down his shoulders. His hands hung low and loose and simian.

She hugged the boots to her chest. Al had told her the soles were made of the same material as aircraft tyres, or perhaps he'd even said from aircraft tyres themselves. The boots smelled of old sweat and talc. No one wore socks with EBs; they had to fit the foot like a second skin, so that a climber could feel out and grip the smallest wrinkle in the smoothest rock. Not the sort of items you should separate from the owner. Intimate as condoms, in fact, but Sam didn't necessarily know that.

The last time she'd seen Al wearing them was on a nudist beach near Land's End. He'd been bouldering bare-arsed, with a silk Paisley scarf tied across his brow like a headband. His shadow had fallen across a German tourist who lay toasting on the sand below, and she'd stared up in shock, poor woman, at the genitals that dangled overhead, pink and blind as newborn kittens in their mother's jaws.

She fingered the stained green suede of the uppers. 'I'll look after them for him,' she said emphatically.

The boots spent the night at the bottom of the bed. Every so often she opened her eyes and looked down at them. They must have been balled up in Al's panniers for weeks, and now they curled back on themselves like two crescent moons, as though the rubber of the soles was trying to revert to its original form. Two semicircular sections of aircraft tyre, except that, for the moment, the aircraft had been grounded.

A dim grey light rose above the rooftops and then, unexpectedly, the silver rim of the sun. The date was the fourteenth of February; her alarm clock insisted on it.

She forgot for once to brace herself against bad news; instead she felt a resurgence of the honeymoon excitement she always felt on her way to meet Al. As she showered and dressed, her mind flew ahead of her, already resuming their big adventure, picking up where they'd left off. When she tried to put on mascara her hand shook so much that she had to wipe it off and start from scratch. She forced herself to slow down and do the thing properly: eyeshadow, blusher, the lot. She made a well in her holdall for the EBs and stuffed the alarm clock in beside them. She dragged her overcoat from the wardrobe and let the hanger lie on the floor where it fell. The coat reeked of smoke. She could not wait to be with him.

Through the glass porthole she saw Al, swaddled like a newborn in a pale-blue cellular blanket. He lay on a stretcher trolley, wired up to an assortment of machines. From his mouth a ridged plastic tube led to an apparatus she assumed must be the ventilator. Dr Glen stood beside the trolley with a clipboard, signing papers.

235

Delia saw her at the door and hurried out. She wore a navy raincoat over her uniform. On her head was a jaunty forage cap which made her look like an air hostess.

'How is he?'

'Well, we've sedated him now, of course, for the flight. But when we arrived his eyes were open. And he recognized his name.' The professional coolness had fallen away. There was suppressed excitement in her voice.

Broom's heart lurched. She looked at the still figure on the trolley. 'You mean he spoke to you?'

Delia's eyes were pale blue and tired. 'Well, no, but he squeezed Glen's finger on command. He responded to your name, too. We told him you and his sons were here.'

The trolley began to move, Dr Glen pushing from behind while an orderly guided at the front. The patients on the beds on either side observed its procession down the centre aisle of the ward. It looked stately and important, like a coronation carriage.

'But that's wonderful!' Broom said breathlessly.

Delia gave her the glimmer of a smile and wedged the ward door open.

Broom stepped back as Dr Glen, sweating in his heavy duffel-coat, wheeled the trolley through. 'I hear Al was awake!' she said.

The doctor looked sharply at her and then at Delia. 'His temperature's still up. I'm a bit concerned about a chest infection.'

Broom's mind considered coughs and colds. The doctor kicked the brake on the gurney and tightened the webbing straps that secured the stretcher. Either the blue blanket was too short for Al, or else it had

236

somehow ridden up, exposing his big bare feet. She wondered if she would be allowed to pull it down and tuck them in.

The memory opened like a door into another room. Blue blankets for boys and pink for girls. In the maternity ward all the mothers had bassinets by their beds but she did not. They told her it was the rule: breech babies were whisked away to the nursery immediately after they were born; the mums weren't allowed out of bed, either, for twenty-four hours, in case of internal injury.

She'd waited trustingly for Sean to be brought to her, but nothing had happened. Two days later she became hysterical and demanded to see her baby. From the dismay on the faces of the staff she saw that it was true. She and Sean had simply been forgotten. When the apologetic sister handed her the bundle she burst into tears of fright. Her arms felt limp and useless; she no longer trusted her own strong skilful artist's hands. They'd called it Post Partum Depression; she'd been so horribly afraid that she would drop him.

With a great unwillingness she said, 'Is that serious?'

'Let's just say I'll feel a lot happier when we get him back to St Thomas's'

Delia had positioned herself at the head of the gurney, within reach of the apparatus. The doctor slapped the brake off and shoved. 'OK. Nice and easy.'

Broom stood aside as the gurney swooshed away from her on rubber wheels. The process of her thoughts seemed to have slowed to nothing and reversed. She had not adjusted the blanket.

Delia looked fretfully at her watch. 'What's taking him so long?' They had been waiting for half an hour at a checkpoint between two airport outbuildings. Broom got out of the ambulance and walked up and down, smoking. An armed guard eyed her from his prefab hutch.

In daylight the terminal was a glass shack, a wind-punched outpost on a polluted plain that stretched as far as Syria. 'The armpit of the Mediterranean', Al had called it on the phone: every lorry route – and every oil pipeline – in the Middle East converged on it. She observed the guard through her sunglasses. He wore grey, unlike the city police, and didn't smile at her. Even in Britain she was bad at uniforms, but at least back there you didn't have to worry about the guns. According to Al, Turkey had one of the largest armies in the world, if you included paramilitaries and special units, and a large proportion of them were stationed in the southeast, on account of Ocalan's Kurdistan Workers Party, the PKK. 'Down here it isn't wise to call a spade a spade,' he'd said. 'A lot of Turks refuse to countenance the name of Kurdistan.' She dropped her cigarette butt at her feet and ground it into the tarmac. The red-and-white control barrier stayed down.

After another ten minutes Dr Glen appeared, muttering angrily about forms in triplicate and the clapped-out wheels of bureaucracy. 'Would you believe it, they're still keeping us waiting for the passports!' The barrier squeaked up and the ambulance drove through.

A Turkish Airlines airbus was parked in the modest shadow cast by the control tower. Far out on the apron a small plane sat with the sun full on it; it was white

238

and sleek and shaped like a swordfish. The tarmac stretched away on all sides, flat as a tambourine-skin. There were no other aircraft in sight.

From the door of the terminal, passengers were emerging; a stewardess was lining them up on the tarmac. Just then Sam and Dexter came through the glass exit door with their bags and joined the queue. They looked towards the ambulance, and Broom waved to them, although she knew they could not see her.

The ambulance took a wide arc across the apron and stopped on the far side of the tiny plane. Broom got out with the doctor. The two pilots were shadowy behind the smoked glass of the cockpit window.

Greg emerged, tapping his watch and shrugging despairingly. 'So what the merry heck is it this time?'

'Passports,' the doctor snapped. 'Need you ask?'

There was a clash of gears as the driver engaged reverse. Dr Glen began to walk backwards, directing the ambulance in. Broom walked out past the wing and waited. The wind was chilly, gusting; there was a faint smell of aviation fuel. After a moment Greg joined her. 'Looks like there'll be some hanging around.' His smile was cynical. 'The usual cockups.'

They stood together, staring at the plane. It was pure of heart and lively of line and light as a feather. Like Concorde, she thought, but in miniature.

'What kind is it?' she asked.

'A Lear jet. Lovely, isn't she?'

'Pretty amazing,' said Broom.

Greg's face brimmed with satisfaction. She could see why a man might easily fall in love with such a thing: a machine so beautiful, indeed, that it was almost impossible not to credit it with intelligence. She felt

239

like reaching out and stroking the sweet white slope of the wing, an impulse which was quickly overridden by her recent history with metal.

Delia was still inside the ambulance, doing something to the underpinnings of the stretcher. Dr Glen began to haul it out, while Delia and the ambulance driver hoisted from the rear. Broom saw the walrus tusks of the respirator, the broad blue-blanketed chest. The doctor began to back his way up the folding steps of the plane. There was a hiatus while they searched for a workable angle.

'Need a hand?' Greg called.

The doctor swore. 'No room,' he said impatiently. He braced himself against one side of the ovoid doorway. And then they were sliding Al into the plane, her trussed Valentine, tilted this way and that, dreaming, oblivious.

Under the tilt of the tailplane she could see the meagre façade of the terminal and, in front of it, the lengthening snake of the passengers. Dexter was a head taller than anyone and he was waving, his long arms semaphoring urgently. Greg caught her eye. 'Is there time?' she asked him.

He shrugged. 'Without passports, no one's going anywhere.'

She wrapped her scarf round her neck and hurried across the apron. To the right of the terminal building was a line of thin pine trees and the wire-netting ramparts of a car park. A man with a radio detached himself from a group of officials gathered in the terminal doorway and took a few steps towards her, but made no move to block her path. The passengers watched incuriously from their queue of suitcases.

'So what's happening?' Dexter's lips drew down at

240

the corners as he pulled on his cigarette.

'Can I?' Broom plucked it from his fingers and took a drag. The interior of the terminal was plastered with NO SMOKING notices, but out here, illogically, everyone was smoking. 'They're loading Al in.' Sam's eyes were on her. He looked dazed and lethargic, his mood turned inward. 'He was awake, earlier,' she said. 'Isn't that great?'

'Yeah, great,' Sam said hollowly. She had an urge to hug some hopefulness into him, force the bugger to trust someone.

A peristaltic movement had started at the front of the queue. A stewardess, having gathered up the first batch of passengers, was shepherding them towards the plane. Just ahead of Dexter a youth with a conscript's haircut bent to pick up his kitbag, which had a rolled prayer-rug strapped to the top, like an afterthought. On the back of his black T-shirt a slogan said MY BODY IS A NIGHTCLUB.

'We're moving,' Sam said with sudden animation, shouldering his rucksack.

Broom turned and stared across the tarmac. Out on the apron the small jet sat becalmed, like a white bird no one had set free. 'But they can't go before us. No way.'

She dropped the cigarette and ran towards the man with the radio. Pointing to the Lear, she shook her finger at him like a schoolteacher. 'That plane must go first! It is an emergency!' She began to mime wildly. One finger for the plane that must go first, two for the airbus, which must go after it.

The man's face was blank. In his hand was a small stack of passports. He glanced down at them and fanned them out, frowning.

241

She saw with a shock of surprise that the one on top was Al's. 'You have our passports,' she said sternly, reaching for them. 'We must have the passports.'

The official snatched back his hand.

In desperation she repeated the mime routine, her voice rising high and arrogant on the wind. She had forgotten the Turkish for husband.

The man shrugged at her and stood his ground. Plainly the female was foreign and hysterical. His radio made quarrelsome sounds. He held it against his cheek as if to soothe it, speaking out of the side of his mouth. Out on the tarmac the ambulance was leaving. It nosed out from behind the Lear and skirted the perimeter of the apron; then it gathered speed and headed back towards the checkpoint. He followed its progress with deliberate eyes, as if to emphasize that nothing she could do was worthy of his attention.

Sam and Dexter had reached the front of the queue. In a moment they would be boarding. They turned and looked back anxiously.

Greg was coming across the apron. His stride was fast, but somehow neat and jaunty. A gust of wind blew his hair up into a corrugated red wedge. When he reached them the official frowned judiciously. He appeared to be relieved.

Greg's face was set. She jerked her head at the passports. 'What happens if the airbus gets clearance?'

'Not a good idea.' He said evenly, 'Look here, mate, you've kept us waiting long enough.'

The official took a step backwards and gestured towards the control point. The aerial of his radio pointed straight at it, like the barrel of a gun. The passports, forgotten, jutted from his other hand. She raised her eyebrows at Greg. 'Are you thinking what I'm thinking?'

Greg nodded. 'Go for it.'

Her lips were parched, her heart hammering. She grabbed the passports and ran. Behind her a burst of static came from the walkie-talkie. Greg was shouting, 'Leg it, leg it!' Her coat flapped out behind her. Her scarf wriggled from her neck and fell away. Greg's feet pounded behind her. When he caught up, she thrust the passports at him like a relay runner passing the baton.

She was almost at the plane, but Greg was home and dry. She slowed, panting. What she saw when she glanced over her shoulder was purest slapstick: the official chasing madly across the tarmac with the radio glued to his ear; behind him, at the gallop, came the grey-uniformed militia, a herd of extras, flattening their holsters down against their thighs like bouncing breasts.

Dr Glen came out of the plane cursing blue murder. He took the passports and counted through them. 'Nice work,' he said grimly, stuffing them into the inside pocket of his duffel-coat. 'You'd better let me handle this.'

The official sprinted round the end of the wing and skidded to an anticlimactic halt. Dr Glen advanced on him. His arms flapped menacingly, his duffel-coat ballooned out behind him. Not a light bird, she thought, a dry hilarity skirling in her chest, not like the plane: more of a pelican, really. The militiamen, arriving in dribs and drabs, spread out untidily, not quite encircling the plane. In the distance the airbus began its slow taxi towards the main runway. She wondered if Sam and Dexter were at the windows,

243

watching the melodrama.

'This emergency flight *is taking off.' The doctor was breathing fiercely through his nose, like an All Black at a Rugby International.* 'So stop mucking me about.' *The official held up a cautioning hand and held an earnest conference with his radio.* 'And while you're about it you can tell your sodding superiors they've had* twelve hours *to complete the formalities.'*

The word 'emergency' fell on her ears like a rebuke. Tears rose on cue, a thick grateful tide behind her eyes. 'Get on the plane,' the doctor snapped, and it flashed through her mind that the militiamen might fire their little pistols after all. She made it to the door and skipped smartly up the steps.

The right-hand side of the cabin had been stripped down to make room for a stretcher bay. Delia indicated a spare seat on the left side, at the back. Broom clambered over the equipment that clogged the aisle and strapped herself in. Al's feet were level with her, still bare, leisurely, angled at ten to two. Delia bent over the monitor, calmly adjusting things.

The standoff on the tarmac continued. Dr Glen was gesticulating, his neck thrust bullishly forward, his large face pink and puffed with rage. Through the starboard window a Jeep appeared, heading fast across the apron. It skidded to a halt some twenty feet from the plane. There were soldiers in the back but the man who leapt out was unarmed. Producing a fountain pen from his breast pocket, he presented a fistful of papers to the doctor. The doctor uncapped the pen with his teeth and slapped the documents down on the wing. He thumbed through the pile, signing rapidly, flattening the sheets with his elbow to stop them frisking in the wind.

The hatch door to the cockpit was open. Greg had dived in and was already at the controls. Banks of digits glittered on the instrument panel. Declan was on the radio, talking to Approach Control.

Delia buckled herself into the seat in front of Broom's. 'You'll find sandwiches under the seat, and a bottle of mineral water.' She smiled ruefully. 'Unfortunately there's no toilet.'

Through the window Broom saw the doctor thrust the paperwork at the official and dash for the plane.

Greg's head came round the hatch. 'We used to have a potty, but we kind of got used to crossing our legs!'

'OK, lads.' Dr Glen hauled the door shut behind him. 'Go, go, go.'

Greg stuck his thumbs up. He was grinning. 'Couple of secs.'

The turbo jets began to hum. Then the hum became a whine, which deepened to a muted but purposeful roar. Through the flicker of the exhaust haze Broom saw that the airbus had come to a halt. The Lear pitched forward. She reached out and gripped Al's big toe, which was warm and calloused and filled her palm like a pebble. After a bare hundred metres they were airborne, slithering steeply up some unseen vector in the sky. As the coastal plain tilted and dwindled she saw, beyond the dirty plumes of oil refineries, the tarnish of sun on the sea. Then they turned north towards the mountain barrier, and the snow-bright morning shone up at them from the glaciers.

Dr Glen sat at the head of the stretcher, his back against the wall that divided the cabin from the cockpit, his bulky thighs crammed uncomfortably together. In the ambulance he'd mentioned a corridor

245

of privilege at fifty thousand feet, into which commercial aircraft could not stray. High in this stratosphere there was little or no turbulence; it was the aeronautical equivalent, he said, of wrapping Al in cotton wool. When the plane levelled out he patted Al's shoulder and smiled at her.

'He's a lucky chap, eh? I dare say it's a darn sight easier than cycling home.'

'That's true,' she said. It was also ironic. Al liked to do things the hard way. He wouldn't be too keen on this million-dollar ease.

The doctor gazed out of the window, a pensive expression on his face, his hand resting protectively on the blue cellular blanket.

Al's chest rose and fell rhythmically. The turbine noise had faded to a whisper that was quieter than the engine of his breath. There was the pop of a ring-pull as Greg passed a can of Coke to Declan, whose fingers fluttered over the control panel, performing delicate arpeggios. She thought it was a shame that Al couldn't know how well they were caring for him, up here in the realm of miracles – so high and aloof, now, they could have tongued the terrible ear of the gods. In her mind's eye the spear of the nose-cone pierced the oxygenless air like an arrow – Cupid's arrow, undoubtedly. She leaned back against the headrest and squeezed Al's toe, thinking of Samaritans and saints, letting herself slip into the comfort of exhaustion.

Later, Delia pointed out the Matterhorn. The brilliant sunlight in the cabin turned her pasty skin to gold. To the south Broom saw, unmistakably on the far horizon, a white thumbs-up sign.

Inshallah, as the Arabs say, they would carry him safely home.

From the sitting room came the startling sound of the telephone.

'Well, hello there,' said a voice classless and clear.

The vision came, eidetic and unbidden, before the name: exactly how the red ski-sock had rolled down over the ankle. Broom's heart sank. 'Oh, hi. How's the foot doing?'

'Och, no sae bad,' drawled Micky Flint. She let it pass. 'I was wondering, if you're at a loose end later, how about a spot of dinner? My treat, naturally. As in, I owe you one.'

'Really, you don't have to,' she protested. In the kitchen the glasses in the sideboard began to rattle in concert with the fridge. Like the approach of a train along a railway track, the vibration spread via the old oak floorboards to the sitting room, where it shook the ashtray on the coffee table and rustled through the huge paper heads of the floral display on the dresser. Their wire stems sang against the cut-glass vase. 'It really isn't necessary...'

'Come on,' said Micky. 'Let me twist your arm.'

Tears of irritation rose to her eyes. He was asking her to escape the echoes that were all her own; he was asking her to be convivial. Wanting to be seen to go out to dinner wasn't the same thing as actually *wanting* to go out to dinner, but already she was dressing herself in red chenille, already chasing away the feeling that everyone, everywhere, was managing their lives better than she was. 'It's extremely nice of you,' she said reluctantly.

'Terrific,' cried Micky. 'Say, nine at the Relais Savoyarde? It's on the folksy side but, you know, it's crazy, I must've been in the Alps a dozen times and I never ate *raclettes*.'

Broom went back through to the kitchen, to the limited world she had built. When her eye fell on the table she felt a sudden strangeness, as if she'd caught sight of her own face reflected in a shop window. It wasn't as if she didn't have her gouaches with her, her Chinese inks and brushes; they were sitting beside the tape-recorder, staring at her. She stood stock still, gazing down at the storyboards. Every last sheet was in black-and-white. The term was *grisaille*. A painterly simulation of sculpted monuments, used in the Renaissance. Tone without colour. From the outset, without knowing it, she'd been thinking and working in monochrome.

Acc: iceboy@freeserve.co.uk

I love the text of the future: its palaces,
its silk sheets, its houris

my book of the future
is a bed, a city

My bed is a book of dreams
folded back

Each leaf of the book is temptation
My book is a bed of many sheets

Changed every day, like royal linen,
like concubines

Nighthawk

Lockhart couldn't be quite sure what he felt. He got up from the iMac and prowled the room in the half-light, feeling like a burglar who rummages behind drawn curtains for the cash he's convinced is secreted in the shoebox or jam jar or hot-water bottle. At the back of his mind there was a question he was postponing – something about a supplier name that cropped up perhaps a little too often.

At first he'd felt relieved. It was true that the IT start-up costs seemed inordinately high, particularly since he could have fixed Fraser up with more than one eager beaver who would have designed the website for £300. It was strange that Fraser hadn't asked for his advice on this. The building and refrigeration costs also seemed a bit over the odds, but presumably his father vetted all the major tenders. All in all, there was nothing that couldn't be put down to expansion costs, or to simple inexperience.

He found himself standing in front of the wall cupboard where they used to keep their toys. The tongue-and-groove boarding of the doors was clogged with the paint of decades; runnels and swags had petrified in the course of their descent. Even the iron latch wore a thick bobbly skin of it. He lifted the latch and looked inside. The upper shelves held board games: dusty sets of draughts and chequers and Monopoly. Lower down were the stamp albums and annuals. He saw Superman and Spiderman and Batman, all with chins as cleft and chivalric as Alan Shearer's, all fighting the good fight in faded primary colours.

On the topmost shelf was a butterfly collection, for which he and Fraser weren't responsible, and one of birds' eggs, for which they were. Although the eggs weren't labelled, he recognized the curlew's and the tiny robin's, and the surprisingly beautiful brown-freckled turquoise of the crow's. You pierced each end with a needle and blew out the white and the blood-streaked yolk until the shells were light and empty as boyish heads. The practice was illegal now, and rightly so. He picked up an oystercatcher's egg, remembering the excitement of the hunt, the woven hollow of the nest hot under his marauding hand.

Nead Insecticides. He realized that it wasn't only the frequency of the entries that was bothering him. *Nead,* if he wasn't mistaken, was Gaelic for 'nest'. With a kind of dread he went back to the screen and opened the System file, searching for something bland. An unremarkable-looking file, perhaps, which might contain another, in which yet another might just be secretly, comfortably nesting.

When he found it the hairs rose on the back of

his neck. He forced himself to slow down and scroll through every detail. He took a sheet of A4 from the printer and made pencil notes, checking the two sets of accounts against each other. His mind flew here and there, protesting vainly, like a grouse trying to guard its nest in the heather. For a moment he was tempted to rub out the pencilled figures. Basic accounting hadn't been his best module at HBS; it was still possible that he'd made a mistake. Until he saw the details of the deposits in black-and-white, the nest-egg, the actual stash, he wasn't absolutely obliged to believe in it.

Apart from the inflated IT figure, the mark-ups were relatively small: twelve per cent here, fifteen per cent there. In total some £12,000 had been siphoned off.

When he thought of his father muddling along with his ledgers and in-trays, fury clenched at his stomach. Fraser was on the fiddle, there was no longer any doubt about that. But you could argue that it was their father's abstruseness that had put him in temptation's way. If he didn't trust Fraser, why on earth had he allowed him to take so much responsibility?

The question wasn't difficult to answer: because he, Lockhart, hadn't been there to take it, that's why. If he'd intervened earlier, none of this need have happened. But he'd ducked out, hadn't wanted to know, had hidden his head in the sand, telling himself that if he kept out of the picture Fraser and his father might inch towards something that passed for entente. When all the time instinct was saying that the two of them were partnered, as they always had been, in some drastic family dance.

The end of his pencil bore the vindictive imprints of his teeth. His hands were trembling. He tried to imagine his brother sitting down every day at the screen and painstakingly constructing his fictions. He'd underestimated Fraser's capacity for calculation, if not his capacity for shooting himself in the foot. Where, he wondered, had he learned his little tricks? Fucking idiot that he was. Didn't he realize that someone, in the end, was bound to find him out? Did he think, perhaps, that their father was feeble-minded?

He twitched the blind aside to see the state of the day. It had become beautiful outside. It was the sort of weather – clear and blue and windy-bright – that would have had Frances Lockhart wickedly mimicking the locals. 'Lovely day, though.' 'Aye. But we'll pay for it.'

He checked the Gillfish email. He made a note of the invoices and scanned the mailshots, noticing in passing that Fraser had designed an elaborate header in which a salmon leapt joyously towards a midnight sun. In Sent Mail there was only one item that gave him pause. It was a poem addressed to someone with the screen name Nighthawk. The style was unmistakably Fraser's. 'The sun is in sackcloth,' he read, 'and we in our merits, shivering.' He scrolled quickly through the stanzas, through 'moths of cold', and 'matchstick days scratched on the prison wall'.

The byline at the bottom was Iceboy. A

personal user name? It was almost as if Fraser was laying a trail for him that, if followed, would lead him to the location of the truth, if not to the truth itself. Because Iceboy might have his little personal filing cabinet, but Lockhart did not have the password.

Anger rattled the teeth of the mouse and drove the ugly little arrow on its quest around the screen. Lockhart was reaching the frontiers of his known universe, but the sense of impotence merely increased his determination not to abandon ship. He fished out his mobile and punched in the Rivestre number. When he got through to IT he asked for Barry. Before Rivestre poached him for the private sector, Barry had been with CESG, the Internet arm of GCHQ. The good ship Enterprise still had a few tricks up its sleeve.

When Lockhart rang off he shut his eyes for a moment, digging his knuckles into the sockets, until an aurora borealis flickered on the darkened skyscape of his mind. It took him half an hour to follow the thread of the instructions Barry had dictated. Finally, with a sense of disbelief, he found himself at the centre of the maze. There were items he stared at for a second and elbowed to the back of his mind, newsgroups and chatrooms that were none of his business.

As Barry had said, it was relatively easy to winkle out the bank details, and after that it was plain sailing. He hardly had the heart to type in Fraser's security number. It was so bloody easy it was pitiful. He saw with perfect clarity his brother's face in the firelight of Uncle Boz's room and heard the outrage shrilling in his voice. When he keyed in Frances's birth date the screen obediently delivered the deposits and withdrawals.

He'd known more or less what to expect, but when the moment came it made him catch his breath. The details were there in black and white, fragile and final, like a suicide note. Monies that had swooped into the secret account, settled briefly on the cliff-edge on the credit column, and vanished thereafter like seagulls in a mist.

Lockhart left the house in a daze, but as he strode along the coast path the landscape forced its way in on him. A thin fleece of snow greyed the fields above the shore. On the moor a piebald pony raced and pranced. Orange splashes of lichen stained the spines of the rock promontories which thrust out into the bay, silhouetted by hurrying white foam.

Far out on the slate-blue surface of the Sound he saw a series of eerie flashes, as if someone with a torch was signalling in Morse code from the deeps. After a second he realized that the phenomenon was caused by a shoal of herring on the rise, their swift silver scales momentarily reflecting the sunlight.

Into his mind came an image of Fraser, racing down to the shore on the first day of summer vac. Fraser had started at Fettes that Easter, and all term he had pined, as Lockhart never had, for Callasay. He stood on the rock spit with his tracksuit bottoms flapping against skinny thighs, his arms flung wide, as if to reclaim the span of the sea.

Then felt I like some watcher of the skies
When a new planet swims into his ken;
Or like stout Cortez when with eagle eyes
He stared at the Pacific – and all his men
Look'd at each other with a wild surmise –
Silent, upon a peak in Darien...

At thirteen, Fraser was given to transports. He loved Keats, he loved Coleridge; worse still, he was happy to say so in public. At a time when Lockhart's primary passions were rugby, mountaineering and girls, not always in that order, he'd had to put up with the presence, in the same House, of a sickly younger brother who, in his own cringe-making words – overheard at his school interview and passed traitorously along the House grapevine – 'intended to become a poet'. From then on Jessie was Fraser's middle name, and although threats and even fist-fights stemmed the flow of taunts, they couldn't entirely stop it. Since Fraser seemed oblivious, it had fallen to Lockhart to avenge what he'd seen as affronts to the family honour and the family name. And so on that summer day, while Fraser declaimed – ridiculously, asthmatically – on the shore, he'd turned his back and marched away until he was out of earshot, and each stone he hurled struck the sea scathingly, slapped a curse on his liability of a brother, and skidded into oblivion.

Brow down into the wind, Lockheart breasted the rise and saw the white curve of the beach, which was bounded to the west by the long low headland of Starragan. Out in the bay floated the circular fish pens, enclaves whose surfaces exploded every few seconds into a turmoil of leaping.

Set back from the shore, and served by a small stone jetty and a concrete boat-ramp, were the twin barns of the Smokery, and a squat breezeblock addition he supposed must be the icehouse. New cinders had been spread to soak up the mud of the yard in front, where a white 20cwt van was parked, its back doors open for loading. The sound of Radio 1 drifted up the hill towards him, a cheery prattle aimed at chasing away the demon sloth, which did nothing to strengthen his resolve. He strode on down, towards the timeless light that lay on the wet slate roofs of the settlement. He had never felt so lonely in his life.

Through the sliding doors of the icehouse he glimpsed a long steel table at which half a dozen women were working, their overalls and hairnets luminous white under the ultra-blue glimmer of insectiverous lamps. They were gutting the salmon, throwing them into deep plastic trays of crushed ice. The salmon slithered as if on ball bearings and finally settled. There was an infinite sadness in their surrender, in that moment of stillness before the last layer of ice interred them.

A man in overalls emerged, carrying a tray of oysters, grim and grey in their barnacled shells. Lockhart recognized Davie Donaldson and managed a shy *'Ciamar a tha thu?'*

'Gu math,' Davie replied impassively, as if he met and greeted Lockhart on the shores of

Callasay every day of the year. 'And yourself?' Davie was broader now, and balding. He slid the tray into an aluminium rack in the van. 'Home for the holiday, is it?'

'Aye, just a few days.' Lockhart smiled apologetically, overtaken as always by a need to justify himself for having left in the first place. Not a word of censure had ever been spoken, or at least not to his face, but the sense of guilt persisted. 'Actually, I was looking for Fraser.'

'Well, he'll no be far.' Davie glanced in the direction of the Smokery. 'He was here a minute ago. Away round the back for a fag, likely.'

'Right,' said Lockhart. Separated from the Smokery by a narrow gusty alley was the new concrete cube of a storage shed. The metal door bore the yellow and black HAZCHEM sign. Fraser was hunkered down with Ronnie in the scant shelter of a stack of pallets; the two of them were talking intently. Lockhart heard the secretive sea-sounds of the Gaelic.

'Hey, Lucky.' Fraser patted the pallet beside him. 'Take a pew. Meet Ronnie, fellow skiver and factotum.'

'Mr Lockhart.' Ronnie stood up hastily and ground his cigarette out in the cinders. The fabric of his trainers was tidemarked by mud and frost-melt. He was fourteen, perhaps, or a young sixteen. He had a snub nose and wide blue eyes and a David Beckham haircut that didn't suit him. He turned to go, muttering something to Fraser, of which Lockhart could make out only the Gaelic word for father.

Fraser's gaze followed him to the end of the

257

alleyway. 'Can you believe I was at primary school with his dad? We're pushing on, aren't we, old son?' He held onto the pallet for support and, grinning, pretended to dodder to his feet. 'So, are you up for the guided tour, then?'

Lockhart took a breath and dived. 'Look, we need to talk.'

'What, a heart-to-heart? Well, that'll be worth the wait!'

'Can we walk?'

Fraser shrugged and glanced at the sky, as if hoping for rain. The expression on his face was midway between wariness and boredom. 'I guess we could go down Starragan.'

At the end of the beach the path became a narrow tunnel through waist-high gorse. They walked in single file, for which Lockhart was thankful, since it made conversation temporarily impossible. In any case he'd decided to wait until they reached the rock-stacks at the end of the headland, which would give Fraser every chance to explain himself. 'Havering' was what Agneta would call it: an old Scottish word she had leapt on with delight. 'Stop havering, Archie.' In the distant era of Broom the word had taken on a kind of menace. Havering was what a man did when he could neither leave his wife for his lover nor vice versa. Criminal indecision was what it amounted to, and Agneta had judged him, found him guilty and handed down the sentence. A frozen month on the floor of Fraser's bedsit, with the carpets smelling of stale beer and, outside, the Euston trains squealing as they clove through the morning fog. Vagrant, tearful nights spent learning the lesson Agneta was determined to teach him. Agneta, it had to be said, didn't mess around. He still feared that toughness of hers, but at the same time he admired it. He had a sudden aching impulse to get his mobile out and call her up, ask if he could borrow a bit of her backbone.

Just then Fraser spun round and walked backwards, his outstretched arms grazing the top of the gorse. 'This is the business, eh? Never mind London...'

The rock-stacks were still a good mile off: black top hats rising from white rims of spume. Lockhart decided to make a contract with Agneta. He would not do the cowardly thing and wait till the last possible moment. If Fraser hadn't come clean by the time they reached the burn bridge at the halfway point, he would confront him.

From the semicircular stones of the old sheep-fold two crows flew up, cawing, and swung away to join a low black flock in the sky to the north, skating on the ice of the air currents. Their descent was unanimous and abrupt, a sudden collapse on the horizon of the field. Fifty yards ahead was the burn inlet, which was crossed by a low railway-sleeper bridge. As Fraser approached it he slowed and held his hand up for silence. He was frowning, pointing at a shadow in the shallow water. Lockhart saw the gunmetal-grey slick of an otter's back. It flickered through the shallows and disappeared under a floating bouquet of sea-wrack. There was a sudden flurry as another otter surfaced, dived and struck. For a second the two animals tumbled catastrophically in the water. Then they broke apart, and the vanquished one fled for the cover of the open sea.

'Two dogs,' said Fraser. 'Christ!'

The victor remained in the shallows, submarine-coloured, slowly patrolling the borders of its territory.

Lockhart sat down on the bridge and dangled his legs over the edge. The railway sleepers were bleached and mossy and dredged with blown white sand. He heard the restless click of Fraser's lighter.

'Remember the mussels? Best I ever tasted.'

Lockhart nodded. 'They were that.' They'd waded thigh-deep in the shallows, filling their pockets. It was easy to distinguish the peculiarly intense bluish-mauve of the shells from the burgundy fronds of the sea-anemones, but the clarity of the water was deceptive. Nothing was ever quite where hand and eye expected; instead it was a few inches to the right or left, and at least six inches deeper, so that you were constantly recalibrating your brain to account for the refraction.

Fraser was gazing contemplatively at the bay. He appeared to be entirely at ease.

'So,' said Lockhart.

Fraser looked at him. 'So what, Lucky?' His cigarette, lodged insolently in the corner of his mouth, beat time to the words.

'I know *how* you did it, Fraser. That wasn't so difficult. What I want to know is where it *went*.'

Fraser ignored the question. Lockhart gazed down at the two still shadows they cast across the

260

surface of the burn. He tried to keep his voice steady. 'Obviously I need to know that it wasn't drugs.'

For a second Fraser did not react. Then he laughed. 'God, you're predictable!'

Lockhart rubbed his hands down his jeans, holding in the urge to hit him. 'So what are you playing at, Fraser?' he burst out. 'What are you fucking playing at?'

Fraser's eyes flickered at Lockhart. 'A gentleman without expectations, dear boy, has to make provision. For salary, read pocket money. Or didn't you notice that?' Fraser scooped up sand and watched it pour in a thin stream from the bottom of his fist. His eyelashes lay against the curve of the socket, long and girlishly curled; his lips pouted reproachfully.

Lockhart said roughly, 'He's your father, for Christ's sake, not a monster. You seriously think he wouldn't provide for you?'

Fraser's smile was spiteful. 'Did I hear you mention the M word?'

'Fuck you, Fraser.' It struck him then that it was within his power to put a stop to this, to wipe away the inequality. On the tip of his tongue was the whole sorry saga. Test tubes and eggs. The clinical history of a couple. If he said it, just came out with it, Fraser would know that he, not Lockhart or his non-existent heirs, would inherit the servants' bells and silences of Gillinish. It would be, as Retta would say, the making of him. But a sense of decorum held him back. It was only right that his father be the first to hear the tale, be given time to absorb its futile ending.

Something white and skeletal waved from a rock cranny at the edge of the burn. A crab's claw, wind-dried, light as paper. Lockhart wondered if he was just making excuses for himself. Perhaps he simply couldn't bring himself to say the word 'infertile', couldn't bear to see it mirrored in his brother's eyes or hear its doleful echo on his lips. That seemed nearer the truth. He just didn't feel like giving Fraser the opportunity to feel outstandingly sorry for him.

Fraser sighed. 'You'd never believe me, would you, if I said I did it for the business.'

Lockhart felt a momentary pang of hope. With Fraser, anything was possible. 'We're talking twelve thousand quid here.'

'Yeah. Average wage of a dustman, I'm told. Since you must know, I invested it in dotcom shares. The old bugger knows the fish farm's undercapitalized but he'd never take the risk...' Fraser flicked his cigarette out across the pristine surface of the water. 'You know the rest. What goes up must come down. I bet you were one of the doom-and-gloom merchants on that score.'

Which was indeed the case, although Lockhart had no intention of admitting it. 'You'll have to pay it back, you know.'

'Fuck that for a game of soldiers!'

He knew that Fraser was blustering. He spoke rapidly, pressing his advantage. 'Look, he doesn't have to know. Not if we play our cards right. I can say it was an IT glitch, costs wrongly duplicated – I'll think of something. But the money has to show up, Fraser.'

Fraser was silent for a moment, staring out to

262

sea. His Adam's apple was working. His eyes looked suspiciously moist. Lockhart prayed that he wouldn't decide to burst into tears. 'OK, OK. So it was stupid. But it's not so easy to get your life back on track, you know.'

Lockhart nodded miserably. 'I know, man.'

'I really wanted to surprise him, would you believe?'

Lockhart wanted to believe it, he wanted to think that Fraser had tried to do his level best. When he saw the Stornoway ferry nose out from behind the stacks and steam west towards Morrisdale he followed it with his eyes, clinging for a moment to the comfort of knowing that in a day or two it would carry him away from Callasay. *Speed, bonny boat, like a bird on the wing, on with the sailors' cry.* Then he remembered the next line. *Carry the lad that's born to be king...* 'Look, if you've got shares left, sell them. In the meantime I'll transfer the money into your account.'

Fraser was silent for so long that Lockhart almost lost heart. Then he hugged his knees and stared at him. 'So I guess this is my cue to pledge eternal gratitude.'

'Don't bother,' Lockhart snapped. Sarcasm he could handle; at least it was preferable to the sort of self-pity that could swamp them both. 'Sackcloth and ashes never suited you.'

'It's all right for you! You've always been Mr Clean. I could be Saint fucking Peter himself and he'd still find fault!' Lockhart said nothing. Fraser's face had taken on the aggrieved expression he hated, all the more so because

263

what he said was true. 'Can I ask why you're doing this?'

'Let's just say I have my reasons.' If Fraser honestly couldn't work it out, Lockhart certainly wasn't going to tell him.

A tarmac-coloured cloud had covered up the sun and the temperature had dropped; above the low landscape the sky was gathering weight. Lockhart stood up and rubbed his hands together to warm them.

Fraser lounged on the bridge, his sharp teeth nibbling delicately at the pith of a reed, his eyes narrowly appraising him. He made no move to get up. 'So tell me, what shivers *your* timbers these days, Lucky? What refreshes the compartments fund management doesn't reach? Or is it all Perrier water and self-denial?'

Choosing to misunderstand what he took to be a reference to Broom, Lockhart patted his girth ruefully. 'Does it look to you like I'm denying myself?'

Fraser's face grew thoughtful. On a note of earnest solicitude, he said, 'I mean, it's not as if you even go climbing any more, is it?'

It was the sheer pettiness of it that got to Lockhart. A small thick pain rose at the back of his throat, something like grief for his youth or whatever else was gone and done with. He thought of snow and blue and height, and of a sustained slither upwards, a sensation that at its best had always felt less like human effort than animal instinct, like the spine memory that tells a salmon how and when to leap the waterfall and swim upstream towards the source. *An Giblean,*

264

April: the month of the spawning. Nature's cycles, Fraser said, were at the very heart of the Gaelic language.

With peculiar clarity he saw Broom struggling with the ugly rubber cap. She had one foot up on the old-fashioned hip-bath and she was trying to get it out or get it in. There was a chemical smell of jelly and a precise frown on her face which angered him. He felt awash with her, in awe of her. Her highflown talk of art like another barrier keeping him at bay.

It was he who had started it. Wanting everything, he'd felt capable of being everything she'd ever wanted. Bugger the contraception, he'd said. Everything we do together, the two of us, *that's* art. And he had meant it, too, hadn't he; he'd been so blisteringly certain that he was right, so romantically sure that they should cast their fate to the winds.

'So do you see her, ever?'

'See who?'

Fraser's sigh was high camp. 'She who shall remain nameless, of course. Mata Hari. Miss Jean Brodie. Whatever.'

Lockhart leapt to his feet. 'God, you don't give up, do you?' Turning his back on Fraser, he breasted the sandy bank, unzipped himself, and pissed a wavering arc into the heather. When he thought of how he had been, the heat of regret rose to his face. Mad times, bad times. Bloody Fraser didn't know the half of it. He shuddered to think of the risks he had taken, risks he had no right to take. As for Broom, well, she should have known better. She was ten years older, she

265

already had a lolloping teenage son, for God's sake. If she'd got pregnant it would have been an out-and-out disaster. I mean, bohemian was all very well, but just how reckless could you get?

Below him the burn blethered over tea-coloured stones. Fraser was humming something softly out at the sea, his long limbs splayed loose and vagabondish on the bridge. A charmed halo of midges hung about his head but did not bite. When Lockhart stepped down from the bank he could hear the words.

'*Rien, rien de rien, non, je ne regrette rien.*' Fraser looked up at him and laughed. 'Dear boy, if you could only see yourself!'

Lockhart could no longer hold back his anger. 'So are you staying here to fucking freeze, or what? I've got a fuck of a lot of doctoring to do before I speak to Father!'

To her annoyance, Broom arrived early. She chose a table with a good view of the room, ordered a *kir*, and sat taking everything in: the lustrous little tables with their lustrous little lamps, the dessert trolley with its *tartes aux framboises* and its mountains of meringues.

Next to the revolving entrance door, enticing customers in from the street, stood an illuminated tank in which dark-blue lobsters pursued their last amours and fought their final battles. She and Lockhart, being poor at the time, had never actually eaten here, but she

266

remembered looking in at the lobsters.

When she thought of Lockhart what came back to her was not the solid substance of a relationship, but rather a kind of vibrato, something frail and fervent that had moved the air between them. It was more than ten years since he'd gone back, cap in hand, to Agneta: long enough to grow out of him, you'd think; long enough to see her feelings clearly. But there were some links, it seemed, that didn't break merely because life would be less problematic without them. History hung in there, stamping its tenacious trace on the present, as if intent on proving that it wasn't anything as ordinary as longing that had been flouted, but rather fate itself, the cosmic imperative. She dreamt, still, about Lockhart, and each time awoke inspirited and enhanced, as if the Muse had been breathing on her; for a day or two afterwards she'd live a charmed life from which nothing, not even genius, seemed to be lacking. Which seemed to imply that she and Lockhart should have gone on knowing each other – and certainly she would have wanted to, if it had been up to her, which it was not. Whatever else had changed in the meantime – the Cold War had ended, the Berlin Wall had fallen, even Thatcher had been consigned to the dustbin of history – Agneta's ban, which was total, remained in force, and in all these years Lockhart had defied it only once.

The call had come out of the blue, Lockhart suggesting that they meet for dinner. 'I know the perfect place,' he said. 'It's called the Bleeding Heart.' When he laughed she understood that money had distanced him, as money does, and that this was how he saw her now.

There was a table for two set prominently before an open fire, and too many waiters making an inordinate fuss of *Monsieur* Lockhart; she'd almost expected the chef to come out of the kitchen and shake him by the hand. The walls were lined with art-deco mirrors in which their reflections, warmed by the important glow of the fire, looked secret and sparkling.

She'd always thought of him as young but that night she saw that he was not. He'd grown stockier, sat more squarely at the table. His face was more severe than the one she remembered, as if the features were trying very hard to keep themselves in place. She stared down at the small fish on her plate – so lonely in its corona of contrasting sauces – and tried to explain about Al, her voice halting and fading, because it was only a year since he had died, and although Lockhart heard her out he didn't exactly prompt her. It was his own life he wanted to talk about, her whispering Highlander, his voice like an insistent arm round her waist, pulling her towards him, his need pressing on her as it always had, demanding her complete attention. In his eyes she read impatience and a hollow jealousy; even so, it had been uncannily easy to forgive him, to be touched by his selfishness, by his inability to countenance the existence – even in the past tense – of another lover. Easy to indulge him, as you'd indulge a child who knew no better.

Afterwards, in the inhospitable drizzle, he'd

toured her round Broadgate, where the real money was. He showed her the glass ziggurat that housed his investment bank, the gym that squeezed his morning orange juice and laundered his business shirts. Little bursts of happy laughter escaped from him. He pointed out his exact office window, counting vertically up and then across.

Grinning, he made light of it – 'Aye, well' – this multinational world, its airborne excitable currencies. When he boasted about the price of his sports coat he was playing at shocking her; it was, OK, a wind-up, but his expression was furtive and greedy.

It felt like his right to claim her hand, as always. He rushed her through vine-draped arcades and across black marble piazzas on which their shoes rang out like coins at the bottom of an empty well, every five minutes Broom saying she must get a taxi but in the event never quite managing it.

Around midnight they sat on the stone lip of a dry fountain and she blew on his fingers to warm them, for although it was February he was wearing only a thin shirt and sports jacket. Painfully, she did not let him kiss her mouth. It would have been more painful, however, if he hadn't wanted to.

She had no idea how he'd squared it with his conscience. The whole thing was plainly so dangerous. First she'd been addicted to him, and then to the High Alps, and all these years later – having dumped her, remember, having chosen Agneta in the end – he could still mesmerize her, still build that illicit little snow-cave in the clouds...

She saw Micky limping across the cobbles of the pedestrian precinct. He was holding a vivacious conversation with his mobile. When he caught sight of her he lifted his shoulders in speechless apology and went on talking. Remembering the sticking-plaster on her chin, she waved self-consciously. It was almost a relief to see real life approaching, like a cold shower, like a punishment. The Muse, for Christ's sake! As if she didn't know the picture all too well. Lockhart was an investment banker. It wasn't love that had lifted him up where he belonged; it was money.

Futurist?' Broom repeated with a puzzled frown. 'You mean like Marinetti? Or the Russians – Rodchenko and that lot?'

Micky did his best to ignore the plaster on her chin, which was painfully obvious and really rather sweet. 'Well, I wouldn't go as far as to say I was serving the Revolution... Although they were at the cutting edge in their time, weren't they? Industrial technology as an aesthetic, embracing the new era, and all that.'

'Only because the new era was Communist,' she objected. 'For the Russians, that is. Marinetti became a fascist, didn't he?'

Micky nodded. Actually he had no idea what Marinetti had become, although he seemed to

recall that he was something to do with
Vorticism. Her mouth had perked up at the
corners but her frown – pedantic – said that life
was very far from being a game to her. He
thought of the way a still gaze could transform
itself into a smile through a minor modification.
The eyelid system could remain immobile; it was
just a matter of a small change in the cornea's
brightness, or in the diameter of the pupil. He
was aware that his will, as if of its own accord,
was training itself on holding her gaze and
forcing it to hold his own.

'So what exactly *do* you mean?'

'Well, without labouring the point, you could
see it as a revolution in communications...' Micky
sucked up a ribbon of melted *tôme de Savoie* and
tried to think himself back to first principles.
'You're a visual person, OK? So, for instance, an
obvious example. Once you accept that how we
impact on others depends fifty-five per cent on
how we look and behave, thirty-eight per cent on
how we speak, and only seven per cent on what
we actually say, then everything changes, doesn't
it?' He grinned an apology for the statistics. In
the meantime he observed that her breasts were
softly rounded and her fairish hair curved
pleasantly enough around her face. Wistfully he
reflected that she wasn't old enough to be his
mother, not by a long chalk. 'It's quite simple,
really. The visual predominates, so if you don't
want form to totally undermine content, if you
want to stay in control of the signals you're
sending, you have to have a strategy...' He
beckoned to the waiter and asked for water.

'*Monsieur*,' the man muttered, and without a courteous word flirted a fast turn on his heel and vanished into the kitchen. He was small, thin-hipped, with a broken nose and a practised pout: North African – Algerian, perhaps. Micky didn't like his attitude one bit. '*Raclettes?*' he'd echoed when Micky ordered, with the sort of sneer that aims to send the cowed customer scuttling to the expensive end of the menu. Micky had flashed him the evil eye and asked if he had some kind of problem with that; he was aware that Broom was staring, but for a waiter the guy was way way out of order. 'Oh no, *monsieur*,' he spluttered, 'I meant only, it is a rough dish, a peasant dish.' 'Exactly,' Micky snapped back. 'If I'd wanted *homard à l'américaine* I'd have ordered it.'

The food, admittedly, was basic. What the dish consisted of was a huge heap of potatoes boiled in their skins, thick slices of *jambon cru* and a platter of Alpine cheeses served with a garnish of *cornichons* and radishes. The portable grill came equipped with mini-shovels, on which you melted slices of cheese before pouring them over your potatoes. Broom was absorbed in a struggle with her little trowel, her cheeks flushed from the insistent heat of the grill.

'All I'm saying is, in front of the camera everything's show business, whether it's a prime minister or a plate of chocolate éclairs. Take your cheese, for instance. It's melting, it's hot, it's runny, but try shooting it for an ad and the lens won't pick up the steam or the surface shine, so you have to simulate, with glycerine, say, and cigarette smoke.'

272

Broom made a disdainful face and dabbed with a napkin at a film of sweat on her upper lip. He watched her take out a cigarette and signal to the waiter. An ashtray materialized on the table like driftwood at high tide.

'The point being,' he continued, 'that it takes an awful lot of artifice to make things look natural. I mean, you said you've worked in theatre, didn't you.'

'The theatre has nothing to do with naturalism. The theatre is theatrical, or at least it should be.' Her voice was flat, impatient: a minor rap across the knuckles. She lit a cigarette and blew the smoke away from him.

Micky flashed her a rueful smile. 'Something tells me you really, really don't approve of advertising.'

'Frankly, I'd ban it!' She gave a sour little laugh. 'Once upon a time young people used to have things they aspired to. Now all they're offered is an aspirational lifestyle!'

For a second he was startled by her vehemence. He'd forgotten that demonization came with the territory, it was the price you had to pay. All the same, it was tedious, and he allowed himself a mordant little sigh. 'I can see you're going to be a hard nut to crack!' There were still a couple of loony-left dictatorships in Africa, he imagined; she could always emigrate. 'I guess you'd be with Castro, would you, on Monopoly? Didn't he destroy all the sets in Cuba?'

'So it's OK by you, is it, if there's nothing in the world that can't be turned into a commodity? If all these people waste their talent marketing and promoting and selling. Instead of doing something real. Instead of *making* something?' She ground out her cigarette and glared at him.

Micky ducked down, grinning, behind the shield he had made of his hands. 'Like, excuse me for living!'

The look he received was seriously queenly, as in 'we are not amused'. Which was a pity, he thought, because she had a nice smile when it happened, wide and warm and not entirely innocent. He picked up her cigarette lighter and turned it over in his palm. A Zippo, plain steel. As clear a fashion statement as you could get, and nobody could persuade him that she wasn't aware of that.

'May I?'

'Of course.'

He tapped a cigarette out of the packet. They were Royales, the same brand he'd bought as a boy in Beirut. The old soft-top pack with the galleon logo; a red Crusader cross on the white billowing mainsail. He lit up and took a nostalgic puff. Blond tobacco, pleasant-smelling. 'You know, you really shouldn't overestimate the power of advertising.' He fixed her with an earnest gaze. 'You talk about wasted talent, but to be perfectly honest, the vast majority of so-called creatives are second-raters. Oh, they'll tell you they're going to jack it all in and paint the great canvas or write the great play or whatever, but the truth is they're just fooling themselves.' She was watching him closely, supping up her wine. '*Of course* it's all froth, don't think I don't know it. But when you've been in the business as long

274

as I have, it's not so easy to get out.'

Broom frowned. 'But by now, surely, you could afford to?'

'In a year or two, perhaps. I have thought of writing a novel. A sort of man-who-fell-to-earth yarn.' He smiled at her mournfully. 'But then again, I could just be kidding myself.'

On the ice-glazed cobbles outside, a red-faced giant of a guy was touting sleigh rides to the tourists. He wore a Cossack hat and a sheepskin greatcoat that reached his ankles. His sleigh was high and handsome, hung with bells; in the harness stood a sturdy cob bedecked with scarlet plumes. The *boules de merde* that steamed on the ground below its hindquarters were straw-stippled and looked strangely wholesome, like wheaten bread.

He waved his cigarette towards the scene. 'He feeds it pints of beer, you know,' he murmured, wondering how easy she would be to lie to.

'So you know Sophie Sauvage?' Micky looked at her with surprise.

Broom shrugged. She knew she shouldn't keep harrying him but she couldn't seem to stop. 'Doesn't everyone? I should have thought she was quite a megastar already.'

'Well, she could be, *if* she'll go the route. And it's a big if. Between you and me, I'm still not entirely convinced about Sophie.'

'Convinced about what? About whether she really wants to sell herself?'

When she met his gaze she realized that his eyes were not brown, as she had thought, but a

275

curious light ochre, like the colour of elastic bands, and also that they were mocking her. He had baited the hook and she had swallowed it: out of misplaced loyalty, out of some misguided we-feeling, she had leapt to defend Sophie Sauvage, who quite plainly was the sort of woman who could look after herself.

Outside, snow had begun to float down again in outsize flakes, and she saw squeamishly that it was nothing if not picturesque, this pantomime snow that came to rest on the Christmas tree in front of the church, on the curling beard of the Cossack, and the straight blond patient eyelashes of his horse. The flakes were in such a wrong and strange proportion that the little scene might have been contained in one of those glass domes you find in tourist shops which, when shaken, fill up with dandruff blizzards. For a moment it was as if she too was contained, suspended claustrophobically in glycerine, gazed at through the curvature of glass.

When she'd probed Micky about politics she'd discovered only that he disliked both main parties with equal intensity but would mount campaigns, if asked, for either. When it came to voting he might or he might not, he said; it really depended on the candidate. 'In politics, as in life,' he said amiably, 'I believe in trusting my impulses.'

'Instincts,' she corrected. 'Don't you mean instincts?'

'Instincts, impulses – is there a difference?'

'Actually, yes.'

Micky quirked a merry eyebrow. His intimate

look sparked a sudden fear that she wasn't in command of all the signals she was sending. She felt her face tighten, as if all the muscles were straining to be back in the safe seclusion of the chalet. She quaffed more wine and tried to suppress her self-consciousness. Micky himself had drunk little; she'd noticed how often he covered his glass with his hand when the waiter tried to refill it. She hoped he didn't think she was flirting, which she certainly had been doing with the restaurant at large: swift glances exchanged, smiles of complicity at the antics of a child or the grand entrance of a platter of lobsters – all the small and pleasing signals that inserted her into a communality of good humour, her eyes narrowing and widening, brightening with the lustre of visibility, each glance she received – of interest or curiosity or even of appreciation – each in its own way easing her out of purdah.

When Micky, eyeing her empty glass, proposed brandies, she was surprised by the alacrity with which she accepted. Evidently she still harboured some hope of pleasure, some kind of determination to squeeze the last possible drop out of the evening. In a moment of alcoholic clarity she saw that civilization was based on the ability to separate one concept from another, and that 'market' was an entirely different beast from 'value', but men like Micky were hell bent on gluing the two together.

Revitalized, she leaned forward, eager to impress on him, against all the odds, a great and strong conviction. 'But look at the way things are going! You only have to read the jobs pages to see

277

how pernicious it is. Even in the arts, what do you see? Marketing the arts, developing the arts, promoting the arts – but not a single mention of the actual artists!'

Micky took a last puff of his cigarette and sighed the smoke out through perfect teeth. 'Tell me about it.'

Broom recoiled from the city sarcasm. Thus the Scots after a glass or two, she thought: on fire with our lost causes, our missionary passions. She reached into her bag and slapped her wallet on the table. It was tooled black plastic, with a bright metal button. She felt sorry for it, trying so hard to look like leather. 'OK,' she said. 'Forget it. Let's just get the bill.'

Micky shook his head. His gaze was narrow and exasperated. 'No, I meant, whatever it is, you could try *telling* me.' Feeding her with his yellow eyes.

On her way home Broom stopped at the telephone kiosk outside the station and tried to get through to Heather. Bulletins from the Alps. She told the answerphone: 'I've just had dinner with an advertising executive. Christfathers, talk about sleeping with the enemy.' Moonlight shone on the steel of the railway lines and the silver spray-paint of the graffiti on the bridge. Realizing what she'd said, she corrected herself. 'Don't take that literally.' She chattered into oblivion for a little longer, then, disappointed, she rang off and walked brusquely home across the ice, looking up at the nightline of the Massif from time to time, for encouragement. She felt prim and proud of herself; at the same time she felt very small, about four or five. At the same time she felt enormous, like an unstable snow cornice about to tip its slurry down the mountain, pushing before it an invisible force of winds.

It hadn't been fear, or not exactly. Rather that Al was not a topic of conversation to be delivered up, and after the first craven flush of gratitude she had come to her senses. The temptation to confide had only lasted for a moment. But Micky's stare had been unnerving. It had spied out the winter in her, that terrible need for kindness. In singling her out it had removed her from the ordinary little excitations of the room, the ebb and flow of the collective. It had told her that she belonged not there but elsewhere, in the ranks of the needy and disgraceful. Which was the truth, of course. But she didn't have to like it.

He'd had the impression that she was warming to him, that by sincerity he might redeem himself. 'You're brave, you see. You put yourself on the line. Maybe you don't realize, but not everyone can do that.' There was a second's full frontal gaze as she took the shock of the compliment, then the lashes flapped significantly down. Clearly his instincts had been spot-on: this was her precious secret and how she saw herself. It was then, perhaps, that he'd miscalculated. 'It occurs to me, do you know Hadrian Green at the Saatchi?'

'I don't believe so.'

'Only that he's a mate,' he said casually. 'I could, well, introduce you.'

'Actually I do have a gallery,' she replied, stiff as the silverware.

'Well, of course. But a bit of extra promotion never hurts, does it?'

She shrugged. 'I guess not.' Tweaking the net curtain aside, she gazed out at the night.

'Unless it's totally against your principles, of course.'

She said nothing, just went on communing with the sky or stars. A soft and superior dreaminess had settled on her face, as if she'd seen something out there that truly satisfied her.

'"Without patrons, art is a bird with broken wings",' he quoted. 'Who said that, anyway?'

She laughed shortly and let the curtain fall. 'Lorenzo di Medici once commissioned Michelangelo to make a sculpture out of snow – did you know that? They say it was his finest work.'

Micky closed his laptop and rubbed the heels of his palms up across his forehead. Maybe he shouldn't have retaliated in quite the way he had, but that snooty look of hers had peeved the arse off him. As in, 'holier than thou'. As in, 'methinks the lady doth protest too much'. Not that it was any skin off his nose, but if she wanted to convince him that she actually scorned the fleshpots she was going to have to try a whole lot harder. It was a big bad world out there; it was no shame if sometimes you had to run after the right people. As Robert Mitchum said to his fiancée when his star began to rise, 'Stick with me, kid, and you'll be farting through silk.' It was, he'd always thought, an irresistible proposal.

The orange light of the street lamp, occluded by snow flurries and by the branches of the cypress tree outside the window, flickered across the floorboards. She lay in the dark, rigid and blushing, remembering how the fulcrum of his elbow allowed his left hand maximum pivot on the wrist, how the fingers bent loosely inward and pulsed to punctuate his phrases. Of course he used his hands as any powerful man does, to emphasize the points he wanted to make, but there was nothing polemical about Micky's hand, nothing bombastic. It was a potent hand, but one that laid down no law: hypnotic, rather than emphatic, with something of the sea-anemone in its rhythmic opening and closing.

After she'd finished her cognac she'd made the mistake of eyeing his, which he had left untouched. It was excellent cognac, expensive; to leave it seemed a terrible waste. 'Are you actually going to drink that?' she'd asked.

He shook his head, smiling, his hand hovering, mischievous, above the glass. A moment later he slid the cognac across the tablecloth. 'I knew you wanted it,' he said pleasantly. 'I was just waiting for you to humiliate yourself.'

Then he'd reached out and locked his fingers, quite gently, around the muscles of her upper arm. She had half a second to register the heat of the grip before the hand was withdrawn, about the same time as it took to register the sadism.

'OK, I'm humiliated, so can I drink it now?' she'd retorted, tilting her head back and sipping defiantly. She saw that he was grinning at her, was watching her, in fact, with every sign of affection. When he pulled out his credit card she could have sworn that he flexed it. She said sweetly – had she really been so drunk? – 'You're all going to hell, you know. You lot.'

But Micky had only chuckled at her. 'Do you mean admen or Arabs?'

Broom pulled the blankets up to cowl her head and felt the sweat rise and slide on her belly. The radiators breathed out their infernal heat, but when she kicked a foot out of the covers a chill ran through her. She wondered if she was feverish, hoped so: better to be feverish than accept that she was, quite simply, on fire. Five years of celibacy fanning the foolish flames.

A good fuck. Words slick and simple as a goal or a nail knocked in.

'What I could do with is a good fuck,' she and her single friends – or rather, since none of them could quite face the possibility that the condition might be permanent, those who were *currently* single – would declare after a drink or two, yielding to the fashion for lowdown, laddish words. They'd done enough head counts to be aware that most women they knew of similar age – attractive, talented women, women of wit and appetite – had ended up alone. It was a problem that none of them, strangely, had foreseen. Simon had left Roz for a twenty-five-year-old; Roz had put on weight and laboured mightily to pay the extra mortgage. Heather, who'd inherited sole responsibility for her ailing mother, insisted, not entirely ironically, that it was possible to diversify your erotics. She was becoming polymorphously perverse, she said, with her cats, her cello and her kitchen-garden.

All three of them buried themselves in work, by choice as well as by necessity: it was, they agreed, a lifesaver. It was also an option that hadn't necessarily been open to the women of their mothers' generation. Feminists all, they'd never wanted to be the handmaidens of men, but neither had they wanted to ape them. Yet here they were, feeling, even at their age, an insidious pressure to prove that they were streetwise, up to the minute, and so on.

Broom moulded herself down into the hollow of the bed, as if by doing so she could escape the crudeness that had squeezed itself into the room and winked at her from every shadowed corner.

A good fuck. Words full of spunk and spite, words that made her feel as if she was colluding, if not exactly in a lie, then at the very least in a kind of conceptual sloth. Such a blokeish shorthand didn't come close to describing what sex was, had been, to her, but all the same she adopted it, as the others did, and it wounded her; and in the fault-line between the wound and the hopeless inadequacy of the language was a half-admitted, spasmodic pleasure.

She knew, of course, that Al wouldn't have wanted her to deprive herself of any of the comforts of the flesh. 'Go for it, girl,' he'd say, if he was looking down, if he wasn't too busy setting out the chairs for meetings and photo-copying the celestial agendas, 'go for it.'

As on earth, so in heaven. Hadn't he hinted, more than once, that he'd like her to spread it

283

around? Sometimes after love-making, when she wanted to slide off happily into her sea-sleep, he'd subject his cock to comparisons. 'Come on now, be honest. Wouldn't you prefer something a bit younger?' Nagging and niggling, regretting lost empires of adolescent vigour.

In middle age, women dream of lost trains and missing handbags; men get peevish about their potency. *Torschlusspanik*, Miriam would have called it. Literally: closed-door panic.

She'd tried to laugh him out of it. 'I've had young, thank you very much. If it's all the same to you, I'll stick with the old.'

'There's no reason why you can't have both...' He was wheedling, rapt as an addict, inveigling her in. Until she'd erupted at him.

'Oh yeah, you'd really like that, wouldn't you. That would really make it easy for you.'

The office was decorated in conciliatory colours: beige carpet, blond fabrics, lilac walls with Laurencins. Miriam was a little older than Broom, and attractive in the snub-featured way the French call jolie laide; *she dressed like a Frenchwoman, too, in pale close-fitting linen suits and high-heeled peep-toe shoes. Her ankles were slim, her smile lenient, her bare calves solid and summery.*

She showed them to two chairs angled slightly towards each other; her own chair, which she brought out and placed in front of the desk, formed the apex of the triangle. There were files and papers on the desk.

On the top of a slim pile of books Broom saw Saint-Exupéry's Little Prince, *stranded on his asteroid.*

Al rolled up his sleeves and sat with his forearms levelled along the slatted arms of the chair, surveying the room with undisguised suspicion. Feeling his attention drain away from her and find a new adversary in Miriam, Broom smiled strenuously. It was the Tavistock, for God's sake. She hoped he wasn't going to ask for her credentials.

All week he'd been maintaining – on the grounds of nothing but prejudice, as far as she could see – that the majority of psychotherapists were quacks. Worrying away at her, until what was uppermost in her mind was neither fear nor hope, but rather a cool curiosity about how he would acquit himself.

Miriam had greeted them cordially, and now, cordially, she waited.

Broom was determined not to be the first to speak. He wanted *to come, she reminded herself; it isn't as if I had to force him. He was afraid of getting the heave-ho, he said, the letter of dismissal slipped through the door. She'd already done it once and the memory seemed to haunt him. April was the month they'd been apart and a month was as long as either of them could bear. Afterwards he'd come trembling to her door with tulips, and since then he hadn't been able to mention the word 'April' without flinching. So she should have felt powerful, but that, for the moment, seemed to depend on Miriam, on whether or not she could handle him.*

While she waited for Al to tire of the staring game, she inspected one of the paintings on the wall. She had never much liked Laurencin. Her wistful pastel shades she found too feminine by half. A woman in a

285

frothy dress sat at a table beside a vase of flowers: a young woman of the bourgeoisie, perhaps, waiting trustfully for her fiancé. She looked pale and malleable, as if she had no skeleton supporting her; her hands were formless: white dabs of whipped cream in her lap.

Al shifted decisively in his chair. His grin flared, irritable. 'So change me, then,' he demanded.

Miriam's eyebrows flickered up. 'Do you want to change?' she asked pleasantly.

'Well, I don't want to go on being such a toe-rag,' he muttered, with a sidelong glance at Broom intended, she imagined, to placate her.

She examined Miriam for signs of susceptibility. Miriam might be charmed, but she wouldn't, not yet – not until she had heard him say his piece, his pros and cons.

The initial assessment had been conducted by a stately pearl-blonde therapist who looked like the Duchess of Kent. When she'd asked Broom to list the positive things she felt about Al the words had tumbled from her mouth like fox cubs from a burrow. Paeans of appreciation. What must she have sounded like? A teenager with a crush, a case of arrested development. Al had gaped at her and blushed. But the therapist had seemed pleased. At the end of the session she stood up with her clipboard, smiled broadly and said she would definitely refer them. Afterwards Al admitted that he was relieved. There had been a test and they had passed it. 'Suitable cases for treatment,' he said with a shaky laugh as they headed for the pub.

Bursts of sun raked the room. Once again the word 'incompatible' lurked in the shadows, but at least it

286

hadn't been pronounced yet. She wondered if Miriam had inherited the notes.

The recap had taken five minutes at the most, but it was already clear that Al was running out of steam. His face was vanishing; soon only the grin would be left, hanging like a Cheshire cat's in the air. At the thought that she too would be required to go back over the same ground, she felt suddenly exhausted, as if she might simply ooze off her chair and puddle on the Persian rug at Miriam's feet, where the sun came and went, highlighting the mosaic colours.

'And so...?' said Miriam, turning to her. She knew that the important thing was to sum up as briefly as possible and as neutrally: avoid, at all costs, the resentful whine of the victim.

Miriam listened, her fingers lightly cupping her cheek. It wasn't just the lovers he already had when they met, she explained, some of whom had faded out of the picture, or had been squeezed out by the space she had claimed in his life. The real problem was that he refused to make any of the promises that might have made her feel secure. 'Not marriage,' she said, with a rueful smile, to prove she hadn't entirely lost her sense of irony. 'I've already seen the light on that one. Just some kind of guarantee that he won't rush off today or tomorrow or the next day and sleep with whoever takes his fancy.'

Miriam clasped her hands across a sunburned knee. 'Would you say, then, that Al makes a distinction between love and sex, but it's hard for you to do the same?'

It was difficult to hold Miriam's eyes. She said timidly, 'I suppose.' Perhaps there was, after all, something significantly abnormal about her, a moral

287

spinelessness from which women like Miriam didn't suffer. She stared at Miriam's toenails, which were varnished the uncompromising red of rowanberries. Miriam would know how and where to draw the line. She wouldn't tolerate the things Broom had put up with, things Al had sneered at in the white heat of the moment. Of course she could give as good as she got, but 'Socialism in one cunt, eh?' was more lethal than laughable. Not in a million years could she repeat it to Miriam.

'I keep telling her that my heart is faithful,' Al said. 'It belongs to her and her alone. But that doesn't seem to be enough for her.'

Miriam studied him. Her nod was courteous. 'What you're saying is that your relationship with Broom means a great deal to you.'

Al's grin was fleet and grateful and hopelessly endearing. 'You're telling me it does! I adore her. She fills the sky for me.' He swung one leg over his knee and grabbed his ankle, shooting a bashful glance at Broom. 'I'm bowled over by her, in a way no fifty-year-old man should be!' His foot jigged excitably; his socks were nylon, sludge-coloured, from too many washes.

Once again she was whisked up to heaven and held there, telling herself that this should be enough, even though she knew at the next moment she'd be falling. She watched Miriam absorb the careless clothes, the radiant eagerness. She thought of satellite systems, relaying messages across the invisible armature of space, bouncing them safely back to earth. Her cheeks flamed. She didn't trust herself to smile.

'So do you think it would be fair to say that Broom has made an effort to adapt herself to your existing

288

relationships, but the compromise hasn't really been reciprocated?'

The truth had a plainness to it, a steady, even-handed light. She focused on Miriam's hands, the glint of her rings as she pushed back the heavy fringe of her hair. They were good hands, large-knuckled and strong-looking – strong enough, perhaps, to rein him in. So argue yourself out of that one, she thought.

Al scowled. 'Well, if you're going to put it like that!'

'Intimacy does generally require some kind of compromise,' Miriam offered mildly.

'Well, obviously,' said Al. 'I wouldn't be here, would I, if I didn't believe in compromise.' He sat back and folded his arms, like a man who has made his point.

There was a glint of amusement in Miriam's eyes. 'So by coming here you've already made quite a concession; yes, I see that.' For a moment Broom wondered if she was teasing him.

Al beetled his considerable brows. 'Look, I know we have to get things sorted before I go. That's what I'm here for.'

'Ah yes. Your trip.' Miriam glanced at her watch. 'Which reminds me, before we run out of time, it might be useful if Broom were to say a little about her fears of abandonment...'

'You mention, Al, that your first wife walked out.' Miriam glanced up from her notes. 'My feeling is that there may still be some painful issues here.'

Al bridled immediately. 'I was only married once.'

Broom turned to look at him. 'Actually, you still are,' she pointed out. Her bag lay on the floor beside her chair; its zip was half-open, revealing her cigarettes. She had smoked a quick one while she

289

waited for Al outside, grinding it out among the other butts in the gravel of the forecourt, but now she wanted another.

'As a matter of fact she didn't walk out, she threw me out. But since that was twenty-five years ago, I hardly think it's relevant.'

All week he had been brooding about hidden agendas. He didn't like the direction things were taking. He admitted that he felt coralled by Miriam. Broom said cautiously that she seemed fair-minded. Al said darkly, 'That's because you didn't get the stick!' She thought of saying that it wasn't exactly plain sailing for her either, but the ripples of alarm the sessions stirred in her seemed too murky and archaic to discuss. She worried about that keen and candid gaze of Miriam's, and what it saw in her. The excitement written on her skin, the naked pride of possession when she looked at him. She worried in waves, superstitiously, about any blessed thing that might conduce some kind of archetypal envy.

Miriam examined Al over her glasses. Her surprise was plain. 'You and your wife never divorced?'

Al made no attempt to hide his exasperation. His eyes flashed from Broom to Miriam. 'I'd really like to get something clear here. If I was the marrying kind I'd marry her in a flash, but I'm not, and if that's what's on the agenda there's absolutely no point in going any further!' Gripping the arms of the chair, he levered himself forward, as if signalling his preparedness to make an exit. His face was purposeful and made Broom panic.

She said quickly, 'Sometimes I think, if only I could be more grown-up about things…'

Miriam frowned. 'You see yourself as childish?'

290

'Sometimes I do.' Well, it was true, wasn't it? That was exactly how she saw herself: bad, infantile, uncontrollable. Although she hadn't, for obvious reasons, admitted it, there were times when she came close to despising the clinging jealous creature love had turned her into. The trouble was when you stopped being certain which of your feelings you ought to struggle with, and which ones you ought to be loyal to...

'I know he thinks he's being honest and above-board, but if he so much as mentions fancying someone I feel completely tortured! Even if it's just talk, you know?'

Miriam nodded sombrely. Her face was lit by a sympathy Broom wasn't sure she deserved. Heather – meaning, perhaps, to be helpful – had hinted that she could have married if she'd really wanted to. If marriage had been her priority. In other words, she had some weird stake in unavailable men; Lockhart being a case in point. The perversity of this rang true. Broom didn't care to dwell on the Oedipal implications, but, in all honesty, weren't she and Al a perfect fit? And if so, why on earth was she fighting? She glanced at Al pleadingly. He was studying the sole of his trainer with excessive concentration.

When he caught her eye he let out a stormy sigh and looked away. 'Well, I did sleep with Nicky last week, as a matter of fact.'

A woman carrying drinks across a Brixton bar. Dark cropped hair, an unbuttoned raincoat. She remembered the downward flicker of Al's eyelashes. 'Oh, just someone I used to go out with.'

Her first instinct was to ask or beg to know what she had done. Then her stomach converged on itself and

291

she huddled her arms across the pain. Miriam's hand slid into view, holding a box of pastel tissues. She pulled one out and spread it across her knee, smoothing it flat with her thumbs. It was pale mauve, chilblain-coloured. In the glasshouse heat of the room she stared at it, shivering. What was almost unthinkable, and threatened her with total collapse, was the possibility that she'd become, through no fault of her own, the object of an ungovernable malevolence.

Miriam made a small clucking sound at the back of her throat. At this signal Broom began to sob, a wall of tears suddenly breaking and coursing down her face. There was a definite silence. Through a weight of water she heard Al protest, 'Would you rather I kept it in the dark?' To which Miriam replied, rather flatly and tiredly, 'Perhaps what you have to ask yourself is whether this affair with Nicky is important enough to risk your relationship for...'

Broom heard herself discussed. She supposed she ought to listen. Al sounded dogged and aggrieved; Miriam's voice was measured. Quite frankly, Broom thought she was flogging a dead horse, but she was glad of the voice itself, that lullaby drone which kept her safe and let her cry. There was a clock on the wall, a schoolish thing, for keeping institution time. Perhaps she should just put her hand up and say, 'Absent.' After a while she blew her nose and stopped trembling. She counted the red second-hand around the dial, waiting with a muted patience while life went on without her.

In the coffee shop on the Finchley Road Al took her hand and held it. 'Of course I'm going to call it off with Nicky. Even if it was a big sacrifice, which it isn't, it would still be worth making...'

292

There was a grand piano in the corner and a bentwood hall stand hung with sober hats and coats. Outside, the sun was stark but the shadows in the café put years on him. 'I'd do anything for you. You know that, don't you?' He stared at her, his eyes dark with shock and tenderness.

'The restrictions you fight against now,' Miriam had said, 'you may actually come to relish. One day you might even find them a source of security.'

From Broom's lips the words would have sent him snorting and pawing into protest; the miracle was that Miriam had made them sound so reasonable. He'd listened solemnly, lacing his fingers together and gazing down at the basket they had made.

Then she'd turned to Broom. 'Equally you might have to accept that there are things about Al that can't change, or at least not as much as you would wish. It's possible that you may not be able to get everything you need from this relationship...'

The weights and the balances, she thought: the real miracle is that we're still together. Al bit into a honey-cake, spilling a white dust of icing sugar down his shirt front. She watched him brush at it with the back of his hand, thinking of the skill that had held them steady, and had even, perhaps, persuaded him that she didn't actually want to steal his soul...

'If you really want to know, I'm just so pissed off with myself! To think that I can get to my age and still be, well, like I am...' Setting the cake down on his plate, he looked bleakly at it. 'When I come back from my trip, I can see I'll seriously have to think about going to therapy.'

Was it a sop to her? He didn't seem to be trying to charm her. From the neighbouring booth, separated

293

from theirs by a veneer partition, came the clink of butter knives, the timeless, decorous murmur of Yiddish. *They might have been in Berlin or Hamburg in the Weimar Republic: an old married couple, welded by a hurt that weighed like history. She passed him a napkin. She was, or seemed to be, incapable of not loving him. Of just stopping.*

With a joyless glance at the clock above the counter he bent to pick up his saddlebag, from which his bicycle pump protruded like a weapon, and sat it on his lap.

After six weeks at the Tavistock they'd evolved no protocol for parting. Usually they'd stand together in the forecourt, he with his hand on the bar of his bike, she smoking, procrastinating, afraid to go back to her separate asteroid, as if leaving would open a gulf from which the demons of distrust could once again erupt.

'What you said about how frightening it is: I'm beginning to see what you mean.' *Al grinned mirthlessly, hugging the saddlebag to his chest. She wondered how much the admission had cost him.* 'I'll say this for Miriam: she certainly knows how to lay it on the line.' *For a moment he hesitated, his face lit strangely by relief.* 'Maybe you should come back with me. In the circumstances. I mean, if you think it's a good idea.'

She thought of the bed that once had tempted and repelled her, but that now seemed like the one place where they could both be safe. Un grand lit carré, *a bed wide as the sea, that's how the old song went, and that's how it would be; they were probably too shellshocked for sex but at least they could comfort each other.* 'But don't you have a meeting?'

'Cancelled.' *He was watching her anxiously.*

'Good.'

'So that's a definite yes?'

She saw the smile swell up behind his eyes and cleave his face in two. He glanced absent-mindedly at the bill and dropped a five-pound note on the plate. Normally he would have put his glasses on and scanned it for suspicious increments.

'Definitely.'

Outside, the sun and the traffic fumes hit them. On the other side of the road, beyond a barricade of crawling lorries, a blue sign post pointed the way to the Freud Museum, which Al had never visited.

They walked together to the tube, the bike wheeled awkwardly between them. At the entrance Al gripped it by its curving horns and stretched across to kiss her. 'Don't quote me on this, but I'm bloody glad we've got these extra sessions in September.' He stepped back and raised his hand in a wave. His smile was vehement and self-mocking. 'There's a lot to be said, I guess, for a frank exchange of views!'

Broom's heart melted. As she ran down the steps it occurred to her that what he really meant, of course, and in his own way was struggling to acknowledge, was something else, something deeper. Something that Miriam might have defined as a frank exchange of sorrows.

The padded envelope had come Express. Inside Micky found a video cassette labelled 'Mallory 2000' and a note: *Thought this might be grist to the mill re Sophie project. 'Mankind achieving through spirit rather than technology' kind of thing... Off to Hong Kong to cross chopsticks with our friends the Slopes. Catch up with you anon. Cheers. Damien.*

The medium is the message, thought Micky, balancing the slip of paper on his knee and gazing at the unfamiliar handwriting. It was typical of Damien that, no matter how pushed he was, he would find time to take a personal interest. In the cut-throat world of business that really counted for something. It felt good. It felt inclusive and encompassing, as if a benign eye was watching you from afar and never missing a trick.

He remembered the mega-box of Belgian chocolates that had materialized on his desk the day after they'd pipped Leagas Delaney for the Henkel account. Since he wasn't in the habit of broadcasting his sweet tooth, it was fucking impressive, really, the quality of surveillance. It made you feel like, Hey, here's a guy who makes it his business to find out.

Which wasn't to imply that Damien was a soft touch, no way. Nor would Micky have wished him to be. Damien had a mantra he expected you to follow to the letter, and woe betide the suit who couldn't stand the pace. In your own account group you'd increase your turnover by twenty-five per cent year on year and double your personal business every four years. In terms of profit you'd take twenty per cent on the gross, four per cent on the net, you'd never, ever, lose a client and you'd always *sell* the creative work. And beyond that you could do, well, more or less what the fuck you liked.

Whatever makes you happy, Micky.

Micky went to the window and peeped out at the muffling snow, feeling like a bug in a rug, like a kid in a hidey-hole who knows deliciously that he can be winkled out, if need be, but only by those that matter. With a little bob of his head he sent his appreciation winging its way across continents to Damien.

He slipped the tape into his Halliburton and ordered Eggs Benedict and a pot of coffee to be sent up to the business suite. He took the stairs two at a time and soundlessly, feeling sweet and silly and audacious. On the second landing, faced momentarily by his reflection in a full-length Empire mirror, he pointed his forefinger, jerked up his trigger-thumb, zapped himself once, twice, thrice. The silent bullets spun him back and forth like stuntmen's slaps. He gave himself a blackguard's smile. With Damien at the helm, Svensen wasn't just another bunch of suits, it was family, for Christ's sake; it was as close as you could come to Cosa Nostra.

In the business suite he shoved the tape into the VCR and punched the remote. Whoever had taped the programme hadn't wiped the ads. He caught J. Walter Thompson's bean-toy puppy kak for Andrex, and the infamous tortoise-shags-v. small-Motorola – now a v. endangered species itself, thanks to a concerted complaints campaign by Friends of the Earth. Damien had been tickled pink by the news. He always enjoyed seeing his rivals shoot themselves in the foot.

The camera swooped up a Himalayan valley. Micky watched the grey-green foothills unfold, followed by the glaciers, grimy as washing in the backyards of Birmingham. Then pale blue ridges rose up, until finally Everest filled the screen.

At Base Camp, in a circle of domed tents, the Stars and Stripes fluttered on a pole from which strings of prayer flags radiated like spokes. An earnest German in pebble glasses aligned the topographical features – the Rock Step, the Yellow Band, the site of the 1975 Chinese camp near which Irvine's ice-axe had been discovered. Bods with names like Jake and Conrad deliberated *ad nauseam* about the likeliest location of Mallory's body and, even more importantly, his camera, for only a photographic record could establish beyond doubt whether or not he and Irvine had made it to the summit.

Skip the logistics, thought Micky: just tell us what *happens*. A waiter slithered in with his lunch-tray. He signed the chit and fast-forwarded.

He'd seen the photos of the body in *The Times* but this was different: the high-altitude indigo of the sky, the sun shining straight down on the clean gold parchment of the skin. A Himalayan wind tugged at the ten torn layers of silk and cotton and fine Shetland wool that had kept George Mallory warm. The naked back was hairless, sleek as a tailor's dummy.

The camera focused briefly on the arch of a calf, exposing a protrusion of splintered bone. Otherwise there was relatively little damage. Micky moved closer and squatted down in front of the screen. At some point Mallory must have stretched his hands above his head in a desperate attempt to gain purchase on the slabby rocks, but the impression was of a child, sleeping face down and deeply, spread fingers kneading at his pillow. How far had he fallen, Micky wondered. A hundred feet? A thousand? Had he slipped free of the rope and fallen straight as a die, or swooped circuitously on the beating wings of the wind?

Something caught Micky up and cupped him momentarily in its hand. Teasing subliminal flashes of a film that was his – his dreamtime and his documentary, his whence and his whither. His skin tingled with the traces of memory. Then the camera jigged away and the feeling was gone.

A box of Swan Vestas was produced from Mallory's pocket, and a Gamages invoice, dated 1924, unpaid. There was a faded letter Mallory had written to his brother, but no sign of a camera. The earnest German turned away, mopping at the tears that had pooled inside his goggles.

Micky found that he was moved. He wondered how Sophie would react if she were there. Would she crack up, like the American, or would fascination draw her close?

Climbing is the only sport in which death chooses the winners and the losers.

He saw her kneeling beside the body, in tacit acknowledgement of the price mountains could exact from the fragile mortals who challenged them. Bowing her head in tribute to the man's commitment.

A climber with a British accent produced a Bible and mumbled from the Psalms. '...As a Father, he is tender towards His children...' Micky watched in frustration, teetering on the brink of understanding, willing the camera to return to the body and focus on its frozen passion, the wondrous sheen of its flesh.

The climbers, who had stood in solemn silence, broke ranks and scattered over the rocks. They were gathering stones, bringing them back, heaping them on top of the body.

Micky shook his head, aghast, as the corpse was blotted out by the growing grey cairn. What made them think they had the right? Out of some half-assed concept of respect they were burying him, destroying every trace. One of the most potent images of the century – an ikon that should be preserved in perpetuity for everyone – was disappearing under a dull grey cairn!

He snatched up the remote and hit the rewind. The stones flew left and right, exploding away from the body. He saw the climbers trot backwards and replace them on the scree. When the smooth bald back was disinterred he paused the tape and stood drinking his coffee in gulps. His mind was airborne now, raised to a pitch of alertness that was almost erotic. If you could film a climber falling, you could also film him resurrected, bouncing to his feet, soaring upwards until all the damage was undone and he alighted, gently and gracefully as a bird, on his original stance.

It occurred to him that Sophie's frostbite could also be rewound. The narrative would begin with a swollen slug-black thing in a surgical dish, and then the scalpel would swoop up and back, and the severed section would be reunited with the joint. At this stage the finger would be waxy-white, a chilly candle slipped inside a thermal glove. Later a pink and lively digit would appear, one that could curl round the handle of a toothbrush, smoke a pensive cigarette, or hold the comb that winnowed through a tangled mop of hair. He wondered if Sophie ever felt the loss, or mourned the missing joint, or woke from wistful dreams that reinstated it.

Once again he saw Mallory sleep, pristine, in his amphitheatre of space and silence, and quite suddenly his thought process was clear to him. No image so epitomized the risks that Sophie took, the stakes she played for. OK, the flow of her limbs up an overhang, or the space falling away in thousand-metre strata below her feet: all that kind of stuff could raise a *frisson* of fear in the onlooker. But the trouble was that Sophie herself was simply so alive – adrenalin pumping through her like electricity through a cable – that the eye of the mind, paradoxically, didn't really register her as mortal, but rather as some Lara Croft-type goddess, involved in a game which was digital, and therefore endlessly repeatable. You could sense the fear to some extent, but you couldn't truly grasp the essence of the thing that could be lost. When death was out of shot, how could you really truly understand what *life* was? As long as that crucial component was absent, you were missing out, surely, on full exposure to the experience...

Micky felt the rush of a creative high, his synaptic shutters clicking open to reveal vistas of excitement. He could see it clearly now: his missing link, his marriage made in heaven. The Trampa logo. The title: *High Risk*. Superimpose a quote from Sophie. *'Real adventure bares the soul.'*

The contrast between Mallory, encrypted in death, and Sophie in red-blooded action. Totally visceral. Nothing else could drive the message home as forcefully.

Oh, you bright boy! Oh, you clever Mick, you! He arched his clever feet and rounded his shoulders. Sweeping his arms back and up, he swivelled on his heel, scissored them, and floated round in a Tai Chi pass. When he came to a halt his outstretched hands pressed gently at the obedient air. He observed them for a moment or two and let them fall.

For Words and Pictures they could mock it up, splice the Mallory image in with some shit-hot footage of Sophie. It would mean going way over budget, but so what? The results would more than justify the expenditure; the results, in fact, would be just awesome. Then, once the account was in the bag, why not go for the full monty, fly Sophie out to Nepal? Toby's arm was eminently twistable, and when it was make-or-break time on the global market, outfits like Trampa weren't going to go in for penny-pinching.

Micky's eggs were cooling but he had lost his appetite. Damien was the man he wanted to speak to, like a.s.a.p., like immediately, but Damien had given no indication when he would be back. Not that he couldn't go ahead without Damien's say-so, but he'd prefer to check things out and have his input. Maybe Alice had a number for him, or could send a fax; she'd said she was manning the office over the holiday. Alice was Jewish, bless her little kosher socks, and apart from that the bonus was worth it.

Again the night's snowfall had been excessive. Since dawn the valley had echoed with the sound of the gun that, according to the Tourist Office, could trigger avalanches on fifty known slide-paths over a range of five miles.

As soon as Broom spread the storyboards out on the table she knew that the morning would flow nowhere. How could she ever have thought that the Faust project would be easier or more pleasurable than painting; an escape, for a while, from the demons of self-criticism? It was clear that the opposite was true: when the stakes were lower, failure was even more ignominious. Doom settled like a crow between her shoulderblades and told her that everything she tried to create would come to grief. She was, in fact, a fraud. She was what she'd always feared she might be: a second-rater with vast pretensions.

Without the rectitude of work the prospect of the day appalled her. She'd accepted the commission under false pretences. She'd have to tell Daniel that she wasn't up to it; she'd insist, of course, on repaying the advance. He'd be angry with her, and with reason; worse still, he'd be disappointed in her, because she'd let him down.

In a burst of panic she backed away from the table and stood trembling by the french windows, pressing her belly against the cold glass of the pane, as if a scan might thus be made that would pronounce in her favour and prove what was in there was not stillborn, that she was not, after all, a *fruit sec*.

She had a sudden urge, childish in its violence, to rip up the roughs and snap her chalks in two and spatter her Chinese inks across the kitchen floor. Instead, she let out a moan – hateful in its absurdity, for no one heard – and, throwing on her anorak, she banged out of the apartment and headed towards town.

The landscape was a room that crowded in on her. She forced herself to notice things – a yellow post-box, a golf umbrella striped in orange and blue, two baguettes poking like a V-sign from someone's Codec bag – but noticing was not seeing, and nothing was lucid. Everywhere she looked, all her lovely distances were closing down; even the Massif withheld itself under a gloomy skirt of fog. Her nose dripped. She blew it and walked faster, trying to think not of what was behind her – shame like a dog, locked and cowering in the chalet – but of what was ahead: the slush of the main streets, the beckoning lights of the shops. If form was the mirror in which you sought the contours of the self, perhaps she had to accept that the mirror was broken. There was no template lurking there, no hidden correspondences. Nothing she could mend or fix.

She fled into the *confiserie* and managed to effect a purchase: *marrons glacés*, eight fat ones in a gilded carton, a Christmas gift for Daniel. Instinct drew her towards the pharmacy in the arcade behind the *poste*. Heather was fond of Roger et Gallet soaps: *Lavande, Iris, Oeillet mignardise*. She pushed open the door. Inside, the

304

bordello smells were comforting. The bottles on the shelves invited. Lotions *corporelle*, improving shampoos, phials of plush perfumes such as L'Air du Temps and Sortilège. There were pots of chamomile and feverfew, Bach flower remedies to lift the female mood, HRT pills in pink and beige sachets, whose trade names called to mind obscure post-Soviet republics.

In a fever of anxious greed she stood by the soaps, sniffing the pretty boxes.

At the skincare counter she sampled half a dozen creams and bought none: *crème multi-régénerative, anti-rides*, and so on. She poked her finger into the jars and smeared the stuff lavishly on the back of her hand. The cream looked milky and tempting. She wanted to bring her smeared skin to her lips and lick it off. When a teenage assistant sidled up and confided charmingly that she herself could vouch for the Ultra-lift, Broom hiked an incredulous eyebrow. '*Ah, oui?*' At her age, with her skin, who did she think she was kidding? She turned back to the soap display and chose *Muguet des bois* and handed it over to a girl with a master's degree in Grooming. Behind the counter the Clarins model on the poster was radiant and *naturelle*; her sun-struck hair and sky-blue eyes exuded an air of national superiority. Frenchwomen, thought Broom; however do they do it? That immortal sisterhood of *chic*: vanity understated but also unabashed. It was impossible not to ache to be included; equally impossible, however, not to feel a definite urge to clown and camp it up, prove that the whole thing was craven and dishonourable...

305

She paid for the nattily wrapped soap and left the shop, shutting the door on its buttery lights and little flatteries. Outside, she paused to read the daily *météo* printout in the window. The forecast was for more snow to come, *beaucoup en montagne* but also *en plaine*. She searched in vain for the magic word *'ensoleillé'*. It was as if even her ally the sun had deserted her, taking with it the last of her lustre. She put her sunglasses on all the same, and turned up her collar and saw her reflection, bulky and characterless, in the plate-glass window. *Une femme d'un certain âge.* A woman, moreover, who was beginning to see why Garbo never forgave herself. For to be old was bad enough, but to be old and sad was quite beyond redemption.

As always when the light withdrew from her she heard at the edge of the shadows an echo of her father's voice, comic, bombastic, husky from cigarettes. 'I'm surrounded by bloody women and I canny even get ma tea on time!' A scolding she'd always assumed was meant not for her but for her mother and grandmother, meant to make them scuttle. Some kind of nod or wink, perhaps, granting her immunity. She'd only been twelve or thirteen, a late developer – too young, surely, to be included in the bloody women category...

Her face tried to fight back. Robbed of elasticity, it attempted to smile at itself, as if the appearance of cheer would drag the muscles out of danger. She was conscious of a forsaken, aimless drumming on the inside of her skull. As she set off across the square the rhythm stood in for her own; her feet moved briskly to its jaunty beat. Not until she'd settled herself on the terrace of the Café des Couronnes did the words catch up with the music. *You are my sunshine, my only sunshine...* Carl Perkins jamming with Elvis and Jerry Lee Lewis. Funeral music. It was the track she'd requested, sweet and raucous and ravaged. Dexter had searched the archive for days until he'd unearthed it.

Snowbanks were backed up against the kerb. When the waiter came out she ordered a *café crème*. Under sagging cloud she lit a cigarette and stared at things, blankly wishing them comfort. The green mittens she had taken off and stacked one upon the other, the octagonal gold rim of the coffee-cup, the silver spoon with the chamois crest on the handle. Automatically she took out her small hard-backed sketchbook, transferred her cigarette to her left hand, and took her 2B pencil in her right. The clean page was bland and white as cloud.

'Can I join you? Do you mind?'

She looked up, startled, and saw Micky. He was standing over her, his hand flirting with the back of a chair that was demonstrably empty.

Once again she was shaken by the mysterious mechanisms that are called coincidence but which work to connect one life with another. Beirut, where Al had learned his infant lessons from the Jesuits. *Give me the child of seven and I'll show you the man.*

'But you don't look like...'

'...an Arab?' he'd supplied last night, as she groped for the acceptable term. 'My father was Irish. His name was Jerome, like the saint, ha ha.

He pissed off when I was a babe in arms.'

Jerome had met his mother, Latifa, Micky said, while working for one of the big US construction companies in the Lebanon. After her parents were killed by Phalangist snipers in 1954, she'd agreed to marry him. 'She was alone, she was vulnerable...' He'd shrugged then, his fluent hands appealing for understanding of Latifa, and the poverty of her choices.

'Not at all.' The lie was out of Broom's mouth before she knew it. Too late she thought of all the plausible excuses she might have offered. Montjoie was a small town. Now she would be running into him everywhere.

When he took off his sunglasses she saw that his face was not as she remembered it, and once again she was conscious of a sensation of slippage. His woollen hat, pulled down to his eyebrows, hid the cosmetic blackness of his hair; his jaw looked more emphatic, his skin stretched with cheerful ruddiness across his cheekbones.

Calling for a *chocolat chaud*, he sat down and said, as if there had been no interruption, no night between, 'Let me tell you about Latifa.' And when he said that his whole face changed again, like clouds do. The upper lip mournfully lengthened, two deep grooves etching themselves from nose to chin, while into his eyes stole such a genuine expression of sweetness that she was transfixed by the sudden resemblance to Al. The likeness was accentuated by the way he sat back and folded his arms across his chest like a challenge, so that she clasped her cold hands between her knees and, with the hollowness of

308

inevitability, said, 'Yes, of course,' feeling that she had no choice but to listen.

Latifa's life-story began in Palestine. In 1948, said Micky, after word spread of the massacre at Deir Yassin it was clear that no Arab was safe in the state of Israel. Sunni or Shia, Christian or Druze, they were all the same to the Jews. This, at least, was what Latifa's parents firmly believed.

Latifa was sixteen when the Swaids left Galilee and fled across the border to join their Lebanese cousins in the mountains of the Chouf. Their farm had been abandoned – the orchard, the tobacco fields, the whitewashed stone house with the grapevine caressing the side. The house had been locked and shuttered in the hope – vain, as it turned out – that it would not be burgled, and that one day, when the troubles were over, they would be able to come back to their village and reclaim their rightful property.

In a tin box on his lap Latifa's father carried his title deeds, his tax returns and, wrapped in a silk handkerchief, the solid iron doorkey with its ornately decorated handle. The title deeds, which dated back to Ottoman times, bore the royal coat of arms and the monogram of King George VI, and were signed and sealed by the British Mandate.

They travelled by donkey-cart, with a few goats trailing along behind them. Latifa sat in the back of the cart with her mother, her bicycle, the best copperware from the kitchen, several sacks of oranges and dried maize cobs, and a fine Ottoman carpet that had been intended for her dowry.

If the average person cries sixty-five litres of tears in a lifetime – a fact Latifa had learned quite recently in school – her parents must have used up half their allowance in the five days it took to reach the sanctuary of the Chouf. What she recalled later was how determined she was to sit up far straighter than was prudent – given the sniper-fire that sounded intermittently in the foothills and olive groves a few hundred metres from the road – simply because she could not bear to see herself as helpless in the face of events, nor to be seen as such by those who stared from the roadside at the passing cavalcade of refugees. Her parents were old, and because of this they were afraid, and although she was sad for them and their trouble she held something of herself apart from them, and for hours on end sat in a silent blaze of irritation, so unwilling was she to admit that she, Latifa Swaid, must suffer as victims suffer, must feel defeated as victims feel defeated.

Out of that same defiance she had put on her best red dress with the gold embroidery at the hem, and all sixteen silver bangles, one for each year of her life. When she held her arm over the side of the cart her fingers swam through hot tides of dust and all the bracelets jingled, and if she felt her hand dragged back by the sorrowful undertow of Galilee she knew that her will was strong enough, not only for herself but also for her parents, strong enough to urge the cart on towards the country where a better future lay in wait for all of them.

A snowplough came, stately, into the square,

bright yellow, with a cutting prow. Its hydraulic noise drowned Micky out. He pressed his lips together, frowning, while he waited for it to pass.

'The wretched procession inched north. At nights when they bedded down at the roadside the Great Bear was a skeleton that curved across a quarter of the sky, and the donkey munched on maize-cobs, interrupting its feed only at the thud of distant mortars or the shriek of a ravaged gear-box on the road, when it would raise its head and stand quivering, the whites of its eyes filled fleetingly with moonlight.

'And although in the daytime Latifa was dutiful and wiped dust and tears from her mother's face with a handkerchief dipped in rosewater, her mind stood always apart, counting its plans like worry-beads. First she must finish her schooling; then, afterwards, she would study medicine and qualify as a doctor or a surgeon, for if everyone were to sit around beating their breasts who would be left with the strength to do anything or change anything, and so how would all the wrongs – for wrongs she knew they were – be righted?

'She was the sort of person who gives too much, who gives herself away to everyone. She died young: that's the way it goes, doesn't it? At thirty-six, when she was still young, you know, still beautiful.'

Broom sat mesmerized, watching the slow march of her suspicions. Here was a man who loved his mother. Not a gay man, perhaps, but possibly one that Miriam would describe as mother-ridden. His enchantment with Latifa was so infectious that she could almost hear the swish

311

of her dress, feel the weight of the thick gold threadwork at the hem. Presumably she had loved him very much. It was hard to imagine what it must be like, to know that you'd been held so close and so preciously, like a new egg.

'In Beirut,' he said, 'everyone's so keen to be heroes, they forget about the real heroines.' Broom nodded mutely, studying his face. It was his eyes now that would not meet her own. Just then the café owner came out to inform them that it was snowing and that he had no umbrella for the table. *'Oui, d'accord,'* they replied, *'ça ne fait rien.'*

'Won't you come inside?' he invited, sternly, but they said no, and pulled their hats lower over their ears, and stuffed their hands in their pockets, and sat on.

Broom plodded back to the chalet in a deepening blizzard. The wind was veering into the north. There would be no mountain hike this afternoon. She thought of the softness of Micky's skin, the cunning space-age micro-fibre of his sports clothes, all the logo'd glitz and gloss that worked to fill the world with painful doubting envy. Yet under the surface lay sites of darkness, an archaeology of damage: Beirut the burned and broken city, catastrophic as Dresden. Listening, she'd begun to be aware of a shift or easing in her own condition, as if some transfer had been effected, some equalizing of the general weight. She was sorry, now, that she'd been so quick to judge. As always, her recoil from others, her prickliness, had been a kind of self-protection.

When she'd leaned forward to assure him of her attention, kindness came up from her as if from a well, and although it was of a sort that was meant for others some of it spilled onto her, so that she found she could touch her hair more tenderly, and even forget about the wrinkles on her face.

Broom had of course no memory of the war but her imagination constructed images that merged with the scraps of information she gleaned from books and films and occasionally from her unwilling parents. By April 1941, fifty thousand civilians had been killed in the Blitz. What she knew was that her mother had been in London at the time, working as a clerk in the main post office in Trafalgar Square. Every night when the sirens sounded she went down into Maida Vale underground station with the other tenants of the boarding-house where she lived; those included a world-class soprano, a conjuror, a couple of struggling actors and a lady spiritualist whose eyes were milky with the onset of cataracts.

The spiritualist explained that she and her many colleagues across the country were fighting their very own Battle of Britain. Every night, she said, whether apart or together, they sat in silent concentration, holding the British Isles within their Cross of Light. This in no way resembled the Swastika, which was a perversion, she explained, of the original symbol, but a cross of light within a circle. She and her colleagues sent out this pure white signal of love, because they believed that Hitler's armies were the harbingers of hate, particularly the hate of other races. It was a battle, she explained, of light against darkness.

By 1943 the spiritualist churches were proliferating. So many loved ones had been lost abroad and so few bodies had been returned for burial. Surveys showed that a quarter of people across the country, and two-thirds of women, believed in the paranormal. The Ministry of Information could no longer afford to ignore the phenomenon. They saw that such popular currents could be marshalled in the interests of national morale. Within a short while the same poster appeared in every air-raid shelter and underground station: a cross with a rose at the boss, surrounded by a circle, and the legend 'The Forces of Darkness Halt before the Cross of Light'.

Broom's father was in the RAF by then, flying sorties over Germany: Bremen, Hamburg, Düsseldorf, the Ruhr. Later the bomber squadrons penetrated further, droning dangerously south and east, to Halle, Leipzig and the Elbe. In the 700 bomber raid on Dresden, thirty-five thousand people were killed in a single night. Much later Broom learned of the ninety asphyxiated young girls discovered sitting in a basement as if still alive, about the people sucked feet first into the firestorms, about the deranged zoo animals – tigers, zebras, even a giraffe – found wandering among the ruins of the streets. Of course her father wasn't aware of any of this; nor could he have known that the dome of the

Frauenkirche, which was almost as tall as St Paul's, miraculously stood until the next morning – a day that happened to be both Ash Wednesday and St Valentine's – when, with a whisper of submission, it collapsed.

On his way back to the hotel Micky had stopped at a novelty-shop window full of toy marmots. They had snug brown fur and two cute white squares of felt for front teeth that made you want to stroke them. There were ski marmots and climbing marmots, windsurfers and scuba-divers. The scuba-diver came equipped with flippers, an oxygen cylinder, the works. It made him laugh out loud: it was so obviously, so perfectly, the Christmas gift for the boss who had everything...

If Micky himself had been the architect of Damien's life he couldn't have designed it better. Damien enjoyed beach summers at the Hamptons and winters in Mauritius; for skiing he kept an apartment in Val d'Isère close to the slopes and, more importantly, to Dick's Tea Bar. In his Westminster house he had paintings by Kitaj and Kiff and Clemente, and a sound-system so expensive that he would tell no one what it cost. As a counterbalance to these indulgences he had a social conscience that took him trekking in the Amazon for Save the Rainforest, and swimming with dolphins off the coast of Clare to raise the profile of the campaign for dolphin-friendly nets. From where Micky stood, Damien's life was zestful, creative and perfectly appropriate. It was also enviable, OK, but for some reason envy didn't enter the picture for him. Quite the opposite, in fact. He was glad that it was a good life, and in its own way exemplary, as far as he could see. For what sense would there be in following a general who gave his foot-soldiers nothing to aspire to?

The lugubrious voice on the *météo* line confirmed that the coming weekend would bring a window in the weather. According to Sophie, some of the more spectacular routes were easily accessible by *'frique* – the north face of the Faille, for instance, or the vicious-looking *gendarme* on the Diable – so one good day should give them time enough to sort the shoot.

He called Alice back and requested the usual suspects. According to her email, Damien had gone scuba-diving on the Kotobashi launch and was temporarily unavailable. It was, Micky decided, an implicit OK. If Damien felt the need for a conference, wild horses or, more to the point, tiger-sharks wouldn't keep him off the Satphone.

Alice had only just arrived at the office, thanks to a road-rage incident in Park Lane, on top of a cracking hangover. While Micky listened to a string of toxic expletives he contemplated his surroundings through Alice's eyes: the room kindly lit and softly spotless, the desk gleaming, the mountains modest as maiden aunts behind the misty voile curtains. It occurred to him that he was, after all, in no great hurry to leave the area. He might even consider buying himself a little studio apartment along the lines of Damien's, which friends like Alice, and perhaps the odd deserving case like Broom, could use when he wasn't in residence. If he had time he might even nip over to Val and recce a few estate agents. He could take the opportunity to check out Renate Kessler – arguably the best female downhiller in the world and no dog either – thus killing two birds with one stone, as well as justifying the outing. It would be as well to have something up his sleeve, just in case Sophie blew it.

There was a pause while Alice's superlative brain logged on to the matter in hand. 'Why don't I try for Fluff Henderson?' Her cough was vintage Gauloise, and it lasted. 'Does a lot of mountain stuff,' she added indistinctly. 'Won that big prize, yeah? If he can't we'll go with Christof. I mean, if you're sure it's all OK with Damien.'

'It's cool. Keep trying him, by all means. But believe me, when he sees the footage he'll thank me. *Carpe diem*, love.'

'Roger, you jammy bastard.'

Micky agreed, with a commiserating laugh, that some people certainly had it easy. 'I've got Luca on hold, so we just need make-up. His wife's had another *bambino* but he's still up for it. You know Luca – have scissors, will travel. Get back to me a.s.a.p. on Henderson, will you?'

'Will do.'

'Carruthers, you're a marvel.' Micky smacked two kisses into the receiver and rang off. It was all coming together. By the time Damien surfaced from the South China Sea the package, with any

317

luck, would be signed, sealed and tied up with red satin ribbon.

Christmas in Hong Kong. Micky smiled a nostalgic smile. He'd been there often enough himself to know the kind of hospitality that was on offer.

Inevitably, speculation about the CEO's sexuality was rife, but although Micky wasn't above lending an ear to office gossip he'd never allowed himself the luxury of joining in. If you ride with the herd, as they say, you get shit on your shoes, and as far as he was concerned Damien had a right to expect a certain amount of loyalty. From what he could make out, in that department Damien was a romantic at heart. Rumour had it that although he wasn't one for expensive gifts of jewellery or lingerie, when he went out with a woman, no matter where she was in the world, she'd receive a flower the next morning, and if they'd been listening to a particular CD she'd get that as well.

It struck him that he didn't know what kind of flower Damien sent to his girlfriends; his information didn't extend to the actual species. A singular flower, clearly. Definitely not your bog-standard bouquet of carnations or chrysanths. A rose would be the front-runner, although perhaps a rose might be a little too loaded. An orchid, then. Something with enough star quality to stand on its own. Something that would signify.

Perhaps he should steal a leaf, as it were, from Damien's book and send a flower to Broom. It would be a nice touch. Broom whose name called to mind those melancholy yellow wands that waved from the rocky outcrops on the summits of the Chouf. A hardy mountain flower. More of a shrub, actually. Not the sort of thing you'd find at your average florist's.

When in doubt, delegate. He added a note to the list in his organizer: *Flower – ask Reception.* He would name a price and stipulate a single bloom, but leave the choice of species to the experts. The card must be handwritten, though. *Manners maketh the man*, thought Micky.

In her dream Broom ran the gauntlet. She had to make her way between two columns of men who spat on the ground as she passed. She was in no particular country, but there were echoes of Islam, of North Africa. She stumbled along the corridor the men had made for her. In the face of their scorn it was impossible not to feel ashamed, even if she didn't know what *of*. She wished her hips and her breasts would vanish. She became aware, then, of an alteration. As she proceeded along the line, the molten gobs of spit congealed in front of her, the blobs and spatters on the pavement solidifying into lapis, cornelian, jasper; forming, where they fell, a glittering mosaic inlay.

What she remembered was Al's grin, innocent and democratic. *'Ici ma chère amie.'* They were standing at the desk of the small sea-front hotel on the Cap Afrique, signing the register.

'Call me *ma femme,* for fuck's sake,' she hissed,

319

smiling vehemently at the *patron*. But it was already too late. The town wasn't yet on the tourist track; word spread quickly, a ripple of gossip along the harbour-front, or this is how she imagined it. A certain hooded gaze in which she read contempt. Al the optimist hadn't wanted to believe her.

What she remembered was the ribbon of blood running down her wrist, the surprise and censure in the eyes of the diners. It was Christmas Day; they'd been having lunch outside a restaurant on the quay, a few doors along from the hotel. After the first course she'd gone inside to the Ladies. She sat on the loo, peeing happily. Then there was a crash. She looked up and saw a fist. Glass sprayed down on her from the shattered fanlight. She caught a glimpse of a grin and shouted. There were two of them. When it struck her that they had gone to the trouble of standing on a chair she was briefly amazed. Then she saw that the flying splinters had sliced her hand open.

What she recalled most vividly was the red spatter on the tiled floor of the dining room as the language racketed clumsily out of her. *'Des gens ont cassé la fenêtre pour me regarder. Ceci c'est un pays civilisé ou non?'*

Behind a potted palm there was the flicker of a white jacket as one of the culprits slipped soundlessly through the bead curtain that led to the kitchen. The *patron* fetched iodine and dressed her hand with lint. *Madame* must be mistaken. No such thing could possibly have happened. Not in his establishment. *Madame* had closed the door too abruptly, *peut-être,* thereby dislodging the glass.

She'd wanted to go to the police but Al had talked her out of it. 'That might not be such a good idea,' he said sombrely. She could feel him weighing things up, struggling to believe her version. Sexism v. racism. Europe v. Africa. The checks and the balances.

After she flew back to London she saw from his journal that he'd gone on arguing with himself, and had come down, belatedly, on her side:

No matter what concessions she makes in the way of dress or demeanour, the very existence of an independent woman is an affront to the male Islamic world view, whose internal logic sanctions the punishment of those women who break its code...

She'd had to force herself to read the full analysis. I've become a cause, she thought cynically: so now he can fight for me. Later when she came back to it more calmly she detected an element of remorse. The journal entry was not only an endorsement of her position on what Al called the fault-line between Europe and Islam, it was also as close as he could come to an apology.

'Shall I put "Wife"?' said Nurse Ronnie-short-for-Veronica, glancing up from her clipboard. She was breezy and athletic, with a bracing Irish brogue, and bore absolutely no resemblance to the fragile one that Broom already knew.

'God, no!' she cried. 'He'll kill me.' She felt ragged and proud, euphoric as the patient who'd been

321

wheeled from the lift as she brought Al in. High as a kite on the pre-med.

Professor Rhys-Evans turned from the bed. 'In that case, my dear, we'd better not, had we?' His smile was expert and sustained her. He was quick and slight, with energetic small hands: the best neurologist in the country, Delia had said. The tweed of his Sunday suit was a crosshatch of all the heather and bracken hues of Snowdonia. It evoked an ordered world in which people had Sunday lunch and oxblood shoes and Labradors. She imagined him being paged on Hampstead Heath, thrusting the dog's lead at his wife, hurrying straight to the hospital. Possibly Philip's Radcliffe buddies had pulled a string or two. 'A challenging case, Professor. You remember young Hargreave, of course? His brother. They're flying him in from Asia Minor.'

In the February dusk the lights of St Thomas's shone out like a beacon across the grim maundering river. Sam and Dexter were still in the air somewhere, getting rat-arsed, she presumed, over Central Europe, unaware as yet that Al had been safely signed, sealed and delivered.

He was breathing by way of a tube inserted into the base of his throat, a ribbed plastic oesophagus through which the ventilator pumped oxygen directly into his lungs. The machine made a measured hiss, a sound like the sea breathing. In the background was a hum of nurses talking, nurses under instruction, nurses passing on case reports at the changeover of a shift, exhaustively detailing procedures: adrenalin levels, nutrition, physio, ice-blankets, antibiotics.

Because of the risk of infection, Didi's tulips had been surrendered at the door. Ken McBurney had ushered her into the ward but she'd taken one look at her fallen father and let out an awful howl. Tears spurted from her, and curses. She shook and sagged and had to be taken out to the lobby by the lifts, which had padded benches and ashtrays for visitors. Broom left her with Ken, pacing, filling the cramped space with angry smoke; the sister had given her a Valium.

The professor, who'd tried and failed to reassure her, shook his head sadly. 'This is no place for her, poor lass.'

Through the glass partition that divided the nurses station from the ward, Broom could see the tulips standing in a jar on the steel draining-board of the sink. Someone had tacked a Valentine card to the wall. Hearts and roses. After a while the sister emerged and asked if she could have a quiet word. Her face was worn and calm, her hair strictly drawn back into a ponytail. Her name badge said 'Sister Alison'. She glanced at the admission form, frowning. The switchboard, she said, had been jammed with calls. 'I'm afraid we're going to have to limit them. What we usually do is ask one member of the family to co-ordinate the reports on the patient.'

'I'm sorry,' said Broom. 'I'll see to it.'

The sister handed her a leaflet. Broom looked down at it. Mead Ward. The name like a promise of milk and honey.

'Also, he has no toiletries. If you could bring a toothbrush, and his razor, so that we can shave him.' She looked closely at Broom. 'Of course you can call us any time, day or night; don't hesitate. But right now I really think you should go home and get some sleep.'

She woke in the night with a ship on her mind, a superstitious ship that carved the waves, its white sails tilted to the wind.

Twenty-five years ago, in the January her father died, she'd mistaken his birth date, advancing it, bizarrely, by a day. Of course she'd known that he was ill, but her mother hadn't told her how far gone he really was, and hadn't seen fit to summon her to Scotland and the hospital. Broom's mistake meant that the card arrived early. He'd seen his birthday card that year, but not his birthday.

Although he'd begged for a last cigarette, the comfort had been denied him. This detail she didn't discover until after the funeral, when all the dry-eyed aunts had gone and she sat facing her mother across the fireplace, silent, smoking, rigid as a brass candlestick. Cigarettes were bad for you, but not as bad as death, and she hadn't been there to say it, shout it, or for that matter to do any small or simple thing that might have made him chuckle and delighted him.

She thought of the Greek dredger she had painted for Al, with such insouciance, as if that first birthday ship hadn't already taught her to steer clear of all sea-impulses, the tilting ship her father saw before he sailed away.

She put the light on, swallowed a Valium, and looked for the leaflet the sister had given her. Her hands were shaking. She tried three times to key the digits on the phone. Ships were bad omens, symbolic of death. How could she have been so slow to get the message?

Acc: nighthawk@freeserve.co.uk
Re: envy

My brother will never treat me as an equal
To do so would mean facing up to his own envy
This is my mantra, which saves me

Knocked out by your plans for Mallory. Given
the need for confidentiality, I feel privileged to be
the confidant: my lips are sealed, of course. My
tap will not drip. (Not that anyone up here listens
to me anyway, I might add.) Your comment about
Lara Croft *et al* is so true. We're all so insulated
from REAL EXPERIENCE, all time-servers in
the dumb-fuck prison of narcissism.

My brother who spies on me steals my soul
My father who denies me steals my holy fire
This is my mantra, which saves me

I see now how patient you've been with my
dumb-fuck's soulsearching.

Grace approaches

Iceboy

The day was soft and damp. A constant drizzle of fine snowflakes soaked the shoulders of Broom's coat. It was avalanche weather, with no frost to hold the slopes in place. For safety's sake, she'd taken the *petit balcon* path on the Couronnes side, which was only a hundred metres or so above the valley floor, and sheltered by trees: the unspectacular side, which lacked major climbs and which Lockhart, therefore, had ignored.

It had been slow-going, the snow wet and claggy underfoot. Mist-ribbons clung to the tree-tops, and the Will-o'-the-Wisp chorus kept sighing through her head, faint, eerie, like the souls of the departed. *Dans les bruyères / Dans les roseaux / Parmi les pierres / Et sur les eaux / Mourantes flammes / Rayons glacées / Ce sont les âmes / Des trépassés...*

Act V: the Harz Mountains. The chorus was a prelude to the enchantments of *Walpurgis Nacht.* '*Mon sang de glace!*' cries Faust, and then the mountain opens thrillingly, like the wings of a tabernacle (she envisaged one peak unfolding into three, a triptych), to reveal a golden palace, Cleopatra, Helen of Troy. The obvious solution for the chorus, the one traditionally resorted to, Daniel said, was a series of gauzes behind which vague apparitions took shape. It seemed too literal to her, although for the moment she couldn't see past it.

Earlier, waking cautiously, she'd found that her

brain had put itself in neutral, as if unwilling to risk a repeat of yesterday's *crise*. There had been a small squeeze of tears, vague adolescent yearnings. Below her the town lay, steaming gently, like a beast in a field. The streets were crammed with shopping crowds. A huge Italian tour bus was reversing at snail's pace out of the square, snarling up the traffic. A police car, its blue light flashing, nosed through the jam towards it. She could see the church with its Christmas tree, and the imposing mansard roof of Micky's hotel.

Her head felt hot and greasy. She pulled off her hat and began to descend the treeless defile under the pylons of the *télécabine*. If she followed them down to the Couronnes station she could call in at the Codec and stock up on supplies: bread, wine, some kind of seasonal bird to roast. The route, she realized, would take her past the hotel, unless of course she turned off above the church and went out of her way to avoid it, which would be tantamount to admitting that Micky had the power to influence her movements, to turn her, even, into a skulker. This thought was followed by the suspicion that she was tricking herself, pride masking a secret desire to run into him. Behind its dull veil her brain, perhaps, was shaping its intent, and every little thing she did or thought was becoming an absurd exaggeration of his importance.

She felt trapped and tired, suddenly, and stopped to light a dank cigarette. The Zippo was ice cold against her palm but the all-weather flame flared up faithfully. An empty *cabine* slid up the cable towards her and whirred overhead. Stuffing her hat into her pocket, she marched on down.

The road from the *télécabine* station dived steeply towards the town; the pavement had been gritted, but there were patches of ice under the reddish slush. She picked her way past the side of the hotel, where a neon sign over a slipway indicated underground parking.

Crossing at the intersection of the Rue des Martyrs, she risked a glance up at the hotel façade. Cream stucco, newly painted shutters. The ironwork of the balconies was a matching duck-egg blue. A woman in a pale suede coat and hat stood at the top of the steps. Her luggage was as blond as her outfit, and Micky was carrying it. The redhead with them was unmistakably Sophie Sauvage.

Broom ducked swiftly under the awning of a gift shop and took refuge behind a postcard stand. A red Renault waited at the kerb. A uniformed parking attendant got out and handed the keys to the suede woman, while Micky loaded the luggage into the boot. There were Gallic pecks on the cheek, right and left and right again. Their goodbyes were leisurely, each gesture honed to a filmic precision. They looked prosperous and important. The grey day had not even pinched their faces. She felt squalid, lurking there, her eyes fixed on the two women, on the glow and glitz of them.

Retreating inside, she found herself in a crowded cavern walled with cuckoo clocks. There were obsidian ashtrays, goatskins, spill-holders made of chamois horn, carved wooden mice with amethysts for eyes. A foot-long pencil had a glass globe on the end which, when shaken, sent snow storming round the plastic summit of the Aiguille du Sud. She stared blankly at the display cases, pretending to herself that she might find something in the gift line that Sean would like.

The cuckoo clocks were synchronized to within a few seconds. It was five to three, local time: soon there would be a cacophony. Even now Sean's plane would be crossing the Cascade Range, while Beverley steered some harum-scarum borrowed car along the freeway to the airport. If he hadn't opted to go to Seattle, would she have come out to Montjoie in the first place? Sod's law dictated it was at Christmas, when you felt most childish, that you had to make the most grown-up choices.

She was deliberating between a sheepskin hat with jolly ear-flaps and a two-metre panorama of the Massif when she felt herself observed. Turning, she saw Micky, standing in the queue at the cash desk. He held up a small furry toy and waved its paw at her. It looked like a marmot. A little gift for a little someone.

Immediately she felt red-nosed, straggle-haired, a sight. She raised a tentative hand. He hadn't mentioned children, but there could be nephews, nieces, godchildren. A man of his age: naturally he would have accumulated a certain amount of baggage. She remembered how Al had taken Nina in his arms and, supporting her like a surfboard, sailed her out above the table to blow out the three pink candles on her cake. However often she'd wished that Al's brood would simply dematerialize, the thought of Micky dandling an infant was rather reassuring. In principle at least.

A substantial family blocked her view as she squeezed her way through the throng towards the cash desk. She could no longer see Micky, but only his glove puppet, his silly familiar. The marmot hoisted an imaginary glass in the air and tilted it to its mouth. Micky was craning, his face a question mark above the crowd.

'My French friend has a diabolical *soif*. He wants to know if the charming lady will have a drink with him.'

Broom shook the paw that was extended. 'Well, OK, maybe a quick one.'

The marmot hid a bashful head in Micky's coat. A basso profundo issued from his lapels. *'Vous m'avez sauvé la vie, madame.'*

She waited on the pavement while the toy was being wrapped. When Micky came out with the parcel she laughed. 'They don't growl, you know, marmots. It's really more of a squeal.'

He took her arm, leaning into her rather than steering. His breath had a flowery smell that reminded her of old-fashioned violet cachous. They seemed to be going nowhere in particular, *flâneurs* on some boulevard of ease.

The Bar Mexicana looked onto the wide cobbled courtyard in front of the church. It was not a climbers' bar, unlike the old Couronnes, but smart and steely, the interior laid out with canteen trestles and lit by alarmingly white lights. A low wall topped by potted privet plants marked off a minimal *terrasse*, but it was a terrace without

330

a view. Inside, TexMex played on some hidden jukebox, loudly.

Al had labelled each tape-box on the spine. 'The Tape With No Name'. 'The Tape That Rides Alone'. 'The Ideologically Unsound Tape', which cracked climbers up on car journeys to Llanberis or the Peaks. That was the worst one, the one which reminded her of Saturday nights in the time-warped pubs in Perth and Pitlochry, and made her slice a finger graphically across her throat. *All my exes live in Texas, that's why I hang my hat in Tennessee.* While the back seat erupted in groans, Al would hold out his hand for another dose of dolly mixtures – a passion he indulged only when driving – and train a gleeful grizzled smile on the Interstate ahead.

Micky had his hand on the saloon doors.

'Let's sit out!' she cried, glancing up at the brief awning, which sheltered half a yard of the terrace.

'You're joking!'

'Honestly,' she lied, 'I never sit in when it's daylight.'

They were scraping pus out of Al's lungs. Every day the physios came with a small gadget like a Hoover and sucked it out. In the lab they were growing cultures. The chest man said that if you were going to kill a bug you wanted to know exactly what kind of little beggar you were dealing with. In Turkey, he said, they just bought in all the latest antibiotics from the US and chucked the lot at it; no wonder they were seeing such an increase in resistant strains.

At nights, if only to give the nurses a rest, she rode

331

the bus north across the river. Back in Hackney, Heather exiled her cats from the kitchen and fed her, or tried to: good nourishing meals with salad and potatoes. Then they'd drink whisky.

Later in her own flat, she'd remember to undress, wash. The telephone squatted on the floor beside the bed. She circled it, eyeing it mistrustfully, as if only constant vigilance could defuse its potential for awful surprises. When she turned her back on it she could feel its cold breath on the base of her spine. Even from the kitchen it was visible, dusty and malign, tethered to the wall socket by its twisted cord. On the other end of the line was Sister Alison, whose job it was to think of something comforting to say to her. 'Stable.' 'No change.' 'Comfortable.'

The voice was lenient and cradled her. Sister Alison didn't think her mad when she chattered away to Al as if he could hear her every word. In Mead Ward, where the nurses were too well trained to turn a hair, nothing felt particularly bizarre. Which didn't mean that there weren't some things she kept strictly between her and the bedpost, obeisances she made superstitiously in secret. Lord Death, if it pleases you, stay back from the door.

In Mead Ward you were free to believe in anything you liked. Runes. UFOs. The Miracle of Lourdes. Broom, being the artist, believed in Beauty. Now that Al's eyes were beginning to open, she wanted to give him something to look at. She turned out her jewellery box and polished her silver earrings; she painted her nails bright scarlet, like Miriam's. At nights she lay on the sofa with her eyes closed and the TV off, concentrating on what to wear. The green velvet top, the long black skirt with the slit, the satin-look stockings. Each morning in the greyish light it took half an hour at least to redesign her face.

Dexter, a man of few words, was putting his faith in music. Most nights he called in at the hospital after work and for half an hour the two of them would overlap. He had brought in a Walkman and a batch of cassettes, compilations mainly, on which singers with hokey names like Lefty Frizzell and Sleepy la Beef had heartaches by the hundred and tears that fell like rain, and everyone had leaving on their minds.

'So don't go,' Miriam had suggested, in the last session. 'You could actually make that choice...' He'd been hand-wringing about leaving Broom alone for all that time – she might get totally pissed at him, or meet someone else and decide to pack it in – but now he hoisted his eyebrows and gave Miriam a look that was both baffled and superior, like Isaac Newton facing a flat-earther. Miriam's grin was mischievous. 'I mean it. Stay here and work on your relationship instead. Spend the £5,000 on therapy!'

After one of the nurses had adjusted the headset on Al's shaven skull, Dexter would plug him in. The first time this happened, a definite frown of surprise flickered for a moment between his eyebrows. Accordion music trickled from the headphones. Dexter placed the player on the bedside locker and sat down to begin his vigil by the bed. His smile was distant and devout; his fingers nodded out a natty waltz-time on the sheet.

When she bent to kiss Al goodnight her earring dangled down and brushed against his cheek. The track had ended. She was close enough to hear the tape-hiss. Then another track began. From deep inside the cave that was his sleeping head, a tinny oracle

333

assured her that the borders of evil would fall to the smugglers of light, for Mescalito was riding his white horse, and the Free Mexican Airforce was flying tonight.

'Latifa went to an UNWRA school,' said Micky. 'Needless to say they didn't train her as a doctor, but she did manage to get some training as a nurse.' He was drinking Mexican beer straight from the bottle. On the label Broom saw a sunset or sunrise, a half-wheel with fine gold spokes. He was watching her closely. 'For years she worked at the Barbir Hospital in West Beirut. She worked there through the civil war, the Israeli shelling, the phosphorus bombs, the lot. I think she wanted to protect me from it at the time, but later, when I was older, she told me things. Just before she died she told me that one night a family of twelve were brought in from Bourj al Barajneh camp, all of them with their skin on fire. There were two five-day-old twins who were already dead. The doctor told her to take the babies and put them in a bucket of water to extinguish the flames. When she took them out an hour later they were still burning. Even in the mortuary they smouldered for hours. In the morning, when she removed them for burial, to her horror the two bodies once again burst into flames.' Micky's voice was flat and curiously absent. 'I'm sorry.'

Broom's hand went up to seal off her mouth. Her head nodded, too heavy, suddenly, for her neck. The story – the gruesome details – seemed familiar; she must have read about it at the time, numbly consigned it to a category called War, called the Middle East. But when had it happened? Her hand trembled as she tried to light her cigarette. It seemed inexcusable that she couldn't remember.

Micky had pulled off his hat and was brushing the snow from it with quick, finicky gestures. On his face was the same sullen expression she had seen often enough in her own mirror: the one that expects to be rejected, that knows no one wants to hear the truth about a tragedy, because what they hate most of all is their own helplessness.

'Don't apologize,' she said urgently. 'You shouldn't apologize.'

Momentarily the cloud lifted and the sun came sheeting across the square. Micky gave her the ghost of a smile. 'Somehow I sort of knew I could tell you...'

The phone in his chest pocket cheeped twice. He took it out and perused the text message. 'Well, the company calls...' He stood up with a sigh. Replacing his chair, he braced his hands on the back of it, hunched and leaning. His scarf dangled from his neck. There was a small red logo sewn into one end, near the corner: some kind of animal with horns – an antelope, perhaps. 'But thanks. For the debriefing, I mean. Really. I appreciate it. Some people charge a hundred quid an hour for that, you know.'

She gazed at him, bewildered. He had put his sunglasses on and she couldn't see the expression in his eyes. 'You're going?'

''Fraid so.' He shrugged and, bending swiftly, planted a kiss on the crown of her head. 'Catch you later, yeah?' He hurried to the kerb, turned, smiled once. She watched him skip across a bank of slush the snowplough had deposited in the gutter. She noticed that he wasn't limping at all; in fact he looked light-footed and nimble. She was aware of her gaze following him with a kind of stunned obedience, like a dog tracking the movements of its master. At the intersection of the Rue des Martyrs, without turning to look back, he raised his hand in salute, as if to ratify some bond that had been forged between them.

Long after he had vanished, Broom sat brooding on the troubles he had charged her with, while her legs grew stiff and heavy, and in her mind's eye the flames dimmed and died, flickered balefully, and once more burst into flower.

Later, at the kitchen table, she opened her notebook. At the top of the page she wrote the word RUINATION.

For Marguerite's prison scene, soaked wall-paper would sag from a low ceiling to form a pendulous breast shape whose nipple leaked not rain, but milk.

The trading-screen idea for Faust's study was wrong. It would have to be scrapped. Other images were crowding at her mind. She saw sites of building and demolition. Heaps of sand, scaffold poles, concrete-mixers.

She drew three drums of asphalt, smoking blackly.

At the bottom of the page she wrote: *A vision of Hell: to be so very attached to what eats you.*

In the morning Lockhart took the Land Rover and drove to Morrisdale, where he bought a video of *Brief Encounter* for Retta, and a bottle of her favourite Bristol Cream. When he rounded the bend by the forestry plantation and came in sight of Gillinish he remembered his dream.

On the carpet runners in the corridors Fraser had painted a yellow boundary line. This demarcation divided the house exactly in two, and on the one side he'd placed their mother's weaving loom and telescope and easel, plus the few items of furniture that belonged to her, and on the other he'd stacked everything that was their father's, so that the rooms in one sector were so crammed and wedged with wardrobes and dressers that hardly a door would open, while those in the other ached and echoed like the empty ballroom. And along the centre of the yellow line, spaced out like marker buoys, were the birds' eggs Lockhart knew he mustn't step on.

Last night Fraser had gone to the pub again, but this time he hadn't invited Lockhart. He had come back late. Lockhart had heard him around 1 a.m., vomiting in the bathroom. He'd called out to ask if he was OK. 'Aye. Tip-top,' said Fraser.

Lockhart carried his purchases up to the Blue Room, realizing, too late, that he'd forgotten to buy wrapping paper. The one thing he could buy

Fraser was time: a few weeks or months of grace. After that he was on his own. Fortunately most businesses were closed over the holiday, so there was no immediate risk that his adjustments would come under scrutiny. For the moment the main thing was to cover Fraser's tracks; thereafter the bank draft – dispersed creatively, in believable increments – would plug up the worst of the deficits.

He went into the nursery and logged on. He'd managed to stall his father last night at dinner, but today was D-Day, serious housecleaning. The email box waved its flag at him but he ignored it. No one was asking him to be the guardian of Fraser's morals. Barry, who was unshockable, said you'd be surprised at the amount of porn you found kicking around on people's hard drives. Barry's lips, of course, were sealed, which was no doubt why people treated him with extreme respect, bought him Krug at Christmas, slipped him their comps for Wimbledon and Wembley.

It was dark when he finished tinkering with the spreadsheets and consigned the damning evidence to the waste-bin. Then he sat back in the silence and heard the sea again, distantly sweeping, scouring away at the silver beach. His eye lingered reluctantly on Last Sites Visited.

If he'd been in the Alps the faint buzzing in his ears would have been a warning of objective dangers: rotten ice, a *couloir* prone to avalanche, the pressure drop that signalled an impending storm. A click of the mouse would settle it. He inched the arrow up until it pointed accusingly at IMBLA.

When footsteps sounded in the corridor he pressed Quit guiltily and swung round to face the door. It was his father, however, who knocked and called his name, then came in hesitantly and stood at the end of the bed, keeping his distance from the computer.

'Just to let you know I'll be having dinner at the dominie's. It's the school carol concert tonight, at the tree... Retta said she'd leave you some cold cuts.' He was shaved and changed and his cheeks were red and shiny, like fresh mutton. 'And so how are you going along with it?'

'Well, it's a bit of a pig's breakfast, but I'm beginning to see the wood from the trees.' Lockhart swivelled his chair back. Together they regarded the computer, sighing. The desk-top glowed at Lockhart, but kept its secrets. 'These glitches happen more often than you'd think. Not so easy to spot but luckily fairly easy to put right – with a bit of support, I have to say, from our IT wizard at work!' Lockhart was talking fast. He shut down the iMac, slapped its translucent flank, and stood up decisively. 'The good news is that what look like big losses on paper are actually a break-even scenario.'

'Is that right?' John Lockhart said doubtfully.

'Absolutely.' Lockhart gave him the benefit of his boardroom smile. 'It would have shown up on the customer accounts at some point, but of course I'll get on to them straight away. Or, rather, a.s.a.p. I should have it sorted in a couple of weeks.'

The gratitude on his father's face was too much for Lockhart. He moved briskly to lower the

339

blinds, bending to peer through his reflection to the misty and mendacious dark beyond. 'Fraser's asked me to monitor the accounts for the next few months, just until he, you know, finds his feet.'

Lockhart hadn't lied so well or so frequently for years; not since Broom, in fact. He'd forgotten how incremental it was – first the little white ones, then the sickly shades of grey, until finally you got to the great gut-blasting black jobs where the truth was a disaster aching to happen. Another thing he'd forgotten was the particular mix of pity and impatience you began to feel towards your victim.

'It's very good of you, Archie. I know you've a lot on your plate.'

'Not at all! I'd feel better if I knew I was keeping an eye on things.' His voice sounded clear and forceful in his ears. He accompanied his father to the door. 'The joys of being on line, eh?'

'Aye, so they say.' His father gave the computer a last dour look and turned his back on it. 'I hear you can even buy a baby. Makes your flesh creep, does it not?'

For a chilly weightless moment Lockhart stood with his hand anchored to the doorknob. He shrugged manfully. 'Aye, it does that,' he said.

When his father had gone he returned to the workstation and stared at the blank grey square of the screen. On impulse he rang Barry. Barry was not in the office. He massaged the back of his neck while he waited for the call to be transferred.

'It's me again. Where are you?'

'In Willesden, with the wife on one knee and a bottle of eggnog on the other. Where else would I be?'

Lockhart looked at his watch. It was only 3.30. Then he remembered that it was Christmas Eve. 'Look, I'm sorry to bother you and all that, but what's IMBLA?'

He heard a disgusted snort. 'And season's greetings to you too, mate! International Man-Boy Love Association. Poofy pin-ups. OK?'

'Thanks,' said Lockhart.

'Be my guest!'

'Right.' He couldn't quite bring himself to say 'Merry Christmas'.

'*Un cadeau, madame. Pour vous. Regardez.*' The cellophane box had been delivered to the ground floor. With a conspiratorial smile Madame d'Ange showed Broom the accompanying card. Then she turned quickly and scurried off along the hall, her broad cardiganed back saying that her tenant had a secret which she would not probe.

Christmas is coming, Broom read. *Love, Micky.*

Inside the cellophane coffin lay a flower born and bred in a greenhouse. At first glance it was an exotic cross of iris and orchid, with orange stamens coiled like springs and red blunt-ended petals whose shape reminded her of jaw-bones. Broom knew her wild flowers but not her cultivated, which were Heather's preserve, although she doubted that even Heather would be able to put a name to this particular foreigner. She took it out of its box and laid it gingerly on the kitchen table. The flower was so large and so insistently aesthetic that it looked not like a real flower at all but rather the representation of a flower, a designer version, copied from a painting, perhaps, by some follower of Georgia O'Keefe. She turned the card over.

PS You're an OK lady.

A couple of summers ago, in Heather's garden, she'd watched the total eclipse of the sun. Heather had filled a bucket of water to catch the reflection, but even so the glare was worryingly bright. Broom put on her glacier goggles; Heather donned three pairs of sunglasses. As the shadow inched across, the sun shrank to a thin but piercing crescent, until it was hard to remember that it *was* the sun and not the moon. After half an hour the light became arctic.

The air, which had become increasingly still, gained altitude. The garden, which was at sea-level, had climbed miraculously to six or seven thousand feet. The shadows paled and thinned until they looked like drying stains. This was no evening light with softly slanting rays, but a cold overhead glare, cruel as a fluorescent strip on their not-so-young faces. Goose pimples rose on their skin.

Although it was August, they put on their fleeces, agreeing that they'd never realized before how totally they depended on the sun. The sun gave them life. They relied on its constancy, its integrity. Without it the earth had entered a stoppage, a terrible sleep. Already the bees had gone to ground and the orange poppies in the flower-bed had yawned and closed up their petals.

In the lugubrious parentheses there was no more busyness. Broom learned later that all over the city traffic had stopped as people got out of their cars to stare. Offices had emptied. Even the trading floor of the Stock Exchange fell silent as all eyes fixed on the more dramatic transactions of the sky.

Upside down in the bucket only the sheerest sliver of the sun remained. For a moment she saw the shadow of the moon as death's fat apple, and hugged herself morbidly, shivering.

They'd realized then that the air was drenched catastrophically with perfume. It was as though the flowers, alarmed by their failure to attract the bees, had stoked up their scent and showered it out across the garden. Although she and Heather were at a panicky age themselves they were too awestruck, at that moment, to remark wryly on the obvious analogy. If scent were sound, they agreed, the decibels would be unbearable. Whatever else happened at the fag end of the world, this last-ditch outpouring of the flowers would make sure that it smelled apocalyptically sweet.

She replaced the flower in its cellophane box and carried it out to the balcony. The petals caught the sunlight, processed it and beamed back a different frequency, the red flower simmering like a flame on its chilly bed of snow.

That first morning, in the vestibule outside Mead Ward, she'd pulled the packing tissue from the quilted toilet bag and replaced it with toothpaste, shaving soap, the shiny new razor.

The professor had sailed out to greet her. 'Good news, my dear!' He pumped her hand, beaming. 'God knows what kind of sedation your Europ Assistance chums had him on, but quite frankly if you'd asked me last night I wouldn't have given the poor blighter half a chance... But this morning he's much perkier, and now that I've seen the scans, I'm delighted to say I was wrong.'

Broom's ears drummed. She felt a brief sharp pain for the peril that had passed her by. 'He's going to be OK?'

'I should say so! Give him three months and he'll be doing the Times crossword!'

The professor's gaiety was infectious. Broom didn't do crosswords, but if crosswords were his yardstick for recovery then they were good enough for her. 'And climbing?' she said eagerly. 'The first thing he'll want to do is climb again!'

The professor hesitated. He sidestepped nimbly, sweeping his arms wide to shepherd her towards the ward. 'Well, I'm not so sure about that. With this kind of case there's always a slight possibility of fits. Let's wait and see, shall we? It's early days yet... But come in, my dear, come and take a look.'

She thought of wheelchairs and walking-frames and speech therapists. Rehabilitation. An odd word,

344

one which didn't really seem to connect with the living, breathing body. It sounded more like re-housing, refurbishments to be carried out while the occupants were lodged elsewhere. It didn't suit Al at all.

At first glance he looked strangely symmetrical, now that the plaster cast had been cut away to reveal both shoulders. The swelling had subsided considerably, so that his head no longer looked remarkable. His cheeks, she noticed, were rosier.

She handed the toilet bag to a nurse whose badge-name was Hazel. Hazel with the hazel eyes. It was the sort of trick she used with the new student intake at the beginning of term. If it was going to be a long haul she ought to start remembering. She'd have to cancel her classes, arrange for a substitute. Her painting would have to go on the back burner for a while, become a harmless little hobby, like flower arranging or DIY. The decision was instant and didn't even shock her. She felt like telling Hazel that Al would be the world's worst patient – cantankerous, incensed by his infirmities.

The professor whipped a pen-torch from his top pocket and leaned over the bed. 'Open your eyes for me, Al,' he said, so commandingly that she half-expected Al to sit up straight and tell him to fuck off.

His eyes opened, quite quickly, without evident effort. The pupils were large and black, crowding out the colours of the iris. They reacted sluggishly to the professor's pin-point light. In college she'd learned about the orbicularis group, the subtle circular muscles around the eyes and mouth that define character. On Al's face they had smoothed, slackened.

His expression was neither happy nor unhappy. It

was simply non-existent.

'Follow my finger, Al,' said the professor. She thought of Dr Coppelius, ordering his wooden girl to nod and smile and dance. But it was happening: the muscles did their basic work, swivelled the eye sideways. The obedience of it hurt her heart. She didn't want to think of the good little boy in there who was going through his paces. The eyes rested on her for a second. They inched on, and returned.

She looked helplessly at the professor. 'Is he seeing me?'

'Well, in a manner of speaking.'

The moving finger tracked on and was ignored. The unwavering gaze was fixed on her. It occurred to her to walk round the bed, to test him out. She moved quite slowly, trying to smile. His eyes followed her with a vague but compelling interest, like a flower following the sun. He seemed to be staring at her hair, the bright hair that had always attracted bees and babies. The word that came to mind was 'phototropic'.

'Top of the morning to you!' The brogue was Irish this time, and the voice was familiar. 'I mean that literally. So did you get it?'

'The flower?'

'What?' He was calling on his mobile.

'Yes, thanks. I got it.'

'Listen, I predict a window of opportunity at around three thirty, if you're free.' His voice was shuddering and crazing, like rain blown sideways across a windscreen. She made out 'Faille' and 'recce' and 'Café des Couronnes'.

'You're breaking up,' she shouted, as the words fell away into the abyss. 'You're gone.'

She went out to the stone landing at the top of the steps that led down to the garden and peered up at the sunlit summit of the Faille. A thin scarf of cirrus clung to the Arête des Cristaux but it was clearing. She stood for a moment, wondering why she was standing there and what she was hoping to see.

Back in the warmth of the kitchen she inspected her Chinese ink bottles. There was a red she needed, a red called Geranium. The Calvin Klein girl needed it too. Not that she had any curves worth corseting but at least she deserved some colour, a bit of cleavage.

Her father always said kids should run wild, but what about women? She remembered the cotton brassières, stiff and sinless as cricket bats, the girdles and roll-ons her mother wore. Back then buttocks were singular and tubular: no part of a Scotswoman was supposed to wobble.

In fairy tales a girl could as well bloom as she could wither. She could have a father who adored her, who gave her flowers with red petals that hooked at her heart. A boy could love or hate his father but a girl would always want to be lovely to him, and that's where it all came unstuck.

The brush shivered in her hand. She felt clumsy and loose. The red ink flowed into the outlines of the dress and spilled over.

She's filling out.

She'd felt their eyes on her, shy and swerving, like moths. But there was no way of telling whether the whispers held approval or dismay.

Al said she had an exuberant body. Earthy. 'Nothing subtle about you when you want to get yourself fucked,' he'd said in the car on the way back from Cornwall, turning to her with a look of decorous triumph, as if he'd just cracked the crux problem on an E3 5c. 'One thing I *have* sussed about you. If you don't get food, sex or exercise just when you want it, you're going to throw a wobbler...'

Hardly a delicate picture, but she liked it because he did, because what he seemed to be saying was that here were needs that he was pleased as punch to satisfy. Once again his smile spread through her, a smile of serious wattage, like the amplified gleam of a lighthouse. He was, she'd decided, a simple man. He preferred to know exactly where he was with women. So perhaps in her own way she could be simple too. After all, there had been men before who'd merely filled a gap – a week, a month, a year. Men whose names kept slipping from her mind, like the names of the Shadow Cabinet.

She felt breathless and breakable, and wanted just for once to take a risk, to spill out her energy, single-mindedly, like the flowers in Heather's garden. It wasn't by being good that she'd won Al, but by fighting tooth and nail. She'd been good for five years, in fact she'd lived like a fucking Carmelite, and it hadn't resurrected him. Of one thing she could be sure: Al wouldn't want her to wither ladylike and white; he'd call that a criminal waste of resources.

Micky dropped Sophie at the Café Russe, in whose kitchen her boyfriend Roland was slaving, she said, like some single-handed Stakhanovite, and turned out of the village onto the Route Nationale. There was a long straight stretch down the valley to Montjoie on which he could let the Range Rover have her head.

To put it bluntly, he was pissed at La Sophie, not only on account of the boyfriend, but because she'd cut the outing short. She'd got her period, and felt, she pronounced with relish – as if the whole world really wanted to know the details – like seven degrees of shite.

He did some deep breathing, focused, made himself take in the splendours of the view. The wet black tongue of the tarmac hissed past beneath the wheels. By the time he swung the car off at the roundabout his hands rode lightly on the steering wheel. He cruised into the square and parked outside the Café des Couronnes.

The altitude had made him thirsty. 'I see you managed to find your umbrellas,' he remarked sarcastically as he gave the *patron* his order.

'Today the sun is shining, *monsieur*.' He indicated the orb with a graceless shrug of the shoulder. His skin looked damp and jaundiced. The stubble on his chin was blue-grey, like the mould on a rotten wine-cork. A lover of the cellar, evidently, not of the great outdoors. Micky had to admire the guy's nerve, his casual refusal to cover up the patent lie he'd told them earlier in the week. Not for him the sweet satisfactions of sussing out his clients and telling them what they really wanted to hear.

Even Jesus, Micky reflected, had known how to adapt his message to different audiences, had improvised, no doubt, as well as any Method actor. Unlike the dour *patron*, Micky had benefited from a similar training. He had Father Petrie to thank for his subtler skills in this department. It was the Jesuits, after all, who had invented sophistry.

A small queue had formed outside the concrete blockhouse of the Téléférique du Sud. Micky watched the descending cabin skim the tree-tops, sway past the final pylon and whirr down into the docking bay. He glimpsed Broom then, on the other side of the square. She paused at the kerb and crossed the street, striding towards him with her head down and her hands in her pockets. Even so, she had a certain elegance, and although she didn't parade her sexuality it was definitely there. She would clean up well, he decided. Classic clothes would work: cashmere, pencil skirts. A serious heel. He stood up and kissed her heartily on both cheeks and waited for her to sit down.

'So you've been up top already?' she enquired.

Micky signalled to the *patron*. 'Well, you like to know what you're letting your crew in for. We located a couple of possible spots, by which I mean not too utterly gut-wrenching!'

Broom picked up his keyring and dangled it from her finger, letting the mini-Maglite stroke a circle on the palm of her other hand. 'You drove over?' She seemed surprised.

'From London? Sure.' He indicated the Range Rover, which stood at the kerb, its stately bulk dwarfing the Citroëns and Renaults. 'Company car. Costs me nine thousand a year in tax, but it's worth it for the hassle it saves.' He grinned at her. 'All the fun and none of the responsibility.'

Once again he wondered what age she was. She might be pushing fifty, but then again she might be older; these days, with HRT, it was getting harder and harder to tell. Sunlight twinkled on the fine blond hairs above her upper lip. One theory about Monroe was that she'd had a lot of body hair, which powder-dust clung to and caught the light: thus the famous radiance. Monroe, however, would not have aged well, because you needed good bones for that – just look at the difference in decay rates between, say, Bacall and Bardot. To be brutally honest, thirty-six was the optimum age for most women, their shining summit. You could be forgiven for thinking that Diana, in her spooky way, had sussed this out.

Behind the sunglasses Broom's face was expressionless as she tilted her head to survey the summit needle of the Sud. At this range you could see no sign of the restaurant that was advertised, but it was good to know it was there. He thought of the upward flow of produce – the crates of quail's eggs and capons, the scallops and the crayfish, the tubs of goose livers and the chilly pails of oysters. He thought of the alchemies happening right now at the heart of the ice, the *soufflés*, the *flambés*, the Baked Alaskas wrought in fiery ovens. A gap had been detected in that barren brightness, a gap that cried out to be filled, and who better qualified to fill it than the French, who had always been experts at exploiting a country's prime resources.

'Wonder what their Christmas dinner's like. Must be a bit like hob-nobbing with the gods up there, huh?'

Broom let out a snort. 'With two hundred Italians in unsuitable shoes, more like.'

'Or a Japanese film crew doing an ad for tampons... I kid you not. The models froze their asses off in the wind, and the snow was the wrong sort. They had to bring up canisters of the artificial stuff and shoot it behind the toilet block.'

'An apocryphal tale, I take it?'

'No, absolutely,' said Micky, who had it on good authority from Christof, although the setting, it was true, might have been Klosters or Kitzbühel.

'I thought the Japanese had enough mountains of their own.'

'Must be the wrong sort of mountains.'

Broom's laugh trilled out, full-throated and excitable. The response was disproportionate to the stimulus; it was as if no one had pressed that particular button in a long time and the jackpot was overdue. Micky had simply happened along at the right moment. Not that he was complaining, of course. Something in the shake of her shoulders was sending signals, something reckless and manless. She'd said she had a son, he remembered, but when he'd asked about other ties she'd implied that she was a widow.

Covering her mouth with her hand, she laughed sideways at him, emitting a series of smothered giggles. It dawned on him that she was flirting; the nice thing being that she wasn't very good at it. Strange, he thought, as he laughed along with her: at some point your fantasy of what *could* happen engages with someone else's definition of what *will* happen. The significance translating itself into a feeling of warmth or magnanimity of which desire seems to be only a minor component, no more than an invigorating additive.

He hooked his chair up by the scruff of the neck, carried it round the table and sat down facing her, blocking out her view of the mountains. Her hand played warily with the Swiss Army knife on his keyring. She stroked it with her forefinger. It was smooth and scarlet with a silver cross, a masterpiece in miniature. He took the keyring away from her and placed it on the table. Then he gathered her hands together and chafed them between his own.

'Correct me if I'm wrong, but I get the impression that you don't find me too objectionable.' Their knees were almost touching. He heard her hold her breath.

She said accusingly, 'I thought you were gay, at first.'

'Ha!' said Micky. 'And now, what do you think?'

Broom took a long time to answer. He turned her hands palm up and examined them. They submitted trustingly, as if to a family doctor. When he took possession of her wrists she made no move to resist him.

'I think you're too young.' Her voice so lacked conviction that Micky had to make an effort not to laugh.

'Flattery will get you everywhere!' he retorted, feeling the flush of adventure settle on his cheeks. His heart thumped boyishly. 'As it happens, I think you're a very attractive woman by any standards.'

The shadow of the umbrella had slipped across her face. Micky reached over and took off her sunglasses.

'Don't!' she exclaimed, lunging forward and snatching them out of his hand.

Micky felt the shock of red-hot adolescent rage. For a moment he was too confused to look at her. He sat back abruptly, glimpsing through the open door of the café the curve of the bar counter and behind it the *patron*, leaning, watching the little scene with a glacial smile. He raised his eyebrows at Micky and then his glass of wine.

'Sorry,' Broom muttered, pursing her cheeks regretfully, but it was too late, the moment had floundered into foolishness. The jerk-off barman had queered his pitch and there was no way back to the realms of banter. Micky cupped his cheek in his hand and picked at the label of the Perrier bottle. The tear-drop shape was timeless and accommodating, an object lesson in branding. For a second there he had nearly lost it, his mind brimming with wild and purposeless thoughts.

Reculer pour mieux sauter, he told himself. Perhaps he had misread the signs. You could misjudge not only what a person wanted to hear, but also the exact degree of pressure that would trip the switch, open the sesame, as it were. It didn't happen often, but it happened.

'Actually, I've got a confession to make,' he said after a moment. His voice was low and lustreless, his wings adroop.

'A confession?'

'What would you say if I told you I lied about my father? I mean, about him leaving.'

Broom's arm slid onto the table and lay in a loose arc, as if in mimicry of his. 'But why would you lie?'

'It's not very pleasant having to share your mother with a drunk. You don't exactly feel like advertising it!'

'I guess not.'

Her voice was soft, perplexed: empathy in waiting. All he had to do was tap into the correct undercurrent of worry and remorse. He heard his ragged sigh. 'When I was at the seminary Father Petrie used to talk about the terrible disappointment of the saints. Anyone who had ever lost a beloved person, he'd say, through violent death, or death aggravated by injustice, anyone who had ever mourned someone they really believed was great and good and of importance to humanity, anyone who had ever dreamt that it was all a mistake, that the person was still alive, and then woke to what he called – eloquent old devil that he was – "the bitterness of unchanged absence" ... could imagine the devastating impact of the

355

Crucifixion. Well, I didn't know a whole lot about that, but I could have written a dissertation on the bitterness of unchanged presence. Not that Father Petrie would have believed me. He'd never hear a word against Jerome. "Salt of the earth", he called him.' Micky gave Broom a sidelong glance. 'Just another devout Catholic set on seeing his son enter the priesthood.'

'The priesthood!' Broom pushed up her sunglasses onto the top of her head. Her eyes were wide with surprise.

'See what I mean?' he said wryly.

'It's certainly hard to believe.'

'Might not have been such a bad deal, when you think about it. A man of the cloth. When it comes to women, they really have it made.'

He was conscious that the *patron* lurked still in the dim interior, but for the moment Broom was a barricade that blocked his sight-line from the door. 'To cut a long story short, the Jerome I knew wasn't devout, not by any stretch of the imagination, and unlike his namesake he wasn't famed for a furious chastity either! Oh no, saint he was not, although to be sure I'd've martyred the old sod ten times over given the chance, sealed him in the early Christian catacombs so deep down that even when the Resurrection came he'd never have made it back to the surface!'

She was sitting unnaturally still, a little hurt smile nagging at the corners of her mouth. Had he gone too far? He sensed that she was uncomfortable with the 'sins of the father' stuff, which would be par for the course. Girls and their precious daddies; he could smell a protection racket a mile off. 'I'm wittering on.' He felt in his pocket for change and threw some ten-franc pieces on the table. 'I'm also freezing to bloody death.' He laid a hand on her arm. 'I feel like driving. Do you mind? We could nip up to the Col, snatch the last bit of sunset.'

Broom nodded. She got up and followed him silently to the car. To Micky her gait seemed as slow as a sleepwalker's. He had to resist an urge to grab her by the arm and hurry her along. On the back of his neck he could feel the malevolent gaze of the *patron*. With exaggerated courtesy he opened the passenger door and handed her in.

Swishing up the S-bends on the side of the gorge, where the mist of waterfalls obscured the depths below, Broom thought of the aeroplane dream she used to have when she was a girl. A plane that didn't take off, but lumbered instead through towns and landscapes, its wingtips clipping telegraph poles and chimney-pots; a plane like a bus or a dodo, that wasn't designed for flight.

Micky drove with precision, his wrist slick and sexy on the gear-stick, his pleasure obvious. They parked on the Col itself, where the road summited and slid unremarked into Switzerland, and sat facing France and the afterglow. She had been granted permission to smoke.

High up in the cockpit of the Range Rover, she gazed at the array of dials on the dashboard. She was trying to picture the Corniche, not the one above Nice, with its oleander terraces and fabulous bluffs, but Micky's boulevard of cafés, and the garden where an Arab boy hurled his

357

stick at a pigeon and Latifa frowned as the rose
petals spilled seawards. They'd been eating ice-
creams, Micky had said: multicoloured sundaes
topped with paper parasols; it might even have
been his birthday.

Above the distant sprocketed edge of the
Massif the pink of the sky was deepening and
spreading. Micky was leaning back against the
headrest, hugging himself, staring at a point in
inner space. Broom listened silently, sweating in
her heavy jacket; she was beginning to feel dowdy
and dutiful. 'This is just for instance,' he'd said.
Clearly it was something he needed to talk about.

'Then I saw Jerome in the doorway of the café,
his face red and, well, "oafish" is the word that
comes to mind. The underarms of his nylon shirt
were all dark and soggy with sweat. He came over
and stood glowering down at us, like it was all
our fault or something. We could smell the
whisky on his breath. Latifa tapped her watch
and said, "Where have you been?" You could see
how tense she was by the cringy way she was
smiling. "Only in every fuckin' caff from here to
Kingdom come. You said the Pittoresque." "No,
Le Pigeon," Latifa said, "I said the Pigeon." "You
never bloody did!" he shouted. By now his face
was so slack and stupid that I really needed to
laugh. I was sucking ice-cream up through the
straw, not looking at him, and of course it made
a rude noise, like a fart. Then of course I did
laugh, and the proverbial hit the fan... "You don't
fool me, boyo. I'm on to your tricks!"'

There was a second in which a sympathetic
noise started to come from her. Then Micky's fist

shot out sideways and squared up two inches from her jaw. In the ruddy light the face he thrust at her was corrugated, pantomime-cruel. Broom froze. He had judged the distance perfectly. Then the fist was withdrawn and her face felt naked and knotted with shock.

When Micky shook his head at his history she began to breathe again. She pushed the arrowed button on the door and the window shooshed down six inches. Having fumbled a cigarette out of her packet, she lit it and blew the smoke angrily through the gap.

'It's the shame I remember as much as anything. The shame of that shirt, for a start.' Micky's shoulders rose and fell in a sigh of revulsion. 'Latifa was begging him to stop. All around us people were staring, and not only because people always looked at Latifa. Then he grabbed me and jerked me up so that the chair fell over, and started dragging me towards the door. Latifa was running alongside, pleading with him; she had her purse in her hand because she hadn't paid the bill yet. Then he got her by the arm too and dragged both of us through the café, where you could see the men's faces in the dark, flickering in front of a black-and-white TV, straight past the cashier and out to the kerb, where the car was waiting with its door standing open and its engine still running, like a kidnapper's.'

'Christ,' muttered Broom.

'Well, Christ didn't exactly come into it!' Micky rubbed his eyes hard with the heels of his hands.

'They look inflamed,' she said.

Micky gave her a bleary smile. 'Maybe that's because I haven't slept for several thousand years.' When he turned the key in the ignition all the dials on the dash lit up. She snapped her seatbelt home, wound up the window and waited for take-off. Micky's hand was poised on the gearstick. She had no idea where he thought they might be going.

'Look, I'm sorry to land all that on you. It's a mug's game, I know, dwelling on the past. A waste of emotional energy.'

'Well, not necessarily.'

'So I'm forgiven?' There was a carphone in the bulwark that separated the two seats, clipped into a little open coffin. He reached across and took her hand in his. He looked down at it for a moment and then at her. 'Come back to the hotel. Drink some champagne with me.'

In the hotel room Broom let out a gasp of pleasure and flew immediately to the balcony. Micky called Room Service, who told him regretfully that there would be a delay. 'Forget it,' he snapped, dismissing the flurry of apologies. 'How can a bottle of plonk and some nibbles take half an hour?' The minibar yielded a quarter-bottle of Moët; he poured himself an inch and filled a glass for Broom.

'Some view,' she said, coming back in.

'That's what you pay for,' said Micky. 'I won't tell you how much.'

'I can imagine,' said Broom, surveying the facilities of the room with a marked lack of interest. Then she sat down on the Louis Seize chair and began to unlace her hiking boots.

'It's comfortable – that's what counts,' Micky said airily, setting the flute carefully on the desk beside her. 'I'm just going to take a quick shower. Sweaty business, these eternal snows.'

She had pulled off her boots, which now sat side by side on the thick pale pile of the carpet. They were big and brown and scuffed, the toecaps pitted with triangular scars, like arrow-heads. She took off her socks and bent to stuff them inside. Her feet were small and white, with stark red varnish on the toenails. He looked at them uncertainly. 'Will you be all right for a couple of minutes?'

She glanced up at him through a tangle of hair. Her smile was fleeting and polite. 'Sure.'

At the bathroom mirror Micky craned his head back and tipped Optrex into his right eye. When he came to the left eye the dropper trembled wildly, the clear liquid swimming down his face like tears. He steadied his elbow against the wall and succeeded at the third attempt.

In the shower he soaped his balls and prick and turned his back to let the torrent sluice the tension from his shoulders. Then he faced into the jetspray, letting it play, baptismal, on his forehead. He opened his mouth wide until it filled up like a fountain bowl, and spouted water through his teeth. He thought of the 5.30 rising at the seminary, the frigid dribble of the shower. Even someone who'd had a vocation in the first place would have lost it pretty sharpish.

Already the hot water was working its wonders. The huge feeling that had come over him in the café was fading from his head. As for Jerome, the old sod was no longer a threat to anyone. The nuns always said it was the civil war that had done for his wits, which showed how little they knew. One day he would tell the dear sisters – in fact he was actively looking forward to it – tell them the drink had merely carried on the work that the devil had started, and all their decades and novenas couldn't cure the fire and foam inside his father's head. The only pity was that the Israelis hadn't finished the job when they scored a direct hit on the asylum. Instead he'd been fished out and shipped off to a modern annexe where, presumably, he was still in residence, still decked out, no doubt, in the scapular some well-meaning novice had sewed from an old bedsheet, with a red cross stitched to his breast, still sailing the corridors of the acute wing like a Crusader ship come to quell the Muslim hordes.

Micky stepped out onto the bathmat and reached for a robe. His erection was rising, and stood by now at an angle just above the horizontal. Like a cannon, he thought, towelling it with affection: like a muzzle-loading brass cannon, ready to fire a broadside.

He opened the door to the bedroom and went through humming 'Air on a G-string'. Then he smelled smoke and remembered with a split-second jolt of surprise that she was in there.

Broom crushed out her cigarette and stood up. 'If I can just clean my teeth.'

Micky folded down the counterpane and lay waiting. The pillows were plump, the sheets immaculate as Easter lilies. In the bathroom water gargled and spouted.

When she returned he sat up hospitably and patted the bed beside him. It was on the tip of his tongue to say something reassuring – for instance, that he preferred older women, which wouldn't have been a lie, or not exactly: at this point in his life, more of a *tabula rasa*. The mind in its original uninformed state, as Locke would have said. A clean slate, a pure white sheet that waited to be sullied.

Broom had already started to undress. She got out of her jeans and sweatshirt efficiently, like an athlete stripping for the shower. Too late it occurred to him that he should have closed the curtains, in deference to her modesty. She was compact, muscled. She cast off her underwear and dropped it in a heap. Black Lycra, appropriately: somehow he couldn't imagine her in silk. Her legs were powerful, although he glimpsed a hint of laxness about the inner thigh. Her breasts stood out strongly, the nipples eyeing him. Clearly she had never breast-fed. The thought filled him with an acute and sorrowful tenderness.

So far she had suffered his scrutiny without flinching but now she struck a pose and smiled defensively. 'So?'

Micky made a frame of his fingers and snapped her with his thumb. He let his breath out slowly through his teeth. 'Gorgeous.'

She shrugged at this, but he could tell that she was pleased. 'I work out.'

'I can see that,' he said appreciatively. He saw

363

her hesitate, as if even at this late stage some nugget of refusal was trying to harden in her mind. 'Come here,' he sighed, reaching out both hands to her, like St Jerome blessing his lion.

She collected her champagne glass from the desk and padded barefoot across the carpet. Hoisting it above her head like the Statue of Liberty's torch, she took a long stride up and clambered onto the bed.

Micky trailed Broom's fingers over the thick dark hair on his chest. 'My pelt,' he said ruefully, tucking in his chin and pouting down at it. The hair was silky, with a scant curl to it, and smelled of something exorbitant. Beside her his body felt slender and insubstantial.

'I like hair,' she said, in automatic reassurance.

'You do?'

'Yes. Hair is good.'

Expelling a contented sigh, Micky closed his eyes. 'That's all right, then.'

Broom lay on her stomach with her nose crushed against the pillow and her hand captive. If only he would sleep. She turned her head cautiously and squinted at the digital alarm. 4.45. The curtains were open and, outside, dusk was falling but not fast enough. She thirsted for darkness, oceans of it, as if only in darkness could she locate the fault that was in her.

After her father had done his business sadly with the belt, she would lie frozen with betrayal

364

and shame. The cottage belonged to a game-keeper and the walls were wooden and thin. The sounds that came through were bedsprings and mutterings. Sometimes her father's voice rose sternly, as if in reproach. One thing she'd heard him tell her mother was that you should never hit a child in anger; you should wait and punish them in cold blood, and make sure they understood the reason. She'd liked the idea that her mother could be made to toe the line, that there were laws laid down to protect her. Stealing was wrong, for instance, but lying was worse, so it was better to own up immediately.

She'd never stolen for gain, though, more for the hell of it. The impulse part of some wildness that was in her head. Lemonade stored in the Co-op basement; canned goods that promised to be peaches but turned out to be beetroot. She could remember the hideout she'd made in the skeleton of a car that nested, rusting, in the tall bracken by the river, but not who'd been with her. Village kids, boys most likely, full of spleen and disappointment. They'd chucked the bleeding beetroot into the undergrowth, where the slices shrank and shrivelled and gathered flies. She was the one who'd said they had to save the juice. Since she'd been the ringleader, the onus lay on her to save the day and its devilment. The juice was red as wine and turned them into celebrants. Crazy kid that she was, capable even then of conjuring up some kind of magic sacrament. Not even bothering to cover her tracks, either. As if she'd actually wanted to be punished.

Between her legs was swampy and slick. *In cold*

blood. As an idea it made no sense at all. Unless you were dead, blood was warm even in winter and salty like tears when you licked it from a cut. Nevertheless she'd taken what her father said as Gospel, because at that age your parents had the power to say that black was white and wrong was right. If your father didn't love you, you were bad; if he did, he must know what was good for you.

Micky's chest rose and fell steadily under her hand. His nostrils pointed at the ceiling, small dark oblongs, like sockets waiting to be plugged. According to Al the barbers in Damascus lassoed the little nose hairs with a thread and jerked them out: it was simply part of the service. The thought led on to undertakers, who plugged the nose with lint or wax to stop the fluids leaking out. She inched her hand away from Micky, and then her sweaty body. Finally she retrieved a cool space at her side of the bed. The sheets were of pure white cotton, hand-hemmed; an embroidered label warned that they were the property of the Intercontinental Group. She heard the faint beginnings of a snore.

He had done what she wanted, willingly, and she had reciprocated, but the last thing she'd wanted was intimacy. What she'd wanted was what gay men want because it disgusts them: sounds, sensations, the seedy back room of a nightclub without lights, a dance floor stinking of sperm. The click of a belt being unbuckled, the smack of lips that signalled a little factory of spittle. A stranger's cock up your arse, doing you an anonymous favour.

Mercy on the body, perhaps, but not the soul. Sex without love, the grown-up version. Al would have been proud of her.

A cold pinpoint of light watched her from the desk. Micky's cellphone was still on, or else recharging. She thought of the way the broken base of a lemonade bottle made a curved lens that concentrated the rays of the sun. When you got the angle right you could make a white spot of brilliance in the grass; then you blew and blew until the miniature haystack hollowed out and browned. At first the flames were invisible against the day's brightness; only the scorched smell and the blue beginnings of smoke told you the fire was burning. In the fish-eye of the lens dots of clouds leaned darkly in towards the speck that was the sun, a seed that could set the bracken ablaze, whole moors of heather flaming as far as the horizon. Once she'd let the spot settle on the back of her hand, but only for a moment, just long enough to see the blond hairs curl and shrivel, while in her mind's eye the beam seared straight through and bored a black hole like stigmata.

With my body I thee worship...

She slid out of bed and carried her clothes into the bathroom, her bare feet soundless and uncertain on the marble tiles. There was a quake or a gasp embedded in her solar plexus. She rushed her clothes on and tiptoed out, boots in hand, to the somnolent safety of the hallway.

The air temperature outside was falling fast. She could smell the night exhalations of the town: diesel, fresh bread, woodsmoke. As she sped towards the chalet a dank mist slicked her cheeks. At the top of the steps the exterior light was on. Almost before she saw the glitter of frost on concrete she knew what kind of memory was coming. The frozen doorstep, and on it, like a heart beating stoutly for her, the open diary.

With my worldly goods I thee endow...

After the funeral she'd inherited, along with a few keepsakes, a large pasteboard suitcase, which Al's kids, in a frenzy of house-clearing, wanted to get rid of. Inside were one or two karabiners, a frayed climbing harness, a sheaf of old papers and bank statements, and a school atlas from the era when the British Empire still spread its beetroot stain across the globe.

The suitcase would not store; it fitted conveniently into no cupboard or corner. In the cramped flat she kept tripping over it. Nine months later, on the last day of the year, her loyalty ran out. She decided on a clean sweep, and dragged the thing down four flights of stairs to the street, where she left it for the council dustmen to dispose of.

That night there was a snowstorm, with violent winds. She'd got drunk at Heather's New Year party and stayed over. When she returned next morning the suitcase was gone, but the contents were smeared across the square, stuck to tree trunks, park railings; she saw bank statements iced in and glassy, like a frozen mosaic on the pavements.

Her first instinct was to disown the diary, to step over it and look the other way, as if a kitten she'd tried to drown had crawled its way back to her doorstep. The open page stopped her. When she bent to look at it she saw her own name written formally, in full. The month was July, the July of two years ago. The day was Tuesday: her first date with Al, when he'd limped to her front door and they'd been strangers.

Your cheatin' heart will make you weep, you'll cry and cry, and try to sleep. She shouldered her way into the hall and flicked the time switch. The suitcase image wasn't one she wanted on her mind. It spoke of leaving, of moving on. Of being left with nothing.

She got the kitchen door open and leaned against the jamb, dragging off her boots. Her knees felt disastrous, two jellyfish trying to hold steady against the abrupt descent of a lift. The kids had instructed the insurance company to sue the life out of the lorry driver, but that was after Al was dead and buried, when she no longer had the energy to protest. When her eye fell on the whisky it occurred to her that someone had certainly been cheated, but she couldn't work out exactly who it was. She poured herself a glass and lay down on the leatherette sofa, wondering if she could organize a coma. Sleep. Cessation. Nothing. A word like a truck, a Turkish truck loaded with consumer durables, a ten-ton word that could roll right over Micky.

On the day after Al died she drove with Roz and Simon to a cottage they had hired near a village called Diss, which was, it turned out, the Roman name for the Underworld.

Mercifully the fields were flat and Baltic and stirred

no feeling in her. The objects that inhabited this spurned landscape – birds, tractors, transmission masts – were elbowed apart by sky. Between them there was no relationship of tone or colour that she could understand, or wanted to go looking for. She walked silently behind Simon along sunless furrows. There were gravel pits, dolmen-shaped stacks of sugar beet.

'We've got heaps of food, and you must just help yourself to the booze.' Roz pointed to the bottles lined up on the sideboard. 'You don't have to say a single thing unless you really want to.'

In bed she lay straight and still as a winter furrow and listened to Al's complaints. The voice in her ear was unbearably plaintive and puzzling. 'But you can't just drop me now!' it said. As if he hadn't yet gone, as if there was still something he wanted from her. Something that still remained to be done. Did he feel, in some dead and muddled way, that she really had dropped him, like a hopeless butterfingered mother? Or was it his own body he was reproaching, the body that for fifty years had given him so much pleasure and had now betrayed him? Or was it, perhaps, the sound of herself, the part of her that love had lodged in him?

Mornings were muffled by rain or browsing cloud. She resisted them until hunger forced her to get dressed. At intervals throughout the second day she was gripped by a sense of being in a small underground cell. There was a high chink of light she squinted up to, and, on the floor, smashed shards of pottery.

Occasionally Roz or Simon swam in like visitors and spoke to her, but since she had no news, she could

370

think of little to say in response. After a while she realized that her mind no longer belonged exclusively to her; instead it had become a receiver for messages.

Her first thought was that he had a bloody cheek. The rationalist who poured scorn on the very notion of the unconscious wasn't above plugging into its channels when it suited him, busily trying to convey how he'd felt in the hospital, and how he now felt — smashed, in pieces. After weeks spent translating the signs of the body, she was being asked to deal with a brand-new medium. Direct agitations of the cortex. An infant technology. Like John Logie Baird with his cathode-ray tubes, straining to receive transmitted light patterns.

Some of the images were weak and muddy. More than once she found herself in the middle of the bedroom, rotating through 360 degrees, trying to tune herself, trying to align her aerial.

In London it was harder to listen in, because of the interference. Ken had left a frantic message on her answerphone. Al's kids were at each other's throats, it said; she had to help them organize the funeral. She rang him back. It was just one more thing her mind wanted to say no to.

'Why me, for God's sake? What about Philip, or the parents?'

'We're talking the massed ranks of the Party here, not a family funeral! My mobile hasn't stopped ringing all weekend. Look, the kids are insisting they want to do it. I'm not asking you, honey, I'm begging you.'

Afterwards, she spread a sheet of newspaper on the kitchen table and stood her walking boots on it. Mostly she wanted to slip down into sleep and stay

371

there, but Ken wasn't going to let her off the hook. The activity, he said, would do her good. 'Then do it for Al's sake,' he said.

There was mail on the hall carpet. On a padded envelope she saw the energetic slant of Al's handwriting. Inside was a roll of film he'd posted six weeks ago in Cairo. A sheet of lined paper torn from his notebook was wrapped around the canister.

This is not a letter but I love you.

The words were like the touch of his hand, and the touch was electric. She could smell wet tents, the damp sweet morning sweat of his hair. She dropped the note and stood over it, tears pouring out of her suddenly at the sight of the wobbly line of kisses, big and strong at first, then shrinking, trailing off like little stars into infinity.

She intersected, once again, with his itinerary. A mosque tower mirrored curiously in the harbour, a white sheet forgotten on a balcony, the shriek of an invisible peacock from the marshes of the delta. There was the early-morning square where he waited for the post office to open, eager for the poste restante and the wooden compartment marked F to H from which the clerk would produce her letters, one or two or maybe even three; there was the acacia-shaded café where he would devour them, trembling a little from lonely desire and the small strong bursts of caffeine that battered at his heart.

She picked up a boot and began to sponge it. The note lived and breathed. It could have risen up laughing or singing and walked away. It was her boot, by comparison, that was posthumous: dank and empty, still crusted by the mud of the Underworld.

Micky slept for a few hours and woke alone, for which he was thankful. He reflected that older women were easier to please – more demanding in bed and less demanding out of it. All this was common knowledge where he came from, of course; it was the English and the Americans who simply didn't know what they were missing. As they approached middle age they seemed to believe that a young woman would make them feel younger, when in actual fact the opposite was the case: youth glowed too brightly and put them in the shade; it made them look like foolish old wrinklies.

He thought of Marianne, who lived across the landing in the apartment block on the Rue Saint Antoine, and did his mother's hair. Magazine pictures of Catherine Deneuve and Princess Grace were taped to the cupboard doors in the kitchen that doubled as her salon. Her own hair was bleached to pale fawn and fell in two labial wings on either side of her face. She was divorced and thirty-six, the magic age; she wore stilettos with bare legs, and stuck plasters on the sore patches behind her heels. When his mother was on late shift he was supposed to sit in her kitchen and do his homework, but by the time he reached fifteen it was clear that what Marianne had to teach him – after her clients, with chiffon scarves tied like helmets over their styles, had paid and gone – was in all ways more alluring than St

Ignatius' Spiritual Exercises.

The night hours stretched spaciously ahead of him. Christmas Eve. As a child he'd loved the solemnity of wrapping things and feeling rich: sweets and shells and white pebbles collected on summer Sundays at the beach and saved for months, all for the sake of the anticipation he would feel when he watched Latifa's fingers unwrap, with mischievous slowness, each little gift. He thought of the Nordic night-glimmer of tinsel, and how unsuitably it glared in the southern sun, and the TV screen on which the Pope addressed the multitudes, and how Jerome would shout at him to sit up straight and pay attention while he was being blessed, but later in the day the scenario would always change and Latifa was his to delight and his alone, because by then Jerome had gone to see a man about a dog and simply did not figure.

He lay cruciform across the empty bed, remembering the vast relief of Broom's sigh. He was shocked and laughing and flattered. Five years without sex! It was unimaginable. It was quite literally un-fucking-believable. When he asked about the dead lover she was curt and clammed up, but you didn't need words to know when someone was choked. In actual fact he'd felt a bit choked himself. Needless to say he'd dropped the subject immediately, because the last thing he wanted was to come across as an emotional intruder.

There was a griping pang of hunger in the pit of his stomach. He remembered that they hadn't got as far as dinner. He reached for the Room

Service menu and leafed fretfully through it but couldn't settle on a single thing. Presently the hunger pangs subsided but the thought of her starvation stayed with him and suddenly he was wide awake and worrying. He had a fleeting memory of soft thick hair, the momentary dampness of tears across his chest.

Right now, if he was in her shoes, he'd be feeling fairly exposed. Humiliated, even. Perhaps he should have reassured her more. He hated to think of her slinking off in the dark with her tail between her legs. He didn't know what kind of guy she was used to – there were plenty of shits about who thought it was strictly uncool to be chivalrous – but any decent guy would be genuinely concerned.

The bed smelled of femaleness and sweat. Micky got up and showered and robed and cleaned his teeth. He became aware of another, separate current of disturbance. Something was nagging at him. He'd had a more than OK time himself – no complaints on that score – and undoubtedly it was gratifying to be the agent of so much pleasure (I mean, with some people it could feel as if you were the one who was taking advantage), but he was beginning to wish that she hadn't been quite so grateful. If there was thanking to be done, surely it was the man's place to thank the woman, not vice versa.

He swept the steam from the mirror and frowned at his reflection. Standing there with the razor in his hand he realized that it wasn't morning yet; far too early to shave. His eyes were deep and dark. He looked blurred and shadowy, like an understudy. It struck him then that a lot of guys would get insecure: they'd think, well, maybe she could have been in bed with anybody; any dumb prick at all would have done the trick. Was it really so flattering? After all, nobody liked to feel they were just performing a useful service.

He ordered coffee and a *croque monsieur* and towelled his hair briskly, trying to dismiss his doubts. It wasn't like him to be so paranoid. Then he sat down at his laptop to design his Christmas mailshot and do his festive duty.

Within half an hour a pack of emails were skimming across the globe and Micky felt better. Some had galloping reindeer and some had holly leaves on which cyber-snowflakes gently gathered. He'd taken extra special care with Damien's. Although Damien hadn't mentioned where he was going for the holiday, odds on he'd be nipping over to Val d'Isère. He wondered if he would be back yet, and whether it would be uncool to ring.

Acc:nighthawk@freeserve.co.uk

Nighthawk, what my father sees is simply that all the crows must die. Every day the box of cartridges brick-heavy in the pocket of my jerkin, and the print of my boots blue in the frosted grass at first light as I tramp the headland where today the ewes stand very still and separate, not huddled together in the stone semicircle of the fold as they do in storm or snow, heavy already, gravid, and, yes, helpless, but who protects the crows, Nighthawk? I in my Nazi jackboots must make war on them long before the lambs are even born. I must shoot them because my father believes it will make a man of me. I must shoot every last one and witness their guts bursting like little pink berries. I must pierce them through the eye and hang them like washing from the branches of the hawthorns till the whole headland smells sharp and musty, smells of death.

At first their bodies are still warm, pliable; you can curl their necks in softly against their breasts, stretch their wings out to their broad and beautiful span, fan out their feathers. You hang them, and their blood is brief, a few drips spotting the dead bracken under the tree, and then they are stiff and absent, like vacated chairs, the oils and unguents drained from their feathers, the blue-black life-gleam gone, the colour turned dry and dull as old coffee grounds. When the wind blows they sway stiffly on the branch, light and empty, rustling against one another like paper bags, and all because my father believes that whatever he builds the crows will tear down, they will make rags of all his plans and his ever-present need for order. This is the contribution he demands I make, the only pound of flesh that is important to him, an impossible labour he asks of me in order to fulfil his vision of an island where not a single crow exists, a clean clear island dotted with his spotless white lambs...

Iceboy

Acc: iceboy@demon.co.uk
Re: forgiveness

Don't get me wrong, Iceboy, I'm not asking you to forgive your father, I'm asking you to forgive yourself.

Forgive yourself your rage. Forgive yourself for not being what he wants, or wanting what he wants. Forgive yourself for wanting to realize your own desires for objects and values, et cetera, et cetera.

At the seminary we had it dinned into us that nothing and no one is beyond forgiveness but the devil himself. Father Petrie, bless his little cotton socks, would say you were guilty of one sin only and that was the common one of pride. The comforts of theology, Iceboy. If you'd ever had to study it you'd know that the Reformation put the kibosh on the notion of a forgiving God.

It is neither right nor credible that God should forgive those who themselves will not forgive others.'

Or again – 'Although it is difficult for us to forgive others it is much easier for us to do so than to believe that God forgives our own sin.'

The Nuremberg Catechism, for your information – Father Petrie believed in knowing the enemy. It goes way back to when they were just beginning to work out their pitch. You see, for the Prod. God, everything always has to be conditional. At least as a lapsed Catholic I could go to confession if I wanted to, but you don't even

378

have that choice!

Of course it's always tempting to indulge in guilt, even to spend years perfecting it, but on the other hand you can flick the willpower switch and decide to indulge in something more sustainingly pleasurable and less grudgingly punishing to self and others.

As I said before, it's your choice. In this day and age we have to be able to do this for ourselves and each other because no higher agency is going to do it for us.

I agree totally that you mustn't allow yourself to be humiliated. What I'm trying to get across to you is that if you could only kick the guilt habit you'd be 100% more able to stand up to him.

The warmth of my compassion flows out to you.

Nighthawk

What the apartment lacked was a decent-sized mirror. There was a small square one above the bathroom basin but nothing full-length, nothing that gave back her whole body, not even if she balanced on the edge of the hip-bath or stood contorted on a stool, no way of seeing what Micky had seen.

'In a manner of speaking' wasn't nearly good enough. Blind instinct, that was the term. From the very beginning a baby wanted to be utterly important in its mother's eyes; it wanted to *figure*.

According to Heather, even before it could see her for certain it was straining to be seen, and if it wasn't seen, or not properly, it sensed this too ... then the invisibility became a basic fault that the baby felt obliged to decipher or even – talk about getting the wrong end of the stick – to correct.

How could a small thing like a baby take on such a mammoth task? The answer, of course, was that it couldn't... Imagining this deluded and dutiful infant, Broom wanted to weep for its smallness and for the great effort it put into piecing its mother together, composing her. Centuries of effort, oceans of pigment, acres of gold leaf, and for what? For the sake of the bent attentive head, the divine linkage of the two gazes, the two haloes inclining towards each other until they almost touched? The template of all templates?

'I don't know how you do it!' Al's sister Vicky hissed as she stood beside Broom, holding a rolled umbrella, two heavy handbags and a swatch of cardigans and coats; she stared at the figure on the bed, her round face growing redder and redder. It was almost as if the sight of her own brother was too much for her, or even – judging by the explosive disgust of her whisper – that it repelled her. Broom wanted to say that it was hardly a penance, that the real test was not the daily vigil at Al's bedside, the real test was crossing the river each night like a ghost with no guarantees and leaving him.

She had given up her precious bedside chair but Al's mother had made no attempt to claim it. Instead she stood stock-still in the middle of the floor, like a new girl at school waiting to be directed to her form room. When Broom went over to kiss her, Jennifer fixed her with a bright gaze and began to talk about the frost on the lawn when they left Birmingham, and the uncommonly light traffic on the M1. Broom wondered what on earth was wrong with her. Al was sleeping, so she'd been spared that eerie persevering gaze. All right, she was shocked, but shock hadn't stopped anyone else: Ken with his eyes misty behind bifocals, Keith and Barbara, white-faced but controlled, Sam and Dexter who were old hands by now, even her own sturdy Sean — not one of them had flinched or passed up the privilege of the empty chair.

'I just hold his hand and talk to him,' Broom whispered. 'You do actually get used to it.' It was all she could do to smile.

Later she excused herself and left them to it, paced unseeing as far as the Festival Hall and up some walkways past the triumphal bust of Nelson Mandela, her mind carrying on its quarrel with Jennifer, asking her exactly what she'd expected and how exactly Al had fallen short of her ideal, when he was still the man he'd always been, her first-born son, the apple, surely, of her eye.

When she went back into the ward Jennifer was sitting by the bed, holding Al's hand. Her back was straight, her small feet lined up neatly as shoes in a hotel corridor. She turned to look at Broom, an oddly self-deprecating expression on her face. 'I'm getting to quite like this,' she said, on a note of girlish wonder. 'I think I could really get used to this.'

Her need for approval was so palpable that Broom's heart clenched. She stood there in no-man's-land

381

smiling at Jennifer as if her life depended on it. 'Yes, it's nice, isn't it?' she said, for if it was a bit late in the day to be learning such basic skills, late was definitely better than never.

Micky dozed a little before dawn and when he woke and went to the window the day was a brand-new leaf. Clouds were flowing along the bowl of the valley and lifting; small children sledged decorously on the shallow meadow-slope behind the Maine. He thought without regret of the rainswept emptiness of London streets, the brutish good cheer of the pubs. On Christmas Day everything in France stayed open: the cafés and the restaurants would be full; even the shops would be offering their fresh baguettes, their truffled patés and their cheeses. There would be a bustle, everyone out and about. The citizens would be dressed more smartly than usual, and their kids would be excitable but not hysterical, and no one would be drunk or disarrayed except perhaps the giant Cossack and his horse.

He turned on France Classique to dress by and struck gold – a Messiah from St John's Smith Square, with Emma Kirkby. He emptied the ashtray into the wastebasket and sang along. 'O come unto me, all ye that are heavy la – ay – den...'

He carried his orange juice out to the balcony and gazed with satisfaction at the real McCoy. It was exactly what Christmas should be: the sky clearing by the minute, the fairytale firs, the houses trim under their steep white snowhats. Christmas as advertised, a definite pitch-winner. The sun still lurked behind the bulk of the Massif but the first *cabines* were already plying up to the Sud. He must remember to ring through to Reception, get them to make a reservation. His shout, of course. For no more than a fleeting second he felt the rich person's impatience with others' lack of means. If Latifa was watching she would want him to be kind; she would want him to make someone happy.

He'd made it his business to know the street name and the number; he would simply nip round to the chalet and surprise her. When she answered his knock she'd find him on the doorstep, large as life and bearing gifts. What greater pleasure than not to be expected, but to arrive and be greeted with the shyness that reveals the secret heat of wishes? Already she had sweetened up and softened; she was beginning to know what was good for her. She was a woman of substance. The world, as they say, was her oyster; she would tilt the shell and suck it down lustily, its pearls and its pleasures. The thought made his lips tingle. He found what seemed to be due east and made a little bow but not to Allah. It tickled him to think that she didn't know he saw her as his special little mission.

'And he shall feed his flock, like a she – e – e – eh – perd...' He tried for the high note and fell, chuckling, off the cliff. His brain was clear, his eyes eased by the unaccustomed hours of sleep. He felt, all in all, like a man who could work miracles.

Broom saw her mother at the far side of the room, faint at first, like a lighthouse through a mist. A small pulsing brightness that raised the possibility of ease. The sea ploughed all around, doing its nature-duty. She could hear it throbbing, although she couldn't see the broken ice blue of the waves. Her mother lay in a bed Broom wanted very much to snuggle into. Sensing an unspoken invitation, she was exhilarated, and approached the bed. The mattress greeted her with a kind sound when she clambered in. Her mother wore something white that might have been a nightdress. A sleepy wheeze of breathing came from her but Broom couldn't find her face. She waited for arms to go round her and hold her tight, but the body her kisses encountered was segmented, soft, legless, like a chrysalis. There were no arms.

Keep the hips still and the heart suffocates. The thought startled her awake. Because of the way she was lying – stiff as a sword, with her arms pasted to her sides and her legs lined up, like a Norman tomb effigy – she imagined at first that she was in a tent, zipped tightly into a single sleeping bag. She sat up with a jerk and switched the light on. When she swung her legs out of bed the scintillating smell of sex rose up from her crotch. The whisky bottle stood on the coffee table, the tumbler lolling empty on the rug.

'My dear, you really mustn't blame yourself,' Miriam had said. 'From what you've told me it's clear that you did absolutely everything you could.' Her eyes veered towards Al's empty chair, as if out of a habit of adjudication. For a moment she was silent, wrestling with some private thought. 'He was a fine man. I'm so desperately sorry.' She raised her shoulders in frustration. 'If only we'd had him just a little while longer.'

The look that passed between them had cut Broom to the heart. It was no more and no less than a tacit acknowledgement of failure; it said, unmistakably, that with a little while longer they could have saved him.

She left her underwear on the floor and pulled on thermals and a fleece. In thick hiking socks her feet were too big for her trainers, but she shoved them on anyway and shuffled down the hall with the laces loose and clicking on the floorboards. On the concrete landing outside she gulped in the freezing air. Her mind was full of questions, dismal and unanswerable.

She saw again the Laurencin painting on Miriam's wall, the limpness of the woman, the passive blobs of her hands. Back then a girl could sue for breach of promise but she didn't even have that prerogative. If he had jilted her (the word bubbled up bizarrely from another century – not 'dropped' or 'dumped', but 'jilted'), at least she could have raged, fought, slashed his car tyres, cut up his shirts...

Of course it was easier to blame the living and the breathing, but it was hardly Micky's fault if her lover had died on her.

385

Once again she felt a teetering alarm, as if on some inner fault-line cracks were opening, geysers of malevolence preparing to erupt. Alive, Al could be given a good talking to, or even a belt round the ear; fleshless, he was a shadow she dared not box with. If she hit him he would break, and try as she might to repair him she'd never be able to put the pieces back together again.

She knew it made no sense, but that was hardly the point. Logically speaking, the dead were safe as houses; they no longer needed to be protected. Then again, if houses were so safe, why was she out here seeking safety, searching the darkness for a glimpse of the high enclosing rim of the Massif, as if only the mountains – solid, immovable – were strong enough to absorb the impact? Why this sense of having committed a dangerous act, when she knew perfectly well that all this could go on in her mind, yet nothing would actually have occurred? She of all people should know that the dead weren't weak and breakable at all, they were fucking obdurate. They had the power to ignore you for all eternity.

Although the valley was ink black, there was a paling in the eastern sky above the beetling brow-line of the Massif. Broom pulled her sleeves down to protect her hands, then gripped the metal rail and leaned out until she could see, round the corner of the building, the first dawn rays highlighting the solitary summit tip of the Faille. It wasn't fair, none of it was fair. But if there was a place where justice lived she wanted to be up there, up in the land of the animus, infused by the promise that what she thought, and, more importantly, what she felt, would one day be weighed and put in order.

From the neighbouring chalet came the bleep of an alarm clock. Christmas Day or not, someone was on early shift; soon the rest of the town would be getting up, shoving bare feet into slippers, coughing in bathrooms. The sun was charging in from the east and Europe was awakening. Miles above the earth, satellites were taking pictures of the darkness that lay ahead of the running rim of light. Half a world away, in Seattle, Sean was celebrating Christmas Eve with Beverley.

Expire is the opposite of inspire. The thought entered her ear like an overheard remark, the sort of casual bullshitty thing that might drift down from a group of climbers on the pitch above and make you groan but leave you wanting more. She felt just light-headed enough to ponder the truth of it, or at least some truth it might presently give birth to. She stood at the rail, feeling the dawn wind creep round the corner of the house and whisper across her skin.

First she had to forgive herself for being left. Then she had to forgive Al for leaving her.

Christmas morning was clear and frosty. The sea was quiet on the sand. Wading birds worked the shoreline. From the lower margins of the moor came the ratchet call of the red grouse.

After breakfast they adjourned to the sitting

387

room, where there was no tree but at least there were presents. Lockhart had wrapped his the evening before in the Blue Room; then he had switched on the old portable TV – although channel-surfing lost a great deal of its appeal when you didn't have a remote control – and crawled under the duvet. In the end he'd watched a programme about a Midwest church where men and women in electric-blue shirts jigged to hillbilly music with rattlesnakes coiled round their wrists. The band sang a jaunty song of which he could remember only the chorus: 'Drop-kick me, Jesus, to the goal posts of Life.' The theory being that since everything was in God's hands it was only His intervention that stopped the rattlesnakes destroying the believers. Lockhart hadn't been convinced. What stopped them, clearly, was sheer surprise at the situation they found themselves in. Huddled under the duvet, he'd identified with the rattlesnakes. He hadn't had the heart to call Agneta.

His father had given him a Mont Blanc pen. Lockhart watched him fold back the tissue wrapping from the golfing pullover – bought, on Agneta's insistence, at Lillywhite's – lay it reverently across his knee and stroke the cashmere with a timid Presbyterian delight.

Fraser was playing Santa Claus. He passed Lockhart a heavy drum-shaped object. *'Archie, love from Retta.'*

'Well, I can't think what this is,' said Lockhart, feeling obliged to enter into the spirit of the thing. A sherry would have oiled the wheels but the decanter hadn't yet put in an appearance.

'A landmine?' Fraser offered.

Lockhart stifled a laugh as he peeled the paper from a bumper tin of Quality Street. 'Not far off.'

John Lockhart appeared not to have heard; he was staring into the fire, the cashmere sweater draped across his knees. His shoulders had a convalescent slump; he looked bemused, like a man caught on the barbed wire of other Christmases.

It was Fraser, surprisingly, who came up trumps. When Lockhart saw the books he let out a whoop. They were climbing classics, as least as old as he was: Hunt and Herzog and Hillary.

Fraser looked pleased. 'H as in hero,' he said, grinning.

'How did you get your hands on them?' Lockhart sniffed at the plain dark schoolish weave of the covers.

Fraser shrugged modestly. 'I did a book search on the net.'

In the flyleaf of the Herzog was a photograph of Lionel Terray on the fixed rope above Camp 2. A combination of high colour-contrast and slightly shaky registration made it look as mythic as a movie poster; the ice chips that sprayed from Terray's front-point were so sharp and bright they could have stabbed you in the eye. He held the page open to show his father. '1950. Brilliant, isn't it? The first ascent of Annapurna.'

John Lockhart craned politely. 'Aye, well. It's a different era.' It struck Lockhart that 1950 was the year of the photograph in the library, the year his parents had got engaged.

Fraser crushed his cigarette out in the ashtray

389

and almost immediately lit another. He sat cross-legged on the rug in front of the fire, his presents lined up before him like toy soldiers. He had leafed through the Mandelstam Lockhart had given him but mercifully hadn't read aloud from it. Retta's cuff-links had been returned to their presentation box; his fingers tapped a military rhythm on the lid.

Presently it would be time for church. Lockhart excused himself and went next door to use the land line in the library.

When he heard Agneta's voice he had an acute urge to dive into the receiver and be shot at warp speed down the line, like some proton in a particle accelerator.

'It's a madhouse down here,' she said. 'Are you surviving?'

Fluid trickled down his sinuses and thickened in his throat. He cupped his hand round the mouthpiece and clamped the receiver to his ear. 'Sure. Yes. But, you know. Missing you.'

Agneta's laugh had an edge. 'Speak up, darling. I don't think I quite caught that!' She was teasing him, enjoying his discomfiture.

The silence of the sitting room pressed so heavily against the door that his 'I love you' sounded like a boastful bellow. Surely Fraser and his father could hear him. 'Things are a bit tricky. It's hard to talk about on the phone.' He was speaking into his fist. 'I'll tell you when I see you.'

There was a chorus of giggles in the background. 'Hang on, the twins want to say hi...'

'Say "thank you" for your presents, kids,' someone shouted, as he tried in vain to remember what Agneta had bought for them.

'Happy Chriss-mass, Un-cul Ar-shee,' they carolled.

'Happy Christmas to you too, you two.'

Outside the window the elongated shadows of the rhododendrons were exact frost-monsters chalked out on the greening lawn. He thought of the boisterous central heating in the Brighton house, the twins prancing permissively in pyjama tops on a carpet with a pile as thick as a polar bear's pelt, his wife, who should have been at his side but who was having a merry family Christmas a thousand miles away. He reminded himself that he ought to be, indeed was, glad for her.

'I take it you've started on the *sekt*,' he said enviously, when she came back on the line.

'Absolutely.' Her voice softened. 'Hey. Look after yourself, lovely. Don't let that Fraser grind you down. It's not your fault if he's a complete dingbat.'

The McFadzean pew was at the front of the church, directly below the pulpit. Although it was too big by far for the three Lockharts, none of the other worshippers made a move to enter. Aeons ago, when Boz and Nessa were alive and the family was large enough to fill it, Lockhart and Fraser would file in every Sunday in their matching tweed coats and Startrite shoes, and sit crushed together at the junior end, furthest from the aisle, Lockhart with orders to hold Fraser's hand and feed him Mint Imperials to keep him quiet during the sermon.

They sat now in feudal isolation, craning up at

the gnomish figure of the Reverend Hutchinson, who leaned above them at a beatific angle, like Buster Keaton from a gantry.

Lockhart nudged Fraser. 'What age must he be?'

'About as old as the Queen Mum,' Fraser whispered. 'Only she has better frocks.'

The invisible organist belted out an intro. To the right of the pulpit hung a board onto which hymn numbers were slotted. Once upon a time Lockhart wouldn't have needed to check them in the index: he'd have recognized the standards by their numbers and known at a glance if there was anything to look forward to. 'Onward, Christian Soldiers'. 'Away in a Manger'. 'We Three Kings of Orient Are'.

The congregation rose. He and Fraser shared a hymnbook.

Star of wonder, star of light,
Star with royal beauty bright,
Westward leading, still proceeding...

Beside him Fraser swayed to the lugubrious lilt of the tune; his voice rang out, a sweet enthusiastic tenor. He'd forgotten that Fraser loved to sing. He was conscious of his brother's fingers, flattening back the pages of the hymn-book; apart from that he was bodiless, a transparent presence in the corner of Lockhart's eye, linear as a Cranach angel, and resonantly fair. When the notes of the organ died away they sat down again and Lockhart's heart was a shiver in his chest.

As the Lord's Prayer began he heard a rustle

above his head and saw a bird darting. There was a swallow's nest in the rafters, where one of the crossbeams met the eaves. The nest, lumpish and moulded, was a dull pastry colour. His father, he remembered, was treasurer of the renovation fund.

In the old days the brass collection plate had been passed along the pew and they'd dropped their shillings or sixpences proudly on the pile. Lockhart saw that offerings were made more discreetly now, in small square buff envelopes marked 'Church of Scotland'. No doubt they also accepted standing orders and direct debits. The usher hovered, hands folded, in the aisle. Lockhart folded a five-pound note and slipped it under his father's envelope. He didn't pass the plate along to Fraser.

Once the collection was over people began to leave. The church emptied within moments; no one hung around to kneel or pray popishly, but filed quietly out to the porch, the men with their black hats in their hands, the women signalling to one another with nods and muted smiles. In the meantime the Reverend Hutchinson, age and frailty notwithstanding, had nipped out through the vestry and hurried round to the main door to stand in sun or snow and be ready to receive his flock.

Lockhart had a suit on under his parka but he didn't own a hat. As a mark of respect he removed his gloves while they queued to shake hands.

The Reverend's fingers were sparrowlike and cold as gravestones. 'Mr Lockhart. Fraser. Good

393

to see you back, Archie.' He nodded firmly as he named them, as though reassuring himself that his memory, at least, was still intact.

At the bottom of the steps people paused on the gravel path to chat, their breaths mingling in a collective steam-cloud on the frosty air. The men replaced their hats and said their season's greetings; several who, like Fraser, couldn't wait until they reached the churchyard gate, lit up cigarettes.

John Lockhart went to the Volvo, which was parked by the lychgate, and opened the boot. A moment later he returned, carrying in both hands, like a soup tureen, a pot of Christmas roses. The flowers were white and perishable; one night's frost would finish them.

Lockhart knew that their father wouldn't ask them to accompany him to the family plot, he'd simply assume that they would do so. He thought of the gold-lettered headstone, the immodest shine of its polished black marble. Unlike the granite stones of Boz and Nessa and their antecedents, which were rain-roughened and humbled by moss, Frances's gravestone displayed no more sign of bowing to the imperatives of Callasay than she herself had shown in life, but stood apart, a lonely monument to futile rebellion.

John Lockhart stood with the pot in his hands. On his face was an expression of strained solemnity. People glanced at the flowers and nodded silently, averting their gaze. Several ogled the blue sky and pronounced it a grand day. As Lockhart agreed soberly that it was indeed, he saw the fiendish glint of gaiety in Fraser's eye and hysteria rose in him. Just one wink and he would be done for, his house of cards collapsed. The laughter, when it came, would be tidal and terminal, like teenage orgasm. He coughed sharply and shook hands with the dominie's wife, stilling his bursting face, praying that just for once no one would say, 'And we'll pay for it.'

She was beginning to see it as a climb of up to half a dozen pitches. Al knew she was waiting at the top for him, but at every stance he had to fix his belay, bring up the second, rerack his gear, gather his forces. He would climb slowly and deliberately, and every runner he placed would be bomb-proof, and he might take an age to get there but he'd make it in the end.

She'd been learning how to keep him comfortable. Nurse Hazel had shown her how to moisten his lips with a Q-tip dipped in a pinkish solution; she'd even asked her to help change the sterile dressing that staunched the seepage from the tracheostomy incision.

Nurse Ronnie had come on shift at ten to put him through his paces. He had squeezed her finger and put his tongue out on demand and received congratulations. After the tracking test his eyes connected once again with Broom, who was following the procedures from the foot of the bed. This time there was more urgency in his expression.

When Ronnie had finished changing the IV bags, Broom moved to him and took his hand. She was aware immediately of a subtle shift in the balance of power. Instead of lying limp and letting itself be enfolded, his hand struggled to enclose hers. He was twisting his neck, straining to look at her. His grip tightened. Sluggishly at first, he began to pull her hand downwards.

'What is it?' she asked, thinking that he wanted her to scratch an itch for him or smooth a pucker in the sheet. The force of his will startled her. Her hand was no longer her own, but a function of his fierce wish to travel downwards. His body was tense, the tendons in his neck strung taut with effort.

There was an oxygen monitor clipped like a clothes peg to his finger, tubes in his arm through which drugs entered, and, lower down, the unkind catheter. So many crucial items he could dislodge.

When it dawned on her where her hand was heading, she was horrified and whispered strictly, trying to extract it from his grip. Hot-cheeked under the scathing lights, she glanced through the glass partition at the nurses' station, hoping that no one had seen.

Al's body shifted, plaintive; she thought she heard it sigh. His hand, abandoned, lost its way for a moment; she could see it in the gap between the top and bottom sheet, deliberating in the semi-darkness. Then it inched on. She watched helplessly. If he did what she thought he was going to do she couldn't be a party to it. The respirator hissed like a disapproving crowd at the hand on its unseemly odyssey. Clearly he was going to do it anyway.

Broom put her face close to his and whispered in his ear. 'Darling,' she chided, 'there'll be plenty of time for that.'

She saw the brief rebellious pout of his lips as his

fingers encountered the annoying catheter, dismissed it, scented out the mushroom cap: that warm and comforting button. The rest she knew by heart: the forefinger stroking the anterior, the thumb breasting the flowering rim. Even in unconsciousness, the patient expertise of it.

For weeks she'd touched him only as a nurse would or a mother; in all that time she hadn't touched herself.

The images came at her, frantic and drenched with sex. Her face flamed. Her shoulders were rigid with embarrassment. What if the nurses could see right through her, could read on her face something other than devotion, could, on the white and sterile screen of illness, project the private pornographic sweats of health?

The ward was T-shaped, with three large bays marked off by cupboards and lockers. In the bay on the left was a teenage boy who had broken his spine in a snow-boarding accident. Since he'd been brought in not a sound had come from him. Although the nurses moved constantly around his bed, they had stopped trying to cheerlead him through the tests. The staff nurse was explaining something in a low voice. The boy was hidden from view by the banks of monitors, but Broom could see his mother and sister, standing with their arms folded, listening with blank, flushed faces.

She went to the sink and soaked a paper towel and held it across her face. When she opened her eyes again she mistook a grey square of wall for the mirror, and stood for a second, gripping the rim of the sink. How could she be sure what kind of signal he was sending? Whether it was really meant for her, an acknowledge-

ment. Which would at least place it in the realms of the human. Or else – what? Blind instinct, beyond good or bad, beyond reason or love or religion?

When Ronnie swept back in with her clipboard Broom looked at her pleadingly. Al's eyes were closed but there was no mistaking the shape of the movement under the sheet.

Ronnie absorbed the situation at a glance. She stood by the monitor screen, noting down read-outs. Her starched wings crackled as she shrugged. 'First thing they all do,' she said. 'Check it out. Men, eh?' She rolled her eyes at Broom and spun insouciantly on her sensible heels, her angelic pockets weighed down by thermometers.

The doorbell in the *confiserie* tinkled constantly: people were queueing for their *bavaroises* and *bûches de Noël*. There were English mince pies on the counter but clearly only the chalet girls would be bothering to boil Christmas puddings.

Micky bought croissants – *amande* and *chocolat* – and a sun-wheel of marzipan fruits on a big wickerwork platter. From the window he glimpsed the hulking *patron* of the Café des Couronnes. He was leaning on the rail of his terrace, enjoying a *petit verre* with a workman who'd been strewing shovelfuls of salt and cinders on the frozen snow of the pavements. Micky left the shop, detoured via a series of icy alleyways to avoid the creep, and came out eventually onto the Rue Flaubert, where he

398

picked up a bottle of Krug at the *épicerie*.

Broom answered the door in a white bath towel and a pair of Norwegian hiking socks. 'Very saucy,' said Micky. 'Do I get a hug?'

She peered at him, shivering. She looked ravaged and waif-like, which suited her. 'You'd better come in.'

Inside the apartment it was warmer, although not as warm as it should have been. There were dishes in the sink and bare linoleum on the kitchen floor; socks and knickers hung drying on an ancient iron radiator. Through the open bedroom door Micky glimpsed a wardrobe the size of a Sicilian mausoleum, and a bed that was unmade and inhospitably single. Evidently she wasn't the type who'd appear in your dressing-gown next morning bearing trays of toast and honey; which was, thought Micky, cool by him.

The kitchen table was awash with layout sheets. He took a step back and angled his neck to get a better look. 'Hey, storyboards!' he exclaimed, holding the sun-wheel across his chest like a shield.

Broom pushed wet hair back from her face. 'I take it you're not working today.' Her tone was just short of reproving.

'No way. Tomorrow it's all systems go on *la belle* Sophie, but today I'm fancy-free.' Feeling suddenly nervous, Micky held out the bag of croissants. She'd allowed him a peck on the cheek at the door but he couldn't help noticing that she wasn't exactly wriggling with excitement. 'I've brought breakfast, if you're interested.'

'Well!' she said with a glassy hostess smile,

taking the bag and peeping inside.

They were briefly and simultaneously speechless. Micky unzipped his parka and waited to be invited to take it off. He found that he was staring at her skin, that same speckly Celtic skin he had managed not to inherit from Jerome. Once he had come upon Latifa in her slip, washing her hair at the basin. When he was about thirteen she'd taken to wearing long sleeves and high collars; even at the beach she covered her shoulders with small bolero jackets. He'd assumed her sudden modesty was in deference to his age – some kind of compliment, perhaps, to his budding manhood. More fool Micky. He'd backed noiselessly out of the bathroom, but not before he'd seen the two circles that marked the tops of her arms. They were tarnish-coloured, but they certainly weren't bracelets.

Broom's arms were strong and shapely. Soapsuds were shrinking on her bare shoulders. He thought of getting a good grip on her, right there, kneading, maybe even pinching a little.

She turned swiftly and whisked the underwear off the radiator. 'Let me just get dressed.' Flashing the social smile again, she disappeared into the bedroom, leaving him wondering why he still felt he had something to make up to her. The real issue, he suspected, was the dead lover. Maybe someone should tell her that perpetual mourning had fallen out of fashion. Five years was a long time and at her age it was time she couldn't afford to waste.

He hung his parka on a chair and decided to make himself useful by putting the croissants in to warm and the champagne in to cool. There wasn't a great deal in the fridge – some paté in greaseproof paper, half a bar of Ritter Sport, a takeaway carton of carrot salad. He stashed the Krug and shut the door hastily. Looking into someone's fridge was a lot like looking into their open mouth, and he had no intention of invading her privacy. Fridges were such a giveaway. They made you speculate on people's personal habits, hungers you really didn't want to think about – like whether a woman stuffed herself silly, or else, having denied herself all day, crept to the kitchen like a mouse in the night to nibble at leftovers.

Feeling like a proper little housewife, he rolled up his sleeves and rinsed coffee grounds from the cafetière and filled the kettle. Micky the New Man. He didn't particularly mind the role as such; it was more the title that bothered him. With a header like that, no wonder the concept hadn't caught on. New Man didn't initialize, it had absolutely no ring to it; it was, in fact, utterly unmemorable. Initials were as important as alliteration or assonance, which was why Yuppie had stuck, and also why poets made the most effective copywriters. Duppie might work. Domesticated Urban Prick. Duppie, he seemed to remember, had some kind of zombie subtext – enslavement, obedience, the captive bodies of the soulless. Which, if you felt like being cynical, wasn't too far off the mark.

Bathwater clanked away noisily down distant pipes. As he waited for the kettle to boil he had a sudden and quite clear image of taking a bath with her, of the way she would sit facing him and lean forward until the soap-dabs on her nipples transferred precisely to his. It was so visually authoritative that for a moment he thought he must have played this game with Marianne or some other long-forgotten lover, in Beirut or Paris or New York, or perhaps had only wanted to.

When the telephone rang he realized that she wouldn't be able to hear it. He picked up the antique receiver. Servant, social worker, and now secretary: for one morning, he wasn't doing badly.

'*Allo?*'

'Hi, darling, are you there? It's Daniel.'

The voice was deep and magisterial. There was a bullish, impatient edge to it, which grated on him. The famous director, then, about to descend. The Jewish patriarch. He listened for a moment or two, gazing pensively out at the grandiose profile of the Montjoie, picturing someone beefy and balding, someone who would always take up more than his fair share of space.

'*Qui? Ah non. Vous vous êtes trompé. Il n'y a personne à ce nom ici. Désolé.*' He replaced the receiver quietly and lingered at the table, leafing through the sketches. As well as the storyboards there were two sheets of costume designs. The get-up for the female character – drab overalls and galoshes – made him think of Palestinian cleaning women. Mephistopheles wore khakis and loafers without socks and the sort of designer scalp-stubble widely favoured in Fitzrovia, which was a bit of a cheap shot but somehow didn't surprise him.

He pulled a colour transparency from a box and held it up to the window. It was a painting, semi-abstract, with a circular silvery motif at the centre – a moon or a sun or maybe even an eye – and some kind of massy forms obtruding from the outer corners. He took out another. This time the core motif seemed to be submerged in a well or a bucket, but it was hard to tell without a viewer. On that scale and in the diffident daylight the paintings looked sombre and obscured. They didn't remind him of anyone in particular, or at least no one he could immediately put his finger on, but they did have a certain something. Presence, he supposed, was the word he was looking for. Damien had a definite eye for a good investment. He wondered how he would rate them.

'Don't tell me, you've come to see my etchings.'

He wheeled round, startled. She was standing in the doorway with her arms folded, watching him. She had put on denims and a black zipped fleece and some improving make-up round her eyes. She looked, he thought, distinguished: angular and characterful, like the mid-life types Gap had used to good effect on the rumps of London buses.

'Are these yours?'

'For my sins.'

'They're excellent.'

'The sins or the paintings?'

'No, really,' he insisted. 'I'm impressed.'

A smell of scorched pastry wafted from the oven. 'Shit!' cried Micky, grabbing a tea-towel from the back of a chair. He found a clean plate

403

in the drying-rack and bent down to rescue the croissants. 'I nearly forgot. Your mate rang. Dan, is it? Some kind of hitch. I think he said chicken-pox.'

'Oh no!' Broom looked stricken. 'The kids?'

He put the plate on the one section of oilcloth he'd managed to clear of artworks and handed her the table mats. 'I'm sorry; you were in the bathroom. I thought I'd better get it.'

'So he isn't able to come down?'

Micky shook his head solemnly. 'You aren't upset, are you?'

She stood with the table mats in her hand, peering distractedly around for her lighter. 'He's the director. We've got a lot of work to do.' She was toughing it out but her voice was hollow and fragile.

Micky felt like taking her in his arms and kissing her tenderly, but she had already armed herself with a cigarette. He reached across the table and squeezed her hand regretfully. 'And he's, like, a boyfriend?'

'No way. I've known him for centuries.'

'Ah,' said Micky. His irritation rose and crested. If she wanted to go on worshipping the dead hero it was up to her, but there was such a thing as pricing yourself out of the market. And like all special offers, Micky's had a closing date. Nothing ruined a woman like disappointment, he could personally vouch for that. He could tell her plenty of things about Latifa, if she cared to ask. About her patience and her prayers, about how she clung for years to the belief that by the grace of God or Allah her marriage would be cured. If

404

he cared to dredge it all up, which he did not. By your choices you create yourself, as they say. Latifa at thirty-six was perfect, and if thereafter she was not exactly dead she was as good as, so it was kinder to both of them to freeze the frame right there, for no son should ever have to watch his mother go to seed.

'Hey!' he appealed. 'Help me out here.' He gave the unresponsive fingers a final little jiggle. 'Don't be glum. OK, I forgot my Santa hat, but the champagne's cooling and this' – he produced the sun-wheel from its carrier bag with a flourish – 'is for afters!'

Broom flattened her hand across her chest, like Emma Kirkby gearing up for a concert aria. She was smiling foolishly at the platter. 'How did you know I can't resist marzipan?' In her eyes he saw the grateful glint of tears.

Outside, the sky had cleared to duck-egg blue and it was Micky's lucky day. Not just a dumb prick, he thought: not just a Duppie. 'Intuition,' he said, grinning, and tapping the side of his nose. 'Maybe we have more in common than you think.'

'Can I open it?'

'Be my guest.' He stabbed the cellophane wrapping with a knife, peeled the edges back and watched her wonder what to choose. Her hand fluttered above the wheel of fruits. Her face was a slow burn of guilt and greed. 'Go on, spoil yourself,' he urged delightedly. 'And while we're on the subject, there's another proposition I might just be able to tempt you with.'

Broom looked at him blankly, her mind still

fixed on marzipan.

'I'll give you a clue. *Haute cuisine.* With the emphasis on the *haute.*'

'You're joking! The Sud?'

Micky nodded.

'It costs an arm and a leg!'

'As long as it doesn't literally! Unless you have other plans, that is?'

She shook her head. 'No.' A worry winged its way back from somewhere and settled on her face. 'But I can't! I'm expecting a call from Sean. He's in Seattle with his girlfriend.'

He'd forgotten about the son, and didn't particularly want to be reminded. He said airily, 'Well, according to my calculations that gives you a good nine hours to play with. And you could always phone him later, from the hotel...'

Broom put a marzipan peach on her plate and clasped her hands, staring down at it like someone about to say grace. He watched her suss it out. She was, he thought, blushing.

'There are a couple of tapes I've been meaning to show you. I'd like, you know, your professional opinion.'

'We could walk down from the Plan afterwards, couldn't we? I could bring the map.' There was no mistaking the eagerness on her face.

'That's more like it,' cried Micky. 'That's the spirit.' He speared an almond croissant and dropped it on his plate. 'I've been thinking maybe I should do a restaurant guide – top eateries of the world, that sort of thing.' He waited for her chuckle. 'What publishers would call a High Concept book. It's a definite gap in the market.'

Broom took a preliminary nibble at the peach and set it down. A smile had spread across her face, wide and gap-toothed and boyish. 'By the way, forgive me for saying so, but you're a really crap skier!'

'Yeah, yeah, yeah,' said Micky.

Midway through the second week she decided to cook a meal for Sean. Maybe he doesn't want you to protect him, Heather had said; maybe he feels left out. It was time she included him, time she made at least a gesture towards normality.

She bought tortellini and cream and a bottle of Montepulciano, and stood at the kitchen counter, shaving mushrooms into razor-thin slices. Just before she'd left the ward, she'd looked back to check that Al's eyes were closed, because she hated the thought of vanishing when he could see but couldn't raise a finger or say a word to stop her. He looked thin and Byzantine, like some Syriac saint. An ascetic in headphones. Not that he would be lonely, with Dexter beside him, filling his head with Cajun and bluegrass and God knows what else. On the contrary, it must be pretty busy in there, echoey and flashlit, like a church full of tourists. When her own voice wound down, Hank Williams or Pete Rowan waited to take over.

Some tracks made his nostrils flare. His mouth seemed to want to mutter to the words. Although the chest man was still fighting the good fight against all his little bugs and beggars, the professor said he was

407

pleased with his progress. The word they were using now was 'stable'. They had dropped the 'critical, but'.

There was a kind of aurora fulminating at the edges of her eyes, a visual whisper that bothered her. It made her think of the small beige clothes moths that had hatched last year in her hall cupboard. All winter they'd been eating the underarms of her old climbing sweaters; in spring, emerging from a lace of darkness, they flickered like liminal messages around the flat.

She clipped on her glacier goggles and set to work on an onion. Al was in good hands, the best. She had to remember that. Even if there was a long way to go before she could wean herself from the habit of anxiety.

'You're kidding!' said Sean, coming in with his key and doing a double take. He hauled off his Goretex and dumped his camera bag on the floor.

She pushed the goggles back and plonked a kiss on his cheek. 'It's the only way to stop your eyes stinging.'

Fog-damp clung to the stubble on his chin. He smelled of sweat and railway soot. He raised his eyes to heaven. 'Ah, right...'

'You've been at college?'

'Yup.' Two days teaching photography were his bread and butter, around which he organized his freelance work. Reclaim the Streets, Stop the City, Save the Trees, and so on. Oh, she approved, of course, even if some of the gigs he covered worried her witless. Which, she supposed, was as it ought to be. The mother-and-son conspiracy. Luckily his shoulders had turned out to be too broad to squeeze down Swampy's tunnel. 'Actually, I got auctioned. The fashion students were doing a fund-raiser for their degree

shows. *This little French girl called Amalie bought me for forty quid.'*

Broom laughed. 'So what's she going to do with you?'

'Fuck knows. Guess I'll have to wait and see. I've been helping them to produce this Man of the Month calendar. Nudie pics. The girls chose the guys and the guys chose the props. You know, to cover their bits. We had a stag's head and a goldfish bowl, and one guy used his laptop, which was actually the freakiest. Someone even brought a skull.' He grinned. 'Well, they are art students, after all. Actually, the pics are really sweet.'

She looked at him gladly. Light, deep-set eyes, her own domed brow. Reddish-brown hair shorn radically at the back and sides and curling on the top. One hundred per cent Scot. Born and bred in the flatlands of England, yes, but take him within twenty miles of a mountain and he'd vanish up it without a word. Afterwards he'd disclaim responsibility. 'Just blame it on the genes.'

When she served up he raised his eyebrows at the mound of pasta on his plate. 'I see it's Feed the Child time.'

'Old habits die hard. Don't knock it.'

When he'd poured them each a glass of wine, he said cautiously, 'Sounds like things are going better, then? Would you say?'

Broom considered the question. She could tell from his voice how much depended on the answer. Even during the worst times he'd stubbornly stuck up for Al. OK, he could see the downside, he said, but Al was basically a good bloke. Substantial. 'Unlike some of the guys I've had to put up with over the years,' he might have said but, to his credit, didn't.

She saw them walking ahead of her, at the tail end of a straggling column of climbers. Al in his Oxfam sweater and ragged Ron Hills, Sean loaded down with camera bags. Two broad backs from which merry laughter came. The image filled her with pleasure. Al was gesticulating, listening closely for Sean's reply; he'd been planning the trespass for weeks. Since 1941 the coastal stretch had been classified, one of those blank white spaces on the OS map. The clifftops were barren and extreme, as only battlefields can be. Grey plastic casings of anti-personnel mines littered the tussocky grass. She remembered bringing up the rear, gingerly, skipping over spent ordnance.

She raised her glass and clinked it against Sean's. 'Anyway, let's drink to it.'

'Bloody right!'

The phone rang while she was recounting Sam-and-Dexter tales from Turkey. Sean had been egging her on, chuckling with happy horror. She was still talking as she went through to the bedroom and lifted the receiver.

'It's Mead Ward. Sister Alison speaking. I'm sorry to have to tell you, but things have taken a turn for the worse.'

She stood outraged, pressing her hand to her face. 'Yes,' she said, as her mind registered a kind of cruelty she could not associate with Sister Alison. In the silence it struck her that the bedroom reeked of onions, and for a moment she couldn't understand why this should be, or how it might have been prevented.

'I'm coming straight away.' The voice that barked out of her was rude and angry, like a drill sergeant's. She hadn't yet begun to shake.

410

'Yes,' Sister Alison said quietly. 'I think that's best.'

In the kitchen she stood by the table, gripping the back of her chair. Sean's plate was empty; he was mopping up the last sheen of sauce with a slice of baguette. The satisfaction she felt was automatic. Who would have thought he'd be such a good eater? A good sleeper. A happy baby. She knew what Sister Alison was trying to say, but that didn't mean she had to believe it.

Sean looked at her and froze.

'That was the hospital.'

'Oh Christ.'

She shook her head fervently. He stood up and held on to her. She didn't trust herself to lean her head against his chest.

'We'll have to call a taxi.' The radiocab number was on the noticeboard. She unpinned it and handed it to him.

When he came back from the phone she was standing by the window, staring out at the night. He stood behind her and gripped her shoulders hard. His thumbs moved in the hollows of her shoulderblades, where the trapezius inserts.

'They said ten minutes.'

She saw the diagrams in her anatomy book: the great flat muscles wrapped across the back like bat's wings. He had good hands; healer's hands, she'd always said. She let go and shut her eyes and for a moment it was hard to believe that the shadowless ward existed.

The jeans she'd changed into when she got back from the hospital would have to do. She brushed bread crumbs from her sweater and retrieved her shoes from their hiding place under the sofa. Her Valium were in

411

*the kitchen drawer. She rooted about and shoved them
into her handbag.*

*'Take your time,' said Sean, as she stood at the
mirror, struggling with her comb.*

*The taxi bounced sedately south. The driver was
listening to Radio 4. An astrophysicist was attempting
to explain in layman's terms the difference between
the planets and the stars. He was talking too fast,
squashing his sound-bites in. The speed of the
sentences spun her brain. She flashed on the new
moon through open tent-flaps, Venus setting in a clear
pre-dawn darkness. Her mind felt empty at the axis,
like a cored apple. When she tried to hold on to the
images they swirled away.*

*A sign on the partition thanked her for not smoking.
She read the taxi licence number as usual, considered
committing it to memory.*

*Sean leaned forward suddenly and rapped on the
glass. 'Actually, it's urgent, mate. If you could maybe
put your foot on it!'*

*The curtness of his tone took Broom by surprise.
She caught the driver's baleful glance in the mirror,
then his eyes slid away as he accelerated.*

At that altitude the sky was indigo and the sun
was ubiquitous. As the cabin neared the summit
station of the Sud, Micky's face began to gleam
like hers, like a mirror, as though some painstaking craftsman had applied gold leaf to every
square inch of his skin. The thought of what she
was doing – going up so high and so smoothly,

that and the money – made her feel girlish and irresistible. With every twenty metres of ascent another year peeled off her. Lockhart had taken photographs that first time: lit up, she'd looked unearthly, a celestial being, her face brimming over with a child's excited love.

The cabin passed the final pylon, rocked and docked. They clomped with the other pilgrims through the chilly concrete bowels of the building and climbed a flight of iron steps. She'd borrowed Madame d'Ange's ice-axe, which was an old-fashioned item with an elongated wooden stem: a museum-piece really, but perfect for walking. The descent route she'd set her heart on was a feasible traverse, much used in summer, from the midway station at the Plan du Juron to the *balcon* path above Les Gorets; she had shown it to Micky on the map, but he remained to be persuaded.

At the top of the steps they emerged on the concrete terrace, which even in summer wore a layer of ice obdurate enough to survive not only the sun but the constant scuff of tourist feet, and which was already crowded, with Italians mostly; you could always tell them by their shoes. Broom began to shiver slightly, like a dog who scents the arrival of his master. Already she was breathless, leaning on the ice-axe for support, her lungs tussling with the scanty air. Once again the Montjoie had surpassed her expectations, and because the form it took was indestructible – an unalterable beauty, the face that never faded – it put her out of reach of disappointment, so that in a single rush of blood to the head she knew that this was what she, the artist, belonged to, what she'd been waiting for, what she deserved.

'Isn't this the business!' said Micky, gawping around happily. She followed him to the rail and peered over.

The drop to the town was three thousand metres and absolute. Dizzy with privilege, she looked down, thinking of her mother, and of the Veronicas of the world, all that shadowy baggage left behind under the dimpled cloud that hid the valley floor, those other, weaker selves who called out to her, resentful and deserted, knowing that she'd made it to a land where their little cries of envy were too faint for her to hear.

Micky rubbed his hands together. 'Now. About aperitifs. How does a *kir royale* strike you?'

'Why not?' she said gaily, still surprised by the ease with which she'd bowed to his insistence that he pay for absolutely everything, that to protest would only spoil his pleasure. Put like that, it was an offer she couldn't refuse. But there was another, deeper resonance, as though the prospect of being provided for satisfied some part of her that had lain in wait for a long time, and that now, preening itself, slunk out of hiding.

Once upon a time there was a Scottish schoolgirl who dreamt not of marriage with its dullness and duty, nor even of earning a decent living, but of art and, in her muddled way, of patronage. An older man – platonic, of course: a more or less ghostly benefactor who'd quietly take care of everything; until she became famous, that is – celebrity, of course, was central to the agenda. There would be a studio, male models

414

with sleek pelts and classic torsos she'd take as lovers. She'd almost forgotten about the fantasy. As a variation on a theme of 'Some day my prince will come' – not to mention a neat way of having your cake and eating it – it was really quite impressive. Perhaps any woman, given the choice between being wealthy on her own account or having money kneel at her feet, would secretly prefer the latter, would prefer to be kept and spoilt and cosseted.

She lit a cigarette. The flame of her Zippo was small and pale and starved of oxygen. Across the valley, the Couronnes range hunkered down to reveal unknown ranges beyond. To the north, curving like a scythe blade from the granite spire of the Sud to the shoulder of the Juron, stretched the narrow snow ridge she couldn't quite believe she'd tiptoed along all those years ago, weak-kneed and roped to Lockhart. She felt weightless, remembering her fear, and the anchor of his voice behind her, imposing discipline, the correct placement of the feet and the ice-axe, that steadiness of his above the immensity of the exposure.

'*Pardon. Merci. Pardon.*' Micky sidestepped through the throng towards her, the drinks held glamorously high and spilling. All around him people were sunglassed and wreathed in film-star smiles. Although their clothes spoke of affluence, the radiant light lent them a kind of innocence. They looked ageless and lovable, hobbling about the slippery terrace, arms linked, puffing out their frozen breaths. It was all so easy, really: you paid your two hundred francs, clicked through the turnstile and in twenty minutes, with nil expenditure of effort, you stood on the top of the world.

'Bottoms up!' said Micky, wiping champagne froth from his sleeve. He produced an embossed menu card from the pocket of his parka. 'Pity we can't eat out here too, huh?'

'*Slàinte.*' She clinked her glass against his and took a gulp. Over his shoulder a line of midges crawled up the summit dome of the Montjoie. The slope swept grandly down to the expanse of the north col, and from there the eye sailed east and away, over a ripple of ridges, gilded and linear, on a sea that stretched across Italy and Switzerland to the mauvish smudged summits of the Tyrol. Once or twice the crowd brushed or even jostled her but there was no sensation of suffocation. Her mind was light and dancing. She felt unassailable, her haranguing sentry-voices silenced; she could drink her pink champagne and share in the collective smile, for up here happiness was her portion as much as anyone's. My portion and my potion, she thought: the artist's tipple. The one that promised to open doors to a region where everything was possible and everyone was pure of heart and probably immortal, where you could even – to be Faustian about it – comprehend the incomprehensible. It was a potion taken in careful sips by sensible folk, saved up and savoured, but unfortunately she'd never learned the knack of rationing. Above ten thousand feet her temperament showed its true colours, the vertigo of happiness tipping her over now, as she pointed across the rail, into flurries of tears. 'God's truth, is that the Monte Rosa?'

'Search me,' said Micky, glancing up from the menu. 'I see they've got Loch Fyne oysters. How about that?'

'At thirteen thousand feet?' Her laugh tinkled on the sharp air. 'That's what I call out of your element.'

Micky's finger moved on down the card. His lips were pursed judiciously. 'Maybe so, but they've definitely got my name on them.'

Dusk arrived with the port and the Queen at the end of Christmas lunch. Shortly afterwards Fraser disappeared to do his outdoor chores, and his father, dismissing Lockhart's offer to help, stood up to follow. Before he left the room he laid a hesitant hand on Lockhart's shoulder. 'Maybe later, if you've the time, you and I should have a bit of a chat about the future?' His cheeks were warm from the port and his smile had a wistful, almost girlish eagerness.

Lockhart found it difficult to meet his trusting gaze. 'Right you are, sir,' he said hastily, fighting the feeling that he had been, or was about to be, rebuked.

When he had cleared the table and stacked the plates and glasses in the dishwasher he took himself to the sitting room and settled down by the fire with Herzog. He read undisturbed for the better part of two hours, immersing himself in the tale like a seal in the winter Sound.

417

Although the ascent was certainly inspiring, it was the retreat, oddly enough, that affected him more fundamentally. At first he told himself that he wasn't going to blub, but, as it turned out, the nobility of the men – there really was no other word for it – got the better of him.

Like the great leader that he was, Maurice Herzog claimed no credit for himself; instead he stressed that his and Terray's summit triumph owed everything to the effort and sacrifice of the others in the team, who'd manned the supply lines from the lower camps. And this, thought Lockhart, from a man who'd truly paid the price. With both hands and feet irreparably frost-bitten, Herzog's life had hung in the balance. Day after day, with the blood in his veins thick as black pudding, he had suffered excruciating arterial injections.

From the bend of the elbow Oudet gradually tried higher and higher up towards the shoulder so as not always to stab the same place. Twice he touched a nerve. I did not cry out but sobbed spasmodically. What an eternity of suffering. I could do nothing.

'Stick it, Maurice,' Terray whispered. 'It'll soon be over; it's dreadful, I know, but I'm here beside you.'

Yes, he was there. Without him I could never have borne it at all. This man whom we thought hard because he was strong, who made himself out to be a tough peasant, showed a tenderness and affection towards me that I have never seen equalled. I hid my face against his chest and he put his arms around my neck.

Lockhart wept. The tears that slid down his face seemed to him like a distillation of all the simplicities that had ever existed in the world. He wept gratefully, and also hopefully, big softie that he was, glancing at the glowing fire for confirmation and blowing his nose in trumpeting snorts. The book lay open against the incline of his knees. He had reached the halfway mark. He leafed ahead, looking at the pictures, seized by a sudden need to know the outcome.

A tap on the window startled him. The curtains were still open. He got up reluctantly and peered through the frost-powdered glass. A fingernail was scratching a black hole on the outside of the pane. Fraser's eye looked in at him.

'Turn out the lights.'

'What?' Lockhart unlocked the catch and pushed the window up.

Fraser gesticulated towards the invisible sky. 'You're spoiling the show. Come out and take a look.'

When Lockhart rounded the corner of the house he saw the first searchlight ribbons of the aurora. A cigarette glowed on the perimeter of the terrace; Fraser was lurking on one of the stone benches. For no good reason Lockhart could think of, the shotgun was crooked across his arm. All he needed was a balaclava.

However ludicrous the sight, Lockhart felt a primitive signal of alarm. He laughed nervously. 'Got a night-sight, has it?'

'Ha bloody ha,' Fraser retorted, snapping the

419

stock shut and leaning the gun against the bench, so that the barrels sighted at the sky. 'Me and Andy McNab, eh?' He shifted along to make room for Lockhart.

'Hey-up, there she goes!'

A flickering arch had formed across the north horizon, towards which subsidiary bands of light flashed and beckoned: livid pinks and smoky crimsons, ice blues and cold polluted yellows. The silence was intense. Although Lockhart knew perfectly well that this particular lightshow didn't come with sound, he found himself waiting, as always, for the crash of thunder.

Fraser pulled a hip-flask from his pocket and offered it. 'Some things are still worth freezing your bollocks off for, eh?'

Lockhart laughed and tilted the flask to his mouth. 'Cheers. Where's the ceilidh band, though?' The whisky was not malt but blended; firewater, in fact, but he had come out coatless into the freezing fog and swallowed it gratefully. 'At the end of the day you're never sure if it's hellish or heavenly or what.'

'Maybe it's both.'

'Maybe it is.'

A curtain of light shimmied across the sky, shrank to a wavering tongue and licked subserviently at the central arch.

'Bang goes the telly reception,' said Fraser. 'Not to mention your mobile.'

'Aye, well. Here's to magnetism.' Lockhart took another reckless slug and passed the whisky back. Technology would have to wait and try again another day, but at least there would be no surfing tonight for Fraser. A hint of a breeze blew in from the water. Lockhart blew on his hands and tucked them between his knees. Fraser yanked off his scarf and handed it over. The wool smelled of smoke and sheep and cordite. Lockhart wound it round his neck and tucked the ends inside his jacket, crossing them over his heart.

'The books are ace.' He hesitated, wanting to tie things up with an appropriate sentiment, maybe even to say something about honour, if he could phrase it in a way that Fraser wouldn't misconstrue. 'I got quite carried away with the Herzog.' Their eyes met. He gave Fraser a smile, the best he could manage. 'I shed a tear, to be honest.'

Fraser looked at him curiously. 'You know, I never could work out why you stopped. Because it's not an age thing, is it? I mean, take Bonington: he's still going great guns.'

Because it was time we tried for a family. Because if you've got responsibilities you have to be prepared to take them seriously. The words rang hollow in Lockhart's head. Once again it was on the tip of his tongue to tell Fraser, get it over with. 'Bonington's got a living to make!' His voice sounded unnecessarily sharp. 'He's not just doing it for love, I can tell you that much.'

'Like, sorry I spoke!' Fraser shrugged and took another slug at the whisky. The face he turned to the heavens was martyred and mutinous, Frances to the life.

Lockhart felt like a first-class prick. 'I stopped because Agneta asked me to.' The lie was just pale enough to be permissible. 'She's had a lot to put up with over the years,' he added lamely. This, at least, was wholly true; there was no arguing with it.

They stared in silence at the agitated sky. From the east a blue plume rippled in and rose in accelerating spirals, as if sucked up by some celestial whirl of winds. For a moment of acute self-pity, Lockhart imagined his father's shocked face and his sympathy. *Poor girl, she'll be taking it hard, is she? That's bad luck, Archie, aye, you didn't deserve that.* He sat hunchbacked, clutching the cold stone lip of the bench, feeling the rant rise up righteously inside him.

The selfishness of climbers is totally sickening. The way they cling to their habit like addicts, insist on their God-given right to go on taking risks. The way they let nothing and no one clip their precious wings.

The gun slid sideways as the bench quivered. Fraser was shaking with silent laughter. 'Still in the doghouse, is it?'

Lockhart caught the barrel before it fell. He jumped up, shivering, and stamped his feet to warm them. Against the sky the house was a dark bulk in which his father waited to hear him lay it on the line. Already he was rehearsing the walk to the door and what he was going to say, the man-to-man, the honourable guff that wiped the conscience clean. 'I made a decision, OK? She didn't force me.'

'I guess we're both on parole, then. D'you reckon that makes us quits?'

'Meaning?'

Fraser threw his cigarette butt on the ground.

The small light landed at Lockhart's feet and glowed cheerfully in the gravel. He gave Lockhart a pitying glance. 'She still hasn't forgiven you, has she?'

Lockhart scraped the gravel up with the side of his shoe until the butt was dead and buried. 'Screw you, Fraser.'

'Or else – no, wait, don't tell me – could it be a case of self-imposed penance? The guilty penny in the plate?' Fog-breath billowed from Fraser's mouth. His smile was gathering strength. 'Like you haven't made enough sacrifices already?'

'Just shut the fuck up!' Lockhart turned on him furiously. He could say what he liked but Fraser wouldn't believe a word of it. He wasn't even sure that he believed it himself. 'Shut the fuck up and listen. Agneta and I … we can't have kids. As in *infertile*. As in no wee sons and heirs, right? Get the picture? As in it's all yours and that's official!' Lockhart's nose was running. His voice filled the coruscating gloom, but it no longer mattered what he said. He swept his arm out at the dark acres that were Fraser's, the cows and the sheep, the grouse on the moor and the fish in the Sound and the dappled sleeping deer. Fraser's shocked face had a skylit gleam; the fairground colours came and went on it. 'No, don't thank me, Fraser. You're welcome. Did you ever seriously think I wanted it?'

Lockhart took a step back. At his feet the gravel glittered with hoar-frost. He was shaking. 'I'm going in now, OK, and that's what I'm going to tell him. And after that, Fraser, I guess it's up to you.'

Dessert came in a cloud of meringue and cream, with Château-d'Yquem on the side. Micky had ordered it without consulting Broom but there were some *grands crus* that even she had heard of. By bribery or deception he had secured a table with a view, but since the windows of the restaurant were small and double-glazed and sat deeply in their sockets, like eyes screwed up against the severity of the elements, she could see little of the panorama that lay outside, however often she wiped the steam from the glass with her napkin.

After the brilliance of the terrace, the interior was a disappointment. There were crossed alpenstocks on the thick concrete pillars that supported the low ceiling, and wooden plaques of chamois carved in bas-relief. From gnarled beams which were quite cynically fake hung chandeliers bristling with pine-cones and candles. Every table in the room was full. At a bar that simulated a rock-face, a few optimistic customers still waited to be seated. A group of German skiers who'd been singing *Lieder* by the log fire broke off and blew a nose or two, having reduced themselves to sentimental tears.

Micky wore a crown of tinsel, and he was talking in codes. 'Two Cs in a K...' He cocked his head at Broom, soliciting her guess. She'd noticed before how many men seemed naturally to inhabit a psychopathology of digits and initials; they totalled car numbers, read shop signs backwards, assessed the triumphs and disasters of their lives in Brownie points and football scores. Five-nil; a goalless draw; and so on. Bless their hearts. She shook her head, smiling indulgently.

'Scriptwriter's shorthand,' Micky prompted.

'Not a clue.'

'Your classic commercial for soap powder or gravy mix? Come on.' He flattened his hands on the tablecloth and leaned forward to whisper. 'Two cunts in a kitchen.'

She was laughing before she had time to think better of it.

'Mind you, these days it's more likely to be two transvestites.'

She put her head in her hands and rocked with laughter. 'That's disgraceful.' Her shoulders shook so much that the ice-axe, which leaned against the back of her chair, slid sideways and clattered to the floor. When she bent to retrieve it her head swam.

Micky nodded, beaming. 'We're not the only culprits. The medics are no better. Miles's wife used to be a GP somewhere in the reed-beds of East Anglia and she had to ask why NFN appeared so often on the patient records. They told her it meant "Normal For Norfolk". Well, you know what they say about inbreeding up there. FLK's another one. "Funny-Looking Kid". That's for infants they don't think are quite, you know, pukka, but they aren't sure what's wrong.'

Broom flapped her fingers at the offender, sprinkling derision. Al to the life. 'Take the shame.' But surely there was no harm in hanging loose, letting her hair down for once. Chilling out, Sean would call it. Laughter, like being shocked, was tonic. Her fingers tingled with it, as if her body was saying thank you. Light-motes danced in on her eyes from the candelabra's crystal facets, and from the low arrow-sharp sunrays that pierced the veil of condensation on the double-glazing. Why shouldn't she enjoy the seedy guessing game, and the mead-sweet wine, and the kindness of money? She let her head fill up with Micky's froth. USIs, she thought, Unsuitably Shod Italians. POWs, Pissed-Off Waitresses. Tears of laughter jetted from her eyes.

'What?' spluttered Micky.

She mopped her eyes with her napkin. 'How old did you say you were?'

'How old do you want me to be?' Micky zapped her with a psychoanalytic stare. The scrutiny slipped into a smirk. 'Let's just say, older than you think.' Presenting a three-quarter profile, he stroked a finger down the contour of his cheek. 'It's the bones that do it,' he added archly.

When the waitress brought the bill Broom's eye fell on the total. The card Micky dropped in the saucer looked like solid gold. If the decor was drab, the bill was dazzling. As splendiferous as the altitude. The price not of a dinner, but of a soul.

MNO, she thought: Money No Object. She watched a red-beaked chough land on the window-sill, reconsider, and skim away on the thermals.

In London he would take her to the opera. She saw herself handed out of a long car that sighed

426

to a halt and ushered into the stalls by his containing arm. Then, in a drunken rush, but comprehensively, she remembered a dream snatched from her short unsatisfying sleep, in which, youth restored, she made her debut at Covent Garden. In her Orchid Fairy tutu she raced through the unknown bowels of the Opera House. Late and frantic on account of corridors obstructed by landslip and scaffolding and subsidence, she searched wildly for the stage and the spotlight, beat on the locked doors of dressing rooms. At the last minute she daubed her girl's mouth with someone else's carmine as she limbered up *en pointe* in her stolen shoes. Hearing the bars of the intro, she composed herself, ready to float out and perform her first pirouettes for her father, only to be told curtly in the wings that her contract had been cancelled because she was late, so late, twenty-five years too late, in fact, for her father...

Micky's eyes seemed to glow at her like coals. His technicolour face loomed like the thirty-foot close-ups in the long-lost Odeons of her youth. Between the table and the door marked *Toilettes* stretched an expanse of floor she wasn't confident of crossing. She stood up unsteadily.

DNR, she thought. Do Not Resuscitate.

*Well, a hundred miles from nowhere out on the desert
    sand
One-eyed Jack the trader held some turquoise in his
    hand.
Oh, the wind blows cold, on the trail of the buffalo
Oh, the wind blows cold, in the land of the Navajo.*

The tape-recorder sat on the bedside locker, the lead coiled round it, beside a neat stack of tapes. Once again Broom glanced up to check on the monitor. Her brain accepted what it had been told of the war that was being fought out in his lungs and also, now, in his bloodstream. But there was no doubt that the oxygen saturation figures were creeping up: 70. 75. 80.

Breathe for me, she told him. *Count it in and out. Slow and steady on the steep bits. Remember what it's like. Your legs ache and there's that catch in the bottom of the lungs before the breathing moves down into your stomach. Breathe and count and breathe and count: no one ever said it wouldn't be an effort.*

The air in the ward was still and thick. The cold that wafted up from the ice-blanket was a relief. Al lay on a slant, his feet an undignified yard higher than his head. His features had a swollen floating look, like those of an underwater swimmer. It hurt in a new way to admit that he no longer looked like himself.

Something the taxi radio said came back to her, something about the sun, how it pulsates and sings; how, every five minutes or so, it breathes in and out.

She put her face close to Al's and lied in her teeth. It

428

was a clear day in May, she told him, a mild, lark-song kind of day, the shorts-and-T-shirt kind, even on the tops. They were slogging up Swirl How, heading for the mile-long ridge that leads to the Old Man of Coniston. Or else up Stickle Ghyll, crossing and recrossing the bouldered beck below the tarn, en route *for Harrison's. The rest of the Langdale Pikes were looming up ahead, high ground but safe, where the breath flows free and easy and boot-soles thrive on the hospitable springiness of the turf.*

Our brio, she thought, our will to bliss. 'So breathe,' she told him. She knew he wouldn't flag as long as she didn't, as long as she kept on feeding him Bow Fell and Scafell, Cloggy and Kinder and the sheep-cropped cliffs of Pembroke, images that would keep him in the country.

The effort of concentration made her sweat. Between each of her thoughts something seemed to be missing, like classified zones on a map. Her nail-varnish was chipped; pale bays were beginning to appear between ragged red promontories. Her mouth went on breathing and counting. She checked the screen again. The illuminated digits had flickered up. They were holding at 90.

Nurse Hazel stopped by the monitor. For a moment she stood gazing at the screen, tapping her ballpoint lightly against her cheek. Her face was expressionless. Broom waited for a word of confirmation but it did not come. Nothing amazed a nurse, apparently – certainly not Nurse Hazel, who pocketed her pen without even noting down the evidence. Not even the small miracle she and Al were making.

The overhead strips had been turned off for night-time and only a single lamp remained above the bed.

429

Beyond the pool of light the clans were gathering, like moths at the edges of her eyes. Sister Alison flickered into view and faded, leaving Al's parents stranded in the lamplight. Jennifer bent awkwardly to kiss Al's topsy-turvy cheek. Beside her, bashful and hanging back like a cocktail-party guest waiting to be introduced, was his father.

'Alan? It's Dad...' His voice was too loud and terminally uncertain. He laid a finger on Al's shoulder.

It was the blood-gas monitor that registered the shock. She watched the figures teeter and fall back: 85. 80. Then she saw them plummet.

The thought flapped in her brain, panicky but clear. The connection. There was something Al couldn't bear, a line of energy that led back to his father, or to what he represented. She looked around desperately, wondering why no one else had noticed the drastic recoil. Why had nobody – not a staff nurse, not a sister – stepped in and put a stop to it?

She squeezed his hand hard. If she understood anything at all it was that she hadn't come this far only to be thwarted. 'Try for me, Al,' she urged, and he did try, she could feel him trying. She studied his face, his squashed and swollen eyelids, his nose, which was broadening, becoming a snout. How sick he looks, she thought.

In Cairo he'd had love flu, he'd admitted on the phone: he'd been sick with loneliness and longing. How triumphant she'd felt, thinking but managing not to blurt out: 'So now you know what it's like.'

On the screen the digits crawled up a point or two, slothfully. She felt the reluctance in him, a listlessness that frightened her because it was no part of his character. His hand felt dry and horny. He was

430

burning up. She wet his lips again with the small sponge Hazel had given her; it was flat, circular, like the ones the post office laid on so you didn't have to lick your stamps.

When Didi cannoned in, Broom looked at her blankly. She registered that her coat was open, her mouth red and agitated. Didi knelt down and buried her head on the bed, long hair and tears spilling thoughtlessly everywhere. Broom was appalled. The noise drowned her out. Didi was wailing for her dad, her dad, without the faintest notion that the word might simply be too much for him. And he'd been fighting so hard, focusing. Giving it all he'd got. For a few minutes she'd believed they could recreate the rhythm. But now, because Didi was thinking not of him but only of herself, all her good work was in ruins.

Another chair was brought and when Didi sat on it Broom pushed her own chair back and got up in a blind fury and walked away from the light.

Ken stood by the payphone in the lobby, wreathed in smoke and talking jerkily. Sam and Sean were leaning against the window-sill, young London men, with their casual sprawly stance and ruffianly chic, staring out. They might have been watching a football game or a posse of passing girls, except that the window looked onto a ventilation shaft and in any case it was the dead of night.

She allowed Heather to take her arm and draw her to the padded leather bench. She lit a cigarette and smoked it hunched over, staring at the ashtray between her feet, a metal box with four flanges that slanted down to form a central slot. Inside were some screwed-up sweetie papers and a plastic coffee-stirrer. It looked like an envelope. An envelope for sending

431

butts and trash.

'He wants to go. I feel I have to let him go.' She thrust her hands into her pockets and leaned her head back against the wall. The Mission Statement of MeadWard was engraved on a brass plaque above the door. For the first time she noticed the get-out clause: 'Or else to enable the patient to die painlessly, and with dignity'. *A proviso that hinted at tricks of the trade, an expertise that extended to the process of death itself.*

'Maybe you have to tell him.' Heather's voice was barely audible. Her head was close to Broom's but she wasn't looking at her, professionally, judiciously, wasn't looking at her, as if, having dropped her bombshell, she was afraid of exerting any extra pressure. Or perhaps she hadn't said it at all, but something else, something that sounded similar but meant the opposite. Perhaps Broom had simply misheard.

Ken hung the phone back on its hook and glanced at his watch. 'Keith and Barbara are on their way.' He took two cigarettes from his pack, passed one over and lit it for her. Ken the working-class boy from the slums of Birmingham. It was the Party, he said, that had taught him to read. She drew on her new cigarette: a Marlborough Light, stronger than she was used to, but tasting of nothing much. Her old butt still smouldered in the ashtray. It occurred to her that she was surrounded by atheists, that not one of them had the habit of prayer.

Dexter lurked by the lift, his face tilted at a waiting angle. 'Are we going to the canteen, then?'

'Sure we are, matey.' Ken's face was reddish and aghast. 'Two sugars for you, honey?' he boomed,

turning to her, his eyes blinking behind his lenses.

When the lift doors closed Broom looked at Heather. 'But is that the right way?' Her voice was a perilous whisper rising in her throat.

Heather glanced warningly at Sam and Sean. 'There is no right way,' she murmured.

Broom knew instantly that she was wrong, mistaken, maddening. In fact there was nothing else but, nothing but correct conduct, love in its purest form, the last right thing she could do for him.

'Fucking pneumonia!' Sam's voice rose viciously. 'Like it's the fucking Crimea or something!' Sean's hand slipped across his shoulder, but with a terse shrug it was repulsed.

Someone, somehow, had to set Al free. Otherwise what was there? Raging and clinging on like a baby, simply because he was leaving her? When it was glaringly obvious that asking for what someone was powerless to give was the worst sort of torture you could inflict on them. Weighting them down with all your little troubles. She should come straight out and tell them. Sam and Didi and the parents. No, honestly. Point out to them what they were doing. What it amounted to. Like sending him off to eternity with a rucksack full of bricks.

She got up and walked back down the corridor to the ward. The resolve grew in her. There would be burdens to remove, assurances to give. Last rites, last duties. As long as he understood that letting him go wasn't the same as leaving him.

Sister Alison was at her desk in the nurses' station. Broom went in quietly and closed the door behind her.

'How long will it be?'

Sister Alison put the cap on her pen and laid it

433

down and looked her in the eye. 'An hour, maybe two. It's difficult to say.'

Broom nodded. 'How do I know he isn't frightened?'

There was a pause. 'The sedation we use at this stage has a euphoric component.'

At this stage. *The meaning was cruelly clear.* 'Euphoric' was a term she liked better, a relief. Mescalito riding his white horse. 'Thank you,' she said severely.

Sister Alison offered her a chair, which she refused. 'I can assure you that he isn't suffering.'

In the ward on the other side of the glass partition Al's parents seemed to be preparing to go. Before long Didi would exhaust herself, then there would be a window of opportunity.

She went out and waited in the corridor. Her head was cool and clear now, because someone's had to be, to do his thinking for him. She leaned against the radiator, kicking it lightly with her foot. Periodically she shivered. All she needed was a few minutes alone with him; she absolutely could not do it in company. She noticed that she was wearing the same sensible laced shoes that had walked with Al in the desert. He'd asked her to take photos of him, intrepid explorer style, profiled against sand-dunes. Lawrence of Arabia, but without the burnous.

If Didi took much longer the resolve might sink away under her, the aura of rightness somehow sifting out of it. Perhaps Al wouldn't be able to hear her. Or perhaps he would hear and hate her for it. But she didn't believe that, did she, not for a moment, and even if she did it wouldn't hurt her. He knew by now everything about her – the pigheadedness of her

434

devotion, her jealousy, the lot. She'd held nothing back, because she'd never needed to. Because he'd been strong enough to take whatever she dished out. But now he wasn't and she must. So she could bear to be hated. Hate was a grown-up sort of verb. Active. But there was no verb that conveyed what the abandoned felt towards the abandoner, only a few nouns nudging impotently around in the void. Despair. Panic. Betrayal. Words that were as afraid of finding their object as of losing it. Afraid of abusing it.

Didi emerged sobbing. Long strands of damp hair clung to her cheek. Broom lowered her eyes respectfully and let her pass. Then she hurried into the ward.

The shine was still in him; it hadn't faded yet. She collected her post-office sponge and her little dish of pink solution. She sat by the bed and soaked a Q-tip and ran it round his lips. A few drops of the liquid escaped and trickled downhill, towards his eyes. His nose twitched irritably. 'Sorry,' she said, dabbing at the runnel with a square of folded gauze, 'sorry.' And then she began to give permission.

Barbara's head rested on Keith's shoulder. She had linked one arm tightly through his; her other hand crushed her velvet scarf across her mouth. Keith stood motionless in his best tweed jacket, gazing at Al's face. His bright blue eyes were unblinking; the tears that poured from them plunged down his cheeks and vanished into his beard.

The sight of his tears filled her with a watery sympathy. With a vague sense of surprise she remembered how cold she'd found him when they'd first met. She thought he disapproved of her, saw her as a bad influence. Bitchily she'd told herself that

435

under his steely dogmatism lay simple jealousy: he wanted to marry Al just as much as she did.

People had been coming in, in ones and twos, more calmly now, kissing Al's cheek or touching his shaven head with a strange swift wariness. The chest man came in specially to shake her hand. He looked puzzled and affronted. 'I simply can't believe it,' he kept saying. 'He put up such a mighty struggle.'

In the unfamiliar silence she stared at the oblong of sticking plaster at the base of his throat. The respirator had been disconnected, the silly blue clothes-pegs unclipped from his fingers. The bed had been lowered at last to a dead level. Although the stillness around him had deepened, it hadn't yet solidified into anything she could define as difference. His skin so warm and quiet that he might simply have been holding his breath and hiding from her, like the bride in the old folk-tale who played hide-and-seek on her wedding night: who ran to the furthest tower of the castle and climbed into a chest that locked, to be discovered a cobwebbed century later.

Someone, somewhere, was counting to a hundred, but the trouble was that before they reached it she had to find him, and she had no way of knowing when she would be counted out. She glanced at Hazel, but Hazel gave no signal. Al wasn't on the street below, boarding his bicycle in the rain; nor was she fumbling with her passport at the checkpoint barrier, no blood or tears, nothing like that. Nothing was what was happening, happening too stealthily for anyone to see, hear. Nothing she could believe in. She wondered what kind of trick was being played, because how could it really be a parting if you couldn't tell when to say goodbye?

Afterwards Dexter sat the other side of the bed from her, hunched and quiet, his long hands draped over the hillock of Al's thighs. For some time they remained like this, opposite and facing, staring not at Al or at each other, but past each other, silently, at nothing, as if they had never expected more.

Before she stood up Broom took a last look at his feet, which once again protruded at the bottom of the sheet. They looked exactly as they always had: vivid, upstanding, ready to swing into action.

At the door the nurses hovered, arms folded, waiting for her to leave. 'We're so very, very sorry.' They were looking at her strangely – not with pity, but in the way that people do when they know something you don't.

She thanked them for what they'd done and shook their hands with a great and brisk finality, working on the principle that this is what the living do: leave hospitals, because when all is said and done they have no business there. Then she turned decisively and walked away from the ward and what would now begin to happen there, as if the abrupt swivel of her heel would in itself provide the event, the marker, the missing end of it.

Broom looked doubtfully at Micky's shoes. A hundred metres out of the mid-station she'd had second thoughts, but had dismissed them. Although commodious enough in summer, the path was now no more than a slight lip on the uniform snow of the slope: safe enough if you

437

knew how to place your feet, but not safe at all if you didn't even have the habit of watching them. She'd told him to walk in her boot-prints, but really they ought to be roped.

She had an altitude headache exacerbated by champagne and crossness, because Micky appeared not to understand the concept of companionable silence. There was no escape from his incessant prattle, short of shouting 'Shut up!' or striding ahead and leaving him in the lurch – which it might just come to, if he carried on crowing about 'overspend' and 'calculated risk' and how some people just couldn't see 'the big picture' but luckily his boss Damien wasn't one of them.

In the last half-hour she'd had a blow-by-blow account of his plans for George Mallory Esquire, Ms Sophie Sauvage, and their forthcoming digital marriage. Initially she'd assumed it was a joke, another caricature of adland's excesses. Then she realized that he was serious. 'Talk about selling your dead grandmother!' she'd retorted, as her fuddled brain tried to deal with his repellent flow – her professional opinion, if you like, because after all he'd asked for it. Micky hadn't turned a hair; if anything, her anger had made him more expansive. He was, perhaps, deliberately baiting her, although she had no idea why he would do this, unless of course it was his peculiar way of getting his kicks. She could hear his wheezing breath behind her, fraying her nerves, forcing her to think what was beyond the bounds of thought. Al was on the side of the angels, so what was she doing with Micky, who wasn't half the man he was? And nothing, but nothing, was going to persuade her to watch his wretched tapes!

Some way ahead she could see the dog-leg where the *balcon* joined the path that zigzagged down from the Cristaux glacier. From there it was a brief, if steep, descent to Les Gorets. She thought of Micky slithering about in his fashion-boots, on his weak and breakable ankles, and her temper mounted. She would have to watch him like a hawk.

Slipping the sling of the ice-axe over her wrist, she plodded on at a pace too slow to feel steady. Fuck him, anyway. For all she cared he could go to hell and take his unholy ikons with him. But, like it or not, he was her responsibility and she couldn't afford to let him lag too far behind.

Micky shambled along in her wake, cursing cheerfully. She closed the doors of her shoulders against him and prayed for silence. By concentrating on her rhythm she could almost blot him out.

A transparent roil of lenticular cloud uncurled in the blue above the Juron; two choughs circled high up and slowly, threading in and out of the Aiguilles. Far below, the tiny toy-town houses snuggled under a hanging haze of woodsmoke.

'*Mon sang de glace!*' cries Faust, and the wings of the mountain open like a tabernacle.

Again she saw the triptych: two wings, flanking a larger central panel. After a moment it came to her. On one wing would be a woman in a white dress and veil, kneeling like a donor: pious Marguerite, perhaps, still waiting for her man, waiting to wed or worship. On the other wing, a nude male – a headlong figure with skin smooth and indestructible as coins. A gold angel, heroic, fallen. She couldn't quite envisage the material. Wood was of course too heavy. Acrylic on stretched silk, maybe. She would need to use a glaze.

Down below in the valley, a church clock chimed out the hour. Four o'clock. The sound was infinitely remote. She tried to focus on the central panel – usually the place of honour and glory, where the painter could let rip. But that wouldn't work for her; it wasn't what she wanted. She could retain the arched frame, yes, the steep peak of it, but apart from that... Apart from that, nothing. Nothing was what she saw there. So she would dispense with the panel. In place of it would be a site of emptiness, the stage yawning to infinity. No cross or Christ figure or pretty fluffy-clouded heaven, just a scaffold pole, strung with prayer flags.

A sunset shadow was creeping up the face of the Faille.

'There she blows!' chirped Micky. 'That's where we're going to do the shoot.' He had stopped beside an outcrop of rocks and was digging snow out of his trouser-bottoms. His socks and boot-tops were packed full. He leaned against the rocks, panting, and wiped his forehead with his sleeve. 'Still, I guess it's good training for the Himalayas, huh?'

She could see the bluff some way below, at the beginning of the tree line. Soon the light would start to fail and the snow would change from firm

440

to iced and slippery. She had never imagined that Micky would be so slow. They were running it close. She hid her anxiety. With luck they would make it down the steep section to Les Gorets, and then they would be home and dry. 'It's late. We should get a move on,' she said.

At the fork where the paths met she stopped to caution him. He was red and sweating. His nose was running. He looked, she thought, pathetic, the very picture of incompetence. He leaned sideways, pinched one nostril, and blew his nose into the snow. She looked away in distaste. 'I do have tissues in my backpack.' She brought out her water-bottle and made him drink. Maybe I should offer to wipe his arse for him as well, she thought.

'For this bit you've got to splay your feet out like this, OK, and really ram your heels in.' She drove her boots into the snow, her feet turned out in the classic ten-to-two position. 'Like so, right?'

Micky's grin was cheeky. He stood to attention and saluted. 'You're the boss-lady.'

'I mean it!' There was an edge to her voice.

'Now you're really scaring me.'

'Look, it's your funeral.' She gripped her ice-axe by the haft, turned abruptly and started down the slope.

She remembered it as a dumb grey day, not a scrap of blue in the sky. Sifts of snow blew now and again on the wind. The only spattering of colour on the monochrome was the bouquets that shivered on the flagstones outside the Hall of Remembrance. Chrysanths and cornflowers, wreaths of red roses or tulips from this or that ex-branch of the ex-Communist Party. Love formal and in public, its hand shaken by three hundred guests.

In her confusion the word for this was 'wedding'.

Earlier the chief mourners had drunk sherry and said nothing. Upstairs, meanwhile, Didi and Sam's girlfriend Julie shrieked in the bathroom like bridesmaids, doing up their hair. Frantic preparations for a ritual that ruled her head like fog and duped her. Dexter manning the sound-system, Ken pulling the whisky bottle from the inside pocket of his coat, Keith straightening his tie for the oration, while she stood at the door of the hall gazing anxiously at the gravel driveway and the distant gate, and when the wind came with its white luggage of snow or bone-dust or blossom she screwed up her eyes against it, searching for the long dark car, not thinking, no, not thinking at all of who lay shoeless in that satin place, silent as a bat-box in broad daylight with a black hole for words, his rouged face pillowed and put to rights... Her mind turning instead to the bouquets and 'bridesmaids', bewildered, her mind saying that it was the groom they were all waiting for, the groom who was late, the groom who was coming.

They had booked the largest hall but it was overflowing. Ken had assured her that climbers and comrades would come from near and far, but she hadn't expected hundreds. Later there would be a mass wake in a pub that Philip had paid for. She'd had no idea that Al was such a celebrity.

A man of conscience. A man entirely lacking in malice.

There was a murmur, a rustling. The mourners nodded as one. From behind her came the stifled sound of Barbara's tears. And it was true, oh yes, every word of Keith's eulogy, but she could see now, as she hadn't then – anaesthetized by whisky, propped on the hard bench between Sean and Heather, on the friends' side not the family's, her hair stroked somehow from behind, Al's laddish grin on the programme in her lap anticipating an almighty piss-up – that it was also utterly impossible. For how could you rage at those who fought the good fight, or bite or tear at a man who was passing into myth? How could you feel the sheer insult of it, or even think the word – which until now had been exiled from her dictionary – or say to yourself, 'I took all that shit, Al did all that to me and *then he died anyway?*' How could you bear the fault-line that was opened, a fault wide as the Grand Canyon, Al on one side and you on the other, and the immeasurable void between?

She thought of the joy and confidence that spring from mutual desire, and something in her trembled. She felt a surge of bile, an unsteady nausea, almost like a shiver in the mountain.

There was, suddenly, a definite wind, like the blast of a fast train passing a platform. Small snowballs scuttled past her, bouncing down towards the edge of the bluff. The feeling that shot through her was less one of fear than an instant sense of affront. It was the wrong time of day for an avalanche: the sun gone from all but the highest peaks, the temperature dropping, the snow stiffening in its ice-crust. As the first tremor swept under her she thought of Micky's stupid sliding shoes.

From behind her came a sound she did not at first recognize. It was the insistent Valkyrie trill of his mobile. Spindrift spilled down from the overhead rush of the wind. She threw out a hand and screamed to him.

Micky's first thought was that Damien had made it out to Val after all and was now summoning him from the heights of some ski-lift or *relais de montagne*.

He dragged at the front zip of his parka. He could feel the neat oblong of the cellphone, sealed snugly in his inner pocket, throbbing against his heart. He had switched the phone to answer mode, but how many rings was it set on? If Damien was taking the trouble to wish him Merry Christmas, the least he could do was pick up.

He got one glove off with his teeth, and was fumbling two-handed at the velcro strip when his feet went from under him. For a sensible second he considered bracing his heels against the slide, but the memory of the ankle injury was still fresh and he didn't want to take the risk. In any case, the powdery rush of air enclosed his body in a way that was somehow very right and familiar, five-star *déjà-vu*, in fact, the glissade like a bed he had no particular desire to get out of. Knowing that the phone might stop ringing at any moment, he slid on his back, craning his neck up to see what the fuck his fingers were doing. It occurred to him suddenly that Damien might be even closer, perhaps in Montjoie itself. He wouldn't put it past him to drive over from Val if the spirit moved him, even to decide on the spur of the moment to stay over and see La Sophie doing her simian thing on the summit-spire of the Faille. Not that Damien would ever interfere with an actual shoot, no way; it was more his style to stand on the sidelines and generally inspire and be a presence.

Micky slid like a child down a chute, two white wings of snow hunching up on either side of him. His initial sense of urgency began to ease and he reflected that it was true after all what they said about adrenalin and the split second that stretches to infinity... He watched a single star twinkling at him from the deepening blue above the ridge of the Couronnes, recalling that some Portuguese whizz-kid at Imperial College had recently come up with the futuristic hypothesis that the speed of light was not in fact constant. So much for the laws of physics, then, and the theory of Special Relativity. He pondered pleasantly on this to pass the time, of which there now seemed a definite surfeit, looping him up on elastic airwaves, rewinding him back to his beginning.

He got the cellphone to his ear just as the ring-tone died. By then, however, it didn't matter, for he already sensed Damien like a great and beckoning smile that was meant for him alone, and in this state of grace he knew his mission was accomplished. 'Well done,' Damien was saying, breathing his message through the tunnel of air as the blue up top shrank to the size of an eye with a single star at the heart, 'well done, Micky,' as he sailed on down on the softly spreading feathers of the snow.

She had dived instinctively left, her mind throwing up a memory of the path. Then the snow took her. As she slid she did it by the book, shaft of the axe held diagonally across her chest, left hand low down near the spike, right hand gripping the pick in front of the adze. With Lockhart's voice nagging in her ears, she rolled onto her stomach, plunged the pick into the slope and flung her weight full on it. She slid, jolting, in a fine storm of spindrift, until the pick dragged a narrow groove that deepened to reveal a black bleed of earth and pine-needles. Pebbles flew up and whistled past her face. Then the pick bit in, took purchase, and she was slowing ... she had stopped.

She lay prone for a moment, staring back up the slope to where the Juron towered above her, still and stern as justice. Ten metres to her left, the first dark trunks of the tree line bristled on the slope. The funnelling wind had ceased. She rolled onto her back and sat up with her head between her knees, hawking up snow, snorting it down her nose, hearing her heart again in the sudden silence, knocking vibrantly against her ribs.

It was almost dusk when she dragged herself up the concrete steps and beat on the door of the first-floor apartment. The door gave way immediately, swinging effortlessly inwards on its hinge. She lurched into the unlit hall and heard the axe-pick clang against metal. Too late she saw the shadowy outline of the tricycle. She tripped over it and went down on her knees, panting.

Just then the light went on and Guy appeared from an inner door, smiling expectantly, a dinner napkin still tucked in at his neck. He picked her up and held her steady while she tried to speak.

In the kitchen Madame d'Ange's daughter let out a soft gasp and looked at her in dismay. She pulled out a chair and made her sit. Then she darted to the cupboard to fetch brandy. Her two sons watched her, their spoons frozen halfway to their mouths. They were eating some kind of dessert, at the table, like grown-ups. When she gave them permission to get down they slid from their seats and backed away.

Guy knelt before her chair and checked her quickly. When she spoke about Micky her voice sounded muffled and gloved, as if cringing from memories of metal. In the greyness of shock she was proud that the directions she gave were precise. Guy repeated them, word for word, into the telephone, his eyes swivelling to her and away. He vanished into another room and re-appeared in salopettes, buckling on his harness. His wife went quickly about the table, clearing away the dessert that had been interrupted, scraping *mousse au chocolat* from the plates.

Broom sat on the hard kitchen chair, gripping the ice-axe between her knees. From their refuge behind the Christmas tree the two blond boys peeped out at her, wide-eyed with alarm. The smaller one had his thumb in his mouth and looked pitifully close to tears. The brandy made a fire in her throat; for a moment her head swam. She saw then what they must be seeing: a creature crusted monstrously with snow, its eyes bloodshot, its hair snarled into thick dreadlocks of ice.

The weight of their fear wounded her. She smiled hard, peeping at them through the tinsel-laden pine branches. Why did their mother not think of shooing them away? She wiggled her fingers at them and popped her eyes to raise a laugh, for it seemed suddenly that only by doing so could she prevent the onset of a huge and shapeless grief. Her jaw was stiff with the effort of smiling. But if she could prove to them that she was human, she could surely prove it to herself.

Upstairs she locked the door and turned on every light in the apartment. She wrapped a blanket round herself and sat down at the kitchen table, fixing her eye on the clock. When she put her head in her hands she felt the shape of her skull. Her mind was empty and in abeyance: on the outside it was white and calcified; inside was a concretion of silence, dark, opaque, faceted, like flint.

At seven she heard Guy's four-wheel-drive stop in the lane. She looked out and saw the flashing blue light of the police car that had drawn up behind it. One *gendarme* got out while another waited, smoking, at the wheel. She could see no sign of Micky.

Guy stamped his boots on the mat before he came in. Behind him the *gendarme* removed his braided cap and tucked it underneath his arm. Guy's eyes were on her, mountain eyes, light and distant. She put her hand on the edge of the table for support. Under her fingers the oilcloth sweated and grew slippery.

'I'm very sorry, *madame*. The team have searched *la pente* – the run-out? – of the avalanche, with dogs and of course with *bâtons*, but we have found no trace of your friend...'

For a second relief lit her up. 'No trace?' The *gendarme* stood on the other side of the table, his cool gaze sweeping the room. She had the distinct impression that he understood Guy's English but didn't care to admit it. She stared at him, willing him to speak. He was young, about thirty, with a small mouth dark as a prune and the air of a man not best pleased to be called out on a search on Christmas Day. There was a dark bridge of moustache above his upper lip; against a tan that suggested winter breaks in the Maldives or Martinique, his clean-shaven chin and jawline were unnervingly white. He produced a zipped polythene bag and placed it on the table. Inside was what appeared to be a cellphone. *'La seule chose que nous avons trouvée est ce téléphone portable. Vous savez s'il lui appartient?'*

'Do you know if it is his?' Guy translated.

The zipped bag had a forensic aura. She took a step back, afraid to touch it. The phone was the same colour as Micky's. Fire-engine red. Like thousands of others. 'It could be.' She looked at the *gendarme*. *'C'est possible.'*

He was watching her with narrowed eyes. Professional suspicion. The TV-cop trip. Why did policemen always feel they had to ham it up? He cleared his throat significantly. *'Vraiment c'est un mystère, madame... L'avalanche n'était pas particulièrement grave et les débris ne sont pas très profonds. Ils font à peine un demi-mètre en général...'*

The flood of French brought tears to her eyes. She looked at Guy. His face was broad and fair, a Savoie face; his expression was troubled but not tragic. 'What does he mean? What mystery?'

With a trace of embarrassment, Guy said rapidly, 'Because the avalanche was *petite* ... very minor, you understand? The debris is mostly no deeper than one half-metre.' He measured the distance obligingly with his hands. The height of an infant, standing. 'We must assume, I think, that the ... that your friend is not there.'

It was absurd, of course. Absurd as hope. She shook her head and frowned at him severely. 'You mean he just got up and walked away?' She made an effort to remember the snow-slide, the spindrift. Micky's graceful slippage. On the *gendarme*'s face was an expression of such brazen disbelief that for a dizzying moment she doubted her version of events as much as he did. She glared at his ludicrous moustache. 'He's not suggesting that I made the whole thing up!'

'Mais non.' Guy laid an apologetic hand on her shoulder. 'But we have seen, you understand, no footprints.'

450

Broom sat down slowly. She saw the cellphone on the desk in Micky's room, a small light winking at her in the stuffy darkness. 'You have checked his hotel? The Hôtel des Aiguilles?'

The *gendarme* gave a non-committal nod. She saw that he had understood her perfectly. 'Monsieur Flint is no longer at this hotel.' He stroked his beardless chin, considering her. 'Perhaps you have been mistaken, *madame*...' The slow spread of his shrug conveyed his conviction that, particularly when dealing with English ladies of a certain age, anything in the whole wide world was possible.

When the phone burst into life she thought immediately of Sean and rushed to pick it up. She heard Daniel's startled bass. 'So you *are* there! Heather said it was the right number. What the fuck was that about?'

'What the fuck was *what* about?' Her voice, to her own ears, sounded small and altered, as if some thrifty seamstress had taken in the corners of her mouth. 'I thought the boys had chicken-pox.'

'What in hell's name gave you that idea? I called to confirm about tomorrow, and blow me if some French type doesn't say he's never heard of you!'

Broom leaned against the kitchen dresser, noticing, for the first time, a red plastic timer, the sort you'd use to boil an egg or check the oven-timing for baking a quiche. She saw Micky with the tea-towel over his arm, solemn and mother-hennish, fussing with the plates. The tension that rose inside her was like a mixture of fear and excitement. Of course she'd believed him; she'd had no reason not to. The really unbelievable thing was the lie itself, its apparent purposelessness. With the sense that in a moment she would understand, she said, 'So they aren't ill?'

'Far from it! They're absolutely A OK. I'm also packed and ready to roll ... assuming it's still convenient,' he added, his voice heavy with sarcasm.

Something else was nagging at her, another element that didn't fit. 'Of course it is,' she said impatiently, thinking of the Barbir Hospital, the dates that didn't add up. Sharon, the Butcher of Beirut. 'Dan, listen. Do you remember the big Israeli air strikes on Beirut, what year they were?'

There was an offended snort. 'The Palestinians, of course, were innocent as the driven snow! Not to mention Syria. That was 1982, I suppose. Why?'

'It doesn't matter. I'll tell you tomorrow.' The room seemed stifling suddenly. For a moment she didn't want to believe that she was awake. The slippery little shit, she thought. Latifa died at thirty-six. In '82 she would have been fifty. Micky had read the Hammer Horror story in the papers. And she, of course, had shed tears of sympathy and swallowed every word of it.

'So who was the joker on the phone?'

There was a kind of vortex in her head, in which the fitful flakes of her thoughts swirled up and tried to reassemble. It was as if in a glass dome the landscape was shaken and the snow floated up in its suspension, and Micky like a

452

house, like a town, like a city, slipped past her and vanished over the bluff.

'Just a guy,' she said. 'A definite prat. He's gone now.'

'And good riddance too,' Daniel said disgustedly. 'God, sweetie, you can really pick them!'

As always, Daniel's common sense was crushing. In the face of it she was tempted to believe, like the *gendarme*, that the whole thing was fiction, even to see Micky himself as a figment of her imagination, and a perverted one at that. A caricature of a man, conjured from the shadows; an anti-ikon, as insubstantial in life as he was in his disappearing-act of a death. It was marginally better than believing that he was made of flesh and blood, and that there was no rhyme or reason to him.

'As a matter of fact,' she said, 'I think he picked me.'

Later she woke with her head on her arms and her cheek pressed stickily against the oilcloth. Her eye took in a still-life two feet square: a blue coffee bowl, the weave of a straw mat, the reds and greens of the marzipan refracted by the not-quite-crystal facets of a wine glass. It was the sort of small domestic world that Courbet might have painted, familiar and solid and quietly lit.

The room smelled of scorched pastry. When she raised her head she saw that her right hand was clenched tight, as if determined to hold on to something precious it had found in sleep. Blocked circulation had turned her fingertips a puttyish white. The knuckles were a chilly mauve.

Her left hand lay across it, diffidently, like a friend who, although much rebuffed, is still inclined to soothe and have her say. She furled and released her fingers, flapping them out, feeling the first seethe of pins and needles.

The muscles of her stomach felt bruised. She straightened up and stretched out her neck. The clock said 9.30. High noon over Beverley's apartment in Seattle. She imagined them curled together in sleep, their young sweat under the warmth of the duvet. Sean was an early riser only when he had to be; there was still time for him to ring.

Of all the thoughts in her mind the one that rang like truth was that death was a kind of falling out with the living, and that the dead were like children who, in a tantrum, call in their loans, snatch back their favourite toy or whatever they have given you, close it tightly in their hand and turn away.

When she stood up to remove the blanket she felt the chill of sodden cloth against her skin. There were puddles of snow-melt on the linoleum beneath the chair. 'You'll catch your death,' she told herself, like some fussy Fifties mother. And then she remembered that she'd already caught it, caught it and held on tight. And now it was time to let it go.

Another milky desert night, another ubiquitous sunrise, and he is still travelling: this is how it is for him, like thirst, like childhood, like walled-in tears. Dry-mouthed in mirage country, he remembers how he found nothing to say about that vast and shallow sea, landlocked, held in a red-rock rim, the sky birdless, the shores empty of fishing boats; although later he and Broom spoke of it, rambling, delirious, as if they had drunk sea water. Fifty kilometres crossed in a racketing taxi on a pontoon road straight as a railway track, while the sun swooned over the cracked lip of the desert.

Has he ever truly known, before, what thirst is? Before – or now, perhaps, or some time in between – another taxi with another dented bonnet bouncing on its hinge. Bile rising to sour his tongue, the smell of hot rubber making him vomit on the cigarette-littered floor behind the driver's seat. The grizzling heat in the car mounting through another day as the sun slides up behind it and stares in through the dust-veil on the rear window, drums on the metal roof at midday like a child demanding to be let in, fixes its glare on their faces through the remorseless afternoon. Beside him a tall Bedouin who glances at him and says something sharply to the driver. He sees the driver's eyes on him in the cracked mirror, dark, like ripe dates fallen among the furrows of his face.

No stop. No water. The sun sets his eyebrows on fire. The word he says next sounds like 'banditokay', and leaves no doubt that he is angry.

On his wrist is the shiny new watch Mother gave him so that he could impress his teachers with his punctuality, the watch he has begun to fear will attract bandits. Now, in the silence, it's the sun itself he swallows, its sand-choked rays; he feels them fierce inside his chest. The sun that hums in his mouth like a wasp. Seeing his memory spread before him like a mockery of water: the turquoise paint of a dry swimming-pool in a white hotel at the mouth of that other desert, palm-frond shadows rippling across the blue. On the concrete bottom of the pool fallen dates lie rotting. Far south of the Chott he is drinking a beer with Broom on the edge of a Saharan swimming-pool, watching the long oasis shadows claim her freckled face. Flies land and graze on the suppurating dates. He is smiling, the words buzzing recklessly from his mouth, confessing that never in his life has he made it with a black woman, not even an Asian one, no, really, does she think it means he's a racist at heart? Her face freezes in the shadows, her eyes flick at him angrily and what they say is 'Sadist'. And even though he knows he should be good it's too late to buckle down because his grin has gone beyond him, so he waits for her to hit him and put a stop to what may otherwise escalate into some definite loss or suffering.

Stifling in the back of the taxi as it slows and lurches to a halt that steals the last stale breath from the breeze, he sees beads of sweat gathered on the grey bristle on the chin of the driver, who turns with his hand outstretched and barks the one word 'Passport'. The queue reaches into the distance and ends nowhere, a queue of heat-struck cars and donkey-carts and hand-barrows, people hunkered down

456

under djellabas on a shell-scarred road that smells of dung.

Throwing open the back door the driver orders them out of the taxi, then with a newspaper on which squirm the red and black tadpoles of Arabic he mops briefly and bitterly at the sick on the floor and throws the balled-up paper with its adhesion of cigarette butts onto the scrubby verge.

In the other lane armoured vehicles roar past one after another like a frieze in the British Museum, the conquering army proceeding right to left across his line of vision from where he sits on the running-board. After them come open trucks of bravely jolting soldiers, who pass lemonade bottles from hand to hand and tilt them to a brotherhood of sucking mouths. His throat opens wide to be one of them, to let the miraculous liquid pour straight in, but unbelievably they have waved to him and gone. An empty bottle tossed from the truck spins and settles faithlessly in a pothole by the nearside bumper of the car, and tears rise up in him, as if to fill the bottle's emptiness, salty tears that make him gag, dark tears that spurt from his closed eyelids as the male passengers turn away from him, shrugging; tears which must be stopped.

The place he hides in, a place convulsed by silence beyond which a donkey's tail swishes monotonously, fills up with a red presence, the embroidered hem of a girl's dress glimpsed through a chink in his fingers, and the bloom of dust on two sandalled foreign feet. The smell of oranges is overpowering as the red hem dips into the road and the cut fruit swims towards him on a sound-wave like the metallic clink of the sea against small pebbles. Since he is too weak and faint to reach for it she holds the half-orange to his lips, her

457

skin smelling of rosewater and dust, her voice
repeating a soothing name that might be hers as the
bright globules leak and sparkle on his lips and ease
his tongue and wash in to inhabit the desert cells of his
body. His wet mouth like a well that fills up when the
rain forgives. His head sinking against a woman's
breast, a deepness plump and easy as sleep into which
Broom's voice follows him like love until it fades.

On his first night back in London Lockhart woke
in Agneta's arms, smelling the lavender oil she'd
sprinkled as usual on the pillow to help her sleep.
He tidied a straggle of hair off her face and
tucked it back behind her ear; even when he
whispered her name she did not stir.

Lockhart was sweating: after the rigours of the
Hebrides London's micro-climate seemed
positively tropical. Disengaging himself carefully
from her embrace, he pushed the duvet down to
his waist and lay with his arms behind his head,
staring into the hospitable semi-darkness and
listening to the city: bebop sounds from a party
across the street, the familiar clangour of distant
sirens.

What had woken him was a dream of such
detailed clarity that it seemed less like a dream
than a window on some parallel universe, one in
which he had not come clean with his father and
must in that adjacent future for ever face the
consequences.

In his dream it was lunchtime and he was

heading down to Birley's to pick up a prawn-and-avocado sandwich. He was passing the bowling green on Finsbury Square when his mobile rang. The police message came through curt and clear: a Cockney voice talking of Callasay. He noticed the mispronunciation before the news sank in, the accent on the *las*: Ca-lassie. The voice informed him that his father, John Lockhart, was dead, crumpled on his side in the gravel yard behind the house, the 3.03 from the gun room broken across his body. His younger brother, Fraser Lockhart, had admitted the crime and had been taken into custody. He had made no resistance to the arrest.

Lockhart heard himself reply with clipped obedience that he would come to the station immediately. He had every intention of doing so; his feet, however, refused to change direction, and simply went on walking; it seemed beyond his power to stop them. They took a right turn and marched him past the side of M&S, past the window displays and the dummies in their wan spring fashions. In Wilson Street they propelled him under a glass archway, which would cut the signal out. Black marble gleamed on either side of him. Ahead, Broadgate Circus opened out, sheer-walled, like a cirque among mountains, and at the centre was the ice rink, round and white and glittering like a tarn. On the stepped terraces office workers muffled in coats and scarves ate sandwiches or sushi.

Lockhart walked swiftly down the steps to the rink, the cellphone silenced in his pocket. Around him the tower blocks rose, glassy as

459

frozen waterfalls, tugging his eyes towards the sky. When he stepped onto the ice several skaters swerved, cursing, to make way for him, and then resumed their circuits. He stretched out his arms and felt the midwinter wind flap under the armpits of his suit jacket, and his will rose up, light and silvery, like a salmon. There came a point when he no longer felt the chill of the ice through the soles of his Oxford shoes, and he sensed that the air itself was beneath them.

The skaters stopped dead in their separate sprays of frost to stare at him. Lunchers at the tables outside the cafés swivelled their heads, eyes narrowed, ready for the thin clever laughter of the City, white napkins dropping to the ground like handkerchiefs. Lockhart heard the tinkle of knives and forks on the marble tiles of the piazza, and at the tables saw the faces of acquaintances fill with such a tumult of concern that he called out to them to tell them that they really mustn't worry. The vertical pressure mounted like a cloud-engine under his feet and raised him through increments of light until the sky spread softly clear above the crests of the towers; his shirt loosened itself from the waistband of his trousers and the bright rebellious tail of his tie fluttered up to tease his face as he floated, realizing with the weightless sadness of relief that he had gone beyond the call of duty. And when he looked down he saw the shrinking circle of the ice, and the summits of the City were barren rocky islets between which the men bobbing in their business suits were slick and dark, like seals.

In the morning Broom sat at the table and made a shopping list for lunch. She tidied the kitchen with more care than usual, washing the dishes and mopping the muddy boot-prints off the floor, even remembering to bring the frosted flower in from its exile on the balcony. She was about to tip the box into the dustbin when she found herself thinking in a new way of Veronica, of her primal need for protection, which suddenly didn't seem such a shameful flaw or weakness, but, rather, the simple opposite of abandonment: the need, common to everyone under the sun, to be enfolded.

If Al had lived, would he have done this for her? Could he, when she crawled into his arms, have held her close and harboured her? For certainly some great hidden dreaming part of her had gone on believing it.

Hopes were the hardest thing, the most difficult to mourn. Hidden hopes that held you so tight you didn't even know you were clinging to them. Hopes that froze you not only in the past but also in the magic numbness of the Future Perfect – not 'would have' or 'could have' but 'will have', next year or next decade or next century. The truth was that the past was not hers to alter, and Al's template was all his own: no matter what she did or thought or felt, she could neither drive him away nor bring him back.

At one o'clock, with lunch prepared and laid out on the oilcloth, she went out onto the balcony to watch for Daniel. Under the first staggering sunrays she turned up her face and thought of Al, of his light, and also of his darkness. Death was death and that was the end of it, but something in her had always said otherwise, said that badness could still hurt the dead, and truth or goodness aid their progress. Yet life was something there wasn't much of, not for anyone. And no matter how strong the pulse of her vitality, in the final reckoning she wouldn't have so *much more* of it than Al, even if she lived to be a hundred. Looked at that way, there was no need to go on paying such a high price for her extra portion.

The sun, which had been bisected by the summit-stem of the Sud, broke free now and flowered undivided. She shut her eyes against the glare and saw Al's initials in brilliant dayglo on the inside of her eyelids, like one of Micky's logos.

A.H. It looked like an exclamation of surprise. Ah. Which was what the heart said on first encountering the beloved. Ah, it said, then it thought of singing and dancing.

The publishers hope that this book has given you enjoyable reading. Large Print Books are especially designed to be as easy to see and hold as possible. If you wish a complete list of our books please ask at your local library or write directly to:

Magna Large Print Books
Magna House, Long Preston,
Skipton, North Yorkshire.
BD23 4ND

This Large Print Book for the partially sighted, who cannot read normal print, is published under the auspices of

THE ULVERSCROFT FOUNDATION